DARK
INHERITANCE

W. MICHAEL GEAR AND KATHLEEN O'NEAL GEAR

DARK
INHERITANCE

WARNER BOOKS

A Time Warner Company

NEW YORK

Copyright © 2001 by W. Michael Gear and Kathleen O'Neal Gear, Trustees and their successors in Trust under the Joint Trust Agreement dated March 20, 2000

Warner Books, Inc., 1271 Avenue of the Americas, New York, NY 10020

Visit our Web site at www.twbookmark.com

W A Time Warner Company

Printed in the United States of America

First Printing: March 2001

10 9 8 7 6 5 4 3 2 1

Library of Congress Cataloging-in-Publication Data
Gear, W. Michael.
    Dark inheritance / by W. Michael Gear and Kathleen O'Neal Gear.
      p. cm.
    ISBN 0-446-52606-1
      1. Anthropologists—Fiction. 2. Chimpanzees as laboratory animals—Fiction. 3. Animal genetic engineering—Fiction. I. Gear, Kathleen O'Neal. II. Title.

PS3557.El9 D37 2001
813'.54—dc2l
                                            00-032491

To Pete and Linda Wirth
For a friendship that stretches
back to that kitchen counter
so long ago . . .

DARK
INHERITANCE

Prologue

Geoffrey Smyth-Archer stood at the aluminum-framed window and stared out at the manicured grounds. A cold drizzle fell. Everything looked perfectly in order, the lawns recently mowed, the shrubs carefully trimmed. Beyond the silver chain-link fence with its razor wire topping he could see to the Sussex farm country. Round bales of hay, wrapped in black plastic, spotted the fields.

Geoffrey had been called to the Smyth-Archer Chemists, Sussex complex, for the first trial in a new drug protocol. He didn't enjoy this, but sometimes his position as head of SAC demanded his personal appearance.

"Are we about ready?" Geoffrey asked, rocking on his heels, hands clasped behind him.

"They will call for us soon, sir," Richard Godmoore said in the well-modulated voice of the English aristocracy. Godmoore, director of genetic research, carried himself stiffly when a superior was present, acting as if he might fracture into a thousand brittle pieces should any fault be found with him or his department. Now he sat self-consciously behind an ornate walnut desk, the top dotted with ordered piles of neatly stacked papers.

Godmoore's eyes strayed involuntarily to the overstuffed chairs that lined the wall, as if he'd be happier were his superior seated.

Geoffrey resumed staring through the aluminum-framed window. At six feet two, his long frame disguised strength and agility honed on tennis courts and by the two miles he swam every day at his club in London. For this occasion, he wore a dapper gray suit, white shirt, and conservative dark gray tie. Some said he had been given the face of a god, strong-jawed, the cheeks patrician, his nose straight. Those who knew him— and they were few in number—said his blue eyes had a perpetually faraway look that betrayed his disassociation from the cares of the world. Those who didn't know him said he had no compass, that he drifted willy-nilly through life, an example of how excessive affluence could ruin a promising young man. Both were partly right. He could feel the power within him, irresistible, washing about like the tide. If he ever found a direction, a purpose, it would obsess him, overwhelm and devour him.

The clouds hung low, gray, laden with moisture. Days like this were made for driving. In his mind he leaned back in the leather seat of his Morgan, right hand gripping the thick steering wheel, his left caressing the shift lever. He could feel the suspension working, hear the rich burble of the exhaust. Through the windscreen the Morgan's sleek hood glistened as he looked down its length.

"Freedom," he whispered, imagining the resistance of the clutch as he entered a corner, matching ratios as he shifted from third to second and felt the pull of inertia as the wet tires slipped, grabbed, and tracked around the bend.

"Sir?"

"Hmm?" Geoffrey glanced sidelong at Godmoore.

"Did you say something?"

"Nothing important. Sorry." Geoffrey sighed and straightened his back, hands again locked behind him. Twenty-eight years old, he had been in charge of SAC since his parents' death last year. Their Gulfstream had crashed into a mountainside in central Africa.

"Just one of those things," the investigators had told him, faces taut with that strained look of remorse government officials could adopt at will. "Bad weather, low clouds, and perhaps a bit of pilot error. From the instruments recovered at the crash site, we can't be sure."

Geoffrey had said something appropriate, the sort of thing all those years in the right schools had taught him to say. And then he had stepped out, walked around the old Tudor mansion, and spent the rest of the afternoon in the garage with his Morgans. At the time, he had owned only three. Since his parents' death, he had added another six.

He had felt a blank emptiness. White inside, and formless. A slate clean of emotion. Some residual urge insisted that he should have at least shed a tear for them, felt that yawning abyss of grief in his breast. But if anything, his sadness had been tempered by relief. There had always been a distance between him and his parents. If he hadn't been able to bridge it in life, he certainly could not in death.

Godmoore shuffled the papers on his desk. "It won't be much longer, sir. I'm sorry to delay you, but the technicians need to prepare for these things."

"It's all right, Dickie. They are using my theories. I should be here." What a lie. He'd rather be out driving, no matter that they were using his research. Geoffrey smiled wearily, enjoying the chance to twist the perpetual thorn in Godmoore's conscience. Godmoore had insisted Geoffrey's parents take that ill-fated trip. "I was thinking of my parents, actually."

"Ah . . . yes, well." Godmoore's brown eyes tightened.

The tip had come that one of the field research centers had made a breakthrough on a noxious little plant taken from a Mbutu healer's herb bag. Over millions of years, plants had been evolving chemical defenses against myriads of parasites, bacteria, and viruses. Teams of SAC researchers traveled the globe looking for plants used in traditional medicinal cures. Once identified, their chemical constituents were isolated and cataloged. Ironic, wasn't it, that the miracle cure for cancer might be found in a grass hut.

Geoffrey had had every advantage in life. He had attended the right schools, taken Firsts, stood straight, he spoke with the right accent and wore impeccable clothing. His golden hair hung down over his collar—his only rebellion against both class and heritage. But for that, he might have been the perfect model of the English gentleman. He had always been better at the role of gentleman than businessman. To his father's disgust, Geoffrey had never developed the ability to employ ruthless calculation in business or life.

"The boy's nothing more than a bleeding heart waiting to cry over this injustice or that!" His father's harsh words seeped from the place in his soul where he kept it locked. *"You'd think we raised a bloody priest!"*

As a child, Geoffrey had known few friends. In university, most of his peers had been more interested in finance, administration, and making their mark on the world than befriending him. None of his acquaintances shared his enthusiasm for either Morgan automobiles or genetics. At genetics, he had been a wizard, could have had his pick of jobs. His thesis had been considered "brilliant," and had won two international prizes for innovative scholarship. Nevertheless, to the disgust of his professors, he had turned down the academic fellowships and appointments to go home and tinker with his automobiles.

The one woman he had been close to, Elizabeth Hanson, had finally looked him straight in the eye and said, "Geoff, you're a decent sort, but when I'm with you, it's like being with a cardboard cutout. It's just that, well . . . there's *nothing* inside you."

Before Geoffrey had courted her, she had been seeing an RAF pilot who had made quite a reputation for himself in the Gulf War. Shot down, the man had avoided capture for ten days before helicopters could extract him from the desert.

Elizabeth's words had forced Geoffrey to wonder about what it meant to be human. Did being shot at change the quality of a man's soul? Did an RAF pilot know more about life than a geneticist who tinkered with life's very building blocks? He smiled sadly, and still longed for her company. What was it about him that he just couldn't connect with another human being? It was as if the problem were almost mechanical: like plugging an English electrical device into an American socket— neither the plug nor the current was compatible.

A buzzer sounded on the desk behind him and Godmoore leaned forward to press the intercom button. "Yes."

"We're ready, sir."

"Geoff?" Godmoore stood and indicated the door.

Geoffrey took a deep breath and allowed himself to be shown out into the hallway with its fluorescent lights, white walls, and long line of doorways. As they walked, his heels clicked on the gleaming tiles.

"This might be the moment we've all been waiting for." Godmoore strutted. "If the serum works, we'll have beaten everyone to it."

"If it works," Geoffrey reminded. "A retrovirus like this is a rather difficult thing to flag. It's the etiology that makes it tricky. What magic secret does Johnson finally think he's cracked?"

"Using your coding research, he believes he has found a key to the virus's protein coat, sir. He's cooked up some sort of new sugar molecule that will bond with the virus. The combination of the sugar on the viral protein coat triggers an antibody response. In short, sir, it negates the biochemical camouflage in HIV that allows it to slip past the immune system."

"I see." At a T intersection, Geoffrey followed Godmoore to the left. There they passed through two swinging doors marked AUTHORIZED ENTRY ONLY. SECURITY CLEARANCE NECESSARY.

Behind the doors, a uniformed security officer rose from his desk, checked their passes, and nodded. "Good day, Mr. Smyth-Archer. Good to have you here."

A white-coated lab technician stood to the right of the desk, a smile on his dark face. His slight frame, thick black hair, and fine features suggested northern Indian ancestry. "Dr. Smyth-Archer, I'm Michael Hamanandas, director of laboratory research for the Sussex facility. Dr. Johnson is ready. This way, if you please."

"So"—Godmoore glanced sidelong at Hamanandas—"this is your big day?"

"It is indeed." Hamanandas walked with his hands clasped before him, his official smile in place. "We have invited Dr. Smyth-Archer because his gene-splicing research was pivotal to our success. This is the culmination of several years of work."

"And several million pounds," Godmoore reminded.

"Research is never cheap, Dr. Godmoore, but if this final test is successful, we can design a protocol for government approval and proceed to human trials."

Geoffrey remarked dryly, "If it works, Dickie, we'll be the first with an international patent. Being able to tag the HIV retrovirus so that the body can eliminate it will keep SAC in the black for years, old boy."

"And what then?" Godmoore shot him a jovial smile. "A delightfully healthy bonus? Early retirement? The expectation of a call from the Nobel committee?"

"The Nobel maybe, but no retirement for you, Dickie," Geoffrey said. "I'm afraid you're stuck with the old research ball and chain. As for me, I suppose I'll just have to buy another Morgan for the collection."

"Why don't you drive a Bentley? It would be more in character."

"I've always disliked stereotypes." Geoffrey gave Godmoore a cool smile.

Hamanandas opened a brushed stainless steel door. Stenciled on the door were the words PRIMATE WING—AUTHORIZED ENTRY ONLY. PROTECTIVE CLOTHING SUGGESTED.

"Protective clothing?" Geoffrey asked.

Hamanandas shrugged uneasily. "Ah, yes. Well, sir, you see, the apes don't like us much. They throw things."

"Eh? Oh, right." Geoffrey smiled weakly. The apes didn't like them? Why on earth not? They fed them, didn't they? He had always imagined apes as rather clownish, swinging around, playing with balls, that sort of thing.

He wasn't prepared for the sight of the stainless steel cages, row upon row of them, stacked three high from floor to ceiling. Then the odor assailed his nose. As the door opened, the chimps inside screamed. Immediately, a white-suited tech began hosing down the cages with a stream of water.

"Come, sir," Hamanandas said. "As long as the hose is turned on them, they won't throw their feces at you. The chimps hate water. They'll be cowering until we pass."

Geoffrey hurried along, peering into the dark recesses of the cages, where the chimps huddled and shrieked at the cascading water. At the end of the line, one large male chimpanzee clung to the bars, his face pressed against the steel. The little door sign proclaimed the occupant to be "T-Rex." The black hair was patchy, and here and there raw wounds gaped on the animal's limbs, as if constantly picked at. T-Rex rocked back and forth, lips pulled back in what seemed a strained smile. When Geoffrey met the creature's glazed eyes, he saw violent rage. It took a moment to settle into his soul that the look was one of insanity. Not even the dripping water affected the beast.

Would you be sane, a voice in his head asked, *if you were locked up in a tiny square like that?*

"Dickie, how long are they penned up like this? Where do they actually live?"

Hamanandas answered. "Why, in those cages, of course. They're quite unmanageable, sir. Wild animals."

"And you keep them in the dark all the time?"

"The lowered light seems to soothe them." Hamanandas paused before the next door. "They must be confined. It makes it a great deal easier to take the blood samples we need. If you had them out in a big cage, why, you'd never catch them. Even with the apes confined in cages, we have to sedate them just to draw our samples."

"Can they . . . can they *live* like this?"

"Oh yes, sir. Most have never known any other existence. They are quite used to it. Lived all their lives in cages. Believe me, sir. They are as happy as apes get." Hamanandas opened the heavy metal door and gestured for a shaken Geoffrey Smyth-Archer to go through, but he hesitated, glancing back.

He had always imagined prison to be like that: brutal, dark, wet, and confined. Looking at those big animals, hunched over in those cramped, dimly lit cages, he saw the nightmare come to life. What would it be like to live in this manner, the entire universe no more than a body length long? They couldn't even stand upright.

What if I had to spend all of my life in a little box like that? Who would I be? What would I be?

A lush, green image of rain forest came to him, filled with enormous trees, thick vines, and gloriously colored birds, the fragrant air damp and warm.

Through it, the big chimp's face leered at him, insane eyes eating into his very soul, the big hands clutching the bars, skin thick and calloused. Those hands had looked so human. Geoffrey swallowed hard.

"Sir? Are you all right?" Godmoore asked. Geoffrey placed a hand on the doorjamb to steady himself. He took a final glance over his shoulder at the line of stacked cages, the horror of the dripping water. He shivered at the last screams of rage.

"No wonder they hate us."

"They're animals, sir," Hamanandas added, suddenly uneasy. "I thought you had been to the primate wing before. We use chimps for most of our medical research." Geoffrey knew that humans and chimps share 98.6 percent of the same DNA. Because of the many similarities in anatomy, histology, and biochemistry, the more dangerous drugs could be tested on chimps before a human trial was run. Still, the sight of these poor animals was unsettling for him.

The heavy insulated door swung closed behind him, effectively blotting out that hell as if it had never existed. He stood in a brightly lit lab, stainless steel and glass gleaming. Each crisp white wall was lined with workbenches, cabinets, microscopes, petri dishes, test tube racks, and DNA replicating machinery. Two gel tables stood in the back, one for agarose gels, the other for polycrylamide. Attached to them were monitors, the machines ready to conduct electrophoresis tests on genetic specimens. A big silver centrifuge dominated a workbench in one corner, and a spectrometer had been placed across from it. In the center of the room, like a lonely island, another of the stainless steel cages rested on a dolly.

Geoffrey hesitated, afraid of what lurked within. When he peered through the barred opening, a pink face stared out at him. This was a young chimp, her eyes mild, her expression one of curiosity mixed with worry. To his amazement, she extended an arm through the gap, her pink fingers reaching for him. The look in her gentle brown eyes touched him, and before he could think, he responded, reaching out to grasp the warm flesh. At the moment of contact, a thrill shot through his veins.

Surprised by her strength, he allowed the young chimp to pull him close. Soft grunting sounds came from her throat.

"I see you've made friends with Maggie." Dr. Johnson smiled as he handed a clipboard to Hamanandas and stepped forward. He was a tall man, perhaps fifty years old. His bald head gleamed in the white light of the fluorescent bulbs. He, too, wore one of the white lab coats. "It's an honor to have you present for this, sir. I hope today will demonstrate our progress in the area of HIV research."

"Maggie?" Geoffrey asked, ignoring the rest. "Her name is Maggie?"

The chimp responded, reaching through the bars to pat his arm with her other hand. She seemed unwilling to let go, as if reassured by his touch.

"That's what we call her." Hamanandas, preoccupied with the information on the clipboard, answered without looking at Geoffrey. "Well, good, if these data are correct, we've reached the level of purity we want for the serum."

"Hello, Maggie," Geoffrey said gently. "Are you all right?"

Maggie released his arms, a curious look in her soft brown eyes as her hands moved, forming intricate gestures.

"What's this?" Geoffrey leaned down, studying the graceful movements.

Johnson gave the ape a sidelong glance. "Oh, that. She's an experimental animal." He took the clipboard back and slipped it under his arm. "In the beginning, everyone thought chimps would be perfect for HIV research. The problem was, infected apes never developed AIDS. They weren't susceptible to the retrovirus. I think you know, sir, the best evidence is that we caught HIV from them in the first place. We thought they were a dead-end for research until we realized that we could insert a complement of human genes into a chimp. In Maggie's case, we gave her a complete human immune system. To test it, she lived her first three years with a human family that had six children. We wanted to be sure she was exposed to the regular complement of human diseases. You know, colds, flu, mumps, all the illnesses endemic to people which normally kill chimps. While she was living with her human family, they taught her sign language."

"You mean she's talking? Communicating?" Geoffrey bent closer, watching the movements of Maggie's hands, and the questioning look she gave him. "What is she saying?"

"I wouldn't know, sir." Johnson turned and walked away, lost in the figures on his clipboard. Hamanandas had removed a medicine bottle from a small refrigerator and held it up to the light. With a syringe, he pierced the rubber stopper and carefully drew a clear liquid.

"I don't understand," Geoffrey said as he smiled down at the young chimp. "I'm sorry, Maggie. I really wish I knew what you were saying."

Maggie huffed a sigh. Then she reached out and took his hand again. She gave it a reassuring squeeze, the sort of gesture that told him it was all right, that she forgave him. Then, as if to make one final attempt, she lifted her right hand. She watched him intently, as if willing him to understand. Then she indicated the barred door of the cage, and made a gesture that Geoffrey couldn't help but comprehend.

"Open the cage?" he asked, and to his infinite surprise, she grunted assent and nodded her head before repeating the "open" gesture.

"Dear God, I just understood what she was trying to say!" Geoffrey settled back on his heels, staring into the chimpanzee's eyes. For the first time in months, his heart beat with excitement. What an incredible wonder! This wasn't the gaze of an insane animal, but one of sensitivity and concern.

Maggie repeated the "open" gesture again, this time with great patience, as if signing to a slow and dull-witted companion.

"I'll get you out," Geoffrey responded. "I promise. They need to run a test. Do you understand? A test."

Maggie nodded and sank back against the cage, one leg bent. She said, "Whuh!" then reached out and took his hand again. With her free hand, she continued to sign.

"Dickie, come look," Geoffrey said excitedly. "What is she saying?"

Godmoore bent down. The nostrils of his sharply pointed nose flared as he peered into the cage. "I've no idea, sir. It's meaningless to me. Though, I've a cousin who is speech impaired. Were he here, he'd no doubt know those signs. They look similar to what Blair does."

"Oh, Maggie." Geoffrey laughed, his soul bubbling with enjoyment. "What a wonder you are. Do you believe it? I'm talking to you. Me, a human, and I don't have the foggiest notion of what you're saying to me."

Maggie gave him a smile, and repeated the "open" gesture.

"Oh, yes," Geoffrey promised. "As soon as the test is finished. I promise. I want to know more about you. About what you can do."

As Hamanandas approached, he cleared his throat. Geoffrey disentangled his hand from Maggie's, rose, and stepped back.

The sudden change in Maggie's demeanor shocked him. Her eyes fixed on the syringe in Hamanandas's hand. She let out a soft moan and backed toward the rear of the cage, pleadingly signing "open" to Geoffrey. The technician slipped up behind her, artfully injected her bottom where it pressed against the rear bars, and quickly retreated. Maggie shrieked and threw herself against the sides of the cage.

"Sorry, girl," Hamanandas said. He looked at Geoffrey and Godmoore. "Sometimes a little trickery works wonders. They're not very smart, you see."

Maggie rubbed her bottom, grunting indignantly as she tried to position herself between the bars. Then she looked across, meeting Geoffrey's eyes. She tilted her head and imploringly signed: "Open, open, open."

"Can I let her out?"

"Not today," Hamanandas said. "She's in for the duration. It will be weeks before we know if the serum has any side effects. We need to monitor her reactions, no matter how small."

Geoffrey said, "But you won't leave her in that cage, will you?"

"Oh yes." Hamanandas spoke absently as he took his notes on the clipboard. "Let's see, injected ten ccs of A-302 at four-teen thirty-two hours."

"Dr. Hamanandas," Geoffrey insisted, "where will Maggie be kept?"

"We'll put her out on the row with the rest."

"Oh, no," Geoffrey said. "No, you won't." He took a deep breath. "Those are vicious beasts out there. You'll put her in a big cage. A place where I can come and visit her. I want to learn how she communicates."

Hamanandas gave him a placating smile. "Sir, she is part of our experiment. I don't think you understand the protocol under which we *must* work. As part of—"

"And I am not sure, Doctor," Geoffrey cut him off, "that you understand who pays your salary."

"Geoff," Godmoore said as he stepped between them, "I assure you that Dr. Hamanandas will take very good care of the animal. As it is, she's just had a half-million pounds' worth of research serum injected into her, and I don't think Hamanandas would risk the animal's . . ."

Godmoore never finished. Maggie let out a hoarse cry, stiffened, and fell onto her side. Her throat worked as though she were trying to throw up. Geoffrey rushed to the cage, staring past the bars, but those soft brown eyes had no time for him now. They had turned glassy with fear, the pupils fixed, and the hands that had gestured so delicately clawed at her throat.

Geoffrey cried, "What's wrong? Hamanandas, damn it, *what's wrong*!" He made way as Hamanandas and the tech rushed up, squinting in at Maggie. Her long black hair stood on end, and her lips had pulled back in a grimace. With each breath, her lungs labored like those of a strangling man.

"Oh, no. This can't be happening!" Hamanandas whirled and ran to the phone. He punched a rapid series of numbers and waited for several moments. "Michael here. I need the vet. *Fast!* I think one of our animals is experiencing an allergic reaction." A pause. "How the hell do I know? Just get him here. Now!"

Geoffrey shoved Godmoore and the tech aside. Heedless of their shouts, he pulled the pins that locked the cage door.

"You *can't* do that!" the technician cried, grasping at Geoffrey's sleeve.

"The bloody hell I can't!" Geoffrey cried, shaking him off. He dragged Maggie from the smooth steel floor. Her weight amazed him; the warmth of her flesh against his came as a complete surprise. Every muscle in her body had knotted, rigid and trembling. "It's all right, Maggie," he said in a soft voice. "The vet's coming. Help will be here soon. Hold on."

Her body spasmed, and a thin stream of saliva crept past her strained lips. Not knowing what else to do, Geoffrey stroked her long silky hair, humming to her as a mother would to a child. He could feel her lungs pulling against her throat, struggling for air.

Geoffrey barely noticed the people crowding around him in a silent ring. The long minutes dragged past. Finally, Maggie blinked and lifted her head. For a brief instant her soft brown eyes focused on Geoffrey's face, and he could sense her panic, her silent pleading for help. She lifted her hand, as if to say something to him, then a shudder went through her, and the convulsions struck. Geoffrey tightened his hold, clutching her to his chest as she jerked and twitched.

"Oh, God! Where's that vet? Dickie, find the damned vet!"

"Sir, please," one of the techs said and reached down for Maggie.

"Get *away* from us!" Geoffrey screamed. "You're fired. All of you, you . . . you're fired!" Tears shimmered in his vision. "Don't die, Maggie," he whispered as he rocked her back and forth. "Help is coming. I promise. We'll make you well."

Geoffrey patted her board-stiff body and looked into her unfocused eyes. He knew the moment she died. Her body went limp and her mouth opened in a silent cry.

His heart turned cold and dead in his chest. "She—she tried to talk to me," he whispered. "I didn't understand." A sob choked his throat as he pictured her gesturing "open" over and over. "I didn't understand. I . . ."

Behind him, the door swung open, and the shrieks of the apes exploded. A white-coated vet burst into the room. The two sensations, sound and gesture, linked themselves in Geoffrey's reeling mind: the sane gesture "to open," and the enraged screams from the hell of ape cages.

"Sir, I'm Dr. Levey. Please, let me have her." The young blond vet knelt and held out his arms. He had kind green eyes.

Geoffrey looked down at Maggie. She lay peacefully in his arms. "She's dead."

The vet placed two fingers against Maggie's throat, stared at the white ceiling for several moments, then answered, "Yes. She is. God, all our work."

Geoffrey clutched Maggie to his chest, and the vet's expression tightened.

Levey said, "Why don't you give her to me, sir? I'll take her away, and we'll begin our autopsy—"

"No." Geoffrey shook his head. "Free now . . . Maggie." He swallowed hard. "Free."

One

Moonlight cast beams of silvered light onto the murky midnight water. The slim cayuco—a narrow boat a little longer than a canoe—ghosted up the channel. The canal had been laboriously chopped through the towering rain forest. Ngasala sat in the cayuco's stern, paddling silently, his eyes on the dark forest rising to either side. Two other men sat in front of him, Ntogo in the middle of the boat, and Masala in the bow.

Ngasala was a man of the Bitu clan. His people were the Okak, of the Fang tribe, a population of Bantu speakers native to west-central Africa. He lived in Evinayong, a small stucco-walled, tin-roofed village in the uplands of Equatorial Guinea.

Most of the time, he did what he had always done: hunted for a living. Bush meat could be sold for enough in Evinayong to keep him in drink, buy a little food, and repay some of the debt he owed his kin. It wasn't much of a living, but it kept him from begging. Through his skill and woodcraft, he always managed a good kill. Sometimes he killed a crocodile, or a duiker, the small forest antelope. Often bongos—one of the larger, highland antelopes—fell to his arrows. Wild pigs also provided rich meat. Once, he had shot a leopard with his rusty old shotgun. The pellets hadn't killed the big cat immediately. Ngasala had been forced to wait, and track, and watch for two days until the animal exhaled the last of its soul. Tonight, he wore a headband made from the cat's skin, and around his throat hung a necklace of the claws. Monkeys were the easiest to kill, though. They were so plentiful, a man had to be a poor hunter not to kill several in a single hunt.

This land had once been controlled by his lineage. His ancestors had lived amidst these hills, with their abundant forests and game. They had burned, and cleared, and planted the red soil with oil palms, bananas, and yams.

As the forest night pressed down on him, he could feel the ghosts of his ancestors. They watched his passage from the midnight recesses behind the leaves.

A guard post lay behind them, down at the mouth of the canal, where it met the Mitemele River. One of the soldiers there was Ngasala's cousin Bembe. Earlier, just before sunset, Ngasala had paddled past, saying he was headed upriver toward Evinayong. He had slipped Bembe a bottle of rum. Bembe would have shared the bottle with his corporal and the other soldier who stood guard. When Ngasala had paddled his long cayuco past their post just after moonrise, the three soldiers were sound asleep.

Ngasala knew this canal. When the SAC project came to his forest, they had hired him for an incredible fifty thousand *cefas* a year. All that money just to work on excavating the canals, and building the buildings, and cutting the roads. He had worked hard for a year, and then he had had a fight with his foreman that had escalated to the use of machetes. Ngasala had been arrested and sent to jail in Evinayong; but his cousin Ito had managed to buy his release.

Ngasala had gone back to the forest, only to find soldiers guarding the project lands. They were mostly strangers, well armed and paid to stop poachers. But some local men worked with them. Ngasala had never thought of himself as a poacher.

He had always been a hunter, and a skilled one at that. Now the law said that animals could not be killed on the project lands—the very country where the ghosts of his ancestors walked.

He paddled his cayuco around a bend, seeing the bridge reflecting in the moonlight, the span raised like a pointing arm. The project kept the bridges up to keep the apes in their separate territories. Only humans could work the bridges, each of which required a special key.

"This is the place," Masala said. "We need only follow the road. No one will expect anyone to come this way."

Masala was a big man, muscular, with a warrior's scars on his cheeks. In the beginning, he had worked at the compound, a construction worker mixing and pouring cement for the big buildings. One day they had caught him trying to steal a drill. He, too, had been jailed, and eventually set free. Now he liked nothing better than to sneak into the project, robbing the buildings at night or hunting during the day with his bow and arrows.

In project lands, all hunting for bush meat was done with bow and arrows. The report of a shotgun carried, and it would bring the soldiers. Because Ngasala and his friends hated the project, the meat they hunted most often these days was ape meat. Hunting might be business, but every *cefa* they received for ape meat brought a special smile to their faces.

The third man, riding in the middle of the cayuco, was called Ntogo. He had been kicked off the project for drinking. The white men didn't like the idea of drinking. Ntogo had been one of the keepers at the ape pens. The stories he told were laughed at in the bars and at the parties in Evinayong. Wild stories.

Ntogo claimed that the apes could talk with their hands, and that they could do things with tools that no hunter had ever seen apes do. He said that some of the apes looked strange, with funny heads, eyes, and feet. That some walked more like men than apes. People thought him a fool, and Ngasala thought him a fool, too, but Ntogo did know the places where the apes were kept.

Ngasala skillfully let the cayuco drift into the bank beneath the bridge. As the bow slipped up into the weeds, Masala poked around with a stick to make sure that a green mamba, or a cobra, wasn't hiding in the shadows, then he carefully tied the boat off. They checked their bows and steel-tipped arrows. The barbs had been dipped in poison. Sure that all was secure, Ngasala hesitated, and then grabbed his shotgun from the bottom of the cayuco. Better to have it, just in case. He hung it over his back with a rope sling before following his companions as they clambered up the pilings and onto the project road.

"This way," Ntogo called. "We are close to the place where the apes sleep."

Good, not too far to carry meat. If they could catch the apes sleeping, they could kill six, or maybe seven, and be gone by the time Bembe and his corporal sobered up in the morning.

Ngasala grinned as they broke into a trot, the hard red dirt of the road making for easy travel. His weapons clattered as they bounced on his back. He was Fang. The blood of warriors ran in his veins. Once, his people had been feared. It was said that his ancestors had eaten the bravest of their slain enemies. They had taken the brains and hearts, roasted them, and eaten them to gain the enemy's courage and cunning.

Ngasala could already imagine the warm blood on his hands. He placed each step carefully and chanted one of the war songs his father had taught him as a boy. As he ran, he reached into the little bag at his side and dropped twists of fur and feathers: fetishes for the forest spirits and the ghosts who watched from the shadows. He took a deep breath and held it in his lungs while he nocked an arrow to the bowstring. He carried it sideways before him, ready to be lifted, drawn, and released at a moment's notice. The grass had been beaten down here, and in the moonlit clearing he could see the crude huts. What a silly notion. But Ntogo insisted that the white trainers had taught the apes to construct them.

Ngasala eased forward on the balls of his feet. The hunt was working perfectly. At the rude hut in the middle, he stepped up to the low doorway and looked inside. The gloom defied his eyes for a moment, and then he made out three dark blotches—ape beds made of sticks and grass. He lifted his bow and let fly. The bowstring thrummed; the arrow thunked into the ground. Nothing.

Reflexively he nocked a second arrow and loosed it at the second bed.

Taking a chance, he slipped inside and pulled his machete from the scabbard at his waist. He prodded the bedding, hearing the rustling of leaves and grass. Nothing.

"Eeeep!" The call came from the edge of the forest, and Ngasala whirled and stepped into the night, returning his machete and reaching for his bow.

An ape danced in the pale white light. It lifted a mocking arm and bounced from side to side on its feet.

Ngasala grinned, smoothly lifted his bow, drew it back, and centered the poisoned steel point on his target. Even as he made the shot, he knew it was good. The noisy jungle drowned the sound of the impact, but the ape stiffened, shrieked, and clawed at its belly.

Quickly, before the animal could flee to the trees, Ngasala sprinted forward, pulling his machete. The ape was on all fours trying to rise when Ngasala's machete chopped deeply into the back of the animal's neck. The ape fell flat, the weight of its body pushing the poisoned point through its back.

"One," Ngasala said quietly as his partners approached.

A beam of light shot out from Masala's hand. "I stole this from the project. We can find the others."

Masala led the way, flashing his light up into the branches as they ducked through the wall of leaves and into the forest.

"There!" Ntogo pointed.

Ngasala drove an arrow after a black body fleeing through the branches overhead. "Missed."

Joy throbbed in his veins as they clambered over the roots, their feet sinking into the mulched forest floor. One by one, they loosed arrows at the retreating black shapes when Masala's light found them. When Ngasala's fingers scraped against an empty quiver, he chuckled. So what if he'd only killed one ape? The hunt had been fun like he hadn't had in years.

Masala handed the light to the panting Ntogo, also out of arrows.

"Come, let's go back and collect our prize." Ngasala slapped Masala's back and turned. As he did, he saw the ape. "Look!"

The animal pulled its head back behind the protection of a tree trunk.

Masala took his light back from Ntogo and shined it around. "They are all around us."

"So?" Ngasala asked. "What can they do to us? We are men, they are apes." But he pulled the shotgun from his shoulder before he started forward in the gleam cast by Masala's electric light, stumbling over prop roots in the process.

Suddenly Ngasala found himself in darkness as Masala shone the light up into the trees, flashing it this way and that. "Something just hit me."

"Shit, most likely. You've hunted apes and monkeys before. You know they do that. Shine the light back where we can see."

Ntogo was in front. In the flashlight's glare, Ngasala saw the ape leap out from behind one of the knotted prop roots and jab something into Ntogo's side. The man screamed and spun around, his hands gripping at the shaft of one of Masala's arrows. The ape vanished into the bizarre shadows thrown by the wavering flashlight beam.

Ngasala hurried forward. No more than a foot of shaft protruded. That meant the barbed steel point was lodged deep in

Ntogo's intestines. The poison would already be leaching into his bloodstream.

"Help me!" Ntogo cried. Sweat broke out on his brow.

"Hold the light on him," Ngasala directed. "Ntogo, turn a little, that's right. Bend around. Now turn your head away and I will cut the shaft in two." He slipped the machete from the scabbard, hearing noises in the trees as he did so.

"Hurry," Masala gritted. "I can hear them, they're coming."

Ngasala raised the machete . . .

Masala screamed. The light jerked back and forth.

In the careening flashlight beam, Ngasala saw Masala's silhouette. A hairy black apparition clung to his back.

Ngasala dropped his machete and groped for his shotgun. Masala was choking, his voice gurgling in his throat. The flashlight fell from his fingers to bounce on the moldy leaf mat. In the reflected light, Ngasala watched as other black forms charged forward. He could hear the sickening thud of blows and the snapping of bones. Masala flopped down among the thick roots, his arms and legs thrashing.

Ngasala scrambled backward, panting for breath, terror burning in his blood. Gripping the shotgun, he ran into the night, tripping, falling, staggering up again.

Behind him, the flashlight beam played about. It bobbed, as if carried in a human hand. Masala was alive!

"Masala! Over here!" Ngasala stood up, waving. The flashlight beam sought him out. "Masala? Are you all right?"

The light bounced as it started in his direction. Ngasala turned, studying the route they would need to take. The easiest path was downhill.

"Come on, Masala! This way!" Roots continued to snag his feet. Suckers and vines impeded his progress. He tore spiderwebs from his face and crashed on. Shooting a glance over his shoulder, he saw the light gaining on him.

His foot caught under a root and he pitched headlong down

the slope. When he stopped rolling, he groaned at the white pain that shot up his leg. By some miracle, he had kept his grip on the shotgun.

The light shone down on him, and he realized he was cushioned by a web of vegetation that grew above the canal. He tried to stand and cried out at the pain in his leg. The flashlight bobbed down the hill, blinding him. "Masala, I am hurt!"

But instead of Masala's deep voice, he heard the melodic and birdlike hooting of excited apes.

"Masala?" He swallowed hard. "Masala?"

Panicked, he dragged himself backward up over the lianas, supported by the thick mat.

Shadowy figures ringed him. What kind of apes were these? He'd never seen anything . . .

One of the apes started forward, an ungainly silhouette with a huge belly. High-pitched hoots sounded from behind the flashlight.

Ngasala cried out in fear, raising the shotgun. His thumb pulled back the hammer as he leveled it on the horrible apparition. The muzzle flash momentarily illuminated the ring of apes. Their bared teeth, angry eyes, and clenched fists burned into his brain.

They fled in the instant after the shotgun blast. The flashlight lay forgotten on the ground. In the beam, one hairy body remained; a rattling sound, that of punctured lungs, came from the sprawled beast.

Ngasala clutched his shotgun and hauled himself forward on his elbows, gasping at the stabbing pain in his leg. Slowly, he made his way toward the writhing figure. A female, and pregnant. He placed the shotgun beside him and reached for his little folding knife. Was her time close enough that he could take the fetus? A live infant would bring him a fortune on the black market pet trade.

He flung her onto her back. Blood frothed at her mouth as the last gasps of life choked in her lungs. Opening his knife,

Ngasala placed the point on the swell of her belly and cut. He reached into her warm guts, found the swollen womb, and sliced it open. As the fluids gushed over his hand, he pulled the fetus free. It moved. How odd that it should look so human. But after the creation, because of their misdeeds, the gods made the apes almost men, but not quite.

No, this one was too young. He angrily tossed it aside.

Well, he had two adult apes. He reached for his shotgun and struggled to his feet. The searing pain in his left leg must mean a dislocated hip. He bent over and grabbed the female's foot. Using the shotgun as a walking stick, he tried to drag the ape after him.

After several steps, he stopped, reeling, panting for breath. He turned loose of the ape, wiped his brow, and . . .

A metallic clang rang out behind him. He turned.

The flashlight beam shone on the dead infant. He saw the ape, holding the flashlight in one hand and the machete in the other. The big male's eyes had fixed on the infant, and his hair stood on end. As Ngasala watched, dark forms oozed from the shadows and crowded around the male, chirping at the dead baby.

With the silence of ghosts, they all turned toward Ngasala. Their bared teeth and eyes shimmered in the reflected light.

Ngasala staggered backward, and his legs tangled in the thick vines. Terrible pain shot up his hip. He struggled to prop himself with his shotgun so he could extricate his feet, but only managed to step into a deeper nest of vines. His good leg sank up to his thigh. He roared and thrashed.

The animals watched for a few seconds, then charged.

He jerked up his gun and in that instant realized he'd forgotten to reload the old single-shot.

Apes struck him from all sides. Like hurled sacks of lead, they pounded him down into the vines, clawing and biting, howling in rage.

"Get away!" he shrieked, fighting to throw them off. "Leave me alone!"

Abruptly, the apes leaped up in a flurry of frightened hoots.

Ngasala tried to sit up, his shotgun gripped in both hands, and the flashlight beam hit him squarely in the face. He couldn't see the animal behind it . . . but he saw the machete blade glowing as though aflame, swinging down. Ngasala let out a shocked cry as it sliced through his belly.

He dropped his hand into the rushing wetness that was his stomach. The smell of severed intestines stunned him. A terrified whimper caught in his throat.

The apes went quiet.

A moment later, the beam of light swerved wildly over the forest, and Ngasala heard the machete hit the vines with a dull thump. Shrill chirps and hoots erupted into a deafening clamor. From the shadows, he saw them. They emerged cautiously and began moving toward him, closing in again.

Ngasala gasped when a hairy arm reached down and tugged the shotgun from his left hand.

The big male leaned over. He tilted his head back and forth in birdlike curiosity.

Ngasala froze. As he stared up into those bright blue eyes, his mouth opened in a haunted breathless scream.

He has climbed to the highest branches. There, he perches, swaying, in the treetop. The odor of blood, her blood, clings to his long black hair. He leans his head back and screams at the skull-white moon.

Two

The irony wasn't lost on Richard Godmoore. Though he held the reins in the most powerful pharmaceutical manufacturer in the world, he still placed two old-fashioned aspirin on his tongue, sipped water, and jerked his head back like a crane with a fish to swallow them.

The headache, like all of its predecessors, and all that would follow, had its roots in Geoffrey's ape project. Godmoore sighed and blinked his eyes, looking around his expansive office. Fifteen long years had passed since that day when little Maggie died in Geoffrey's arms. During those years, he had come a long way, right to the top of Smyth-Archer Chemists and this walnut-paneled office with its leather-bound chairs, thick-pile carpet, and large desk carved from teak. From here, through the communications system that dominated the space beside his desk, Godmoore pulled the strings that manipulated the SAC empire, be it field trials in Ohio, the synthesis of viral DNA in Paris, or antibody research in Delhi. By dint of hard work, intelligence, and dogged determination, he had clawed his way to the top of Smyth-Archer Chemists' administrative mountain. He glanced sideways at the photograph that stood on the edge of his desk. In the picture, three individuals were posed: a smiling Geoffrey Smyth-Archer, a serious-faced Richard Godmoore, and a hairy black ape that clung to Geoff's neck and watched the camera with limpid brown eyes.

Godmoore kept the photograph there to remind himself that Geoffrey's ape project had been the boon and bane of his existence. Thanks to Geoffrey's obsession with the apes, he had overlooked some of Godmoore's more blatant abuses during the vicious power scramble that had led to the top rung of SAC's ladder. Blackmail, fraud, bribery, and assorted dirty tricks had embarrassed, disgraced, and destroyed Godmoore's rivals. In the process he had been forced to employ some rather unsavory individuals. Geoffrey had been too engrossed in producing his "superapes" to notice appeals for decency, justice, and fair play. That same ape project now threatened Godmoore's carefully constructed empire.

Few people knew what SAC had invested in the ape project. Godmoore considered it his "deal with the devil," and that devil had cost SAC almost *two hundred million pounds*! Despite the constant hemorrhage of funds, and the creative book work to hide it from the stockholders, SAC had finally begun to show a profit under Godmoore's stern leadership. In all departments, that is, except Geoffrey's accursed ape project. And now, were word to get out on the true nature of that project, the resulting publicity might well choke those profits like a knot in a garden hose.

And tumble Godmoore from his pinnacle of power.

Though he had long ago resigned himself to flushing millions of pounds into that sewer, the ape project provided three salient benefits: First, the ape compound they had built in Africa had the potential of providing good environmental press—save the planet, and all that. Second, and by far more valuable, it kept the passionately idealistic Geoffrey out of SAC management and safely insulated from the decisions necessary to maintain a giant corporation competing in a global economy. And third—and, to him, most important of all—was the secret bank account that he had filled with skimmed funds from the project. Call it insurance in case of disaster.

As he stared at the photograph, Richard Godmoore couldn't help but wonder how Geoffrey could be so brilliant at the molecular intricacies of genetics and so dense when it came to the real world.

The headache still stabbing behind his eyes, Godmoore turned to the sheaf of papers on his desk. It was one thing to build a preserve for an endangered species, but to attempt what Geoffrey was attempting? How would the world react? If it came out, what would the stockholders say? It had seemed like such a ludicrous idea when Geoffrey first proposed it. Who would have thought he would have pulled it off?

What I would give to shut the whole thing down. Kill it completely. Godmoore studied the report that had been faxed to his office that day. All he had to do was make it through the next stockholders meeting and the damn audit. Two months, that was all, and then he'd have a year to slowly divest himself of SAC stock and meekly retire.

He hadn't anticipated problems with the Dutton ape. Dr. James Dutton fit the profile of a well-balanced individual who took exceptional care of his female bonobo, Umber. Had he expected trouble anywhere, it would have come from Dr. Shanna Bartlett and her bonobo, Kivu. Bartlett had always worried him.

Godmoore sighed, propped his chin on his hand, and stared thoughtfully across the room where the pictures of his three children had been neatly hung.

He picked up the telephone that hung on its golden cradle and said, "Yes, connect me with Mr. Parnell, please."

He waited while the connection rang through and a sleepy voice said, "Yeah? Damn, pal, this better be good. It's the middle of the fucking night here."

"Mr. Parnell, the hour doesn't concern me. I have just reviewed your report. I think we have a potential problem with the Dutton ape. I want you to assess the situation and prepare for an extraction. I will await your report."

"Yes, sir."

Parnell cost him fifty thousand a year for the ape project alone. Among his other duties, the man kept an eye on ten million dollars' worth of project apes in the United States. Godmoore considered the expense to be cheap insurance.

If Parnell's speculation about the call on Dutton's phone log was correct, perhaps the time had come to curtail all of the cross-fostered apes. Geoffrey had his African compound to obsess him now; time to clean up the rest before they had another disaster like the fiasco in Denmark with that Sky Eyes ape.

He rang another number. "Brian? Godmoore. I think the time has come. Bring them all in. I want it done carefully, quietly."

"All of them?" Brian Smithwick's voice sounded strained. "But Geoff gave me explicit instructions that—"

"Did you hear me?"

"Yes, sir."

Godmoore hung up and stared at the photo on his desk.

I need two months. If nothing unravels between now and then, I can keep Geoffrey's madness at bay for another year. And by then I can sell my interests in SAC and live the rest of my life in splendor.

"If you learn nothing else in this course, understand that human evolution occurred because of a chance geological event." Dr. Jim Dutton looked out over the crowded classroom. His close-cropped dark hair contrasted with startling blue eyes. A full beard, trimmed to professorial standards, hid a strong jaw. Humor turned his lips and sparkled at the corners of his eyes. He wore a white Western-style three-button pullover shirt tucked in at the waist. Faded Levi's were snugged to his slim hips by a tooled-leather belt, and scuffed Wilson boots stuck out at the bottom. Broad of shoulder and trim, he looked more like a Western rancher than a university professor, let alone one teaching in so arcane a discipline.

At Colorado State University, anthropology was taught in the A-101 lecture hall in the Clark Building. Jim Dutton always packed them into Introductory Physical Anthropology. Not only was he considered a bright and innovative instructor, but also, at least twice a semester, Jim brought in his project ape, a bonobo named Umber, to help him demonstrate human evolution.

From the day he had received her, eleven years ago, she had never acted the way a bonobo should. For years he had known something was wrong. Umber didn't look right. Act right. Too precocious. Too intelligent.

Then, last week, he had answered a phone call from an old friend, and, in violation of his contract with Smyth-Archer Chemists, he had agreed to allow an outsider to have access to Umber. Dr. Tory Driggers should be on her way up from Denver right now, the last leg of her trip in from Tucson.

And when she gets here, she's going to blow a hole right through my pleasant little world. He glanced uneasily at the clock.

With difficulty, he refocused on the lecture. His students sat behind white-topped desks that spread out from the podium in concentric semicircles. Most hunched over their notebooks, furiously scribbling to record the major points.

"And here, much like Caesar's Rubicon, lies the geological divide which led to humanity." Jim used his laser pointer to trace a wandering line across the projected map of Africa. First the bloodred light transected Djibouti, then moved southwest across Ethiopia to Rwanda, and along the long, narrow string of lakes to Mozambique and the Zambezi River delta.

"This is the Great Rift Valley, where Africa is being pulled apart. East Africa is headed out toward the Indian Ocean at about two centimeters per century."

A hand shot up from the front row. Jim nodded to Theresa Andropolis. She was his hotshot for this semester's class, an auburn-haired girl with glasses and doelike brown eyes. "Dr. Dutton, are you saying that continental drift is responsible for human evolution?"

"That's right. Look, people, evolution is a process of chance events. Blind luck, if you will. No matter what the theologians will tell you, it's a chaotic process. It isn't directed toward a goal. Got that? *Write it down!*"

With the laser pointer he followed a black line from west to east across the center of the continent. "Does anyone know what that line is?"

"The equator," several voices answered in unison.

"Right. The equator. And the prevailing weather patterns are from west to east here. Now, pay attention. We're coming up on the reason why humans are humans and apes are apes." He indicated a range of mountains that lay just west of the central African lakes. "Notice this chain of mountains running north-south through the eastern Congo. These are the most important mountains in human history. We wouldn't be here without them. Anyone know the name?"

Jim turned, scanning the rows of blank faces. "They're called the Mitumba Mountains. For the last eight million years they have been constantly pushing up, creating an orographic barrier between east and west Africa. As they grew taller, a rain shadow formed to the east of the Great Rift, drying out the rain forest. Over millions of years we can document the slow creation of the east African savanna."

He walked over to the lectern and looked up at the map projected on the screen. "Think about it, people. At that place and time—central Africa, eight million years ago—the continent began to pull apart. The Mitumba Mountains rose, and in the process they not only dried out east Africa, but separated a species of apes. The great apes to the west, in the equatorial African rain forests, evolved into modern chimpanzees, *Pan troglodytes,* and the bonobos, or pygmy chimps. We know them as *Pan paniscus.* But east of the Rift the forests thinned, and those apes, the ones we call protohominids, had to stand on their own two feet and scramble for their very survival."

A young woman raised a hand. "How did bonobos and chimpanzees end up as separate species?"

"A water barrier." Jim used his laser pointer to mark the curve of the Zaire River in the Democratic Republic of the Congo. "Today we find bonobos south of the Zaire River and gorillas to the north. Bonobos and gorillas exploit the same food resources. They would have been in competition for the same environmental niche. Again, we have a geographical barrier leading to different species."

He looked out at his class. "Today bonobos are rare; probably less than twenty thousand are still alive in the wild. Until the nineteen eighties, they were called pygmy chimps. But with modern DNA studies, it is apparent that they are a separate species. Not chimpanzees, but bonobos." He grinned. "I ought to know, I live with one. And she tells me about it all the time."

That evoked laughter from the class. Someone shouted: "How long have you had Umber?"

"Eleven years."

"And you raised her?" another student asked from the front row.

"She and my daughter grew up together." Jim leaned against the lectern. "They are more like sisters than sisters. But we're getting away from the subject. We'll come back to Umber, believe me. For the moment, you need to understand that humans split off from the ape line about four million years ago. Bonobos separated from the chimpanzees about three million years ago. We know this from the comparison of DNA between the species. I refer you to Charles Sibley and Jon Ahlquist's 1984 work, and, of course, to Gerloff's 1995 work on bonobos. Interpreting genetic time clocks is fraught with problems, but it does provide a reasonable marker for evolutionary divergence."

He looked out thoughtfully, meeting the gazes of his students, challenging them. "So, tell me, how does it make you feel to know that the building of a mountain range eight million years ago was the key event in human evolution?"

Again, Theresa's hand rose. "Why aren't tools and language the key events?"

"Because they were already part of the protohuman experience as far back as five million years ago. Jane Goodall proved that wild chimpanzees make tools, and ape language studies have shown that chimps, gorillas, orangutans, and bonobos can be taught language skills. You see, it was there, preadapted to the species when the climate began to change. Those early hominids in east Africa had the rudimentary skills for dexterity, tool use, communication, social organization, and intelligence. When the savanna dried out, those skills were essential to survival and their development was accelerated."

He smiled out at them, enjoying their rapt attention. "People, it was those preadapted skills and a change in environment that set the stage for the first genus *Homo*."

Theresa's hand went up. "What about bipedalism?"

At that moment, Dr. Tory Driggers stepped through one of the double doors on the left side of the room. She wore a navy blue skirt and a conservative white blouse under a black jacket. A brown leather purse hung from her left shoulder. She climbed up two rows and slid into a seat.

So, she'd made it. The fat was now in the fire. Jim cleared his throat and said: "It isn't every day that we have distinguished visitors in A-101, but I'd like to introduce Dr. Tory

Driggers." A rustle of clothing and papers accompanied the craning of necks as students swiveled in their chairs. "Dr. Driggers is one of the preeminent primatologists in the world. Tory, welcome to Introductory Physical Anthropology."

Tory smiled. "It's good to be here, Jim. Go ahead with your lecture. If I'm not mistaken, you were just about to explain bipedalism."

"Right, bipedalism, walking on two legs with an upright posture. Can anyone tell me why that would be an advantage in an arid savanna?"

Theresa's hand shot up like a piston. "Increased visibility over open areas for detecting predators and . . ." The young woman hesitated. "And since food resources were more widely distributed, the hands were used for carrying."

Jim pointed at Theresa. "That's what you get for reading ahead in the textbook."

Laughter followed as Jim glanced up at the wall clock. "We still have five minutes, but I'm going to spring you early. I want you to read chapters six and seven in Brothwell for Wednesday. And don't forget, the first midterm is coming up a week from Friday." With that, he waved his hand to dismiss them.

Amidst a clatter of swinging yellow chairs, thumping books, and rustling papers, his students stood and funneled toward the doors. At the lectern, Jim fielded several questions and finally headed for the door where Tory waited, her jacket folded over her right arm.

"Tory. Good to see you. How was the flight?"

"Cattle car. I was stuffed between two men. They *always* prop their elbows on the rests so a woman can't use them." She looked around the room. "God, it looks the same now as it did when we were in grad school!"

"Yeah, well, welcome home."

Tory had the seasoned look of forty, fine lines at the edges of her eyes. Tension pulled at the corners of her normally full mouth. An uncharacteristic square set of the shoulders made him wonder what she was bracing herself for.

They stepped through the wooden doors and out into the hallway. The square light boxes overhead cast a fluorescent glow on her straight black hair, cut short in a professional yet feminine style.

"How's Brett?" she asked.

"She's thirteen. And working harder by the day to be even more thirteen." He chuckled grimly. "A troop of baboons would be more relaxing. If you're interested, I could have her crated up and shipped down to Arizona. You could detail three or four graduate students to study her peculiarities, and win my undying gratitude by getting her out of my hair."

Tory grinned. "Liar. You should hear yourself. A fawning parent if I ever heard one."

He suppressed a smile. "All right, she's in an honors program. She's smarter than I ever was. Too smart for her own good in fact. Sometimes I think she's thirteen going on forty. She's a whiz on her computer and reads everything she can get her hands on. And I mean *everything*!"

"Boyfriend?"

"Hah! She scares boys to death. She's playing center on the girls' basketball team, and last summer she was the star pitcher on a boys' 13–0 softball team. You'll see the trophy tonight, believe me."

"Sounds like quite a girl." Tory paused significantly. "And Valerie? Has she ever . . ."

"No." Jim narrowed an eye. "Not a word. She's never so much as sent a birthday card."

"Such bitterness, even after all these years." Tory tilted her head as they entered the stairway and climbed to the second floor. Passing through the B wing, she finally said, "You know, Jim, it could be that she really cares."

"Oh?"

"Put yourself in her place. Maybe she just doesn't know how to bridge the gap."

"She's a reporter, for God's sake. A great communicator. Word is that she's a shoo-in for Triple N's nightly news anchor."

Tory frowned at her shoes. "Keep track, do you?"

"She's Brett's mother. Of course I do."

She smiled, and the lines around her blue eyes crinkled. "I was trying to suggest that maybe she hasn't been in contact because she's afraid."

"Valerie? Afraid? Are we talking about the woman I saw on TV during the Algiers trouble? The one with the AK-47 who was taking shots at the snipers that pinned down her camera crew?"

"I thought you were the Jim Dutton who studied primate behavior?"

"Most people say I just monkey around with the discipline."

"Evidently you'd better stick to monkeys, because you don't seem to know much about humans."

"Good to see you again, too, Tory," Jim muttered as they turned into the C wing and started down the anthropology department hallway with its line of brown office doors. He passed by the anthro office and dug his key out of his pocket.

Under the sign proclaiming J. DUTTON he opened the wooden door to a small cinder-block-walled office, carpeted in brown, with a floor-to-ceiling bookcase covering the south wall. A window provided a picturesque view of the Animal Sciences building to the east and its adjacent parking lot. Beneath the window, a bulky square heater was piled with books and notes. Pictures of a pretty blond girl with long silken hair hung above the gray metal desk. In many of the shots she posed arm in arm with a black-haired ape of similar size. In each, the ape was watching the camera lens with knowing brown eyes.

"Umber and Brett," Tory said as she stepped over to study the photos. Then, after a pause, her voice dropped. "My God."

Jim's heart skipped. Was it that obvious? "I don't usually hear that sort of awe from a colleague when she walks into the office." Jim tucked his thumbs into his belt loops. "All right, Tory. You didn't just fly up from Arizona for a pleasant visit."

Tory bent closer, squinting at the ape in the photo. "Have you looked at Umber closely, Jim?"

"Every day. In fact, she generally wakes me up in the morning by bouncing on the bed and peering into my eyes when I finally, and generally reluctantly, crank them open."

"She's a bonobo, right? Not a koola-kamba? Not a cross between a chimp and gorilla?" Tory backtracked to the bookcase, scanning the physical anthropology texts and monographs on human evolution before she hooked a slim volume out with an index finger. "Here, look."

"That's De Waal's book on bonobos." He stiffened. "What are you after, Tory?"

When Tory opened the book, found the page, and extended it for his inspection, Jim glanced down at the photo. "I see a female bonobo."

"And what else?"

"She's a high-ranking gal, probably an alpha female because all of her hair is missing. That means she receives regular grooming from the subordinate females." He glanced closely at her, the sinking feeling in his gut expanding. *Yes, you see, don't you, Tory?*

"That's right, high-ranking. That's why I chose this photo, Jim. Because her hair has been plucked, so you can see better. Look closely at her skull morphology, and then look at Umber's."

Without even a glance, Jim took the book and carefully closed it. To a casual observer, they were just two apes, one covered by luxuriant black hair, the other almost bald. But to the trained eye, Umber's head looked different, full and rounded.

Tory was speaking, softly, as if to herself: "Umber is a SAC ape. She belongs to Smyth-Archer Chemists." A thoughtful pause. "Dear Lord, maybe there's something to the stories after all."

Jim's brows drew together. "What stories?"

"Rumors mostly. Wild tales that the SAC apes are different." She gave him a searching look. "You didn't expect this, did you? That I'd notice right off the bat? You see her each day, work with her behavior. When was the last time you compared an image of her with a wild bonobo?"

He shrugged, turning to the window to look out at the white walls of the Animal Sciences building. "I guess it's been a while. Two, maybe three days." A pause. "This isn't as much of a surprise for you as I thought it would be. What do you know, Tory? What have you heard?"

In a sober voice she said, "Jim, some of us are becoming concerned. You see, we've noticed that there's a problem with the SAC apes."

"What problem?" His heart felt like lead.

"We think . . . well . . . that they've been tampered with. Changed."

"Changed? Now there's a scientific term if I ever heard one."

Tory ran a hand through her short black hair. "We're not sure. I've been thinking of coming up here for a while to see if Umber is all right, or if she's one of them."

His stomach muscles instinctively tightened. " 'One of them'? That's certainly cryptic."

Tory folded her arms over her abdomen. "This isn't easy, Jim. We're afraid."

Jim straightened and gave her a deadpan stare. "Of SAC?"

"No, Jim. Of the SAC apes." She looked up at him. "Because they may not be apes at all."

He carries her body into the high crown of the great tree and wedges it in a forked branch. He waits, rocking back and forth, lost in time with her. In his trance, the sun rises and sets. Time has narrowed, changed into a narrow tunnel. The others in the band watch uneasily from below.

He picks maggots from her ruined flesh and waves the flies away from the infant's small face. With each breath he draws the stench of her into his lungs, and listens for her voice.

Three

Brett sucked air in and out as she ran, enjoying the feel of her feet pounding the hard sidewalk. She didn't have basketball practice tonight, and took the opportunity to run. From Blevins Junior High School to the CSU Primate Study Center was two and six-tenths miles if she took the shortcut through suburbia.

Dad didn't approve of her running alone, but Brett was no fool when it came to strangers. She had watched the TV shows and knew the frequency with which pretty blond girls ended up on missing persons posters. The thing was, running helped her to focus, and the thought of being abducted acted to concentrate her attention on the world around her. That undercurrent of fear always lay just below consciousness: She would imagine a car pulling alongside of her just when her energy was starting to flag. Then, powered by adrenaline, she would sprint all the harder, her hair streaming out behind her.

Besides, this was a good day to run; the temperature hovered in the sixties. Yellow leaves covered the trees, and the first Halloween pumpkins squatted on doorsteps. The lawns had browned, and to the west, beyond the hogbacks, the pine-speckled slopes of Horsetooth Mountain rose against the blue sky.

Brett rounded the corner onto Overland and slowed to a trot to catch her breath. To the west, nothing lay between her and the Rocky Mountains but an open, grassy field. Traffic whooshed past, mostly four-wheel-drive utilities and sleek sedans. Commuters taking their worries home from work.

Lungs working, legs pumping, she sprinted past the 7-Eleven on the corner of Elizabeth. Trees, ablaze with autumn, lined the western side of the road and cast a web of shadows across her path. The gravel made a reassuring scrunching under her fancy running shoes.

A car honked. A young man leaned out to whistle as he passed. Brett ignored him, irritated nonetheless.

Get used to it, girl, her father's voice reminded. *As pretty as you are, you're going to spend the rest of your life being admired by men.* Admired was one thing, being ogled was something else. What was it about males that they could only see a girl as a piece of sexual meat? Bonobos were way ahead of humans when it came to sex. Even at thirteen, Brett knew that.

She huffed her way to the gate of the Equine Center, cut west through the parking lot, around the new building, and ducked under the fence into the corrals. The soft hoof-churned soil smelled damp and took the imprint of her artistically pat-terned running soles. The subtle tang of horse and manure filled her nostrils. She slipped past the hay barn and waved at the stable hands who cared for the horses. Most she knew by sight.

One by one she climbed the metal-pipe fences that separated the paddocks until she rounded the rear of the Animal Repro-duction Biotechnology lab. Across the gravel road, in the shadow of the Center for Disease Control's bunkerlike build-ing, stood the Primate Study Center: a steel Quonset attached to a small white frame house. A huge woven-wire cage boxed the rear of the Quonset. Umber spent warm days there, bask-ing in the sunshine.

She spotted her father's red and brown Bronco beside Dana Marks's white Toyota. Over the frame doorway, a weathered sign told the world that this was the Colorado State University Primate Study Center. Paint was flaking off the wood. She stopped and stared thoughtfully at the door.

For the last two weeks, something had been eating at Dad. She couldn't quite put her finger on what had changed, but she'd seen it before, when he was fretting about being granted tenure, and again the time Umber had contracted pneumonia. He had always been a rock, solid and unyielding. A constant support. To see him so worried unnerved her.

Brett opened the brass doorknob with its heavy lock and stepped into the foyer—a small cubicle that acted as a mudroom. To the right, Jim's windbreaker and Umber's heavy Filson coat hung on brass hooks next to Dana's parka and a black dress coat.

To the left, a big white poster notified visitors that they had just entered the Colorado State University Primate Research Facility and that access was restricted to authorized personnel. Another official-looking placard duly provided notice that the lab did not discriminate on the basis of race, creed, gender, or disability. Dana had long ago added "genus" and "species" to the list with a thick black marking pen.

Brett slung her daypack into the corner and scowled at the battered door that led into the lab. Normally open, it was ominously closed. She opened it and entered the main office, a square room measuring twenty by twenty. Floor-to-ceiling shelving along the back wall sagged under books, softbound reports, and photocopied journal articles. Her dad liked to tell her it was the most comprehensive ape library between the Yerkes Primate Center outside of Atlanta and Central Washington University in Ellensburg.

Another floor-to-ceiling shelf on the west wall contained rack after rack of VHS tapes, all marked with dates on white labels.

Each provided a recording of Umber's activities on videotape—part of the extensive record keeping that went with the ape project. Not one, but two televisions and their VCRs were stacked atop each other in the northwest corner. Brett had seen her father and Dana spend hours comparing images of Umber from one screen to the other. A computer control panel allowed them to take images from either monitor and incorporate them onto yet a third computer screen. From there, the images could be encoded to disk, faxed via the modem to other researchers at SAC, or printed onto hard copy on the ink jet printer.

Two old wooden desks stood in opposite corners on the east wall, both battered veterans of surplus markets, cluttered with papers and books, a keyboard, and computer monitors. Glowing screen saver programs danced colorful images across the screens.

The secretary, Betty Marble, sat at her steel desk in the center of the room. As Brett walked in, she looked up from where her fingers rattled on the keyboard. A headset indented her tightly curled gray hair, and her blue eyes had a slightly unfocused look behind her horn-rim glasses.

She smiled crookedly and stopped the tape recorder as Brett walked up. "Hi, girl. How was practice?"

"No practice tonight. The coach let us loose to get in trouble at home instead." Brett gestured to the door that led into the rear of the building—also ominously closed. "What's up?"

Betty lifted an eyebrow. "Some muckety-muck from the University of Arizona. Tory somebody. I don't have a clue, but she and Jim came in about an hour ago. He introduced me and closed the door behind them when they went back. Dana's back there, too. It's all very mysterious."

"Naw. Dad went to school with Tory way back during the last ice age. They've been friends for years." Brett indicated the tape recorder. "Today's notes?"

Betty nodded. "Dana was running tests on Umber this morning. They were doing something with cognition. I'm transcribing."

Everything Umber did had to be recorded. At least, everything she did in the lab. At home, Dad tried to keep track, but even he didn't know *everything* Brett and Umber did. Thank God!

Brett started for the rear door.

"Um," Betty began. "I'm not sure . . ."

"It's all right. I promise. Tory's kind of like an aunt, you know? She even sends me Christmas presents and stuff."

Betty didn't look all that convinced as Brett opened the door and stepped into the lab control room—a narrow cubicle ten feet wide and five feet deep. The door to Brett's left opened into the lab proper. Two empty chairs stood before the long desk. What seemed from her perspective to be windows were one-way mirrors that overlooked the lab rooms.

A complex-looking computer console filled the end of the cubicle. This controlled the cameras and audio equipment and was wired into Umber's computer keyboard. Every communication Umber made through her voice synthesizer was downloaded into the lab system.

Brett fixed her attention on the four individuals who stood in what they called the "playroom," a big fifteen-by-twenty space under the domed west wall of the Quonset. Beneath the arching roof, Jim stood with his arms crossed, a serious expression on his handsome face. Brett knew that worried posture, the way his back tensed, how he rocked on his heels. He usually looked like that when she'd done something wrong, or Umber was sick, or the bills weren't going to be paid on time.

Dana, too, had an uneasy look about her. Her shining black hair, in a long braid, hung down to her tooled-leather belt. Her dark brown eyes were large, her nose straight. With high cheeks and a pointed chin that gave her face a heart shape, she looked every bit what she was, a Cree Indian from northern Manitoba. Today she wore worn Western boots and snug jeans that emphasized her athletic legs. A red flannel shirt was tucked in at her slim waist.

Seven years ago, Dana had been an undergraduate studying pre-vet medicine on a Canadian Native People's exchange program grant. She had taken one of Jim's anthropology classes. Since she worked weekends at the CSU Equine complex, she was familiar with the Primate Center building, and had come to visit. That visit had led her to volunteer, and, combined with her sudden interest in anthropology, had changed her major. She had finished her master's degree, writing her thesis on Umber's utilization of the audio keyboard, and now pursued a Ph.D. with her usual dogged determination.

Brett considered Dana to be something like a big sister, but not quite family. Sure, Dana had eyes for her dad, but then what sane female wouldn't? Even Brett's friends at school said Jim was way cool.

Tory had a white lab coat over her suit, obviously to protect the fabric from any kind of insult that Umber's toys might inflict. Many visitors from other primate centers insisted on having a lab coat. Not that they needed one with Umber, but in other institutions, chimps, gorillas, and bonobos tended to throw feces at strangers—and accurately, too.

All attention centered on Umber, who squatted on an upside-down plastic bucket, her keyboard in her lap. Umber wore loose yellow pants, a Rockies baseball team T-shirt, and a blaze orange plastic wristwatch. Thick black hair covered her bonobo body, and unlike a chimpanzee's, her face was black, similar to a gorilla's. Chimpanzees tended to have tan faces. Umber watched Tory with reserved brown eyes, as if searching for exactly why she was in the lab this afternoon. The sensitive microphones picked up even the slightest sound.

"Umber," Tory said in a friendly tone. "Can you tell me what you will be doing for Christmas this year?"

With long dark fingers, Umber tapped out her response on the keyboard. Even without the audio, Brett could have read what was being said, for the words flashed on the computer monitor in the control room.

"Umber, Jim, and Brett will go to Wyoming for Christmas." The mechanical words took on a stiffer inflection through the speakers in the control room. Such audio keyboards had been in use for years with human patients who suffered from speech impairment. Perhaps the most famous had belonged to the noted physicist Stephen Hawking.

"Wyoming?" Tory asked. "And what will you do there?"

Umber gave Tory a bonobo grin, a wide smile that exposed her lower teeth with their stubby canines. Her fingers flicked over the keyboard. "We will see Brett's grandfather. Umber will chase the cows. It will be cold, so Umber will wear her snow-suit." Umber rocked back and forth, tilted her head, and asked, "What will Tory do for Christmas?"

"Visit family in Texas," Tory answered, a curious reserve in her voice. "They don't have cows to chase, I'm afraid."

"Cows are big," Umber's computer voice replied. Then she used her hands in American Sign Language, or ASL, to add: "Big, very big."

Tory replied in kind, her hands forming the silent words. "And ugly, too."

Umber exploded in bonobo laughter, the sound, "Hee-haii, hee-haii," coming through the speakers. At that, Jim and Dana laughed. But Brett could tell it was more nerves than amuse-ment.

Brett sobered at the pensive look on Tory's face as she stud-ied Umber, and took that moment to walk through the door into the playroom. "Hi, Dad. Hi, Dana. Hey, that looks like

Tory! What a surprise. Did you finally get tired of cactus and rattlesnakes?"

Umber tossed her keyboard to one side, let out a greeting hoot, and charged Brett like a pit bull. Brett caught her up in a hug and they circled around like dancers, Umber hooting softly as she stroked Brett's hair. Then her hands danced through the signs for: "How school today?"

"Okay. Mrs. Redderson wanted me to read my book report out loud." She glanced meaningfully at Tory and her dad. "They sticking pins into you?"

Umber shrugged and grinned, making the X over X sign for "torture."

"Yeah, sure," Brett chided.

Tory stepped forward. "Dear God, Brett, you're a woman now."

Brett met her with outstretched arms. "It's good to see you, Tory. Usually I have to wait for some boring old conference."

"You get more beautiful by the day," Tory said with a sigh. "I swear you've grown a foot since last year's AAPA meetings." AAPA stood for the American Association of Physical Anthropologists, which usually met in April.

"Dad says I'm an animal." Brett stepped back, smiling, and instinctively reached for Umber's hand. Umber slung an arm about Brett's waist and grinned as she rocked back and forth, her actions swaying Brett on her feet.

"I thought you were at practice this afternoon." Jim glanced at the clock behind its protective wire mesh. It read four-thirty-five. The mesh had been placed over the clock face when Umber was still little and threw things. Even though she rarely broke stuff anymore, Jim still took great care not to allow glass into the playroom. It seemed silly; Umber didn't cut herself at home any more than Brett did, but sometimes Dad was funny.

"Dad," she reminded with slight sarcasm. "I told you twice, once last night and again this morning, that practice was canceled." She grinned at Tory and Dana. "He gets that way, you know. Preoccupied. You'd think he was an absentminded professor or something." She shot a twisted grin in his direction. "But I wonder about the kind of science he does when he can't even remember about practice being canceled."

"Bad," Umber signed, her fingertips flipping down from her lips.

"The mind *is* the second thing to go," Tory said dryly.

"God, I hate being gang slammed by women." Jim raised martyred eyes.

"So, what's up for tonight?" Brett asked. "It's almost five. We going out for dinner?"

Jim nodded. "Tory and I are. You, young lady, are going home with Umber. You're going to do your homework and be in bed by ten."

"How am I getting home?" Brett crossed her arms and glared as she considered the best way to protest. From the hard look in Dad's eye, he wasn't going to give in. Whatever Jim and Tory were doing, neither she nor Umber were going to be part of it.

"I was taking Umber up the hill." Dana shot an uneasy glance at Tory. "Looks like I can pack in two for the price of one."

"Deal," Brett said, making the best of it. "I'll even fix dinner."

Umber made the fingers-to-mouth "food" sign, and added, "Time to eat. Let's go."

Dana protested, "You don't have to fix dinner, Brett. I can catch something later, when I get home."

"Hey, you're supposed to be a starving graduate student." Brett grinned slyly at her father. "Don't look a gift horse in the mouth. I can make pizza. We've got a crust in the freezer."

"Okay, kid. You talked me into it." Dana shot a sidelong glance at Jim and Tory with what Brett called her inscrutable

Indian look. Two points! She could pick Dana's brain about Tory's mysterious visit.

"Pizza! Pizza!" Umber made the circled Z sign. "Umber eat pizza, too?"

"A couple of pieces," Jim said cautiously. "I don't want you sick again."

Umber hooted in assent, the sound brimming with bonobo pleasure.

Tory straightened and turned to Jim. "I'd like to take a look at some of the tapes you mentioned while we're here. Would that be any trouble?"

"No. I can pull up anything you need." He turned to Dana. "You can take off. The monsters are both under your command."

Dana raised a speculative eyebrow. "Want me to hang around until you're home?"

"It's not necessary. You shouldn't have to lose a whole night because of me."

"It's no problem." Dana gave him an understanding smile, eyes wary. "I'll take my laptop and the matching column data with me. I could use the quiet time."

Lie like a rug, Brett thought. *You don't trust him out with Tory any more than I do.*

There was something unpleasant about all this. Brett could sense reservation in Tory's blue eyes, and see it in the stiff way she held herself. She acted more like a professor than an old family friend. Not only that, Dana had picked up on the unease, though she was valiantly trying to hide it.

Secrets, secrets. So what was the best way to make Dana spill it all?

"Come on, guys." Dana started for the door. "Let me get my stuff." She glanced toward Brett and Umber. "Do we need anything from the store? Or do you have all the makings for this killer pizza?"

"Get fruit," Umber signed as she bounded after Dana. "Make watermelon, cantaloupe, banana pizza."

"That's disgusting!" Brett cried. "See you later, Dad. Watch him, Tory. He's slow to pick up the bill when there's even a faint chance someone else might."

As she turned reluctantly and followed Umber and Dana out through the control room and into the office she heard her father say: "She's a changeling, you know. A black, horned demon left her in the crib in place of my baby."

Brett leaned back through the door and shouted, "That's a *horny* demon, Dad!"

Betty, still typing away at her dictation, jerked upright, swiveling around in her chair to stare wide-eyed at Brett. Dana laughed and stopped at her desk long enough to pick up two notebooks and a slim laptop computer.

Outside, the long shadows of evening stretched down the hogbacks to the west, accenting the ponderosa pine and mountain mahogany on the slopes. Autumn's evening chill had settled with the slanting light. In the pastures, the horses gleamed in the tawny afternoon. To the north, along the shores of College Lake, the last of the yellow leaves colored the cottonwoods and willows. With the air still, the lake surface reflected the trees and sky.

Brett looked down at Umber's warm, calloused hand against hers. The contrast seemed to hit home more than ever. Umber's long fingers and palm engulfed Brett's delicate hand. Umber had a grip that could almost crush a rock, but never had she so much as raised a bruise—unless, of course, they were wrestling, or playing tickle, or tug-of-war; but all was fair in play.

Dana unlocked her Toyota and climbed into the driver's seat, that preoccupied look still on her face.

"Front or back?" Brett asked Umber as she opened the door.

Umber dropped her hand in front of her face, indicating "front."

"You had the front last time."

Umber grinned, hands signing: "Umber was good today. Umber sits up front."

"All right. But don't forget to buckle yourself in." Brett climbed into the back, irritated at not being in the passenger seat where she could try to read Dana's expression.

Brett waited while Dana turned the Toyota and started down the drive. She absently watched the Animal Reproduction Center pass by, then said: "Okay, Dana, spill it. What's going on?"

Dana said, "Going on?"

"What's Tory doing here? I mean, this isn't just an ordinary visit. Dad's been off his feed for the last couple of days. It's like he's been on another planet."

Brett leaned forward in the seat, far enough to catch the uneasy glance Dana gave Umber. As they passed the horses' paddocks, Umber craned her neck to watch. She liked the horses, was fascinated by them at a distance, but horrified when they came close. Anyone who deliberately took Umber near a horse discovered she was capable of leaping tall buildings in a single bound.

"We've just been looking at the data, that's all," Dana insisted. "Don't push it, okay, kid?"

"Dana, what kind of a dope do you think—"

"I said, *don't* push it."

At the sharp tone in Dana's voice, Umber swiveled her head and blinked before she signed: "Dana okay?"

"I'm fine. Long day, that's all."

"Long day," Umber agreed, hands flying as she signed, "Do this. Do that. Many questions."

"Too many questions," Dana agreed before turning south onto Overland Trail. Brett maneuvered herself so that she could see Dana's face reflected in the rearview mirror. The only time Brett could remember that pinched expression was just before

Dana had taken her oral exams for her master's degree, and then again before she'd taken her Ph.D. prelims.

In response to the tension, Umber slumped down, staring wide-eyed at her powerful black fingers as she picked at her coat.

Dana took a right onto Stadium Road. The road ran straight west across the flats for a half mile before bending south in a gradual curve and climbing into a cleft eroded into the face of the hogback. Where the Great Plains met the Rocky Mountains, the border was stark, defined by the abrupt slope of the Dakota sandstone anticline. Cracked rock rose on either side as they climbed the switchback that led south.

Brett leaned forward to whisper, "Something's wrong here," into Umber's ear.

Umber shifted around so she could peer past the head restraint and grunted in assent.

Brett continued to fume as they drove past the fancy houses atop the hogback and down the steep grade to the rocky dam that penned Horsetooth Reservoir. Tilted beds of sandstone cupped the big lake, rising on each side like barriers. Calm water reflected sunset's orange hues and the irregular shadows cast by the mountain slopes.

At Horsetooth Road, Dana slowed for the stop sign. She waited for a gap in traffic, then took a right. "Look," Dana said stiffly. "I know you two. You're going to work on me all night. Forget it. If anything has to be said, ask Jim, okay?"

Home run! Brett sat back, crossing her arms. Something was happening, all right. Something really grim. The most horrible thing she could think of popped into her head.

"Let me guess. Tory's here to offer Dad a position on the University of Arizona faculty. He wants us to move to Tucson. That's it, isn't it? He and Tory are talking about salary, relocation, and all that."

God, and basketball season was just getting started! What

about her friends here? What did Tory and Dad expect, that they could just pull her up by the roots and cast her into the Sonora Desert to wither in the sun? It was inhuman!

"I said I'm not talking about it." Dana clamped her hands on the steering wheel, shoulders hunching as if she were about to bull headlong into the Denver Broncos' defensive line.

Brett pulled her crossed arms tighter against her chest. They wanted her to pack up and move right in the middle of the eighth grade! She *liked* it here. Didn't they understand? Adults didn't have the right to wreck a girl's life like that!

Umber slipped around in her seat again, concern in her intelligent brown eyes as she peered through the gap between the seat and the window. She crossed her arms in the "love you" sign.

"Yeah," Brett said. "I know." She reached out and took the hand Umber extended over the seat back. That warm grip reassured her. She rode the rest of the way in silence as Dana rounded the south end of the lake, crossed the second hogback, and dropped down Butler Hill. Brett stared woodenly as they passed the trailer park and entered the canyon. Steep slopes, thick in mountain mahogany and rock, closed in to squeeze the narrow ribbon of blacktop.

Dana sighed, relenting. "If it's any help, you're not moving. Not to my knowledge. Look, your dad is too important to the department. The grant money he brings in makes up half of the budget for anthropology. That's how universities survive, they skim forty percent right off the top for administration and overhead. The department, the dean of social sciences, everyone would fight like banshees to keep Jim Dutton and Umber here."

"But something's up." Brett cocked her head as Dana geared down and took a left onto a steep gravel road. The Toyota hopped on the washboard as they climbed. Smaller roads branched off, following the contours of the mountain to where three-acre lots had been carved out of the mountain mahogany and pine-dotted hillside. Modern houses, resplendent with glass, decks, and pitched roofs, were spaced irregularly up the slope. In the drainages, wild plum, currants, and rosebushes clung to the last of their bright red leaves. Tawny stands of grass were stippled with protruding rock.

Dana crested the ridge and took a right along the mountain's spine before turning into the Dutton driveway. She pulled up before a gray-sided, two-story house with attached garage. The house stood on a high point atop the mountain with breathtaking views of the uplifted hogbacks giving way to the eastern plains. In the north, the bulk of Horsetooth Mountain rose to the rocky pinnacle that gave it its name. Immediately south, across a barbed-wire fence, lay Rimrock Ranch property.

Even before the car had stopped, Umber clicked her seat belt off and bounced on the seat, rocking the car.

"Wait, now," Dana commanded. "You know, you don't open a door until told to."

Umber nodded, uttering a single affirmative "wheep."

"Okay, Umber, we're stopped. Let's go get pizza." Brett fished in her purse for the house keys.

Umber opened her door and tumbled out onto the gravel drive, then she charged onto the small lawn. The grass had browned with the coming of winter.

Brett growled to herself as she flipped the seat forward, grabbed her daypack, and climbed out. From the pine-clad slopes to the south came the distant echo of a rifle shot. Northern Colorado was two days into deer season.

Dana, too, had heard the shot as she opened the door. "Think he got one?"

"How should I know? I think it's gross." Brett spoke with the authority that came of being young, female, and appropriately enlightened.

Dana gave her a smile. "In the Canadian wilderness where

I come from, that's the sound of the freezer being filled for winter."

Umber jumped onto the step, swinging up on her knuckles, and signed: "Deer go to God. People eat."

"You're as bad as Dana," Brett muttered as she stepped inside and hung her daypack on the coat hook. Umber shucked out of her own coat before hanging it on her low peg.

The entryway opened into a white-walled living room with a cathedral ceiling and two skylights. On the east, plate-glass windows looked out across the hogbacks to the distant brown plains. A breakfast bar separated the kitchen from the living room. To the right, stairs climbed to the second-story bedrooms. Beside the stairs a polished pine log had been mounted in the floor and secured to the ceiling. The branches had been cut off at varying lengths from the trunk, enabling Umber to either climb, hang, or perch depending on her inclination.

Brett walked into the kitchen, where Dana bent over the refrigerator's vegetable bin. Umber peeked around her shoulder, signing: "Good orange. Umber eat orange now."

"Wait until dinner," Brett said crossly, still annoyed by Dana's defection. True loyalty would have implied sharing this latest great secret. "You can eat with the rest of us."

Umber rocked back and studied Brett with her serious brown eyes. Reading the tension in Brett's face, Umber jerked a slight nod. Then she looked at Dana and signed: "Make pizza now. Okay?"

With a weary smile, Dana said, "Sure, 'Come on home, I'll cook dinner!' Huh, Brett? Why didn't I know it was a setup?"

Umber took Brett by the hand, dragging her toward the stairs. Brett tugged back reluctantly, but Umber had that resolute look about her, her silky black hair puffed up. When she got into one of these moods, a normal human couldn't do much but follow along. Umber, though only a girl of twelve, had the strength of three adult men in her long wiry arms. In a one-handed curl that would have thrilled a weight lifter, Brett had seen Umber lift Jim three feet off the floor while hanging by her other hand.

Umber led the way upstairs. At the landing, a balcony overlooked the living room. Behind it, a hallway led to the bedrooms. Umber signed: "Talk now. Umber and Brett talk."

Umber pulled Brett into her room and closed the door behind them. She crossed to the pile of blankets on the bed and retrieved a duplicate of her keyboard voice synthesizer.

Brett looked around and sighed. Umber's room looked like a disaster area. Books, balls, toy animals, and plastic blocks were scattered as if by a tornado's wake. Unlike the rest of the house, Umber's window was barred. The overhead lights were covered with wire mesh. Her bedroom door could be locked from the outside. But, when Brett thought back, she could only remember a dozen times in ten years that Umber had been confined. Not that many more than she herself had been exiled to a "time-out."

"Come sit," Umber said through her keyboard. She patted the blanket nest on her bed.

Brett climbed into the nest and curled up next to Umber's side. "What's happening?"

Umber stroked Brett's shining blond hair with her long black fingers. With the other hand, she tapped her keyboard.

"Tory came today. She, Jim, Dana run tests. Use calipers for measurements."

"What did they measure?"

"Measure Umber's head." Umber used her fingers to show all the places on her head that they had placed the calipers. "Jim is nervous. Dana is nervous. They made Umber nervous."

"But they didn't say anything? Nothing about Dad taking another job?"

Umber stared thoughtfully into Brett's eyes, then typed, "No. Jim not problem. Umber problem."

Brett's heart skipped. "You? How could you be the problem?"

Umber made a futile gesture with one hand. "Do not know. I try to be very good today. Smart. Made Jim worse." She paused, worried brown gaze on the keyboard. Then, as her long black fingers touched the keys, the speakers stated: "Umber frightened."

"Yeah," Brett whispered. "Me, too. And I don't know why."

Umber smiled then, jutting her lower jaw forward as her fingers carefully rearranged Brett's hair in their longtime grooming habit. With her free hand, she signed: "Umber and Brett will be okay. Have each other."

From instinct, Brett ran her fingers through Umber's long black hair, the bonobo gesture of reassurance and security. "I love you, Umber."

In answer, Umber hugged her close.

Four

Traffic clogged College Avenue as the last rays of sunset purpled the sky over the mountains. Many of the cars already had their lights on. Jim glanced sideways at Tory in the Bronco's passenger seat. Her eyes gazed straight ahead. For dinner, she'd dressed in comfortable clothes: a black turtleneck and blue jeans. They waited for the light to turn at the Mulberry Street intersection, then crept northward in the six o'clock fender-to-fender crawl.

"She said 'I will' and 'I did.' That's future and past tense. Not even Kanzi speaks in tenses." Tory glanced at Jim. "How long has she been using tenses?"

"Awhile." He eased the Bronco forward. *How in hell are you going to handle this one, Jimbo?*

He'd only felt this way four times in his life: The first was when Valerie told him she was pregnant; the second time had been just before his comprehensive exams; and again, on the day he'd passed the defense of his dissertation. The last time was when he'd received notification from Smyth-Archer Chemists that he'd been selected for their primate program. Umber had come into his life, and his world had irrevocably changed.

He glanced at Tory. Her expression had gone stiff, worried.

Jim checked the rearview mirror before taking a right onto Mountain Avenue and, in the process, saw his reflection. It stunned him. Grim determination had tightened his blue eyes, and he could feel perspiration trickling down his sides. He wiped his clammy palm on his denim pants.

He drove half a block and steered into the first available parking place. Killing the Bronco's engine, he sat for a moment, hands resting on the leather-wrapped steering wheel.

"Tory, I want you to know—"

"That you're not blind? I already know that," she replied. "You're a good scientist, Jim. Too good to have thought Umber was just a normal average bonobo."

"What's *normal*, Tory?"

She slapped her hands on her lap. "Oh, let's discuss it after a beer. I had a *very* early morning in Tucson. My stomach is a huge gaping pit. I don't care if Umber is a three-headed mutant—if you don't feed me, I'm going to revert to my atavistic hunting-and-gathering African savanna roots and eat the next four-footed furry thing I see." She made a "hurry" motion in ASL, grabbed up her briefcase and purse, and said, "Bring your notes."

Jim stepped out of the Bronco and set the security system. With his notes tucked under one arm, he steered Tory across Mountain Avenue and into the pedestrian mall that led to Linden's Brew Pub. At the doorway, they found a small pack of trendy college types. Jim elbowed his way to the plump dark-haired hostess who stood with a stack of menus in her arms.

Jim beckoned Tory and followed the young woman through the maze of tables, chairs, hanging purses, and elbows to a small table near the window.

"We've got a special tonight on the crawfish. Your waiter's name is Mark. He'll be with you in a minute." She handed them menus, smiled at Jim again, and hurried away.

Jim seated himself and shuffled his notes, marshaling his data, but Tory reached across and placed a hand on his. Her short black hairdo framed her pleading expression. "Not yet. Believe me, we'll get to that, but for now, just talk to me. It's been a while. I'd like the chance to catch up. Try to relax, okay?"

He nodded and sank back in his chair, extending his long legs beneath the table. "I'll try, but I've been brooding since your phone call. Brett probably did tell me practice had been canceled." He grimaced and laced his hands over his stomach. "This thing with Umber . . . Dana and I have known for a long time."

There, he'd said it, and in spite of his agreement with SAC, bolts of lightning hadn't smitten him to a cinder.

Tory gave him a reassuring smile and said with anticlimactic aplomb, "So, how's life otherwise?"

He laughed softly and shook his head. "What life otherwise? Busy, I guess. I teach my two classes, and the rest of the time I run errands for Umber and Brett. I like to think I do science on the side, sort of a hobby from eight to five. Then work really starts at home, or at the ball games, or trying to get Umber to clean her room and take her various pills." At Tory's look, he added, "Specially formulated vitamins and minerals, stuff SAC supplies to keep her immune system up to human diseases. Mostly I spend my off-hours between eleven P.M. and six A.M. in a stuporous supine state with my eyes closed and my mind in stasis."

"Ain't fatherhood hell?"

"You have no idea."

A thin, sandy-haired young man in a white shirt stepped up. "Can I get you something from the bar?"

Jim lifted an eyebrow at Tory's blank look. "I recommend the Red Ass Honey Wheat ale."

"Two of those," Tory said.

Mark muttered something under his breath and vanished into the crowd.

Tory cocked her head. "If you spend all your time being a professor and father, how's your love life?"

"Why, I love life just fine, thanks."

"That's not what I asked, and you know it."

"Let's just say that I'd get more action in a Cistercian monastery." To Jim's relief, the ale arrived in frosty glasses, the crystal malt color rich and red under a frothy head. He lifted his glass, remarking: "To old times, and bold times."

Tory laughed in a way that promised he wasn't off the hook yet and lifted her glass. After she wiped the foam from her lips, she dropped her voice. "Dana is an attractive young woman."

"Jesus, Tory. Give me a break. I'm her academic advisor, for God's sake!"

"It's just that I worry about you, Jim."

"I don't have time for any woman."

"You're having dinner with me."

"Is that a proposition?"

"Hell no. You and I knew years ago that we'd kill each other if we tried anything but sheer, honest, and unadulterated friendship." She smoothed the sides of her glass with her fingertips. "I think Dana likes you. And she looks pretty damn good in a pair of jeans."

Jim took a long drink of his ale. "I'm not a corpse. And yes, sometimes evil thoughts cross my mind. But over the years I've learned when discretion is the better part of valor. In the case of Dana, some things are better left platonic."

Tory tucked her short black hair behind her left ear, and her pearl earring caught the light. "Really? That makes you different than ninety-nine percent of the men in this world. So, why are you alone?"

Jim grunted noncommittally, his eyes straying to the voluptuous "Kina Lillet" blond on the wall poster. Her arms were full of wine bottles, orange leaves, and golden grapes that spilled over a white dress. At that moment she looked a hell of a lot safer than Tory.

Tory made a *tsk-tsk* sound with her lips. "My God, our good old Val sure took her pound of flesh out of your bleeding soul, didn't she? Even after all these years, you're still fucked-up over her."

"I'm not fucked-up," he defended. "That was thirteen long years ago. I've changed since then."

"Bullshit." She laughed. "Tell me, Jim. Honestly. Have you ever really looked twice at another woman since Valerie walked out of your life?"

"Of course I have. I happen to be a fully functional, sometimes sexually active male." He made a face. "And why, for God's sake, do we have to talk about my sex life. How's yours?"

She smiled and sighed. "Blissfully fulfilled. You know Barney Hanson?"

"Primatologist with the San Diego Zoo?"

"The same. He and I go bonobo all the time." Tory's eyes had taken on a gleam. She steepled her fingers before her. Among other things, bonobos were noted for blatant sexual behavior.

"This thing with Barney, is it serious?" Jim lifted an eyebrow.

Tory shrugged. "Who knows? Time will tell."

Mark, their waiter, appeared and asked for their orders. Tory decided on the crawfish; Jim opted for red beans and rice. When Mark retreated, Tory immediately said, "It's been thirteen years, Jim. Maybe you should be in that monastery after all. Get out, meet some women."

"I meet plenty of women. They're just not . . ."

"What? Valerie?"

Jim took a deep breath to ease the cramped feeling in his chest. "I don't know. Maybe. Sure, that's it. It's all Valerie's fault. Now that that's cleared up, can we go on to something really exciting, like departmental politics? You wouldn't believe what happened at the last faculty meeting. We caught one of the archaeologists digging up dirt about people's pasts."

"What do you expect from a glorified grave robber?" Tory smoothed her napkin on her lap. "What's Valerie doing these days? Still clawing her way to the top? Or has she made it?"

"God, I can't even divert you by bad-mouthing archaeologists. What's it going to take?"

"Oh, come on, Jim," Tory said, and reached across the table to touch his arm affectionately. "I knew Val, too. We went to school together, remember? Is she—"

"I think she's still clawing—but she's close to the top." Jim propped his elbows on the table. "I don't know. She does what she needs to do, just like the rest of us."

"What about Brett? Does she ever ask, ever try to contact her mother?"

"No. She tries to act like it's no big thing. We've talked about it a couple of times. It's all very mature. Real dispassionate. Brett grits her teeth and acts so understanding, as if it's her responsibility to keep from hurting me. So, we talk all around it, like Valerie is some sort of minefield where a wrong step could cripple us."

"She must see her mother on TV."

"It's a little game we play. At news time, I find something to do downstairs, or in the garage, or outside. If the weather's really crummy, I go into the den and work on my notes. Brett locks her door, and she and Umber watch Triple N to see if Valerie's on the air that night."

"Brett's a big girl, Jim. I couldn't believe that young lady was the same little Brett I used to hold on my lap." Tory paused. "Is she interested in boys?"

"Damn, what's with you and sex tonight?"

"Who said anything about sex? I asked if she was interested in boys."

"She's thirteen!"

"That's old enough. At least in some places. Maybe not Fort Collins."

Jim said through a long exhalation, "Like I told you earlier, Brett has too many serious drawbacks when it comes to boys. First off, she's a better basketball player. Second, she's much too smart. It's not cool to go steady with a girl with a 4.0 grade point average. Third, Brett's best friend in the world is Umber." He paused. "Did I say best friend? Let me put it this way: Umber is her little sister. I had to attend a parent-student discipline night last year because some boy called Umber a big ugly monkey and Brett beat the tar out of him."

Tory's head drew back in exaggerated surprise. "Seriously?"

"Black eyes, bruised ribs, and a dislocated jaw. Brett took that kid apart, and he outweighed her by ten pounds and stood a head taller."

Tory stifled a laugh. "They ain't making girls like they used to. But then her mother was a real scrapper as I remember."

"Still is, if her news reports are any indication." Jim shook his head. "If there's a hot spot in the world, Valerie's right in the middle of it." He absently glanced down at his fingernails. "I always wonder what I'm going to tell Brett if Val gets shot by some terrorist, or blown up in a war she's covering. I'm not . . . well . . . I guess I'm not ready for that kind of closure. It'll all be so final then."

Tory's keen blue eyes cut past his defenses, seeing down into his soul—as she always had. "Good God, Jim, after all these years, you're still in love with her. What any other woman on earth would give for that kind of devotion."

He shrugged. "She's the mother of my daughter. I owe her something."

"That, or you've got monogamous genes."

"No, I like Levi's, thanks."

Tory scowled. "Valerie walked out of the hospital and dumped

Brett in your arms. You don't owe her shit. Jesus, Jim, what do you think motivates a woman like that? To just walk out? Not even a by-your-leave?"

"She didn't want the baby." He found it odd that he actually had to restrain himself from shouting in defense of Valerie. "I *begged* her to carry Brett to term, Tory. Her part of the deal was that she'd have Brett, and then all bets were off."

"Sorry." Tory caught the tension in his voice. She tipped her head apologetically. "I've no business making judgments about her. I know you both did what you thought you had to."

He smiled. "Yeah, well, it was the right decision for her. She knew what she wanted. She'd never have made it with Brett and me around her neck. In the end, we'd have destroyed each other. We were dancing around each other with verbal knives that last three months as it was."

"Uh-huh." Her eyes told him what she thought of Valerie, and it wasn't kind.

Mark threaded his way through the tables and set the plates before them with a flourish. After asking if they needed anything else, he ended with the one indispensable waiter word in the English language: "Enjoy!"

"Can't they just say something like 'Have a pleasant meal'?" Jim pulled his plate close.

Their attention centered on food, Tory gleefully destroyed a pound of crawfish, while Jim ate his red beans and rice.

Finally, she looked up from the wreckage and gave him a satisfied wink as she wiped her hands with the cloth napkin. They sat in silence a long moment, smiling at each other in that easy manner of old and dear friends. Then the lines at the corners of Tory's blue eyes pinched.

"Well," she said with a sigh. "It's getting late. Let's talk about the data."

He wiped his hands on his napkin and tossed it on the table. "Go on. I'm listening."

She tapped her notebook with a finger. "If you run a couple of calculations . . . Oh, here. I have a calculator in my purse." She pulled it out and handed it to him.

Jim's heart skipped as he took it. Silver in color, it had white keys with most of the numbers rubbed off. "Okay, we took a lot of head measurements on Umber today. What kind of index do you want to run?"

"Cranial capacity. Simple anthropometry. Length times breadth, times auricular height, divided by two."

Jim lifted an eyebrow. "You're talking about using Manouvrier's old formula for humans. Umber's a bonobo. You can't just switch formulae from one species to another and expect to have meaningful results."

She indicated the calculator. "Jimbo, just run the numbers."

He took a deep breath, stilling the sudden fear. His voice felt dry as he said: "A bonobo should have a four-hundred-cc brain." For something to do, he took a swig from his beer. "One thousand two hundred and eighty cubic centimeters."

Her eyebrow arched.

In a leaden voice he said, "I don't need the calculator. That's the number you'd get if you ran the index. That's what you came here to find out, isn't it?"

"Jesus." Tory shook her head. "We didn't think . . ."

"Who?"

"Barney and me."

"So, how much do you know?"

From her briefcase, Tory extracted a photo of a young female bonobo. The image was taken from the left side of the head, like a police mug shot. Next Tory pulled out a Polaroid she'd taken that afternoon, also from the left. "That's a picture of a twelve-year-old female bonobo from the San Diego Zoo. One of Barney's. I tried to match the profile as closely as possible when I photographed Umber this afternoon. Tell me what you see."

Umber's skull was rounded, the frontal bone more pronounced, bossed. Even in profile Jim could tell that the parietal bones on each side of the brain were wider, rounded, like a cantaloupe. In a bonobo, or chimp, the skull was shaped something like an avocado, longer, lower, and sloping. The jutting jaw, so prominent in the zoo bonobo, seemed recessed in Umber.

"I've been watching bonobos for years, Jim," Tory said. "I've worked with them in Atlanta, San Diego, and up at Ellensburg. I've spent time at the field stations in the Congo, at Lomako and Wamba." She tapped the photo of Umber. "This is *not* a bonobo. Whatever it is, it isn't *Pan paniscus*. Want to level with me?"

Jim clamped his jaw. "All right, so what if she's a koola-kamba, a crossbreed? It happens to apes in zoo situations. It's . . . what?"

Tory's lips curled with irony. "That, my friend, is what frightens the hell out of me."

At the tone in her voice, he examined the photo more closely, looking for the characteristics of a gorilla or orangutan in Umber's profile. "But a cross with what? Bonobo-chimp? Bonobo-gorilla? Bonobo . . ."

His heart skipped. The sound of other diners, of clattering plates and silverware, faded into some distant dimension as his mind tried to grapple with the implications. "Dear God, Tory, you're not trying to tell me . . . you think . . ."

Tory bowed her head. "Yes, that is exactly what I'm trying to tell you."

Five

Valerie Radin leaned back and closed her eyes as the cab inched along on the acceleration ramp from the Dulles Airport Access. The northbound ramp onto 495 looked like a glittering string of chrome and glass as it merged slowly with the flow of morning commuters. The cabbie, an Arab named Achmed, hummed along in time to some ethnically atonal music on his tape player.

Lord in Heaven, I'm tired. She fought the urge to nod off. Originally, she had hoped to sleep on the flight in from Colombia, but the hollow images of decomposing human bodies had intruded, along with the caffeine from the endless cups of coffee she'd gulped during the two days before the opening of the mass grave. Even now, three thousand miles from that gaping hole in the ground, the cloying odor of death lingered in her nostrils.

She had left Bogotá at dusk, and here it was bright morning, the dawn of a new day for which she'd had no night. Rush hour.

She slitted an eye and peered out the side window. Yellow light, tinged brown with the normal D.C. haze, reflected boldly on the trees, brightening their resplendent autumn colors. The shoulders of the road looked manicured, recently mowed, with only a hint of trash.

Vacant-eyed, mind-numb with fatigue, Valerie tried to understand what she was seeing. Each of the shiny new automobiles around her was worth an average of, say, thirty thousand dollars. The Cadillacs, Lexuses, Mercedes-Benzes, and BMWs averaged out with the Hondas, Fords, and Hyundais. All that American suburban wealth, each bearing but a single occupant—dressed in nice clothes—toward an air-conditioned office. And in Santa Isleta, the little village nearest to the massacre site, she had seen a total of three trucks, the newest a rattle-trap seventy-six Chevy without a hood, doors, or windshield.

Did those sloe-eyed, somber Indios have anything in common with these suit-covered, aftershave-smelling men? Did those peasant women, their eyes carefully downcast, their dresses crafted from flour and coffee sacks, have any relationship with these women who half reclined behind the wheel, a cell phone to one ear?

Bitch, you're just tired. A couple of nights' sleep, a few good meals, and you'll be ready to joust with dragons again.

She checked her watch. Eight-ten. Murray would want her to call in as soon as she got home.

Murray—good God, what should she do about Murray? They had been living together for six months now. Valerie rubbed her eyes, as if to soothe the grainy burning. Murray Stanton was the executive producer for Triple N's Washington bureau, and a twit—albeit a very influential one. He came from old Massachusetts wealth. He still cultivated that saltwater image, hair always looking slightly windblown, as if he had just stepped off a sailboat. Off camera, he dropped his *R*s in a perfectly nasal northeastern drawl.

Murray slipped around receptions, fund-raisers, and the "right" cocktail parties like a mullet. Adept at the "insider" game, he knew everyone, appeared on the important talk shows, and always had the inside track on breaking stories. When Valerie had left for Colombia, rumor had it that he was being considered for something big at Triple N's Washington bureau.

Good old Murray. With all the tender mercies of a Visigoth, he'd settle for nothing but the top spot. No matter how many throats he had to slit to get there.

The cab nudged its way into the long line of cars waiting to exit onto Memorial Parkway. Rather than risk a dent, the guy in the Infiniti gave way, horn blasting. Achmed seemed oblivious, humming in time to the clashing of bells and brassy 2/4 time.

They fought their way to Fairfax and crossed Chain Bridge. Valerie leaned forward, calling out directions. From some hidden corner of her mind, the Arabic words for right, left, next street, and turn here came to her lips in just the right order and cadence to place her in front of Murray's house on Cathedral Street in Palisades.

Valerie handed Achmed forty dollars, took her blank receipt, and retrieved her suitcase from the trunk. Years ago, she'd learned to travel light. She could live out of her one bag for weeks, still appearing crisp enough after a month in the backcountry for sixty seconds on the nightly news.

As the cab pulled away, her heels rapped hollowly on the walk. Leaves had blown into the corners around the redbrick foundation. She looked up at the two-story house, with its Tudor country-style architecture. Valerie fished the key from her purse, opened the door, and tapped the code into the security system keypad.

Walking out of the foyer, she kicked off her travel-scuffed pumps and glanced into the living room. The white carpet was immaculate; there was not so much as a magazine out of place. But then, Murray's living room was for show only. She'd once tried to make love to him on that white sofa, but he'd refused, leading her instead to the den, where he took her on the floor in front of his ornate bird's-eye maple desk. She had looked up, past his ear, at the pictures, souvenirs, awards, and framed letters that crowded the dark walnut walls. She had always thought of that lovemaking session as but another trophy in his collection.

She shrugged out of her jacket, smelling the heat, sweat, and stink of Colombia—and of the dead—on the fabric. She held it out, pinched between thumb and forefinger, and let it drop, knowing it smelled like the rest of her.

They had finished the shoot early, taped the last of the interviews. Her flight had been booked for tonight, but American had a seat open in first class, so she had left Roberto Naez, her cameraman, at the Bogotá Marriott and caught the earlier flight.

Normally, she would have called Murray to let him know she was coming, but he would have wanted her to stop by the studio to debrief him on the story. It was better this way. She could get a solid eight hours' sleep, brief him when he came home tonight, sleep again after dinner and sex, and meet her crew at the station tomorrow when Roberto arrived with the tapes. Besides, the bodies of the people they had watched dug out of that pit in Colombia didn't care if their story was aired a day or even two later.

As she started for the stairs, her tired brain replayed the images with a camera's clarity. They had taken root in her mind: those little corpses, flesh half rotted from the bones, but the cotton fabrics still brightly colored. One Colombian drug lord was eliminating his competition. A matter of simple efficiency. Did he have to kill his rival's entire family? Two of the girls had been teenaged. Forensic analysis would determine if they'd been raped before they were shot in the back. From some subtle sixth sense, Valerie already knew they had. Something about the way the bodies had sprawled. The little boys and girls had been beaten to death. She had seen enough head trauma around the world. Those crescent indentations in the thin skulls had come from rifle butts. The crushed facial bones, the broken teeth, all spoke of clubbing.

Valerie climbed the carpeted stairs with their brass runners to the second floor. As she unbuttoned her blouse, her skin began to tingle with the anticipation of hot steaming water, of scented soap and a wealth of shampoo cascading from her long blond hair.

She unzipped her skirt and let it fall as she passed the hall mirror, hesitating for a moment to stare at herself. A stranger seemed to look back from her fatigue-bruised blue eyes. A faint smudge marred the side of her straight nose; lord alone knew where she'd received it. Her cheeks, the ones men declared to be classic, appeared hollow, somehow wolfish and gaunt. Even her delicate jaw, with its petite chin, seemed set and hostile.

At thirty-six, her body would have been the envy of a twenty-year-old. She stood five foot six in her bare feet. Her breasts, while full, weren't overly large. When she moved, firm muscle slid under tanned skin. Tightening her belly, she could see a little ripple in her abs. The long white scar running slantwise along her right ribs acted as a reminder of the mortar shell that had almost killed her in a Hutu refugee camp just inside the eastern border of Zaire. Roberto had earned both his wages and Val's undying gratitude that day. He had pulled her to safety and stopped the bleeding, despite her dazed insistence that she was fine.

Valerie undid the severe braid and curled a lip at the stringy mass that cascaded down her back. Well, hell, when had there been time for more than a quick scrubbing with a bar of soap in a bucket of water these last two weeks? She tried to square her shoulders but couldn't manage the energy. When she looked closely at the mirror, her face free of makeup, the lines were visible. God help her, one of these days she was going to have to accept the fact that she wasn't a girl anymore. Too many days in deserts, or rain forests, or standing out in blizzards. She'd paid for each headlining story with one of those wrinkles.

You can see to the damage in the morning. You're tired, that's all. On to the shower. Wash first, then sleep and food. Yes, that was it, the eternal optimism that came of rest and recuperation. It had always worked before.

She opened Murray's bedroom door, intent on the fancy glassed shower with its marble tile walls, gold faucets, and swan-shaped showerhead. Were she not so tired, she'd have noticed immediately, but she was three steps into the room before the figure in the bed registered. "Murray? What in the name of hell are you doing . . ."

The young woman sat up, blinking, drawing the sheet over her naked breasts. Her jaw dropped just enough to emphasize the widening of her eyes. "Who are . . . God, Valerie."

Valerie felt the last of the reserves drain out of her weary body. She slumped against the antique oak dresser, crossed her arms, and propped herself on her hip. "Let me guess, I'm supposed to think you're his little sister. Um, yes, visiting from Cincinnati, or is it Cleveland? And how does the next line go? Whatever you're doing here, it's not what it looks like, right? Then I protest, and you say, 'Wait, I can explain.'" Valerie narrowed hard blue eyes. "How about we cut the bullshit and just deal with the fact that you fucked Murray last night, okay?"

The woman closed her eyes, head back as she took a deep breath. A wealth of raven black hair fell in disarray down her back. Valerie placed her in her mid-twenties. The hickey on her neck looked fresh.

"Why the hell am I surprised?" Valerie asked herself tonelessly. She balled a fist, then kicked the trash can hard enough to bounce it off the corner of the big-screen TV that stood across from the foot of the bed. "Son of a *bitch*!"

The brunette seemed frozen, like a deer caught in the headlights. Valerie sighed, shook her head, and worked her hands in and out of fists. "Relax, baby cakes, I'm not going to use you for a punching bag." She ran a hand over her face and knotted her fingers in her hair as she rocked back and forth, trying to think. "Jesus, why is this happening? Why today?" She glanced at the girl—somehow it was too hard to think of her as a woman. "Who are you? What's your name?"

"Anne. Uh, I mean, Annette. Annette Hamilton. I was just . . ." She glanced helplessly at the clock. "God, is that the time? I overslept."

Valerie laughed bitterly. "I'd say so, honey." She picked up an empty champagne bottle from the nightstand, sniffed it, and decided not to throw it through either the window or the tall mirrored doors that opened into the walk-in closet.

"Special celebration? Or was he just feeling his oats? You know, the old male thing. Prove a little virility. Defy the reality of death by pumping a bit of DNA into nubile young flesh?"

Anne slid her knees out from under the sheet and sat on the side of the bed, head hanging. "Celebration." Then she lifted her head, meeting Valerie's gaze. "And why the hell do I have to answer to you? What Murray does, who he sleeps with, is his business. You don't own him, do you?"

"Maybe not, but my toothbrush's in his medicine cabinet." She pointed at the bathroom door. "It's the one with blue and white bristles." She shook her head. "Forget it, Annie. I'm not going to fight with you. You can have the son of a bitch. I'm taking a shower, packing my things, and he's all yours. I'll even hand you my key on the way out. Deal?" At that, Valerie stepped into the plush bathroom, unhooked her bra, slid out of her panties, and turned the water in the glass shower to hot.

She considered her options, aware that she always made bad decisions when she was bone-tired. In the end, after the water had worked its magic and her muscles and joints felt flaccid and loose, she decided not to trash Murray's house. At thirty-six, she was supposed to be mature, rational, responsible. Instead, she took one of Murray's giant fluffy towels out of the cabinet and tossed her personal effects into the middle.

When she entered the bedroom, dragging her towel behind her, Anne was gone. Valerie used the bedroom phone to call a cab. They told her fifteen minutes. And that, she decided, would be just about right.

From Murray's closet, she took her dresses, slacks, blouses, and shoes. Picking and choosing as she tossed garments onto the towel, she dressed in a conservative black cotton skirt, a white sweater, and her knee-high boots. The rest she folded neatly in the center of the towel. Like some ludicrous hobo, she tied up the four corners and slung the whole over her back. She left her dirty clothes where they lay in the hallway, snarled at herself in the mirror, and descended the stairs.

Anne was waiting in the foyer. Her gaze locked on the towel-wrapped bundle over Val's shoulder.

"Celebration, huh?" Valerie said woodenly. "I guess he can celebrate more space in his closet." She winked at Anne. "And a new woman in his bed. Uh, listen, if I could give you a bit of advice, Murray's a bit like American Express. Don't leave home without him. Or, if you do, be sure to come back a day early. Just to keep track of the slimy bastard."

"You're a real piece of work," Anne said bitterly. "You know, he calls you the 'BitchSicle.' Frozen to the core."

Valerie ground her teeth, pushed past Anne, and opened the door. She flung her bundle down on the stair and dug through her purse. Finding the bit of brass, she tossed Anne the key. "There, you're all set. You can celebrate again tonight. Like a bad dream, the 'BitchSicle' is no more than a memory."

The cab came cruising down the block, the driver with his head bent to read the addresses.

Valerie slung her towel over her shoulder, balancing the load, and picked up her suitcase from where she had left it beside the door. "Oh, and tell Murray I won't try to fuck him over for doing this. He can stay on his side of the building, and I'll stay on mine."

Anne smiled smugly, cocking a hip to lean against the doorjamb. "I don't think so, Val. You see, what we were celebrating last night was Murray's promotion. While you were off screwing around with little brown men, Murray got Dan Feldman's job. He's the Triple N Washington station manager now."

Valerie almost missed her step. Not for anything would she let the little black-haired bitch see how that hurt. Every fiber of her being strained to keep a straight face. The cabbie didn't say a word when she opened the door and slung a bulging blue towel into the backseat. Sliding in beside it, she barked her address and slammed the door shut.

Only after the cab had made the corner onto MacArthur Boulevard did she allow herself to slump wearily in the seat.

Managing a project the size of SAC's African Primate Preserve—nearly six hundred square miles of tropical rain forest—could be downright daunting. But as associate director of SAC Africa, Vernon Shanks was accustomed to quelling small emergencies.

Six feet tall, he had moody brown eyes and a heavy jaw. He drove his red Kawasaki Mule to a stop in front of the D administration building, a concrete structure with a green metal roof. A narrow cement walk ran from the red dirt roadway to the glass front door. On either side, the grass had been carefully mowed, a precaution against the snakes, parasites, and other tropical exotica that periodically crawled out of the forest and made life here in central Africa a little more exciting than the usual assignment in Brighton, Manchester, or Glasgow.

Shanks grabbed his briefcase, pulled his bush hat down over

his close-cropped black hair, and sprinted through the rain to the glass doors. He hung his hat on the rack just inside, then brushed the water from his shoulders onto the foyer floor.

"Dr. Shanks?" Melody Hinsinger hurried down the hall, her lab coat flapping around her short legs. She had rung him up yesterday, called him out of a very important meeting in Compound A, sounding frantic, and had refused to explain the problem over the phone. "How was the drive?"

Like most of the SAC researchers, she was young, in her mid-twenties. Here, in the wilds, dress was casual at best. Hinsinger wore a khaki shirt and shorts. Like so many of them, she had been recruited for the project by Smyth-Archer himself. They were all the best. They knew it, were paid accordingly, and produced—exactly as was expected of them.

"Exciting," he told her, smiling. "I had no choice but to bounce over a huge python stretched clear across the road. He was tremendous, twenty feet if he was an inch. You know, driving over a snake that big, in a vehicle as small as a Kawasaki, has its moments. Especially when the old boy started squirming under the wheels."

Hinsinger nodded absently. But then they'd all had experiences like that. Virgin forest began no more than twenty yards behind the building they now stood in.

Shanks said, "Very well, Melody, what seems to be the problem?"

She turned, leading him down the hall toward his office. "We don't know if we have a problem or not. Alpha Group has disappeared. By that I mean we can't find them. They haven't been back to their village. They haven't come to the feeding grounds, and the remote cameras haven't picked them up."

"What?" he snapped in surprise. She'd just told him that about thirty million dollars' worth of research had vanished. "How long has it been?"

Shanks entered his office and slumped into the blue chair

behind his desk. Bookshelves, stuffed to overflowing, lined the walls. From habit, he automatically picked up the first of the papers on his desk. A report from the maintenance division on the dormitory plumbing. An airfield memo warned that the landing strip would need resurfacing in the next six months. "How long have they been missing?" he repeated.

Melody stood in front of him with her arms crossed defensively over her chest. "Five days. It's not time to panic, Vernon, but we thought you should have a heads up on this."

"Has anyone conducted a search?"

"I've had my people out every day for the last three days. Normally Girl and Baldy give them away. Baldy is a sucker for sugarcane stalks. But we haven't heard a peep."

Shanks considered, fingering his chin. "Could they have slipped past us to Beta or Gamma territory?"

She shook her head. "If they had, the other groups would have reacted." A pause. "Vernon, it's not scientific, but I have a gut feeling about this. You know Sky Eyes. His history. Remember? He attacked that little girl in Denmark. He's first-generation. He's never been very stable."

"And you're implying . . . what?"

The frown lines deepened in her brow. "I don't know. He's twitchy, that's all. Always has been. You know, happy one moment, violent the next. He's attacked people five times in the past year. If you ask me, he's a little mad."

"Maybe a lot mad." Shanks propped his chin on his fist, staring at a flowchart on the opposite wall. "For some reason he's always had a high testosterone reading, and an oversized pituitary. I've never liked that one. I think Geoffrey made a mistake by not terminating him years ago."

"What if he's"—Melody made an awkward gesture— "snapped?"

"Let's just get out and find him, shall we?" Shanks gave her a dismissive wave. "If we haven't located them in another day or two, we'll start considering dire possibilities."

"Yes, sir." She nodded politely and left.

He could hear her feet padding down the hallway as he leaned back in his chair and heaved a sigh.

In the science of genetic engineering, one had to accept the mistakes that accompanied the learning process. Usually such mistakes were eliminated, but Geoffrey Smyth-Archer refused to kill anything. Instead, he'd created Alpha Group—a receptacle for the project's rejects.

Shanks riffled through the papers on his desk, trying to put Alpha Group, and Sky Eyes, out of his mind.

He has given up his vigil at Girl's body. Leaving her corpse behind has left a hollow in his chest. He has come here, the others following uncertainly. Through the leaves, he watches the humans moving along the forest floor below. He hears them calling to him and his band, and then to each other. Soft hoots break out behind him. He lifts his machete for silence. The others comply, but look nervously after the receding humans.

Long after they have passed, he considers the head of the night hunter that is hung from a branch above him. This one had been called Ngasala. This one used the thunder weapon to kill Girl. This one cut the infant from inside her. Now he hangs, bobbing slightly, like some rotting fruit.

Those eyes that had glittered with fear are now dry and sunken. The lips that had parted in a final scream are drawn back to expose white teeth—but instead of a scream the buzzing of the flies issues from within.

Who would have thought that a human would be so easy to kill?

Six

Jim walked with his hands behind his back, breathing in the cool night air. How on earth did he find the ethical high ground in this situation?

First, he told himself, *figure out what Umber is. Then deal with the rest.*

Beside him, Tory's heels tapped on the sidewalk. They were headed north on College Avenue, walking for something to do. She glanced suspiciously at his face, trying to read his expression.

Traffic flowed past, slowing, stopping for reds, and then streaming onward. Behind the coffee shop windows, students sat around the tables, talking over their espresso. Some bent studiously over texts with yellow highlighters, the frown of learning engraved on their young faces.

"You know," Jim said, "within any gene pool enough variation exists to cause different individuals to have a different appearance. That's how natural selection works. Maybe Umber's just on the tail of the curve? A unique combination of genetic traits?"

Tory looked at him askance. "Come on, Dr. Dutton. You took the measurements yourself. Umber has over a thousand ccs of brain. The average human female has around eleven hundred and fifty to twelve hundred. Your normal, run-of-the-mill chimpanzee only has four hundred. So does the bonobo. You *don't* gain six hundred ccs out of the blue, Jim. The instructions to produce it simply aren't coded into the chimpanzee genetic structure."

He shoved his hands into the back pockets of his faded Levi's. "I don't like where this is going."

"I don't either." She tilted her head back, looking up at the few stars bright enough to burn through the city lights. "Tell me about SAC. What do you have to do to keep your grant? What are the rules?"

Jim kicked at a crumpled ball of paper on the cement. "Once a month we download all of our raw data into their system. It's all done electronically through a modem and phone line to England. Each quarter we send them a hard copy report. That includes things like our observations on behavior, evaluation of tests we've conducted, an analysis of research paradigms we're using, hypotheses we've been testing, and statistical programs we've been running. At that time we box up all the duplicate VHS tapes and ship them off to SAC London. The same with any photos, vet reports, that sort of thing."

"What do you hear back?" She folded her arms over her black turtleneck.

He shrugged. "Not much. Sometimes we receive a request. SAC wants us to make a change in the research design, or maybe they'll send us a puzzle box, and ask us to have Umber solve it. Sometimes it gets a little bizarre. Last spring they wanted Umber to plant a garden. So we did. We put in a little patch of carrots, pumpkins, and broccoli and tried to get Umber to take part in growing it. It wasn't one of our more successful endeavors. Umber would rather play on her computer than watch plants grow."

"A garden? For what? Did they give you any reason?"

"No, and that's one of the curiosities about working with SAC. They send in a request, and we do what they ask. Last spring they asked us to teach Umber to throw a javelin. We couldn't even get her to pick it up until Brett dropped by after school. She took to javelin throwing like the proverbial fish to water. And then Umber took a real interest."

"And she did all right?"

"No. Her wrist doesn't have the same flexibility. It was the bow and arrow that she really took a shine to."

"Bow and arrow?" Tory glanced at him uncertainly. In the harsh streetlights her pale impish face and black hair had a faintly blue glow.

"That followed the javelin request. With Umber's upper body strength, she was a natural. She could drive an arrow clear through a hay bale. She could outshoot Brett with it in a day." Jim paused. "You see, there is a little bit of sibling rivalry there."

"But, Jim, surely you have some sense of what SAC is looking for. I mean, you don't function in a vacuum. What do they say when you ask about things?"

He winced. "That's just it. We don't. At least, not often. They send in a polite request. 'Dr. Dutton, would you please plant a garden? Dr. Dutton, we are interested in motor function. Could you experiment with Umber's ability to throw a javelin? Dr. Dutton, we are interested in right-brain spatial relationships. Can Umber successfully manipulate a bow and reliably hit a target at thirty meters?' That sort of thing."

"But no feedback? Surely you ask about what they are doing with the data."

Jim shrugged. "When we ask, they say something like: 'We are currently developing new databases on long-term projects.' Or, 'We are looking forward to your reports on Umber's progress in this field.'"

"You mean, you don't ask for some sort of guidance from them?"

They made the right around the Northern Hotel and headed down Riverside. "We did in the beginning. I was a young postdoc. This was Smyth-Archer Chemists, one of the biggest pharmaceutical companies in the world. You don't blow a chance like that, not and end up a tenured professor of anthropology. If I screwed up, I knew I was going to end up back in Wyoming pitching hay on Dad's ranch for the rest of my life."

"Why'd they pick you?"

"They read a copy of my dissertation on primate socialization and learned hunting behavior. I was raised in Wyoming, with a rifle, on a ranch. I grew up hunting, studying animals. I recognized similarities in hunting behavior between humans and chimpanzees. I postulated that people who study hunting in chimps don't understand the strategy, that for a monkey it isn't always a fortuitous grab, but a planned process. Look, chimps in the wild study their prey, just like a human hunter does. Making that kind of assertion about chimp cognitive ability was controversial. I got a call from Geoffrey Smith-Archer himself, asking if I really believed great apes were that smart. I told him yes, that because of the inherent restrictions of 'the scientific method,' we had underrated their abilities." Jim shrugged. "I guess he liked what I told him."

"So, what happened?" An eighteen-wheeler thundered past, chrome shining in the lights.

Jim smiled. He would never forget that magical day. "They arrived on the fifteenth of June with this squirming bundle of baby ape and a fifty-page contract. Umber was a little over a year old at that time. The two guys who brought her were both charming Englishmen, Brian Smithwick and Daniel Aberly. Very professional. Aberly was a veterinarian. FedEx dropped off a bunch of boxes full of formula, refrigerated medicines, and a stock of prepaid mailers for shipping specimens back to England.

"I worked with Dr. Smithwick, discussing how the lab was supposed to be set up, what equipment to buy, and how to submit my reports. Dr. Aberly set up a liaison with the CSU Vet School to ensure that they'd have the latest information on ape medicine. Finally, I was briefed on how to care for Umber, all the usual ape protocols, like avoiding exposure to the general public, especially children, to keep her from getting sick. I . . ."

When he hesitated, Tory looked up at him. "What?"

Jim said, "I'll always remember that last day. We were sitting in the anthro department lounge and I had just signed that huge contract . . . 'research agreement,' they called it. Roger, the CSU vet, me, Smithwick, Aberly, and Hal Evans. Hal was department chair then. Smithwick told me they had every confidence in me. That they'd researched my life and work. They liked my ranching background and the fact that my beliefs about chimpanzee intelligence mirrored theirs. They thought I was the perfect person to raise Umber, and that while chimps had been cross-fostered before, no one had done it right. They wanted me to treat Umber as a child first, and a research subject second. Make her my second daughter. And they gave me a great deal of latitude in her raising.

"So, I asked what I should do first. Smithwick told me to take a couple of months and get used to Umber, socialize her with Brett and to her new surroundings. Develop that bond of trust, set up the lab, and act as if she were human."

Tory watched her feet as they walked through an intersection, then said, "Did Umber act as if she'd been around humans before?"

"Definitely. She responded to English and had the first basic ASL signs. Better than what you would expect for an ape her age. They had done a great deal of work with her."

"Have any trouble with her?"

"Just the sorts of things you'd expect. Umber was horrified at being left with strangers. I spent those first three months worrying my butt off. It wasn't enough to have a frightened insecure bonobo under my care, I also had a daughter entering the terrible twos. When I wasn't pampering Umber, Brett was trying to stick her fingers into the light socket." Jim shook his head. "And as soon as I got Brett through the terrible twos, Umber started them. If she wasn't emptying the flour canister onto the kitchen floor, or drinking the dish soap, she was stuffing her feces into the heating ducts." He made a face. "Forget war, famine, and plague. If humans ever go extinct, it will be because they had children."

They walked under a street lamp; Tory wore a worried expression. "And SAC didn't demand anything during that period of time?"

"Oh, they sent out observers during that first year to see how we were doing. It wasn't until that fall, after we'd set up the lab, that the first research requests came in from SAC."

"What kind of requests?"

"They wanted us to buy certain toys for Umber: little plastic tools, blocks, plastic letters and numbers. Then we followed a teaching protocol they established. Mostly simple motor coordination, tickle games, peekaboo, that sort of thing."

"That sounds pretty harmless."

Jim shoved his hands into his front pockets as they rounded the corner onto Linden. Passing the boutiques, he said, "Yeah, for the most part. Keep in mind, I'd studied the work of Keith and Cathy Hayes, and Alan and Beatrix Gardner. I'd read everything that came out of Bill Lemmon's work in Oklahoma, and of course everything that Roger Fouts and Sue Savage-Rumbaugh ever wrote. The salient fact that shines through all of it is that when sensitive intelligent chimps are treated like experimental rats, they get weird and psychotic. Just like people."

"Thinking of Harry Harlow?" Tory asked. She was referring to the behavioral psychologist who locked baby rhesus monkeys into a cage. Deprived of any warmth, maternal care, or even a blanket to cling to, they'd gone hopelessly insane. Primates needed intimate care, sophisticated social interaction, and self-security, reinforced by grooming, touching, and hugs.

"Like I said, I grew up on a ranch, Tory. I know animals. I like them and respect them. I didn't want Umber growing up like some of the experimental chimps did. I wanted to give Umber the same breaks I was giving Brett. First off, she's a bonobo. They use sexual favors for social manipulation and interaction. They build their societies around dominant females, a classic matrilineage."

"From what I can see, Jim, Umber is better adjusted than most children I know."

"Yes, well." Jim gave the sky an imploring look. "Time to come clean, I guess. She blew the top off the curve. I followed her progress with American Sign Language and her computer voice synthesizer. At age four, she was performing as well as Kanzi—the adult bonobo at the Language Research Center outside of Atlanta. At age eight, she was constructing complete sentences, using syntax and those verb tenses you are so impressed by. She had a vocabulary of at least thirteen hundred words and knew the English alphabet. The alphabet, by the way, she learned with Brett." He paused. "Sometimes it frightens me to think of the things Brett might be teaching her when I'm not around."

Tory was silent, locked in thought. Finally she said, "Jim, Umber is twelve now. Surely she's demonstrated additional competency since age eight?"

He swallowed hard. "Tory, what would you say if I told you she could read?" He hesitated. "And write. I'm not talking about using the keyboard, which is a spatial skill where the keys represent phonemes. She writes. On paper. With a pencil. In English."

Tory stopped short, mouth agape. "This is a joke, right?"

Jim continued walking. "I'm afraid not. Her spelling is atrocious, and she has problems staying between the lines. As to reading, she isn't into Nora Roberts and Elizabeth George the way Brett is, but Umber reads her picture books, signing out the words. We've got it on tape. If you want to prove it to yourself, buy her a book she doesn't have. Fourth-grade level. Let her read it, then question her on it."

Tory slowed, walking as if in a daze. "This stretches credulity, Jim. For God's sake, I mean . . . what . . . what do the SAC people say when you tell them this?"

Jim stopped dead in his tracks. Tory kept walking for a few paces, then stopped and turned to look back at him.

She tightened her arms across her chest. "Yes, Dr. Dutton? You were saying?"

"Tory, I don't know if it was good or bad, right or wrong, but years ago Dana and I starting fudging the data. To another researcher, it looks like Umber is making steady progress, learning new signs, mastering new skills, but not at the exceptional rate she does."

"Dear God," Tory's voice dropped. She walked back and slipped her arm through his, guiding him forward at a steady pace. "You shouldn't be telling me this, Jim. I don't—"

"No, I shouldn't. Did I mention that contract? The research agreement? By telling you this, I'm in gross violation of that agreement. It has a million nondisclosure clauses, financial penalties that add up to *tons* of money, and probably my left nut, to boot."

"Then why tell me?"

"Because I'm in over my head, Tory! I need help. No ape has ever learned to read English before. I didn't teach her to read. I didn't think of it. If I had, she'd probably be reading at the sixth-grade level. Instead, Brett taught her because it never occurred to Brett not to. Tory, listen to me, Umber does simple mathematics. Adds and subtracts." He gave her a pleading look. "Not just two and two, but twenty-five and thirty-one, with the sum coming out fifty-six."

"Apes can't do that." Tory's face had gone white.

"No," Jim agreed. "And according to the agreement, SAC can land on me like a ton of bricks. Take away everything I own. Ruin me." He swallowed hard. "Now you can understand why Dana and I have been scared half to death for the last two years."

Doug Parnell watched as Dutton and the woman crossed Mountain Avenue to the red and brown Bronco. He had followed them from the moment they had left the lab. Parnell was a beefy man in his late forties, dark-haired, with a thick face and perfectly forgettable features. He liked white long-sleeved shirts that covered the thick mat of hair on his arms. Tonight he'd worn brown cotton pants, a tweed jacket with elbow patches, and brown loafers. Trendy. Just the sort of thing to disappear into the Fort Collins milieu.

Fortunately, Dutton had picked a busy microbrewery for supper. In the throng, Parnell had been able to pass close enough to their table to catch snatches of conversation. The after-dinner talk had been about the ape, the tone grim.

Once out of the restaurant, Parnell hadn't needed to shadow them closely. The directional microphone he carried was a sensitive instrument. From fifty feet behind them, he had managed to monitor most of their conversation. Some of the traffic noise had bled in, especially when the big trucks rolled past, but the computers, with their fractal programs, would clean that up.

Dutton unlocked the Bronco as Parnell punched the speed dial on his cell phone. After the first ring a voice said, "Yeah?"

"Pick me up. They're just getting into the Bronco."

He stepped out to the curb. As Dutton turned on the Bronco lights and backed out, Carl Simms pulled up in the white Ford van and slowed. Parnell climbed into the passenger seat as the Bronco made a right onto Matthews and headed south.

"Keep them in sight," Parnell ordered. He used local guys like Simms to keep an eye on things. He glanced at Carl, adding, "You were right to call me when you did. Flagging Dr. Driggers's number out of his phone records might have bought us a little more time."

Carl gave him a wry smile. "Glad to be of help. Do you want to tell me what this is all about?"

"You don't need to know," Parnell growled under his breath. "Did you get the device into the Bronco?"

"Couldn't. He'd set the security system. That's not normally a problem. It's one of those remote units on the key ring. All I have to do is match the frequencies to disarm it, but why take the time and chance on a busy street? I'll handle that later tonight. He doesn't lock it at home."

Parnell gave Carl a sidelong glance. "Don't worry about it. I'll take care of that little duty myself."

Seven

Mornings had never been one of Valerie's strengths. This one was no exception. According to plan, she should have felt rested, ready to charge hell with a bucket of water. Instead, she'd no sooner been deposited at her apartment building, hobo towel over her shoulder, when some pernicious little microbe— no doubt a denizen of Colombian water—began to work its way through her lower digestive tract.

Having waged guerrilla war with third-world bugs for years, she had fought back with antibiotic salvos, some legal, others not, gathered from across the globe.

By that morning it appeared that she'd beaten the bug. But what should have been almost twenty hours of peaceful sleep had been anything but.

So it was that she felt on the dark side of crummy as she opened the Dodge Durango's door and stepped out. Taking her briefcase and locking the door, she made her way across the parking lot. At the heavy steel door, she smiled up at the security camera and tapped her ID into the touch pad. Inside, she nodded to Nick at the security desk.

"Hey, Val." The guard lifted a finger. "Roberto came in about two hours ago. Said to see him firstest."

"Got it. Thanks." She made her way down the hallway, hesitated as her gut twisted, and clenched her fist on the strap of her leather handbag. The scary feeling eased and she took the elevator to her small office on the sixth floor.

The in-basket on her steel desk was piled with FYIs, photocopies of news stories from the clipping department, reports and briefings, as well as rubber-banded packets of date-stamped mail. Her answering machine listed no less than thirty messages. She pulled out the padded desk chair, slung her purse into the knee space of the desk, and had just started to sit when the cramps stabbed through her.

As she stood, Joan Faulkner, the longtime secretary for the station director, appeared in Val's doorway. She wore a brown tweed suit that looked appropriately conservative and carried a file folder in her thin hands.

"Good morning, Valerie." Joan pushed her horn-rims up on her nose. "Mr. Stanton would like to see you immediately."

"As soon as I go—"

"The station manager said immediately," Joan insisted in that tone of voice that bordered on authoritative but still managed to be professionally polite by the thinnest of threads.

"Murray doesn't waste much time, does he?" Valerie sighed, decided to tough it out, and extended a hand. "Very well, lead the way."

She followed Joan down the carpeted halls, hung with photos of journalists, posters celebrating events, C-prints of politicians, exploded tanks on a Gulf War battlefield, and other natural and man-made disasters that Triple N had covered.

Joan glanced sidelong at her in the elevator as it rose toward the seventh floor. "How was Colombia?"

"Hot. Wet. Muggy and smelly. We got some pretty good footage of Carlos Vacilla's latest mass murder. Lots of close-ups of little children shot in the back of the head. Prime-time stuff. Enough to make Vacilla lay low on the international scene for a couple of years until it blows over." When had she begun to sound so cynical? Or was it the pesky bug?

"Good material, I'm sure," Joan said tonelessly.

Valerie watched her from under lowered eyelids. Joan had been around since the Triple N studio had been built in Washington. She had started as newsroom secretary and been promoted up the line to the station manager's secretary. In the last six years she had survived three different station managers and was now starting on her fourth. Scuttlebutt said that Joan Faulkner knew more about Triple N's D.C. operation than anyone, and that *she* ran the station, allowing the SM to sit as a figurehead.

Valerie followed Joan down the long hall to the glass-fronted reception area. Joan crossed to the walnut door that guarded the station manager's office and leaned her head in. "Miss Radin to see you, sir."

"Send her in," Murray said, voice slightly muffled over the distance.

Valerie stepped past Joan, closed the door behind her, and walked across the large office. Her feet sank in the thick blue carpet. The large windows overlooked Washington Circle below, and from there gave a view down Pennsylvania toward the White House and the Capitol. Overstuffed leather couches faced a big-screen TV that was framed with smaller televisions, each tuned to one of the major networks, the sound off. A computer workstation filled the other corner, the monitor glowing with the Triple N e-mail prompt.

Murray sat on the edge of a giant mahogany desk, with its big green blotter, phone, and lamp. He wore a dark blue silk suit, stylishly cut. A red paisley tie hung just crooked enough to accent his offbeat image and emphasize his salt-spray hairstyle. His smile was humorless, a weary resignation in his hazel eyes. The tan that Chesapeake water and sun had burned into his smooth-shaven face had begun to fade. Well, she thought, perhaps with the promotion he'd have more time for his sail-boat, a twenty-four-foot sloop anchored at Annapolis. His large hands were clasped in his lap, and one foot swung insolently.

"It looks like little orphan Annie got you dressed okay for your first day on the job as station manager," Val greeted as she stood before him. "Congratulations." From the corner of her eye, she noted the boxes to one side. He was still un-packing.

He sighed. "It couldn't have turned out worse if I'd planned it." His expression grew serious. "The first week you were gone, it felt like a huge weight had been lifted off my shoulders. Dur-ing the second, I started dreading your return. On the third, I started thinking about ways to tell you that it was over. I thought I had it planned. I'd meet you at the airport this morn-ing, and we'd discuss it on the way to the station. All nice and professional, just like adults are supposed to do." He spread his hands. "You'd think that after six months, I'd know better than to think anything could go normally in a relationship with you." He gave her an inquisitive look. "You all right? You look green."

"Jesus, Murray, give me a break." Her gut protested. She'd die before she'd let him know how horrible she felt.

He held up his hands defensively. "Wait a minute. Hear me out. Somehow, with you, I was always on edge, always felt as if I was tiptoeing around the sharp edges. I'm not attacking you, and, damn it, don't you stand there and try to tell me that it was all roses between us. Come on. Let me hear from your lips that I made you happy. We were just going through the motions, and you know it." He shook his head slowly and met her eyes. "What? No dying protestations of spurned love?"

"Cut it out, Murray." She propped her hands on her hips and stalked to the window to stare out at the city. "I must be getting old. This shit isn't nearly as upsetting as it used to be. You know, I don't even hate you. I ought to, but I don't. Jesus, how jaded does that make me? I don't even give a shit when I find another woman in my man's bed."

"Maybe you're just being honest," he told her as he came to stand beside her. "You and I come at life from different directions, Val. I want to slice through it like a hot blade. Limit the amount of resistance I have to overcome. You hit things head-on, like a slug from a forty-five. Blast a big hole, batter your way through, and evaluate the little hidden pieces that come flying out with the splinters. That's what makes you such a damn good reporter."

She rubbed her hands up and down her arms, fighting the urge to press on her abdomen. "Yeah, why don't I feel thrilled with the compliment?"

"Val," he said gently. "I don't want this to be difficult. There's no percentage in us fighting each other. I want you to consider some options. Take a couple of weeks off and—"

"Weeks off?" She spun on a heel to face him. "Murray, what the hell are you doing? What options?" At the hardening of his features, she snorted in derision. "Oh, I see. Afraid I'll make waves? Is that it? The boss's old squeeze might be painting the coffee room with poison?"

"Valerie, don't make this more difficult than it has to be. I wanted this . . . well, to be . . ."

She channeled all the disdain she could muster into a scathing glare. "Yeah, Murray? Just thought I'd fly off to Jamaica for a month? Get a little sun? Do a little partying. Get laid by the diving instructor? And when I came back, it would all be forgotten? Just like that?"

He threw his hands up. "All right! Do you want a transfer? Fine with me. Where do you want to go? Frankfurt has a position. So does Moscow. How about Beijing? If anything blows, it's going to be China. You'd be right at ground zero. In at the very beginning. With your Canadian passport, you could probably stay inside. You'd be just like Peter Arnett in Baghdad."

"Anywhere but here, is that it?" She mocked him with a smile.

Murray walked toward his desk, rubbing his forehead. "I don't know, Val. You tell me. How is it going to work, huh? If I send you off to Tehran, is it because I'm giving you preference for a cherry assignment, or am I trying to get you killed? Either way, it's my fault." He hesitated, and turned, eyes pleading. "Frankfurt's not such a bad—"

"I've been there. Murray, snap out of it. You know and I know that at my age, foreign assignment is a dead end. If I'm going anywhere, it's New York or L.A. That's it. And if I go either place, it's with a promotion to anchor. Not just filling in when the anchor's on assignment like I do now."

"Dan Houston isn't leaving L.A., Val, and you know it. And you'd have to use dynamite to blast Virginia Arnold out of New York."

"Then it looks like you're stuck with me, Murray." She ran a finger down the front of her throat as she met his smoldering eyes. "But I'll make you a deal. I won't make any trouble. If you help me, I'll help you."

He chewed his lip uncertainly. "Help you how?"

"All right, old lover, since we're baring souls here, you know that the position of station manager is a short step from corporate. That's fine with me. You've always wanted a slice of the corporate pie. Me, I want an anchor's position, or I want my own show. A documentary. Something I can produce and host."

"God, Val, I can't just up and hand you a prize like that! Jesus, corporate would be all over me! It'll look like I just bought you off!"

"This is Washington, Murray. This town runs on insider deals." She lowered her fists to her sides. Damn, why did she have to do this today, when she felt like hell? "But let's lay that aside for the moment. Forget about personalities, about you and me and what's between us. Forget everything but my ability. If I say I can do my own show, a hard-hitting documentary, *Frontline, 20-20*, and *60 Minutes* all rolled into one, do you think I can deliver?"

He was back to chewing his lip, pensive frown lines eating into his brow. He nodded, the movement of his head ever so slight. "Yeah, Val. No matter what, you've always delivered."

She crossed her arms against the cramps in her intestines. "The bottom line in this business is money, Murray. Ratings mean money. I think I can carve out a bigger hunk of market share for Triple N. You know I can do it. That's my price. I'll slip meekly away, cause you no trouble, and do everything I can to make you a success here. In return, you give me a shot at anchor, or my own show. It's up to you."

He turned and booted an empty cardboard box across the room. "Damn you, you calculating cold-blooded bitch. Everything comes with a price tag, doesn't it? Everything is a negotiation. How did I ever manage—"

"And for you," she kept her voice even, "it's all a matter of keeping score. Chalking up the promotions, the awards, and checking off the people you've met in your *Who's Who* book. Christmas up at Cape Cod will be a real joy as you impress everyone at the dinner table with your little stories."

"Did anyone tell you that you were a pit viper, Val?"

"A time or two. Want to see my fangs?" She arched an eyebrow, refusing to flinch at the pain in her belly. "I don't really think you do, Murray. Now, do we play ball, or do I go down and announce to the newsroom that you threw me over because you were impotent? That, or I could give them a blow-by-blow—literally—of the weekend we spent at the Williamsburg Inn."

His eyes had grown flat, emotionless, as he watched her. "Okay. You've got it." His voice strained at the edge of control. "You do what I tell you, give me a year, and I give you my word, I'll let you have a crack at your own show. Meanwhile, I'm going to make you pay for it, Val. I don't like being pushed into corners, but I'll play along. And, so help me, if you double-cross me, if I hear so much as a peep out of you, I'm going to squash you like a bug. You hear me?"

"Loud and clear, Murray." She gave him a cold smile, turned, and walked toward the door. With her toe, she nudged the caved-in box to one side. "By the way, nice digs you've got here."

She closed the door behind her, gave Joan a satisfied smile, and exited through the glass doors. She waited until she had reached the safety of the stall in the women's rest room to gasp and collapse.

"Hmm? What?" Jim mumbled as a hard finger jabbed him through the blankets. He tried to shake off the foggy stringers of sleep that clouded his mind. God, what time was it? He glanced over at the bedside clock and groaned. It was the middle of the night, for Christ's sake!

Umber pulled on the arm she had found under the blankets.

Jim sat up and blinked in the darkness. "What's wrong, Umber?"

She uttered her alarm sound, part bark, part hoot; he could sense her signing in the dark. Jim reached for his reading light.

Umber squinted, and signed over and over, "Someone in Bronco. Flashlight on. Someone in Bronco. Flashlight on."

"What?" he asked, foggy with sleep. "Who's in the Bronco?"

"Maybe Tory?"

"Tory's in town at the Marriott." He climbed out of bed, growling, and tugged on his pants and boots.

He pulled the rifle from the closet and grabbed for the box of 30.06 bullets on the high shelf. He clicked five rounds into the Sako's chamber and slipped the bolt home on the top round. "All right, let's see what this is about."

The sight of Jim's rifle brought Umber to a sudden panicked halt. Though she was fascinated by the rifle, the loud bang it made terrified her.

Umber cautiously followed Jim down the stairs, but they had no more than reached the landing when they heard the soft slam of the truck door.

Jim ran across the living room, flicked on the light, and threw open the front door.

"Hey!" he shouted as he stepped out onto the lawn. "What the hell are you doing?"

Umber eased out beside him. Jim heard footsteps pounding away, then a "whoof" followed by a grunt as the man ran full tilt into the barbed-wire fence at the edge of the property. The wire made a thrumming sound.

Umber barked and charged forward, hooting at the fleeing intruder. She stopped at the fence, spun around, and bent her finger in the "shoot" sign. "Jim, shoot now!" Then she raced around behind him, getting out of the line of fire, and craned her neck to see what happened next.

Jim lowered the rifle. Umber hooted her uncertainty and dared to walk up to Jim's side. "Shoot?" She made the sign followed by an interrogative.

"No," Jim said uneasily. "He's gone. I've told you time and time again, having a gun means being responsible. The rifle's for shooting food and for protecting the family. He ran, so we're safe." Jim stared out into the darkness, hearing the faint rustling of brush as the man continued to flee. "Umber, please go in and wake Brett. Have her call 911 and ask for the sheriff's office."

"Wheep," Umber replied and headed for the door.

Jim walked over to the Bronco and inspected it. "And bring

me a flashlight," he added. "I don't want to open the Bronco until the sheriff's deputy arrives. They might want fingerprints."

Umber stood in the doorway a few moments, rocking from side to side on her feet, then disappeared into the interior.

Jim took a deep breath and thumbed the safety on before he slung the rifle over his shoulder.

The intruder had fled south. But there was nothing out there for miles but ponderosa pine, scrubby mountain mahogany, and rock outcrops. He would be lucky if he didn't fall and break his neck.

Had it just been a kid looking for something to steal?

As Jim gazed out at the other houses dotting the hills, his shoulder muscles tensed.

He unslung his rifle and cradled it in his arms as he walked to the front step to wait for the deputies.

Eight

The Bronco incident had occurred at around two-thirty. The clock read four-fifteen by the time the deputy finally finished his report, climbed into his cruiser, and drove off down the mountain.

As his taillights disappeared, Brett made the forehead "bastard" sign, like a perverted salute, and for once, Jim didn't chasten her.

Throughout the investigation, the deputy had kept staring at Umber as though he questioned his sanity, especially when she had used her talking keyboard to answer questions about what she'd seen. When he had said, "I don't believe I'm talking to a trained monkey—boy, the desk sergeant is gonna love this one," Jim had clapped a hand over Brett's mouth and physically restrained her.

No sign of vandalism had been seen in the Bronco. Nothing was missing, not even the expensive tape recorder that Jim used to take notes on the road. It lay in plain sight on the seat. When the deputy had dusted the door latch to highlight any fingerprints, smudges of gloved fingers had appeared.

On the barbed-wire fence they'd found the first definitive clue, a long strip of nylon and hollow-fill insulation impaled on one of the sharp barbs. Between the Bronco door and the fence, a single footprint marked the dry soil. The deputy measured and photographed it, noting, "Vibram sole. Really common."

Now, with the deputy gone, the worry set in. Jim sat at the dining room table, elbows braced as he thoughtfully smoothed a hand over his beard. In her yellow and blue Indian print robe, Brett walked around the house for the third time, jiggling each door to make certain it was locked. Her blue eyes had a bright, frightened look.

"Brett, go back to bed," Jim said. "It's okay. The doors are locked and I'm going to be down here with the lights on. Everything's all right."

"Oh, sure, just go up and go to sleep with some pervert wandering around out there in the dark! Just like that! And be raped in my bed!" She made a frustrated gesture with her hands.

Jim gave her a bloodshot stare. "Brettany, I want you and Umber to go to bed. I'll stand guard."

Brett scowled at him, took three steps toward the stairs, then whirled and bolted for the couch. "Not on your life. I'm going to sleep here where you can see me."

Umber hooted softly. Her black hair still stood on end, and her lips had unconsciously curled into a fear-smile that exposed her teeth.

On the couch, Brett pulled her feet up and hugged the satin-cased pillow to her chest. She lay there, motionless, frowning.

Umber looked up the stairs, then signed to Jim: "Bad things hide in darkness."

"Yes," Jim said with a wan smile. "I guess sometimes they do."

Umber softly padded into the kitchen and pushed the button on the coffeemaker—already set to go for the morning. The coffeemaker gurgled and steamed as it warmed to the task.

By the time Umber returned to the table, Jim had his head

in his hands, shoulders stooped. His thoughts had turned crazy. How could there be a connection between someone breaking into the Bronco and the problem with Umber? *God, I'm getting paranoid.*

No one on the mountain locked his doors at night, but that was going to change around the Dutton house.

Where she lay on the couch, Brett had closed her eyes, tangles of hair slipping around the pillow she still clutched.

Umber lifted herself into the chair beside Jim's and reached out, patting his shoulder in reassurance. He rubbed his eyes with his thumbs and stared at her. "Quite a night, huh? I guess we were just lucky you woke up and noticed the light on in the Bronco."

Umber gave him her exaggerated bonobo nod and signed: "Bad dream. Monster chased me. No place to hide. No way out."

"I know how you feel."

Umber studied him thoughtfully. She pointed at Jim, made the sign for "worry," pointed to herself, and drew a question mark in the air.

Jim reached out and took her warm hand. Her black fingers curled around his. "I want you to know that no matter what happens, it's not your fault. Understand?"

"Wheep."

He gently ran his fingers through the black hair on her shoulders. She sighed, happy at his touch.

Umber crossed her arms to say, "Love you. Brett, too."

Jim nodded, and a frown incised his forehead. He glanced at Brett, then leaned toward Umber and, in a low voice, said, "Umber, I think we're in real trouble."

Her soft brown eyes widened as she touched her forehead in the "why?" sign.

"There's a problem with the data." Jim pulled Umber's chair closer and hugged her tightly to his chest. "If what I suspect is true, the whole world is going to come crashing down on top of us. And if it does, prowlers in the night are going to be the least of our concerns."

Roberto Naez and Valerie crouched, shoulder to shoulder, in the cramped editing booth deep in the guts of the Triple N building. Their attention was fixed on the glowing screen showing the Santa Isleta grave. The camera angle was perfect. Roberto's job might be to simply record, but from Valerie he had learned to use his skills to give just the right light, to focus on the smallest nuance, to allow the viewer to interpret the scene through his or her own eyes.

In Santa Isleta he had stood just to the side of the grave, the morning light falling on the bodies and the uniformed soldiers that grimaced down at them. Each soldier had a handkerchief over his mouth and nose, and they wore thick gloves that rose to the elbows. The soldiers had silently lifted the bodies one by one from the gaping hole in the earth.

"I think we may want to edit that." Roberto pointed as one of the teenage girls was lifted, naked, from the grave.

"Figures." Valerie had clipped her long blond hair behind her ears. "Isn't it damned ironic that people will throw a screaming fit, write letters by the bagful, because we show a naked girl, but they couldn't care less that she was raped and shot? Will we get a single indignant outcry that it happened in the first place? God, what's wrong with people?"

Roberto watched as her hands clenched and she ground her teeth. He'd spent his twenty-eighth birthday in Santa Isleta, filming the opening of the grave. For the last five years, he and Valerie had worked as a team, covering story after story. During that time, a sense had developed between them, a subliminal communication. Roberto generally knew what she was thinking before she did. Now, he pushed the pause button, freezing the frame of the naked girl, and leaned back.

Valerie stared into his dark eyes. "What?"

"Brittle today, eh, Fuerta?" He reached up and twisted his long black mustache.

Years ago, in Kosovo, their Humvee had driven over a mine. Valerie had pulled him from the tangled wreckage moments before the perforated fuel tank went up in a ball of flame. As he lay dazed beside the burning wreck, she had determined that his right leg was broken, and that little bits of shrapnel had punctured his chest and abdomen. Sleet had been falling from the sky. He'd insisted she leave him, go for help. The countryside there bristled with snipers and Serb militia. She had refused, and when he had finally passed out, she'd stubbornly lifted him in a combat carry and staggered as far as she could, then she had dragged him when she could no longer bear his weight. Only her dogged determination had seen them through the six tortuous miles back to the IFOR checkpoint.

"Brittle? Me?" she said.

He could see the muscles tightening at the corners of her mouth.

Roberto flipped a pen over onto the desk. "Yeah, you. Wanna spill it? What's up? You're bitchy, sharp, and nasty. It's been three days since you caught Murray banging his new piece of fluff. Usually you're back on your feet by now."

She slipped a hand under her long hair to massage the back of her neck and considered telling him to butt out. He gave her that challenging look, the one that dared her to be honest with him . . . and herself.

"I'm getting old, Roberto." She took a deep breath. "Maybe I'm just tired of all this." She jerked her head at the image of the girl's naked corpse. Despite the smudged dirt and blood, she looked sixteen, with full breasts, narrow waist, and long black hair clotted with filth and decay. "Tired of seeing things like that. Goddamn it."

"You need a break, Fuerta. We been busting ass for months now. It's like you're trying to work yourself to death. Running from something, hiding from something."

"Don't lay that on me. I'm not running from anything."

He arched an eyebrow. "Val, you're pushing yourself because your work is the only thing you got. You don't turn down an assignment, 'cause if you do, man, you got nothing but yourself to live with, and you don't like what's inside you."

She pulled her hand from beneath her hair and slowly closed her fingers into a fist before willing it down. With effort, she unlocked her clamped jaw. "Damn you, *cabron*. If anyone but you said that to me . . ."

He reached up, took her fist, and held it. She'd just made his point for him, and she knew it. "Ever since we did that Scandinavian Airlines story two years ago, you been dancin' closer and closer to the edge. I don't know if you're gonna fall, but I don't want to see you go over. You ready to talk about it yet?"

She shook her head. "No."

"It was that little girl, wasn't it? She spooked you."

Valerie's gaze went vacant, as if seeing the blond girl's body where it lay broken and dead in the snow, the delicate skin like alabaster, the wide blue eyes staring sightlessly at the sky.

"If I was a shrink, I'd say you saw your kid lying there in the snow, and guilt's been eating away at you ever since," Roberto said evenly. "Just pick up the phone and call her, Val."

She muttered under her breath, then added harshly, "It's not that easy, Roberto," and gestured to the screen. "We'd better get back to this. Murray's going—"

"Murray's right behind you," he said as he entered the editing booth and closed the door. His three-piece tan suit looked as though God had ironed it. Every crease perfect. He clutched a thick manila envelope. Head cocked, his eyes focused on the frozen scene of the murdered Colombian girl. "My God, that's great stuff. Even in death you can see the horror on her face."

"We were going to cut it," Roberto said. "Too naked for conservative American tastes. Only dressed people should be shot in the back and thrown into mass graves. It's more socially acceptable."

Murray propped a hand on the console and looked closely. "I want this. Just a split second of it. You know, enough that the viewer will recognize that she's naked, but not see anything." He put his hands up, bracketing her face. "Then zoom to a close-up of her face and freeze the frame. Right there. We'll do the voice-over with her dead eyes looking out at the audience."

Roberto nodded. "You got it. I'll have it ready by six."

Murray shook his head. "Bruno can finish it. You two are busy." He smiled and handed the envelope to Valerie. "Everything you need is in there. You've got tickets for the ten P.M. British Airways flight number 222. You'll be into London at ten tomorrow morning. Someone will meet you at Heathrow after you clear customs. Your hotel is in Kensington."

"Murray, damn it!" Valerie spun, jaw cocked. "We just got back from a month in beautiful scenic Colombia living with rats, lice, bad food, and squalor! Give it to someone else!"

Roberto placed a restraining hand on her arm. Valerie had a reputation for laying big males out on the floor before they knew what had hit them.

Unfazed, Murray gave her his best grin, the one that flashed his pearly whites and deepened the dimples at the corners of his mouth. "Lord, Val, did I ever tell you what a beauty you are when you're mad?"

"Murray, I'm *not* in the mood for any of your bullshit!"

He made a tsk-tsk sound with his lips. "And I thought we had a deal? A year, remember?"

Roberto shot a sidelong glance at Valerie.

"Yeah. All right." Valerie exhaled loudly. "But give Roberto a break." She glanced at him. "Hey, Taco, how long has it been since you've had Thanksgiving with the folks in McAllen?"

"*Muchos anos, pero no es importa.*" He made a throwing-away gesture. "It's okay, Fuerta. I'll go along. See if my chili stomach can take bangers and mash."

Valerie glanced nervously at the envelope, as if it contained a grand jury subpoena, or a letter from the IRS, or something equally distasteful. Then she reached out and took it from Murray's hand. The other hand pressed against her abdomen; this churning in her gut wasn't related to the last of her freeloading amoebas. "Just promise me one thing, Murray. No dead kids, right?"

Murray's lips quirked. "Even I have a heart, Val. This is just straight up-front journalism. A little digging for sources, uncovering the truth, that sort of thing."

"Straight up-front journalism?" She arched an eyebrow. "Then send a features guy. Someone like Hank Shreve. He loves straight up-front journalism."

"I got a feeling about this one, Val." Murray opened the soundproof door, half turning. "Something in my gut says that this could be dynamite if it's handled right. You took anthropology in college, didn't you? Something about bones and bodies and genes? Monkeys and apes, that sort of thing?"

"Yeah." Her blue eyes suddenly lit. "What of it?"

"You're the perfect pick. You'll know what the hell you're looking for."

"And that is?" She crossed her arms.

"In the envelope, baby cakes. My way of saying thanks for not trashing the house or killing Anne." And with that he was gone.

Roberto leaned back in his chair, giving her a bland look. "I'm glad you didn't bust up the furniture or smack his squeeze,

Val. We might have found ourselves heading for Laos, or Chechnya, or some other third-world toilet." He broke into a happy grin. "London? Hot damn, this Tejano is sleeping on clean sheets and getting laid in Piccadilly!"

She opened the envelope and pulled out British Air tickets, several fax sheets, a business prospectus, and photocopies of what looked like pictures of chimpanzees, but they were strangely out of focus.

"So, what's the gig?" Roberto laced his fingers behind his head as he spun around in the chair.

"Smyth-Archer Chemists. Pharmaceuticals company." Val shook her head. "I don't get it. Why'd Murray dump this on us? What's the big mystery?"

One by one she scanned the pages, then handed them to Roberto. Some appeared to be interoffice memos. Words like *methylation, plasmid,* and *ligase* triggered something in her memory. And she was sure that Roberto had at least heard of DNA, RNA, and recombination before.

"Looks like Greek to me," Roberto muttered as he shuffled the pages.

"Genetics," Val said thoughtfully. "It has to do with genetics."

"Huh? Like for breeding and stuff?"

"Maybe."

"So, like, what's a pharmaceutical company doing fooling around with genetics?"

"Got me. But I guess we'd better be packing. I'll meet you at Dulles at eight-thirty." She checked the tickets. "Good man, Murray. At least you booked us first class."

"He'd better have," Roberto said as he stood. "Why the hell else would we do this shit?"

God, she thought, *just promise me that there will be no dead little girls this time around.*

The morning was perfect. A calendar-photo fall day. The still air had a cool crispness. Golden beams of sunlight slanted through a vibrantly blue sky. Jim, Umber, and Tory walked along the shores of College Lake. Given the upset in his life, the world acted insensibly peaceful. He tried to take some solace from it, wondering what had happened to that old centered self of his.

He and Tory had both dressed in jeans and hiking boots. He wore a blue nylon windbreaker. She wore a thick red ski sweater.

Frost whitened the ground. No more than fifty yards ahead of them, a flock of geese waddled cautiously away, their muted honks and squawks carrying in the quiet.

Jim took a deep breath, inhaling the damp odor of mud and lake. As he walked, Umber held his hand, her thick skin warm against his. She wore a wool coat this morning to cut the chill. Her pants were bright green, and she had picked a red sweatshirt emblazoned with a picture of an elk and "Rocky Mountain National Park" in big letters. Specially made sheep-hide boots kept her feet warm.

"Glad you had your excitement last night," Tory said dryly. "I spent my night in the hotel room working with numbers."

"Do I want to hear about it?" Jim tightened his grip on Umber's hand. When Tory glanced sidelong at the ape, Jim added, "Tory, it concerns Umber. She can hear it, too."

Tory said, "All right. You'll tell her anyway, I suppose. In some ways Umber functions at the same level as a seven-year-old human girl. In others, she functions like a twelve-year-old. What she doesn't act like is a twelve-year-old bonobo. We have plenty of data from Takayoshi Kano's studies, Sue Savage-Rumbaugh's, the Badrians', and others. Bonobos don't create the kind of sentences that Umber does. They don't have the same emotional control. You don't even have to lock Umber up at night to keep her from raiding the house."

Umber gave Tory a toothy grin, pointed at herself, and made the palms-out gesture to say: "Umber behaves."

Tory said, "That's part of the problem. Umber behaves too well. Apes can use human language. We've known that for decades. What is at issue is the level at which they use it. Most apes reliably use no more than about one hundred fifty to two hundred fifty signs, though Koko, the gorilla, knew six hundred signs."

"Umber can carry on a sophisticated conversation with an adult," Jim said. "Sometimes she's too sophisticated for me."

Umber gently tightened her hold on his hand and drew it to her cheek so she could rub her face against it. Her black hair felt warm and soft.

"I read something really unbelievable in your notes last night, Jim," Tory said and frowned at the birds feeding along the lakeshore. Dark-eyed juncos and Cassin's finches hopped through the dead grass, chirping and singing.

Jim kicked at a stick that lay in the path. "Which unbelievable thing was that?"

Tory folded her arms over her ski sweater and said, "Umber, could you tell me about God?"

Umber's wide-mouthed face slackened, as if in deep thought. She stepped aside as a flock of geese waddled up, making way for them. Then she craned her neck to look up at Tory. As her hairy fingers formed words, Tory swallowed hard.

"Of all the . . ." Tory shook her head. "You see? She can't do that! Umber, where did you learn that God was the eye inside?"

Umber frowned, making a frustrated gesture with her free hand.

"The eye inside?" Jim asked. Umber often talked about God,

and death, but he'd never heard this before. "You mean God sees inside you?"

Umber shook her head vehemently and signed: "God lives inside," emphasizing "lives" as she made the thumbs-up sign on her chest.

Tory abruptly stopped walking. Wind blew her short black hair around her pale face.

"Tory? You all right?" Jim asked. "You look a little unsteady."

She put a hand to her forehead, as if pressing at a thought. "This will take a while to digest. Only humans discuss abstractions. No ape has ever said the kind of things Umber does, though Koko used to talk about death. Do you remember?"

Jim nodded solemnly. "Yes, I do. But I think it disproves your point. When Penny Patterson asked Koko how gorillas felt when they died, if they were happy or sad, Koko said: 'Asleep.' And when Penny asked where gorillas went when they died, Koko said a 'comfortable hole.' If those aren't abstractions, Tory, I don't know what is. Koko was basically saying gorillas didn't die, they went to a comfortable hole to sleep. Sounds like an afterlife concept to me."

Umber shot Tory one of her peculiar grins, thumped her breastbone, and nodded.

Tory lifted her arms in a "who knows?" gesture. She asked, "What are you going to do, Jim?"

"Do?" he asked, thoughts on Umber's "eye inside" comment. "About Umber? Tory, I have been agonizing over that since your phone call the other day. You tell me. Where is the ethical high ground here? We don't know why Umber does the things she does. So, do we go public with it? Try to book a spot on *Lehrer NewsHour*? Call *Time* magazine? If I do, Smyth-Archer Chemists is going to crush me like a bug. I *signed* that contract of my own free will. I agreed to abide by their rules. If I push this—"

"They won't, not if Umber's a celebrity."

He stared at her in disbelief. "Make Umber a celebrity? I think it would kill her soul." He shook Umber's hand. "And you have a soul, don't you, Umber?"

Umber nodded, and cupped her ear, the sign for "listen."

"Listen to what?" Jim asked, and when she answered, he said, "Ah, the eye inside. I'll try."

Tory shook her head warily. "If the media gets ahold of this, you'll be living in the middle of a circus. Remember the signing ape craze in the early 1970s? Washo, Bruno, and Booee? Remember *Life* magazine doing the spread on Lucy making coffee, mixing gin and tonics, and reading her magazines?"

"The campus newspaper did a piece on us about a year ago. Two years ago, the Fort Collins *Coloradoan* did an article complete with a nice little photo. Umber signed for them and talked on her keyboard. They thought it was cute. End of story."

"Umber didn't talk about God that day, did she?" Tory slowed and turned, looking out at the lake. Cloud reflections drifted across the still surface. "They didn't understand, Jim. But someone will. When they do, they're going to turn your happy little life here upside down. Contract, or no contract."

Umber had been listening patiently, her gaze going back and forth between them. She released Jim's hand, pointed to herself, made the rotating "worry" sign, and indicated herself again.

Jim insisted, "Well, stop worrying, Umber. We'll be okay." He glanced over. "What about you, Tory? What are you going to do?"

She walked down near the water, hands laced behind her. "I don't know, Jim. I'm a scientist, for God's sake. I can't just sit on this. You don't have the only SAC ape, you know. There are four of them in the U.S. that I know of. I think there is one in Canada, a couple of them in England, and maybe one or two in Australia. The only other one I've seen is Shanna Bartlett's bonobo, Kivu. He's a year younger than Umber." Tory brushed the toe of her hiking boot over the dry grass. "I haven't seen

Kivu for almost two years. And even then, I thought Shanna was hiding something. Damn. If she's seeing the same things in Kivu that you are in Umber, I'll bet she's scared to death."

"Shanna scared? I thought she was all salt, nails, and shoe leather."

"That's because you're a man. She's one of those women who puts on a tough front for a man because she's afraid of her own shadow." Tory shook her head. "No, Jim. Kivu is her life. For you, it's Brett and Umber. If anything happened to Kivu, it would kill Shanna."

Umber grunted in curiosity, and asked: "Kivu signs like Umber?"

Tory nodded. "Yes. At least he had the rudiments. At the time he seemed to be doing better than Kanzi. But now, thinking about it, Shanna might have told him to play dumb for me." She paused before adding, "Kanzi's not a SAC ape. Sue Savage-Rumbaugh obtained him through the Yerkes Primate Center, but his mother came from the San Diego Zoo." She lowered her voice, avoiding Umber's eyes. "He's all bonobo."

Umber released Jim's hand and walked over to poke one of her fingers into the mud.

Jim murmured, "Umber isn't a monster, Tory."

"No, but that's what I'm afraid the press is going to paint her as."

"*If* they find out."

"*When* they find out." Tory gave him a weary look. "Jim, what about you? Sure, you signed this agreement. But, damn it, you're still a professional. You have obligations to your colleagues, to the discipline. It seems to me, you've got some pretty hard choices ahead of you."

Jim squared his shoulders. "I'm going to do what's right. Once I figure out just what 'right' is. That contract specifies all of my research belongs to Smyth-Archer Chemists. There is all kinds of wording about patents, and prior right, and other legalese. God knows the penalties are terrifying. Granted, they may have done something to Umber, but was it illegal? I don't think so. Unethical? Where does one draw the line between tinkering with sheep or cow genetics and doing the same kind of tinkering with apes?"

"I don't call an extra seven hundred cubic centimeters of brain tinkering." Tory steepled her fingers and propped her chin on them.

"That's your opinion. And maybe it's mine, too, but SAC can justifiably have an opinion as valid as ours." Jim thrust his hands into his pockets. "Finally, Tory, I also have to consider what's right for Brett and Umber. In this case the needs of science may be in opposition to the needs of a pair of vulnerable girls. What would stirring the hornet's nest of public opinion do to my daughters? And what about Dana? Damn, Tory, when you get to picking at this, there are a lot of different facets." He straightened, glaring into Tory's worried blue eyes. "I'm going to protect my family, Tory. They are my first responsibility."

Tory stepped close and patted him on the shoulder. "I'll do what I can to back you. But you'd better prepare yourself. When this breaks, Umber will be right in the middle of it."

"No matter what was done by whom, Umber hasn't done anything wrong. She doesn't deserve to be punished because of what she is."

Umber turned and hooted softly. Concern lit her brown eyes.

Jim said, "I'm not going to let anyone hurt you, you hear? I promise that on my soul."

Umber charged him, flinging her arms around him as she called out, "Wheeh, wheeh, wheeh," and hugged him until he thought his ribs were going to break.

When his eyes met Tory's a chill settled in the pit of his stomach. She looked as if she'd just watched an old and dear friend condemned.

Nine

The steady drop in temperature inside the van forced Doug Parnell to pull his coat off the back of the driver's seat. The white Ford was now parked in the Marriott parking lot, as unobtrusive as any other late-model vehicle. The earphones had begun to chafe Parnell's ears. Half of what Dutton and Driggers were talking about in the hotel bar didn't make sense, but obviously they were worried about the ape. About the ape's ability to do things apes weren't supposed to do.

Parnell pulled off the right earphone and planted it on the swell of his mastoid so he could rub his hot ear. He leaned back, watching the recorder light blink as the tape machine recorded Dutton and Driggers's conversation. Electronic gear covered the van's entire left wall. The equipment was over ten years old, obsolete for modern intelligence purposes. Nevertheless, it suited Parnell. He had used this same equipment, learned on it, back in the days before Special Intelligence Operations fell under the budget ax.

He liked to say that he had been discharged because of budget cuts. He didn't like to say he'd been booted for taking liberties with the ladies. People who worked under SOCOM, special operations command, considered themselves to be elite.

Professionals. And in those days, under his real name, Parnell had tried to measure up. His one failing had always been a big set of tits, a tight ass, and long legs. During an operation in Turkey, Parnell had been strung out, fatigued from the intensive training. He had seen a girl in a market. That same night, he'd crawled into her third-story bedroom window. The locals had botched the investigation, but he'd been discharged under suspicion. He had learned his lesson. Never leave them breathing so they could give a description later.

Always resourceful, Parnell had taken his training and skills to the private sector. Most of his clients were multinational corporations with a yearning to know about their competition. SAC had contacted him six years earlier to monitor their project apes.

At first the assignments had been sporadic. Then, as more and more apes were placed, Parnell had built a network of investigators to help him.

Parnell returned his earphone in time to hear the Driggers woman say, "The problem is that even Noam Chomsky, the arch opponent of ape language studies, would have to admit that Umber uses complete English. She has perfect syntax with her audio keyboard."

Parnell made a face as Dutton's reply stopped short. Then he faintly heard a third voice ask, "Another drink?"

Dutton's voice, muffled, answered, "A Guinness and another scotch."

Parnell rubbed his jaw. His fingers rasped on the stubble. Carl Simms would be seated several tables away, someplace where he had a straight line of sight for the directional microphone—the little device contained in an ordinary-looking ballpoint pen. Beside Carl's knee would be the briefcase camouflaging the narrow-band FM transmitter and scrambler.

"Jim, since our talk this morning, I've been thinking." Driggers paused. "If it turns out that Umber is really all bonobo, then she's an extreme case of individual variation, the absolute tip of the gene pool. If she's not all bonobo, if she's been, well, changed, then, ethically, we can't just sit on this."

Dutton made a worried sound, and Parnell could imagine him rubbing his face in some futile gesture. "That scares me to death. I don't want my girls exposed to that kind of trauma. The whole world will be trying to horn into our lives. Not to mention the reaction from SAC."

"It's going to come out," Driggers stated flatly. "Too many people are going to notice. So, old friend, I would be planning ahead. When it breaks, what are you going to have done to cover your ass?"

A long silence.

In a resigned voice, Dutton said, "First we have to determine if she's really a product of genetic engineering. Then we have to write up the results, document everything we can."

"And figure out how to disseminate the data without having it traced back to us." Driggers made a smacking sound of fist against palm. "That could be tough."

"I don't want to do that, Tory."

"Damn it, Jim, you're not using your head."

A long silence passed.

Dutton again: "Yeah, yeah, you're right. If it falls apart—"

"When," she corrected.

"*When* it falls apart, I can't come out of this looking like a willing conspirator. It will ruin my career . . . and Dana's, too." He paused. "Actually, I could always go back to the ranch. I don't think Dana wants to go back to the reserve, though. Tory, no matter what, promise me that you'll take care of her. Give her a job, stand up for her. If this thing turns real sour, I want it to look like it was my fault."

"Is that martyrdom lurking behind your eyes, Jim?"

"No. Just responsibility. I got her into this mess. She's a bright, talented woman. I don't want to see her tarred."

Parnell pulled a photograph from his file, inspecting Dana Marks in the van's dim interior. Sharp-looking chick. He wondered what her tits and ass were like.

Driggers continued. "So, it blows up? You're in the middle of a media circus. What about Umber? How do you protect her?"

"I could take her up to the ranch. Dad has a six-mile ranch road with a big Powder River gate that he can lock."

Driggers hesitated, and ice could be heard rattling in a glass. "Are you ready for the speculation? Some media whiz will pull up an image of a hairy chimpanzee copulating with a sweet young blond girl to make a monster."

The sound of fabric and the clatter of glasses interrupted. A waitress's voice could barely be heard.

"You think she's a human-bonobo cross, don't you?" Dutton's voice sounded hesitant, low. "The ultimate koola-kamba?"

"Jim, we don't know for sure that she's a human-bonobo cross."

"She can't be," he protested. "Humans and apes can't interbreed. Apes have twenty-four pairs of chromosomes. Humans have twenty-three. Somewhere in our past, two ape chromosomes merged into a single human chromosome. That number two chromosome makes interbreeding impossible. Assuming a human sperm met an ape ovum, that chromosomal difference would create nonviability at the first mitosis."

"Stop thinking in terms of old-fashioned copulation. People can mix and match in the laboratory these days."

Parnell could imagine their heads, nearly touching, and, in spite of himself, he, too, leaned forward.

A pause, then Driggers spoke again. "Smyth-Archer Chemists has enough labs, enough genetic know-how. They could have tried this . . . in vitro, in the womb, who knows? That's private industry, Jim. They don't have the same oversight that we do in academia."

"If it's . . . If it's true, how do I tell Umber? What do I tell Brett? Good God, Tory, I haven't even nerved myself up enough to discuss menstruation with my daughter. How do I explain this?"

"I never knew that being a single father could be so daunting. But getting back to Umber—"

"Tory, we're going to be laid open like a cadaver in anatomy class. Reporters will be crawling out from under Umber's bed— provided they can wedge themselves in amidst all the balls, Legos, and clutter. Brett is going to be followed everywhere she goes. They'll drive her so berserk that she'll smear a million-dollar camera lens with ape feces and get my ass sued."

"Jim, you don't know for sure that Umber's a . . . a . . ."

"A what? A mule? A mutant? All of a sudden, she's not Umber, but a *thing* you can't even put a name to?"

A pause.

"I'm sorry, Jim. I know she's part of your family. The implications are a little overwhelming. That's all."

"If it's a shock to you, Tory, what's it going to be to the average Joe on the street? Do you know the kind of ratings those anal radio talk show hosts are going to use this for? Just think of it! Umber and I will probably see our smiling faces on those hideous little papers right next to the grocery store checkouts."

Parnell pushed himself back from the console, eyes unblinking. "Understatement of the year, asshole. If the press gets this, they're going to short-stroke Jim Dutton and his little family right onto the TV satellites. Welcome to the spotlight, pal. Your life is about to be carved up like a T-day turkey." Parnell punched the button that sent the recorded conversation skyward to the SAC satellite, and the receiver in far-off England. "God help you, buddy."

SAC now had everything.

As British Airways Flight 222 winged eastward across the Atlantic night, Valerie propped her feet on the footrest, tried to find the right position on the little pillow, and struggled to sleep. The faint vibrations of the plane, the slight changes in altitude, seemed to intrude each time she was ready to drop off.

Beside her, in the aisle seat, Roberto's breath purled in his throat. Valerie cracked an eye and studied his slack face. Dark and lean, he looked every bit the stereotype of a Mexican bandit—right down to the thick black mustache.

She blinked and gazed up at the molded plastic of the overhead bins. Sleep was a lost cause. Absently, she fished her purse from under the seat ahead of her, flipped through the compartments, and dug out her billfold. She removed the photograph from its place behind her driver's license. Thick laminated plastic protected it; it felt smooth and cool on her fingertips. The picture had been taken with a telephoto lens from across the street. She was a young woman now, long blond hair spilling over a down parka. The camera had caught Brett walking out of her junior high school, books cradled in her arms. She'd been talking to friends and laughing at some shared amusement.

For a long moment, Valerie stared into those sparkling blue eyes and thought about what might have been.

God, what a mess I've made out of my life.

"Hey, Fuerta, why don't you call her sometime?"

Valerie turned, meeting Roberto's calm brown eyes. "It's too late, amigo. Too many years. Too much time."

"Never too late, Val." He sighed, crossed his arms, and stretched. "Man, life's too fast. Passes too quickly. You ought to just bite the bullet and go see her."

"Go to sleep, Taco."

"Yeah, you first."

She grunted, sighed, and replaced the photo. "Can't sleep."

He extended his arms, growled, and reached down in the space under the seat in front of him. From his briefcase, he extracted a folder, and folded out his tray table. "Well, Fuerta, since we're both awake, let's see what we got, huh?"

She took the papers he handed her. The file was a workup on Smyth-Archer Chemists. Their corporate structure, assets, holdings, and a market prospectus. Several photos were included. The first was that of an attractive blond man, young, apparently in his early forties. He wore his hair long, and the camera had caught the dreamy look in his eyes. Something reflected there, caught by the camera, caused her to pause.

"Geoffrey Smyth-Archer," she read from the short bio stapled to the photo. "Major stockholder, age forty-three. Residence, Knightsbridge, London. Educated, Cambridge. Ph.D. in genetics granted in 1985. His professors called him brilliant. Compared him with Bateson."

"Who?"

"William Bateson. The founder of modern genetics. Our Geoffrey must really know his way around a pair of chromosomes. Let's see. Parents killed in an African plane crash in 1986." She tapped the photo with a finger. "Knightsbridge? That's the embassy district in London. High rent."

"If you had the biggest chunk of SAC, you could *buy* the embassy district," Roberto muttered. "He must be worth billions—and I'm talking pounds sterling."

She looked into Smyth-Archer's sensitive blue eyes, at the graceful set of his face and the strong line of his jaw. "I'll bet the girls swoon at his feet."

Roberto scanned the bio. "Hey, he's single, Fuerta." He arched an inquiring eyebrow.

"No way, Taco." Valerie scanned the documents. "Nothing here on what this is all about."

"Myles is supposed to brief us. Who's next?"

Valerie picked up the next photo. "Sir Richard Godmoore. Landed family, comes from Kent. Ph.D., Cambridge, 1980. Top of his class. He's been with SAC ever since. Coordinates bio-engineering research and development at SAC's Sussex operation. Gained national prominence during the 'Mad Cow' disease scare in 1996."

Roberto glanced at the photo. "From the picture, it looks like his underwear's pinching his *cojones*. No sense of humor."

"You can ask him about it when we see him." She took the next photo, a square-jawed man. "Vernon Shanks. Associate director, Ape Rescue Compound. Whatever that is. Also a Ph.D. in genetics from Cambridge. Degree conferred in 1986. Responsible for HIV studies in the early 1990s. Has a house in Billingshurst, just outside of the Sussex research facility."

"See any pattern yet?" Roberto asked wryly.

Her eyes had that familiar grainy feeling that came with fatigue. "What do you want to bet? Frankenstein's monster, or mutant ninja cows?" Her lips twitched. "Murray, you bastard, what have you done to us?"

"That will teach you to come home early and find his latest *chingada* flopped out in his bed."

She gave Roberto a dirty look, then ruffled through the papers again. "Genetics, huh? Good God, Roberto, it's been half a lifetime since I took genetics. About all I can remember is how to spell DNA."

"Dolly," he said in reply.

"Who the hell is Dolly? Another of Murray's girls?"

"A sheep. Remember?"

"Oh, yeah, cloned. A perfect copy. Grown, cultured, created, whatever you call it, in Scotland in 1997." She frowned. "Okay, so it is Frankenstein's monster."

"I could get off on this assignment." He smiled. "Man, maybe they could clone me. While one of me is busting ass around the world with you, my other me could be eating cabrito in McAllen. *Que vida es?*"

"In your dreams, Taco. Only in your dreams." Valerie tapped the papers with a long fingernail.

Or had Murray set her up for a fall? A story that would go bust and leave her on her ass?

She picked up the photos one by one, studying the faces, trying to see the secrets that Triple N suspected they hid. Secrets Murray had sent them to ferret out.

She handed the stack of documents to Roberto, leaned back in her seat, and closed her eyes. She began sifting what she knew of genetics from her memory.

Pieces came back: chromosomes, alleles, point mutations, and translocations. Dominant and recessive traits. In her mind, she constructed a DNA molecule: adenine, guanine, thymine, and cytosine. They composed double-helixed strands that unwound from each other like twisted zippers. Messenger RNA formed, moved to the ribosome. Bits of RNA like disjointed lowercase *t*s floated out of an amino acid soup before lining up on the ribosome to form strings of polypeptides, the foundations of proteins.

She had taken those courses with Jim. Long ago, when she was still young and idealistic. His face came back to haunt her, as if yesterday. Handsome, young, enthusiastic, and excited. He had had a vibrancy that swept her off her feet. God, what an attractive man he had been. A Wyoming cowboy, right off the ranch with his boots, Levi's, and broad shoulders. His blue eyes had sparkled with intelligence and an easy compassion that came of knowing animals, loving them, in fact.

She had swooned at the feel of his warm hands on hers. Fallen head over heels in love. And when his seed had caught in her, she had panicked, desperately afraid of being trapped forever when so much life stretched ahead of her.

Now, so many years later, she could only evaluate the price she had paid for that life.

But so well lived, bitch. So very well lived.

Genetics. Brett's face merged with the swirling images of chromosomes, double helixes, and cell fission. All of it reeking of reproduction: the creation of new life.

Is there anything of me in Brett? Or is she all Jim's?

She was going to hate this assignment.

Valerie Radin's face filled the television screen; her serious voice, perfectly modulated, seemed to hang in the room. Brett watched, entranced, as the scene shifted to a brown hole in the ground. Behind the excavation, forested mountains rose like steep-backed green humps against a cloud-choked sky. Men wearing white straw hats stood in a somber ring in the background while green-clad soldiers, white handkerchiefs over their noses and mouths, climbed down into the hole and began to remove bodies, one by one, from the pit.

"The Colombian drug trade is not only measured in millions of dollars," Valerie's voice explained. "It is measured in human blood, suffering, and death." The image zoomed in as the corpse of a teenage girl was lifted from the dirt. Grasping her wrists and ankles, two soldiers carried her naked, sagging body and placed it on a black tarp. In that instant, the image zoomed closer, fixing on her face and freezing there, slightly out of focus, but catching the full horror of her smudged features.

"Those who pay that price," Valerie's voice continued, "are not necessarily the kingpins, but the young and innocent as well."

"Bad," Umber stated through her keyboard. The black hair framing her face shone in the light.

"Yeah, really bad," Brett agreed, and reached over to take Umber's hand where they sat side by side on the couch.

The television showed one final close-up of Valerie's face. "This is Valerie Radin, Triple N News, reporting from Santa Isleta, Colombia."

Valerie's somber expression was replaced by a toothpaste ad. Brett shook her head. "I don't know how she does it. Can you imagine? Digging up graves like that? Seeing all those dead people?"

"People go to God," Umber's keyboard said, and Umber gave Brett a sad frown.

Brett tucked her legs under her, staring expressionlessly at the television. With the turmoil in their household, the old longing came back. Dad tried so hard, but sometimes she really wished she had a mother to talk to. Her heart had alternately hardened and then yearned for her mother. But over the long years, the callus on her soul had thickened. In all that time, Valerie hadn't sent so much as a word. Not a letter, not a phone call, nothing. Would it have been so difficult for her mother to have sent a single birthday card?

"Brett sad?" Umber was watching her, concern shining in those knowing brown eyes. With a long black finger, she stirred Brett's hair, tracing reassuring patterns over her skull.

"No sadder than you." Brett reached over and patted Umber's shoulder through her sweatshirt. "You don't have a mother either."

Umber thought for a moment, then her nimble fingers tapped the keyboard. "Umber has Brett and Jim. Family."

"Family," Brett replied.

"Hug?" Umber asked, and shyly added: "Then tickle?"

Brett laughed and jumped on Umber after she set the keyboard to one side. For a moment they held each other, then Brett tickled that vulnerable spot on Umber's ribs. Umber squealed, twisted, and lifted Brett high with her long arms. In the wrestling match that followed, they ended up on the floor before the television. On the screen, Triple N depicted the latest crises and atrocities convulsing the world, but for the moment, Brett was too involved in trying to keep Umber from pinning her. The match wasn't even close. Brett ended up on her back, red-faced as Umber's strong fingers found the sensitive spot under her armpits and dug in until Brett cried, "Enough! Umber, stop! You win!"

Umber rolled back on her heels, pant-hooting in victory, her lower lip curled in a bonobo grin. She made the grabbing sign with her right hand to indicate "Umber wins."

"Yeah, you always do." Brett sat up, trying to catch her breath. With her fingers, she combed her tousled hair out of her eyes. "You could take State in wrestling. What the coach would do to have you on the team."

"Umber be number one." Then she heard the door as Jim entered, the news safely over. "Eat now. Umber make dinner."

Brett pulled her clothes straight, stood, and met Jim at the door. He wore his blue windbreaker and jeans. His dark brown hair and beard had been blown into wild shapes by the wind. His face had that unfamiliar strained look, but his eyes gleamed at the sight of her.

He hung his coat on the rack, straightened the dark green sweater he wore, then asked, "What happened to you? Cyclone? Tornado? Or is this just a new fashion?"

"Wrestling match. Umber won." She allowed him to hug her, then smiled up at him. "Have a good day, Dad?"

"It was a day." She followed him into the living room as he added, "Might want to put out another plate. Dana's coming for supper tonight. Any calls?"

"Yeah, call Granddad. He said he'd be home all night." She paused, trying to read his guarded expression. "So, what's the occasion? Fun or business?"

He caught the tone in her voice. "Business." He stood for a

moment, a haggard look about him. "Brett, we have to talk about something. All of us."

"Tory coming, too?" Her heart flipped. In the kitchen, Umber had stopped short, arms cradling lettuce, carrots, and a chunk of cheese. Her intent brown eyes had fixed warily on Jim.

"No," Jim's reply was short. "She took off this afternoon. She had an evening flight to Tucson."

"It's about her, isn't it?"

Jim nodded. The nostrils of his straight nose flared. "Wait until supper. We'll discuss it then. Meanwhile, I'm headed for a shower." He glanced at Umber, who stood in the kitchen. "Think you can make something that isn't all raisins, honey, and mayonnaise?"

Umber called out an affirmative "Wheep."

Jim met Brett's eyes and jerked a head toward Umber. "Keep her honest." Then he took the stairs two at a time and disappeared into his bedroom.

At the kitchen counter, Umber looked up from the carrots she was slicing and signed: "What's wrong with Dad?"

"I guess we'll find out." Brett stepped into the kitchen and studied the makings Umber had set out. "What's this going to be?"

"Make Good-cook. Need pan." "Good-cook" was Umber's creation of sautéed vegetables.

Brett went to the cabinet, pulled out a box of rice, and dumped it into a pan with water. "If Dana's coming, we're going to need more than that. And, listen, go easy on the curry, okay?"

"Wheep!"

"I get the feeling heavy shit is coming down tonight."

Umber frowned, put her wooden spoon down, and signed: "Eye inside seeing bad things. Scary."

"You've been talking to God again, huh? What's she say?"

Umber's hands flew: "Monsters. Death. Someone die."

"Well, gee. You're cheery tonight." But her nerves tingled as she said it.

The Compound C apes moved cautiously down the forest trail, led by Old Jerome, the big alpha male. Jerome stopped frequently to look around and scent the air. He grunted to the eight males and three females that followed him. The females were in estrus, and their swollen, bright pink vulvas shone in the sunlight streaming down through the gaps in the canopy.

Mitu Bagawli observed from a safe distance, as was standard protocol for a "follow." His notebook had a clammy feel, and the pen slipped in his fingers as he jotted notes. Curse the dripping humidity, but Mitu had never observed this curious behavior in the Compound C apes before.

Jerome bent to sniff the ground, then knuckle-walked ahead. Every ape behind him stopped to sniff the same spot. Two of the females hooted softly. Rasper, the most aggressive male in the group, picked up a leaf and smelled it, then cocked his ear to the forest and listened. Cicadas shrilled in the trees. In the distance, a leopard screamed.

The Compound C apes went still and quiet, as if frozen in place.

Mitu brushed beads of sweat from his forehead and narrowed his brown eyes as he recorded the events in his notebook. His khaki shirt and shorts clung to his tall skinny body, sweat-drenched.

Jerome pulled down a vine and held it to his nose. After a few moments, he released it and trundled forward. The vine swayed over their heads as the other apes sauntered beneath.

When they'd disappeared around a bend in the trail, Mitu stepped out from his hiding place and followed.

At university in Nairobi, he had started his studies in biology, only to be enchanted by a Jane Goodall lecture. From that moment on, he had made his goal the study of apes, and doing fieldwork. He graduated at the top of his class, worked for a season at Gombe, and again at Mahala. Smyth-Archer Chemists had offered him employment working with Dr. Vernon Shanks in the ape reintroduction program. Not only were they paying him well, but he had already delivered two professional papers and had just published his first article on a shared byline with Dr. Shanks in the prestigious journal *Nature*. Not bad for a twenty-two-year-old son of a tax collector.

Mitu spotted the apes and ducked behind a thick tangle of prop roots. There, he watched them through the weave of knotted roots.

A breeze stirred the forest, feeling heavenly on his hot face. He breathed in the pungent fragrance of rain forest and held it in his lungs for several seconds.

A branch snapped in the forest ahead of Jerome. The big male huffed and stood up. His black hair bristled as he searched the undergrowth ahead. Rasper turned to the other chimps and gave them a broad grin. Calico, one of the "pink" females, leaped around, her arms flailing, and Rasper hugged young Toto.

Mitu scribbled in his notebook. The "grin" gesture displayed both fear and excitement.

A sharp chirp came from the brush ahead. Jerome hunched down, waiting. Feet stirred the forest leaf mat.

Mitu stared unblinking at the spot where every ape eye had focused.

A duiker leaped onto the trail, its ears pricked. When it saw the chimps, it chirped again and bounded into the brush. Deadfall cracked loudly in its wake.

Jerome continued on down the trail. The others followed in an irregular line.

For the next half hour, Mitu shadowed the Compound C apes until Jerome halted at the edge of a grassy clearing. Standing upright, he rocked back and forth as he nervously surveyed the clearing. Wind could be heard where it rustled the tops of the tallest trees. Down on the forest floor, the air stood still, muggy and hot.

An infant chimpanzee cried out from the clearing. Mitu straightened, realizing that it had to have come from one of the native bands of chimps who shared the compound with Jerome's group.

Jerome started forward, cautiously knuckle-walking into the clearing.

The infant cried again, and this time the cooing sound of a mother could be heard. Mitu ducked through a tangle of lianas and hurried to the edge of the clearing. He pulled a small set of binoculars from his pocket, searching the green wall of vegetation around the clearing.

The Compound C apes glanced at each other, then Rasper and Jerome raced forward, tearing across the meadow. The others followed in rapid succession.

Mitu burst through the screening leaves and into the clearing, struggling to see. Several of the apes turned and saw him, but were so intent upon discovering who had invaded their territory they ignored him.

As the Compound C group neared the far end of the clearing, a female screamed, panicked, and scrambled up the green wall of vegetation, her hair bushy from fear. Then her infant shrieked, and she whirled. The baby, perhaps two or three weeks old, still clung to a limb, holding on as if for dear life. By the time the mother raced back and grabbed the baby, Rasper had vaulted into the trees, climbing above her to block that escape route. The mother shrieked in panic and leaped to the ground. She charged away with the baby clinging to her breast, impeding her movements. Jerome and Calico had no trouble cutting her off.

Mitu watched in wide-eyed horror as the Compound C apes

leaped upon her, biting, hitting, and brutally kicking her. Rasper ripped a huge chunk of flesh from the mother's shoulder and swallowed it. Blood streaked his face and dripped down his chin onto his chest.

The infant, forgotten in the foray, huddled in the brush five meters away. As he watched his mother's struggle, he whimpered.

Rasper spun and bounded for the baby. Seizing it by the leg, he charged into the clearing. Running back and forth, screaming in rage, he hurled the baby against tree trunks and slammed it into the ground.

A shrill cry went up from the group around the mother. Mitu looked back and saw that the mother had escaped. Screaming, she scrambled up a tree and took huge leaps through the branches. Two of the lesser Compound C males climbed in pursuit.

The remaining apes raced through the forest in a state of frenzied excitement, flinging bits of rotten wood, waving their arms, tearing off branches and hurling them after the fleeing female.

The baby let out a soft cry, and Mitu jerked his gaze back to Rasper. The big male sat at the edge of the trees, the wounded baby in his lap. As Mitu watched, Rasper lifted the baby and bit deeply into its face, killing it. Blood smeared Rasper's cheeks and splattered his legs.

Jerome led the group over. They sat down, encircling Rasper, watching intently as he tore the infant apart. When he'd finished, he handed pieces around the circle. They sat together, sharing the feast, grinning.

Mitu leaned against a tree, feeling nauseated. He closed his eyes and forced himself to breathe. The coppery scent of blood clawed at the back of his throat. On the verge of heaving, he stepped into the trees, pressed his face against the closest trunk, and fought to concentrate on the damp tangy smell of the bark.

He'd heard about this kind of behavior, read the field reports. Jane Goodall had documented it among the Gombe chimps. One of her chimp groups had fissioned, breaking up into a northern group and a southern group. The northern group had waged a war of extermination against the southern rebels. Within three years, every single chimp that had broken away was dead. The northern group had hunted them down and brutally murdered them. In many cases, they'd turned into cannibals and eaten their victims. But Mitu had never imagined the horror Goodall must have felt seeing it unfold.

Nor had Goodall's Gombe data proved unique. Nishida had documented similar violence at the Mahale mountain preserve further south in Tanzania.

A strange call pierced the forest.

It started as a series of low-pitched hoots, then built to a roar.

Mitu turned, his pulse pounding in his ears.

The sound seemed to come from everywhere at once, echoing through the treetops.

The Compound C apes abandoned their grisly feast and rose to their feet. They faced the direction the stranger female had fled and defiantly pant-hooted in response to the roar.

Mitu blinked, remembered his notebook, and began writing as fast as he could.

"God, Shanks is never going to believe . . ."

His voice died in his throat.

The Compound C apes shrieked and raced toward him, their faces contorted in terror.

Mitu's mouth fell open. Another group of chimps charged from the forest, waving branches, throwing rocks. Odd-looking chimps. Something metallic shone in the sun where one of the apes waved it. And their voices were so . . . human. He couldn't quite place it, but . . .

As they rushed closer, roaring and screaming, Mitu shook himself and dove into the underbrush.

Ten

Dana knocked. The door had been locked since the Bronco break-in. Brett let her in. Dana was wearing worn jeans and a sweater. Her long black hair, in a ponytail, reflected a bluish tint in the light. "Indian hair" Dana called it. A plastic grocery sack hung from her left arm.

"So, how's it going, kid?" Dana asked, reading Brett's strained expression. "Catch any car thieves lately?"

"That was pretty freaky. I think I blew my English test as a result. I kept thinking about rapists. I couldn't concentrate."

"It'll be okay." Dana tried to smile reassuringly. "Sometimes it's worthwhile to be reminded that the world can, and does, bite back."

"I think I liked it better toothless." Brett led the way to the kitchen. "Dad's up in the shower. Want to brace us for whatever it is that's coming down?"

"Not if I value my life." From the sack, Dana removed a small package of hamburger and shot a sidelong glance at Umber. "Can I talk you into a little meat for the local carnivore?"

"Wheep!" Umber gave a curt nod, pointed to the frying pan

hanging on the wall rack, and made the flipping-over "cook" sign, and then signed: "Umber will add to 'good-cook.'"

Brett retrieved the frying pan, put it on the stove, and dumped the hamburger in. As she reached for the spatula, she asked Dana, "Uh, Dad's not doing anything dumb, is he? Like announcing he's getting married to Tory or anything like that?"

Dana hesitated for the briefest of moments, then arched a slim eyebrow. "Not that I know of."

"That set you back, didn't it?" Brett gave her a sly grin. "You could marry Dad."

Dana gave her a warning look. "Don't start on me, kid. I had a long day, and I don't need anyone foisting herself into my life. It's been said that cowboys and Indians mix like nitro and glycerin."

Brett backed off. "So, what happened at the lab today? Find any good data that's going to rock the scientific community back on its heels?"

The expression on Dana's face turned more wooden. "Just statistics, kid. Multivariate analysis. Fun stuff . . . right out to three degrees of freedom."

"Huh?"

"Statistical joke."

"Yeah, sure. I knew that." Brett used her hip to butt Umber out of the way and inspected the progress at the stove. She stirred the hamburger. The smells of cooking vegetables and meat mingled with the spices that Umber had added. "Umber, you're going to make someone a wonderful cook one of these days."

"Better than you." Umber smacked her hands in emphasis.

Brett let Umber crowd her back to the counter and crossed her arms, staring at the floor as Dana set the table. She barely heard Dana whisper to Umber, "What's got her so upset?"

From the corner of her eye, Brett saw Umber sign: "TV mother."

Dana mouthed, "Oh."

Her dad came down the stairs, eyes distant, forehead lined. He'd put on clean blue jeans and a long-sleeved white T-shirt. His hair and beard were still wet. At the landing he asked, "How's it going?"

" 'Bout ready." Brett went for napkins.

Umber waddled from the kitchen, a pot of steaming rice held in a death grip. When she had been little she used to drop everything. She had gotten better over the years, but she still had trouble, especially with hot things. Her pink tongue stuck out of the corner of her mouth as she slid the pot onto the table and retreated for the next pan.

They ate in silence. Jim and Dana shot glances at each other that spoke in a language Brett couldn't quite decipher.

Umber's notion of "just a little curry" left Brett's mouth burning. But then, what could you expect from a creature that ate fruit, shoots, grubs, and insects in the wild? The premonition of trouble down in the bottom of Brett's soul intensified.

"Did you call Granddad?" Brett asked in an attempt to stimulate some sort of conversation. She studied her father and Dana again, feeling that tension.

Jim thoughtfully chewed a mouthful of rice, swallowed, and said, "Yes. Wanted to know if I could get away to go elk hunting again. You know him. It's October. He's going into the Gros Ventre. Says that elk are everywhere. He's going to horse-pack to the head of Soda Creek again."

Jim stared absently at the ceiling. In a wistful voice, he said, "I've never been so tempted. It's nice country up there. Wilderness area. The only way in and out is on foot or horseback. No one can find you, no phones, no one to bother you. In elk camp, life is a whole lot simpler. Believe me." He took a deep breath. "God, I miss it."

"Miss murdering Bambi?" Brett asked caustically.

Jim gave her a strange look. "I should have taken you. You'd understand then. Life comes full circle. No blinders. It's the *real* world, Brett." He indicated the house. "Not this . . . this artificial cultural creation of ours."

"Awesome. Philosophy! Somebody put something funny in your coffee today?" As soon as she'd said it, she wished she hadn't.

He turned hard blue eyes on her and carefully placed his fork on his plate. "I suppose now is as good a time as any." He laced his fingers together and studied them one at a time. "What I'm about to say is between us, all right? I want you all to know what's coming down. We don't talk about it to anyone. Not to Granddad, not to Betty, and especially not to reporters." He glanced from face to face, stopping with Brett. His gaze bored down into her very soul. "Understood?"

Brett swallowed hard and nodded. "What?"

Jim took a breath. "Dana and I have begun to grow worried about some of the things Umber has been doing."

At this point, Umber stopped in mid-chew, her spoon frozen in the air. The black hair that poked out around the neck of her sweatshirt began to rise, and her dark bonobo brow furrowed.

Jim's voice came out soft. "Umber, you have to understand, none of this is your fault. Do you hear me?"

Umber barely nodded, her lips widening as the worry intensified.

Jim braced his elbows on the table. "We're not sure yet. We'll know soon. We think Umber's not one hundred percent bonobo." He smiled, trying to lessen the impact. "Umber, I think you're half human. Do you understand? Not all bonobo."

Umber's hand, with its spoon, might have been petrified in place. She flicked her other hand, making the "what?" sign.

"I don't get it," Brett interrupted.

"A cross," Dana said seriously. "Did Tory confirm that?"

Jim shrugged. "She thinks so. She's taken some blood with her. She'll run it in the U of A lab. Then we'll know."

Umber's brow deepened, her gaze dropping to the plate in front of her.

Jim glanced at Umber, then reached across, placing a hand on her rounded shoulder. "Are you all right?"

Umber managed to nod and looked up bravely, but Brett could read the turmoil behind her eyes.

Umber pointed to herself, made a fist with the thumb extended, put the thumb under her chin and brought it forward, in the sign for "not," then formed her fingers into a "B" for bonobo.

"I don't know for certain," Jim said and patted Umber's shoulder.

Brett stilled the nervousness in her breast. "I don't see the problem here. I mean, Umber's no different today than she was yesterday. And so what? If she's more human, what's wrong with that?"

Umber leaned sideways in her chair until she could rest her head against Brett's arm. Brett scratched her neck.

Dana gave Brett an annoyed look. "For us it's no problem at all." She pointed out the picture window toward the distant plains and the twinkling lights of Fort Collins. "But what about for them? All those nice Americans out there eating supper at their tables and watching the news? If this gets out do you really think they're going to leave us alone?"

As reality began to settle in her stomach, Brett said, "But, I mean, so who's going to tell them?"

Jim wiped at a spot of 'good-cook' on his white sleeve. "It's the sort of story that's going to get out. That's what people like your mother do. They dig up these stories and put them on the evening news."

He caught Brett's expression and winced. "I'm sorry, Brett. I shouldn't have said that. But listen, if Umber turns out to be half human like we suspect, she's going to be news, and a lot of people out there are going to think she's a monster."

Umber jerked up her head and stared unblinking at Jim. She seemed to be holding her breath, her fingers absently tapping out the "no" sign.

Brett pushed her chair back and stepped behind Umber, placing a soothing hand on Umber's arm.

"We know you're not a monster, Umber," Dana said hotly. She flung her arm at the world beyond the window again. "But the Fundamentalists, the newspapers, the television talk shows are going to be all over this. Do you understand? They're going to be coming here, trying to see you, wanting to turn you inside out! Some are going to want to hurt you, others to study. The one thing is, they'll all want to *see* you."

To that, Umber emphatically raised her thumb to her chin and signed, "No way!"

Jim raised his hands. "Hey, easy, ladies. Settle down. Brett, please sit down. Umber, take a deep breath. That's right. Let's be rational about this, all right?"

Brett slid onto the wooden seat and bit her lip at the anger growing inside her. Dana was looking uncertainly back and forth between them.

"The only thing we have going for us is one another," Jim said. "Brett, listen to me. You can't afford to let your emotions get the best of you. You have to be smart about this. Anything else that you do—get mad, scream, hit somebody—is going to make matters a lot worse. Is that fact sinking into your stubborn little brain?"

"Yeah, Dad. I understand."

"If this gets out"—Jim took another bite of dinner and gestured with his fork—"the only way we can deal with it is by using our heads. We have to be smart, careful, and . . ."

Umber bolted from her chair, knocking it over. She broke loose from Brett's reaching hand and, pant-hooting in fear, raced across the carpet, bounded up her climbing pole and onto the upstairs landing.

Brett was right behind her, flying up the stairs, racing down the hallway. She caught the door, almost dislocating her arm as Umber slammed it behind her. Umber dove headfirst to bury herself in the blanket nest in the middle of the bed.

"It's all right," Brett soothed as she ran across the room and wiggled into the soft blankets. She slipped her arms around Umber. "No one's going to hurt you. No matter what, we'll face it. You and me." She could feel Umber trembling, rocking back and forth in panic. The pant-hoots had become swift and breathless.

"Umber?" Jim called softly, and Brett felt his weight settle on the bed. "We'll be all right. I promise."

Gently, but firmly, Brett pulled the blankets aside, saying, "Time for hugs, now. Come on."

With Jim's help, they unwound Umber from the blankets and huddled together, a mass of intertwined arms. Dana stood in the doorway, a worried look on her face. Umber's frantic pant-hoots slowly diminished, and she pulled back, blinking moist eyes. She pointed at her chest and signed two words: "Umber scared."

"Yeah," Brett admitted. "Me, too." She couldn't help but glance at the window. There beyond the glass, the world had just turned ominous and threatening.

At five-thirty in the morning the CSU Foothills Campus slumbered beneath the false dawn. City lights still outshone the budding glow under the eastern horizon. The Bronco door thumped shut behind Jim as he walked across the gravel to the lab door. The air had a cold bite, the temperature in the twenties. The big floods on the Center for Disease Control building outlined the lab in white.

He unlocked the door, turned on the lights, and walked to the desk. Seating himself, he pushed the little moon-shaped button that brought the computer from SLEEP to AWAKE.

"Are you ready for this?" he asked rhetorically in response to the queasy feeling in his stomach. In his youth he had felt the same way each time he crawled down into a rodeo chute to straddle some nasty bull.

He pulled up the computer phone system and turned on the little camera that faced his desk. Tapping in the overseas code for England, he methodically dialed the special SAC number. In the last ten years, he had only called this number twice. Once when Umber had been near death with pneumonia, and another time to gain authorization for a surprise television interview.

The light on the camera gleamed as it indicated the auto-focus had kicked in. The computer informed him: DIALING. As he waited, Jim couldn't help but recall the way he had left Brett and Umber, asleep in each other's arms. Brett's golden locks had been tangled in Umber's glistening black hair. The world "out there" wouldn't see the love they shared, wouldn't understand that special bond between them.

The speakers hummed and clicked. "Smyth-Archer Chemists. Dr. Godmoore's office."

Jim checked the clock. Godmoore should have just returned from lunch. "Jim Dutton for Dr. Godmoore, please. Tell him this is a video call."

"One moment, sir."

Jim waited, his stomach churning with enough determination to make gurgling noises.

The computer informed him: IMAGING. WAIT.

Then the screen blinked to life, Godmoore's thin-faced visage peering back at Jim. He wore a dark blue suit that looked like silk. The close-cropped hair had grayed around the temples since the last time Jim had seen him. Godmoore's eyes narrowed. "Dr. Dutton? Can you see me?"

"Yes, Dr. Godmoore. Do you have my image?"

"I do. Is there something wrong?"

Jim smiled, tension bundled in every nerve. "Perhaps you could tell me?"

"I don't understand." Godmoore's proper English accent sounded clipped. He stared out of the monitor with hard eyes.

"I am calling about Umber, sir. Why don't you tell me just what she really is. A koola-kamba? A genetic experiment? What?"

Godmoore smiled, but the expression carried nothing of humor. "We anticipated your call, Dr. Dutton. You're the first to find the nerve to contact us. Tell me, how long have you suspected?"

"Awhile."

"We have noticed that you've been less than honest in reporting your data over the last two years. What made you finally confide in Dr. Driggers?"

A cold sensation spread through Jim's gut. "Tory works for you?"

"Oh, most assuredly not, sir. But we keep track of our research subjects. I do wish, however, that you had called here first. It would have avoided some complications for us."

"Like press? Public outrage over playing God? Daring to create an entirely new species? Violent reactions by religious leaders who see this as lowering the divinity of the human soul into the animal world? That sort of thing?"

Godmoore gave him a chastising look. "Let us not become too dramatic, Dr. Dutton. The days of Bishop Lightfoot and Thomas Huxley are long gone."

"Maybe in England. Have you ever heard of the American religious right? All of those holier than thou preachers with southern accents and poofy hair are going to have a field day booting Umber through the gospel TV goalposts and right into hell."

Godmoore's gray brows lifted. "Indeed, sir. And I presume you have heard of the English tabloid newspapers? Yes, yes, there will always be those who fail to understand the purposes and means of science."

"Purposes and means . . ." Jim knotted a fist, the first stirrings of anger sending warm tendrils around his heart. "This is about to be blown wide open, and the entire lunatic fringe is going to descend on my house and my family."

"Dr. Dutton, I'm afraid Hollywood has crept into your imagination. We had, and have, our reasons for pursuing this project. It has nothing to do with our vanity as scientists, nor is our project predicated on 'science for the sake of science,' as the old chauvinistic slogan proclaims."

"Then why did you do this?"

"For the apes, Dr. Dutton." He smiled at Jim's confusion, and added: "And, for the moment, that's all that I am willing to tell you. Period. End of conversation. Do you understand? You work for us. Umber is *our* ape. This is *our* project."

Jim's jaw tightened. He could see anger, or maybe angry fear, behind Godmoore's thin face. "I don't think *you* understand, Dr. Godmoore. Umber is a member of *my* family, and I'll do anything in my power to protect her."

Godmoore's brow arched, his lips quivering at the corners. "Indeed? Dr. Dutton, let us take a step back and reconsider. First, we are not adversaries."

"Why didn't you tell me that Umber was a human-ape cross?"

"Please, Dr. Dutton. You know better than this. Science, especially behavioral science, forever seeks to eliminate variables. This was a classic double-blind experiment. Had you known, you could have, probably would have, biased the study. Consider the reports you have forwarded to us over the last two years. You and I both know that Umber is performing far beyond the levels you have reported to us. We have heard that she is reading."

Jim sat in silence, soul in turmoil. *How can they know? He knows about Tory, about Umber's reading, good God, what* don't *they know?*

Godmoore smiled again. "Dr. Dutton . . . Jim, the one thing in all of our studies that surprised us was that none of our researchers reported oddities in their apes. You are the first."

"And Kivu, Shanna Bartlett's ape? He's a cross, too?"

"Among others. We have many project apes in different facilities and circumstances around the world."

Jim slowly shook his head. "That's why we were never allowed to present papers on our findings to the professional community. That's why none of the articles we submitted were ever forwarded for publication."

"I believe you can now see the propriety in that precaution. I also believe that you understand the continuing propriety in maintaining discretion concerning our research."

"God help you, don't you realize that eventually the press is going to learn about this? The professional community is already whispering about it."

"True." Godmoore laced his hands together. "Fortunately, few people pay attention to scientists. They'd much rather worry about athletes and movie stars. We expect a rather slow building of interest. When reporters start sniffing around the SAC apes, we will take the appropriate steps to defuse their interest."

Jim shook his head. How dumb could these people be? "I think the cat's out of the bag, Dr. Godmoore. Tory Driggers won't sit on this." Then his voice lowered. "I'm not sure that I will, either. You don't own me. I'm bringing this up for peer review. Call it damage control before Umber is hurt more than she already is."

"You will do nothing of the kind."

"Give me one good reason why I shouldn't sit right down here and type up an article for *Science* or *American Journal of Physical Anthropology.*"

"Because your grant will be terminated by high noon today,

as you might put it in your Westerner lingo." Godmoore leaned forward, eyes hawkish as he looked into Jim's. "And because Umber is *ours*. We *own* her, Dr. Dutton. She is the property of Smyth-Archer Chemists. You have her on loan from us as part of your research grant. You knew that the moment you signed our research agreement. Which, I am hoping you will remember, contains some rather draconian penalties for unauthorized disclosure. I would refer them to your inspection." He paused, adding: "I assume you kept a copy."

Jim felt the first icy shiver of fear. "I can fight this. Take it to court. Is that the kind of publicity you're looking for?"

"Dr. Dutton, I've told you before, we're not adversaries. We both want the best for Umber. Why are you going to such extremes?"

"Because she's not property. For all intents and purposes, she's my daughter. I'm the one who tended her cuts, held her when she was scared, took her temperature when she had a fever. You must understand, she's as much a part of my family as Brett."

"We don't have papers on your daughter. We do on Umber." An amused twist pulled at Godmoore's thin lips. "And you may take it to court if you would like, but I doubt you'll proceed very far." He glanced at something just out of view. "According to our information, Umber is worth about three point five million dollars to SAC. That's what we have invested in her to date. We'll fight to keep her, and I can assure you that American law, no matter its other failings, will protect our investment."

Jim had the nauseating premonition that Godmoore was right. "I'll still fight . . . for her."

"As you will, Dr. Dutton. But I would have to wonder what you would fight with." He shuffled papers out of sight on the table before him. "According to our information, you still owe over forty thousand dollars in principal on your house, another six thousand on your vehicle, and you have only three thousand, four hundred and twenty-five dollars in a savings account at the bank." He looked up. "College money, I suppose, for Brett?"

Jim's mouth felt cottony. "How do you know that?"

"We have our sources, Dr. Dutton. Oh, come, man, you don't think we would turn an animal worth as much as Umber over to just anyone, do you?"

"You son of a bitch."

Godmoore exhaled wearily. "Which brings us to the next subject, your grant. With your participation in the project suspect, we will have no choice but to ask you to return Umber to our custody. If you are intent on writing that paper for *Science* or *American Journal of Physical Anthropology* we will have a team there, at your lab, by twelve P.M. today. Please have Umber ready to go. Our people will bring a cage and sedative to lessen the stress of her removal."

Jim glared, hard-jawed, his fist knotted. Rage burned around a hollow emptiness at the center of his soul. Godmoore had him. SAC had covered every base.

Jim, the only thing you can do now is play for time. Call his bluff, and he'll hammer you down like a loose nail.

Jim said, "All right, Godmoore, you've made your point. What do I have to do to keep her?"

On the monitor, Godmoore smiled. "First and foremost, we must deal with the Tory Driggers problem. I take it that you can do that?"

Jim swallowed hard. "I can."

"Good. Brian Smithwick should arrive at your office by late afternoon tomorrow. At that time, we will decide which strategy to follow."

Jim glared, steely-eyed, into the monitor.

"Oh, and, Dr. Dutton," Godmoore said coolly, "please, don't do anything foolish . . . anything you would regret if it came to hardball. I'm not in a forgiving mood these days."

Eleven

A scatter of patrons sat around the bar in the Kensington Park Plaza Hotel when Valerie strode into the room. White marble tiles covered the floor. Wooden wainscoting, also painted white, gave way to an ivory patterned wallpaper. Delicate strains of Baroque music drifted down from the ceiling speakers.

She spotted Roberto. In black pants and a red shirt, he sat across from Myles Edwards, one of Triple N's old London hands. Through the windows she could see dusk settling over London.

Valerie crossed to their table and pulled out a chair. "Hi, Myles. You are looking fit."

"Ah, Val, good to see you again. Even better to be working with you." Myles stood and extended a large hand, his grip warm and firm. He had managed to cross the fifty-year mark with grace and flair. The strength implied by the angular set of his jaw, the shaggy gray brows, and deep lines arching off the corners of his nose was diluted by his sensitive hound-dog eyes. They had a moist, vulnerable look that had eroded some of the most stubborn of sources into betraying incredibly damning information. An overcoat rested across his chair back.

Val settled into the chair. "Good to see you again, too. Four hours of sleep just isn't enough. I'm going to be jet-lagged for a week." She shot a thin look at Myles. "Assuming that we're here for a week?"

"Perhaps. My source is a bit secretive, but the material he has provided so far has been provocative. We've had some of our lads working on it, collaring professors—geneticists in particular. Corroborating data."

"What sort of data?" Roberto picked up his ale.

Myles gave them a catlike smile. Valerie ordered a Guinness when the landlord stepped up.

"Cappuccino," Myles decided. "One stout is enough for me these days, I'm afraid." After the landlord retreated, Myles asked, "Are you familiar with the Human Genome project?"

Roberto took a drink from his ale. "Mapping all the chromosomes, or some such thing, right?"

"Right." Myles leaned forward. "It seems that the lads down at Smyth-Archer's Sussex facilities are beyond just mapping chromosomes. If my source is correct, they're already building biological organisms."

"Big deal." Valerie cocked her head. "People have been making all kinds of odd things. Square tomatoes, bigger peaches, that sort of thing. I've even seen pictures of a 'geep.'"

"A geep?" Roberto made a face as the drinks arrived. "What's a geep?"

"A cross between a goat and sheep." Valerie shrugged. "They made one in a lab someplace. The thing's alive, looks a little like both a goat and sheep, but it's sterile. Can't reproduce."

Myles said, "I've read some of the things they do with mice. The geneticists take a couple of chromosomes from one parent, a couple from another, and so on, and then finally put them all together into a mouse ovum. We have mice with as many as sixteen different parents. SAC, it seems, has been doing quite creative things with their genetic engineering. And with more than mice."

"How creative?" Roberto shot Valerie a sober glance.

"We're not sure." Myles hesitated. "But it may be that SAC is placing human genes in animals."

"Human genes have been inserted into mice for years," Valerie replied. "They do that to test for drug efficacy, for cancer protocols, immune responses, that sort of thing."

"Not on this scale," Myles replied in a monotone. "We're talking about mucking around with humanity here. There are ethical and moral implications which must be considered. I mean, my God, you can't just go around making half-human monsters."

"How long has this been going on?" Roberto asked.

Myles answered, "We don't know. We suspect since the early nineties at least."

Valerie leaned forward. "Are you getting reports of strange dogs with human heads eating people's cats, or what?"

"Nothing like that." Myles pulled nervously at his cardigan.

"Didn't the release of the Dolly story translate into a lot of research dollars for a number of genetics labs?" Roberto sipped at his ale. "Have you thought about that, Myles? That maybe the cloak-and-dagger stuff is a setup? Get us to dig it out as a Triple N exclusive, uncover the big secret, and SAC gets a bundle of free press for their next grant renewal or the release of their next product."

Myles shook his head. "Look, it's not like SAC is bending over backward to get publicity on this. I've been in this business for a lot of years. I'd know if I was being led by the nose. My source is scared. Really scared. He thinks that maybe his life might be in danger if this gets out and the leak can be traced back to him. SAC doesn't want *anyone* to know what they're doing."

Valerie gave Roberto a sly glance. "Then that's the story, isn't it? If SAC is hiding it, it's not just a genetics story, not just simple research. This is something operative. Something that could blow up in their faces."

"So, just what sort of monster are we talking about?" Roberto asked. "Anything green and hairy with lots of fangs?"

Myles scowled. "You two are taking this altogether too much in stride," he said and reached for his briefcase.

"You're right," Valerie answered. "Genetic engineering may or may not be a story. The public's tuned it out for the most part now that the novelty has worn off. Cloning isn't a threat except in science-fiction movies."

Myles gave her a dull stare as he opened his briefcase and handed a folder to her. "These are copies of everything we've been given to date. After you go through them, we'll discuss how we're going to approach this."

Valerie opened the folder, quickly leafing through the papers. She stopped at the copy of a copy of a photo. The image was blurry, much of the resolution lost in the copying process. What she saw appeared to be a chimpanzee, but something just wasn't quite right about it.

"Is this one of the experimental animals?" Valerie tapped the photocopied image.

"I don't know." Myles shrugged. "I would assume so if it was included in the papers."

Valerie pulled up a stapled six-page report, a copy of an interoffice memo. At first glance it appeared to be a budget. On the final line, she snapped to attention, old reflexes responding. The column total came to two hundred fifteen million, seven hundred and fifty thousand pounds. A lot of money. She glanced back to the cover page. "Expense estimate, fiscal year, IAR, Compound D. Now, that's a solid clue, isn't it?"

"Is it just me," Roberto asked, "or does anyone else think that SAC has an easy way out of this? All they have to do is come clean, tell the world yes, they put human genes in animals, and bingo, they've cured cancer. End of story."

Valerie narrowed her eyes, studying the chimp photo. "Maybe. Two hundred and fifteen million quid? One year's operating expense? What's IAR? Compound D? Anyone know?"

When Myles gave her a blank look, a slow smile came to her face. "I'm getting interested, Taco. Especially if Myles is right about his snitch being scared." She glanced up, meeting Myles's eyes. "I want to meet your source."

The muscles around Myles's mouth tightened, a reserve appearing in his normally droopy eyes.

"What's wrong?" Valerie asked.

"Nothing."

Valerie lifted an eyebrow in silent question. "Myles, whatever it is, we'll work it out."

He nodded, resistance crumbling. Reaching for his cappuccino, he sipped and gave her a weak smile. "It's silly, I suppose. Vanity and all that. I should just be glad that they thought enough of the leads to send some of their top people, but—"

"Yeah," Roberto agreed in sudden understanding. "You do all the groundwork, start to uncover the story, and the big three Ns send in the Yankee hotshots to take over."

Valerie leaned back, allowing that easy, reassuring smile to slide into place. "Myles, either we work as a team, or nothing will come of this. If this goes big, I'll see that you get your share of glory. If it bombs, we'll take other measures. For the moment, though, we're all in it together."

Myles fingered the handle on his coffee cup, his expression studiously neutral. "I'll make the appointment, Val, but I want to be there."

She met his reserved eyes. "All right, here are the ground rules. Since I'm assigned to the story, I make the final decisions and take the final responsibility. That doesn't mean that I don't want individual initiative when the occasion warrants it. All I'm asking is that you use your head. The single most important thing is breaking the story. After that, we'll sort out the credit. Fair enough?"

"Fair enough," Myles agreed. "I'll make the appointment." He stared into the white froth on his cappuccino.

Valerie raised the picture of the distorted ape, seeking to identify what was wrong with it, coming up blank. "It's right here. All we have to do is figure it out, and we'll split this wide open."

"Tory? It's Jim." He held the phone to his ear and glanced uneasily down the long hallway of the Loring Student Center. Students with backpacks walked past, ignoring him.

"Hi, Jim." Tory's voice sounded carefree, oblivious.

"Have you sent the bloodwork in yet?"

"First thing when I got back. Sorry, I won't have the results for—"

"Tory, kill it. Everything. All of it. Call them if you can and see if they'll return the sample to you. I can't explain. Trust me on this, all right?"

Silence, then Tory said, "No. Not all right. What's wrong?"

Could they have bugged Tory's phone? Was he too paranoid for his own good? He had slipped through the physical anthropology classroom, then out the adjoining laboratory. From there, he'd circled, trying to see if anyone was following him. He had ended up in the student center, at a pay phone.

"Jim?" Tory insisted. "Tell me what this is all about."

He took a deep breath. "Have you got a pen? Good, write this down." He read her the number on the phone. "Call me back as soon as you can reach a pay phone." He hung up.

For six long minutes he waited, and then the phone rang. "Jim," Tory sounded worried. "All right, I'm at a pay phone in the foyer. Now, why am I doing all of this cloak-and-dagger stuff?"

"The answer to the million-dollar question is yes, they are making augmented chimps. Kivu, Umber, and I don't know how many more are out there. They're the first-generation ape, whatever that means. When I called, Godmoore didn't even deny it."

"Then why am I standing down here in the foyer?"

"Because they'll take Umber away from me if I don't help them squash this before it gets out. Tory?" His mouth went dry. "They know everything. They know I've been fudging data. They know you were here, and that I sent blood samples with you."

"Jim, get a grip. How could they—"

"I heard this straight from Godmoore." He glanced along the hall again, checking. Then he related his conversation with Godmoore, word for word.

"This sounds a little far-fetched."

Jim leaned a shoulder against the wall. "Look, I know I sound crazy, but the final reality is that SAC owns Umber. If I don't play along, Godmoore promised me that they would take her away."

Another long silence. "I'll do my best. We knew it was explosive when we talked about it. But, Jim, you know this isn't going to go away. If it's not me, someone else will blow the lid off."

"Yeah, and that scares me to death. What am I going to do if they take Umber?"

He could hear her exhale hard on the other end of the line. "Maybe you should see a lawyer."

With the mouse, Umber highlights the letters F, O, X, in reply to the picture that comes up on the computer screen. She and Brett lie flopped on their bellies on the bed in Brett's room. Afternoon light streams through the windows, illuminating the dresser with its perfume, brushes, and mirror.

"Good for you," the computer voice chimes. "You have spelled *Fox*. A fox is an animal. Foxes are clever."

The picture of the fox vanishes and a tree appears on the screen.

"Can you spell *tree*?" the computer voice asks.

Umber grunts "wheep," looks sidelong at Brett, and uses the mouse to spell out H-O-M-E. Then she chuckles in bonobo laughter as the computer and Brett say in unison: "Wrong!"

Umber feels that happy warmth inside as she forms her hands into the signs for: "Umber is bonobo. Bonobos are at home in trees!"

Brett gives her a serious look as the computer voice asks her to try again. "I would have thought that was funny last week, Umber." She shakes her head and Umber watches her long blond hair glisten as the slanting light catches it. "Now I just don't know. It's like everything's all changed. I feel, well, violated, you know?"

Umber reaches over and pats Brett's shoulder. She wrinkles her nose, signing: "Don't worry, Dad will fix everything."

Brett grunts noncommittally.

Umber plucks absently at the hairs that grow out of her chin. "School dance tonight. Brett go?"

"Get real. Who'd go out with me?" Brett crooks her arm and knots a biceps. "Besides, I'd pop him if he ever tried to kiss me." She makes a face. "Yuck! I don't see what the big deal is about kissing. Who'd want to have some guy's slobber in your mouth?"

Umber responds in whee-haii laughter and, with quick reflexes, hooks an arm around Brett, snugging her close, and plants a big kiss on her cheek. Umber flips the mouse pad and mouse out of the way and they wrestle around on the bed. Brett weasels away only to have Umber snag Brett's belt loops and lift her high. As Brett squalls, Umber's strong fingers find the vulnerable spot on her belly.

Brett thrashes, screams, and laughs. "No fair!" Brett gasps for breath. "You've got two extra hands for feet!"

Umber hoots in victory and rolls across the bed to peer into Brett's eyes. That's when Umber notices that Jim is standing in the doorway next to Brett's Leonardo DiCaprio poster, his expression pained. Anxious at the look on his face, Umber signs: "Want to come tickle?"

Jim smiles, but it doesn't extend to his eyes. "No, you two are doing just fine."

"Hi, Dad." Brett untangles herself and sits up, pawing at her tousled hair. Then she gets a good look at his expression and says, "Uh-oh, what's wrong? We in trouble?"

Jim's shoulders lift and fall. "I don't know. Anything broken that shouldn't be? Is the lock still on the liquor cabinet? Either of you pregnant? Doing drugs?"

"Dad!" Brett cries.

Jim purses his lips and makes a *tsk*ing sound with his tongue. "No? Then I suppose you're missing most of the reasonably popular trouble kids can get into these days." He snaps his fingers. "Almost forgot. You aren't shoplifting, are you?"

"God, Dad. What happened to you today?"

Umber pats the bed, hoping that Jim will come and sit down. Maybe she will hug him. Hugs make her feel better when she is sad. Jim needs a hug.

Jim's face seems to lighten the slightest bit. He steps into the room and lowers himself to the corner of Brett's bed, his eyes taking in the wreckage of the covers. The computer is still showing the picture of the tree, HOME spelled in the bottom right-hand corner. The cursor is flashing for another try. Brett's shoes, a pair of pants, a basketball, softball glove, a stack of schoolbooks, and a scatter of paperback novels litter the floor.

Umber crawls close and hugs him, feeling the warmth of his

body as her strong arms go around his middle. For a long moment, they are silent.

"Let me guess"—Jim eyes the jumble on Brett's floor—"a tornado came through here, right? Or was it a bomb?" He glances into the closet, where additional heaps are piled. "No, none of the above. Would you believe a thirteen-year-old girl lives here?"

"I'll clean it up on Saturday, I promise," Brett groans. Then she takes the offensive. "What happened today?"

Umber watches desperate anger build behind his eyes. She tightens her hug as his shoulders droop and places her hand on his arm. She signs: "You okay?"

He shoots her a melancholy smile. "Yes. I'm okay."

Brett says, "You're not telling us everything. In fact, you haven't told us anything. What's wrong?"

After a long pause, Jim meets their eyes. "I don't know if telling you is a favor or not. But, all right, here's the way it is. I called SAC today. Talked to Godmoore. We were right. Umber's augmented."

"So what does that mean?" Brett asks. "That's not bad, is it? It doesn't make Umber any different today than she was yesterday."

Jim glances around, gaze lingering on the computer flashing "Wrong" where Umber spelled HOME under the picture of the tree. "I don't know," Jim says. "Maybe yesterday she could have spelled 'tree.'"

Brett crosses her arms. Umber continues to watch Jim, her stomach suddenly tight and unhappy.

Jim claps his hands on his knees. "According to SAC, we're supposed to keep Umber's skills secret." His eyes meet hers. "We guard you like a special treasure. If we don't, they'll take you away from us."

Panic surges like little insects eating her stomach, and she thumbs her chin, "No!"

"Take her away!" Brett cries, jerking upright. "They can't! Umber's ours! Ours! *Ours!*"

Umber reaches over, knowing Brett's outbursts. She patiently snags Brett's clenched fists out of the air and muscles them down, barking a warning "huuh!" Meeting Brett's hard blue glare, Umber points at her head in the "think!" sign.

"They *can* take Umber away from us," Jim says seriously, as if trying to impress this fact on the sputtering Brett. "She belongs to them, Brett."

"She's part of *our* family! Who the hell are these people, anyway?"

"Umber's legal owners," Jim says softly. "And they don't care that we love Umber, that we've raised her, nursed her, and protected her. They have the *legal* right to her."

"The law sucks!" Brett cries, and pries her hands out of Umber's grip.

To keep the insects of panic from eating her, Umber reaches up to finger Brett's hair, slowly massaging her scalp in a bonobo grooming gesture. She signs: "Stop. Please. Umber sick, sick." And she is, as if something has gone black inside her heart.

"I'm going to beat the shit out of SAC," Brett declares.

Jim's eyes narrow. "Watch your language. A young lady doesn't 'beat the shit' out of anyone. You might tear off their arms and legs and stuff them down their throats, but you don't—"

"Well, we've got to fight them," Brett insists. "Can't we do something? Take them to court?"

Umber struggles to hold back panic. She barely hears as Jim snorts and says, "I took the afternoon off. Saw a lawyer. He read the contract, and like a lawyer, he said that maybe something could be done. According to him, we can at least file for an injunction. He said that after that we could delay the court date, possibly for quite some time. His words were 'to throw roadblocks in front of them.' To me, that sounded like, 'You aren't going to win, but we can put off the day of reckoning.'"

Some part of Umber's brain notices that Brett's eyes are shining, on the verge of tears. As much as she wants to hug her own self, Umber reaches out and pulls Brett into the hollow of her shoulder, patting her with a gentle hand as she repeats "wha, wha," under her breath. With her free hand, Umber signs, "Brett okay?"

"We could run away!" Brett mutters, her voice beginning to break. "Go where they can't find us!" She sniffs. "Maybe Florida, or Mexico. Someplace far away from here!"

Jim smiles in spite of the situation. "Yeah, right. No one's going to notice Umber in either of those places." His voice tightens again. "And another thing, both of you. They've tapped the phones. If you see any strangers, stay away. Avoid them, no matter what. You don't talk about Umber, Brett. And, Umber, if someone you don't know approaches you, you're not to trust them, understand?"

"Wheep!" She feels the way she does on a merry-go-round, that sick spinning sense in the pit of her stomach.

Brett glares out from tearstained eyes. "You're serious, aren't you?"

Jim stands and fishes around in his pocket. He holds up a little black cube that looks as if it is made of plastic. "Remember the burglar? I looked over the Bronco this afternoon and found this. I stopped by the Ford dealership down on Drake Road just after I got out of the lawyer's. The mechanic down there didn't know what it was. Definitely not part of the Bronco's electrical system." He tosses it onto the bed. "If you look closely, you'll see that it's got a lot of tiny little transistors in it."

Brett and Umber both grab for the cube, but Brett snatches it away first, peering down at it. "What does this mean, Dad?"

"It means that starting today, we're all living very differently than we ever have before." Jim crouches down. "Do you understand? From here on out, we have to live like we're being hunted. We can't take chances. We can't be out of one another's sight."

"That's easy for you and Umber," Brett declares as Umber finally snatches the cube away. "What about me? Basketball season is just getting started."

The little square of plastic is filled with copper connections that are soldered together. It looks like it comes from inside a computer game. Umber's stomach tightens against the insects that are crawling around inside her.

"I'll take you to school and pick you up after practice," Jim says.

"And the games?" Brett's mouth pinches. "I mean, Umber can't wait in the car."

"Maybe Dana can help."

Umber finally gives in, throws the computer chip on the cluttered floor, and hugs herself to fight off the crawling insect feeling. It is all she can do to keep from rocking back and forth. If she does, then she will scream, and cry, and the insects will devour her soul, and God, and there will be nothing left but emptiness.

Twelve

As night settled on Valerie's second day in England, they left the congested London traffic behind. Myles piloted a white Holden wagon southward on the M23, following a line of smoke-belching lorries headed for Brighton.

Valerie sat in the back watching Roberto doze in the passenger seat. They were both tired, jet-lagged and overwhelmed by the information they had been trying to absorb. They had spent the morning on trips to booksellers in search of textbooks on genetics, chimpanzees, and cloning, then used the afternoon to examine library resources. Valerie had concentrated on scientific journals, while Roberto sought out recent newspaper and magazine articles on genetic engineering. Myles had focused on Smyth-Archer Chemists and their activities over the last four years. Now they were on their way to a meeting with Myles's source.

Myles merged right and passed a long line of lorries.

Valerie let herself drift, aware of the Holden's drone as it vibrated down the motorway. In her head, images from the scientific reports ebbed and flowed. The SAC material had been mixed with shipping invoices for lab equipment, all headed for "Compound D" in Equatorial Guinea. Equatorial Guinea?

Where the hell was that? And what, for Pete's sake, was Compound D?

What does it all mean? Why did the source leak this stuff to Myles? How does it fit together? There had been cryptic memos stating things like: "Three infants sedated and transported to Compound D." Her mind juggled the data.

Two hundred and fifteen million pounds? The figure stuck in her mind. Too big. Too much. What had it been spent for?

Roberto yawned and turned around to stare at Valerie. "That guy you used to run around with? He's an anthropologist, right? Maybe it would be worth a call to—"

"Absolutely not." Valerie squinted out the window as they rounded a traffic circle and entered Horsham. "Myles? You've talked to the source. What's the best way to handle him?"

"We've never met face-to-face," Myles said. "I've only talked to him over the phone. As worried as he is, I'd say you'd hit a wall if you went for the throat."

"How did you get the documents?" Roberto asked.

"I did a piece on genetic engineering. Within a week, I started receiving envelopes. Brown paper with an article inside. That sort of thing. Then I received a call about a week ago. The source said that everything was about to come apart, that one of the project apes was going to blow sky high.

"I asked for more details, and he said Smyth-Archer Chemists were at the bottom of it all, and I was the very person to discover what they'd done."

Myles took a left onto a cobblestone street and entered a historical district. "We're meeting him there." He pointed across the street to a pub called The Corked Sow. He slowed, waited for a sleek sedan to pull out, and neatly slipped the Holden into the space.

"What else did he tell you?" Roberto asked.

"Said he couldn't identify himself and didn't want to see me. Too dangerous. He gave me a local phone number in Billingshurst. Said if I needed anything specific, I could call there, say that the plumbing was stopped up, and he'd get back to me when he could."

"That's how you got him last night?" Val asked.

Myles nodded. "I told him I'd put my ass on the line, called in the heavy artillery, and I had questions that needed to be answered. That if I didn't get them answered tonight, I'd consider it a crank. So, let's go see what we've got, eh?"

"How will he know us?" Valerie asked as she followed the men across the irregular street. Historic lampposts cast pools of light on the cobblestones.

"He knows me," Myles said. "At least I assume so since I did that original feature piece. I don't look that different from the way I do on the telly, do I?"

Roberto replied, "Worse."

Valerie grasped the brass handle and pulled open the heavy door. Wooden tables and chairs filled the dining area in front; a line of booths hugged one wall, the bar running down the other. They chose a table off to one side where they could watch the door as well as the length of the room.

By eight o'clock, they had finished dinner.

Valerie switched from beer to coffee at nine-thirty. They watched people come and go. Topics of conversation had run the gamut from talking shop to Arab fundamentalism to the future of the monarchy to global ecology.

By ten-thirty, Myles began to fidget. At a quarter to eleven, he said, "I think this is a bust. Let's call it sufficient for one night. We've still nearly an hour's drive back to the hotel."

"Maybe he wasn't ready," Valerie said. "He probably got scared."

Outside, a fine drizzle wafted down from the dark sky. Valerie slowed as a man stepped out of the tobacco shop's recessed doorway. He appeared to be young, wearing a black leather coat, wool hat, muffler, and dark pants. He had his hands in his pockets, shoulders slumped, but tension reflected from his posture.

"Looking for us?" Valerie asked in a confidential voice.

The man, his face partially shadowed by the hat's low brim, squinted hard at Myles. "Mr. Edwards? That you?"

"It is." Myles nodded and shoved his hands into his coat pockets. "You could have joined us inside."

"No. Someone might have seen." He looked around uncertainly. "I'm half frozen. I thought you'd have left before this."

"We're a determined breed," Valerie said, stepping forward, offering her hand. "I'm Valerie Radin, Triple N, Washington bureau. This is Roberto Naez, my cameraman."

"You're her!" He said it in an awed whisper. "You're really her." He took Valerie's hand in a strong grip. "Mark White, ma'am. I'm with . . ." And he realized what he'd just said.

"It's all right, Mark," Valerie said easily, taking him by the arm. "Come on, we'll just drive around and talk. No one will see you that way."

She led White to the Holden and opened the door so he could climb into the backseat, then slid in beside him. Myles lost no time in starting the engine and driving out from the curb.

As they accelerated down the wet street, Valerie turned to White. "Just what do you do for Smyth-Archer? Work in the lab?"

"No, I'm . . ." He swallowed hard. "Wait, this is a mistake. Pull over and let me out. If they find out . . ."

Valerie placed a hand on his sleeve, adopting her expression of deepest concern. "Mark, just what are you afraid of? Who are you afraid of?"

He gave her an agonized look, face bathed in the light of oncoming traffic. "If they find out I've talked to you, they'll kill me."

"Kill you? Is it that bad?"

"Yes. Let me out!" He reached up and pounded on Myles's shoulder. "Stop the car! Bloody stop!"

Thirteen

Jim stooped to fill his stained cup from the growling coffee-maker. Betty had left for the night and Brett should be halfway through basketball practice. The last Jim had seen of Umber, she had lain down on the little couch in the lab playroom and fallen asleep. Proof that he wasn't the only one lying awake at night and worrying.

Across the office, Dana watched him from her desk. "You don't look well, Jim."

"All things considered, we've got a lot to worry about." He made a face. "Dana, I have a really nasty feeling that I'm out of my league."

Dana rotated her chair on its swivels. "All right, let's look at this logically. What is the worst that could happen?"

"They could come and take Umber. The loneliness would kill her soul . . . break Brett's heart. And mine." He smiled wanly.

"Jim, they may not do anything." Dana stood up, and her braid hung down past her tooled-leather belt. "Did Tory manage to kill the blood test?"

"I don't know." He looked up at the fluorescent lights. "I wish I'd never answered her call that day."

The sound of an engine, of tires on gravel, made him blink. The engine died, followed by the slamming of two doors.

"That must be the Gestapo," Jim said. "Ready for the dreaded knock on the door?" His hands clenched. "Do me a favor? Go check on Umber. Last time I looked, she was still asleep."

Dana walked toward the lab door, and Jim steeled himself.

He could hear shoes grating on the steps, the sound of the door opening to the mudroom. Then came the knock.

"Come in." He turned to appraise the two men who stepped into the office. Both wore gray suits, white button-down shirts, and carried briefcases. Dr. Brian Smithwick had close-cropped dark hair, a long narrow nose, and flashy gold cuff links. The second man had dark hair, flat-looking blue eyes, and the thick muscular shoulders of a football player.

"Hello, Dr. Dutton. I presume that you were awaiting us?" Smithwick asked.

"Yes," Jim answered in what he hoped was a calm voice. "I was just going over some data." And then: "After talking to Godmoore, I don't suppose this is a friendly visit, is it, Dr. Smithwick?"

Smithwick gave him a weak smile. "That depends, Jim. We must come to some decisions regarding your work. And, well, your relationship with us."

Jim's guts turned cold. "So, you've come to ruin my life, have you?"

Smithwick stepped forward and offered his hand. Jim shook, unsure as to whether the crawling feeling was a sign that he should have backed off or just ordinary fear.

"This is my associate, Doug Parnell." Smithwick indicated his companion, who smiled in a threatening way.

Parnell's grip would have crushed rock. Jim barely kept from flinching at the pain. When he took his hand back, he wiggled the fingers, seeing the faintest trace of a grin on Parnell's lips.

"So, what's this about?" Jim asked, resuming his seat. "Did Godmoore send you out to personally cut my throat, or are you just here to give me a little pep chat?"

Smithwick's smile turned a little sad, apology in his eyes. "Neither, Dr. Dutton." He rolled Dana's chair over to face Jim's, and seated himself, leaning forward, elbows propped on his knees. "I'm afraid that events are accelerating rather rapidly. Dr. Godmoore has become concerned about the interest in SAC apes being expressed by certain parties."

"Yes, I know. I talked to Tory . . . Dr. Driggers. She's going to quash the data. She's uneasy about it, but she'll do it as a favor to me."

At that minute, Dana stepped into the room. She smiled professionally and started across the floor, asking, "Am I interrupting anything?"

Powered by nervous energy, Jim stood. "My research associate, Dana Marks. Dana, this is Dr. Smithwick, and Mr. Parnell, both of Smyth-Archer Chemists."

Dana stepped forward to shake Smithwick's hand, saying, "My pleasure." When she took Parnell's she physically recoiled, her expression startled and filled with distaste before she managed to mask it with professional politeness. Reflexively she stepped back to Jim's side, almost sidling up against him.

Parnell watched her with fixed interest, something predatory in his intent gaze.

"Dr. Smithwick has come here to discuss Umber's situation with us." Jim smiled, trying to ease the uncomfortable situation.

"With you, Dr. Dutton." Smithwick smiled. To Dana, he said, "I'm sure you understand, Ms. Marks."

"Of course." Dana pressed her hands together, straightening. "If you'll excuse me, I'll be . . ."

Jim raised his hand, shifting to space himself between Dana and Parnell's unblinking stare. The guy gave him the creeps.

"Anything you need to say can be said in front of Ms. Marks. She shares my complete confidence."

"I'm sure. However, I have my instructions." Smithwick lifted an eyebrow suggestively.

"It's no problem," Dana replied graciously. "Jim, you might be a while. I'll take care of the girls for you. Then there are midterm papers to grade. Call me if you need anything." She picked up her purse and laptop and glanced back. "It was a pleasure to meet you."

"Yeah," Parnell said meaningfully. "We'll see you later."

Dana avoided Parnell's rapacious eyes as she stepped wide around him on the way to the lab door.

After the door clicked behind her, Parnell turned, grinning. "Nice number, there, Doc."

Jim gave him a hostile look, turned to Smithwick, and jerked a thumb at Parnell. "Just what does he do for you, Doctor?"

"I facilitate policy, Dr. Dutton," Parnell answered for himself.

Smithwick raised a calming hand. "Dr. Dutton, if we could return to our previous conversation, we must make some decisions."

Jim backed against his desk, unwilling to retake his seat. "All right. Let's hear it."

Smithwick resumed his chair, leaning back to watch Jim. "We are uncomfortable with the growing interest in the SAC apes." He made a dismissive gesture. "Oh, not just your little conversation with Dr. Driggers, but a growing awareness within the discipline, and beyond, that SAC apes are special."

"What do you want from me?" Jim asked. "Why did you come here?"

"We're here to make preparations, Dr. Dutton." Smithwick straightened the sleeves of his gray suit. "We have come to the conclusion that with Umber's unfolding talents, and the inevitable knowledge that someone is going to leak the information to the press, the time has come to relocate her to an atmosphere that will be more conducive to the further development of her abilities."

Jim barely heard Dana's Toyota start up and the gravel popping under the tires as she backed out and drove off. For the moment, at least, she and Umber were safely away. A yawning abyss opened in his gut. "You mean you're taking her away from me."

"I'm afraid so."

Jim set his cup down hard and straightened. Parnell was surprisingly fast on his feet, grinning as he stepped alongside Jim. But he stopped short at Smithwick's raised hand.

"Dr. Dutton," Smithwick said, "you can work for us, or against us. This can be painful or positive, rewarding or destructive for you, Umber, Ms. Marks, and your department. How do you want to have it?"

"Umber is part of my life . . . and part of my family," Jim said.

"We're not monsters, Dr. Dutton." Smithwick steepled his fingers, his expression strained. "At least, we don't want to be in the position of acting that way. We will, however, take whatever actions you force us to."

"Yeah," Parnell whispered. "I might go help Dana grade her papers. Maybe talk a little primatology with her, huh?"

Jim felt the heat rising in his veins. "Don't you even—"

Parnell reacted like a sprung trap. Jim caught the blur of his movement, and then his arm was in Parnell's iron grip. For a moment, they struggled, but Parnell shoved Jim's arm up behind his back. Searing pain shot up the joint. Jim gasped despite himself.

"Doc," Parnell said evenly, "don't threaten me. It ain't healthy."

"Release him." Smithwick gestured, his cuff link flashing.

Instantly, Parnell turned Jim loose and stepped back, his face expressionless as ice.

Fear mingled with fury in Jim's gut.

To Parnell, Smithwick said, "Doug, would you mind waiting for me outside?"

He sauntered to the door and closed it behind him.

"I apologize for him." Smithwick seemed truly contrite. "Security insisted I bring him along. Corporate mentality, I suppose. However, Dr. Dutton, I am hoping that I'm correct that you are willing to work with us rather than against us."

"The carrot and the stick? Good cop, bad cop? Threat, reward? Now I'm properly set up for the pitch, correct?"

Smithwick nodded absently. "No matter what circumlocution and complicated sophistry you might espouse, the end does indeed justify the means. You have an attractive research assistant and a charming daughter. Whatever you decide to do, I'm sure you wouldn't want anything to happen to either of them."

"And you're telling me something might if I don't cooperate?"

Smithwick tugged on his button-down collar. "I would much rather have you as a willing ally than as an enemy, Dr. Dutton."

"If you take Umber away from me, you'll kill her." Sick to his stomach, Jim took a deep breath. *Think, goddamn it! There's got to be a way out of this!* Then he said: "She'll react like a child taken from her family. It will frighten her, depress her. Her immune system will plummet. She might will herself to die. If you know the Gombe literature, and the Mahale studies, you know that adolescent chimps will do that. I wouldn't put it past Umber."

"Nor would we." Smithwick inspected the ruby ring on his right hand. "And now that you have a glimmering of the stick, let me explain the carrot." He indicated the lab. "You have a nice facility here, all things considered. You've years and years of raw data that you've barely begun to analyze. You have a good job and we can extend it for as long as you'd like. Think of it as job security. We can give you another ape, a replacement for Umber—"

"Out of the question."

"—or you could go with her to her new location. You could spend the rest of your life working with her, or until you grow tired of it."

For the first time, Jim saw a glimmer of light. "Go with her? Where?"

Godmoore inspected his fingernails. "I told you, Dr. Dutton, we're not monsters. If you would like to go with Umber, we can arrange that. As a matter of fact, we would prefer it, because we share your concern over Umber's health. She would be happier with you at her side. We can make it quite all right with your department. Your continued grant will see to that. Take Ms. Marks with you, if you'd like. You'll simply be working outside the country."

"In England?"

Smithwick glanced up, smiling humorlessly. "We have another location in mind. The second half of the grand experiment, as it were."

"And that is?"

"Reintroduction to the wild." Smithwick walked to the coffee machine, scrounged a Styrofoam cup, and poured liquid from the pot. He tasted it and made a face.

"Reintroduction to the wild? Are you crazy? That's a formula for catastrophe. The only cross-fostered animal who came close to making it was Lucy, and she's dead, Brian. Shot by poachers in Senegal. Why? Because she trusted human beings. They cut off her head, hands, and feet and left the rest of her to rot."

"We've a better—"

"It doesn't matter. Umber's an American."

"She's a bonobo."

Jim shook his head. "No, she's not, and you know it. She's a very intelligent, sensitive person. She's lived in a house, been raised in this culture. She watches television, goes shopping for groceries, and cooks dinner on the stove. She takes a bath every night and likes to wear brightly colored clothes. She and Brett read *Teen* magazine and drool over Leonardo DiCaprio. You could no more turn her loose in the wild than you could Brett, for God's sake."

Smithwick seemed nonplussed. "That's another reason we want you there, to help her make that transition. You've spent time in the wilderness before, Jim. You come from an isolated ranch out in the wilds of Wyoming. You have shot your own meat, grown your own food. You've lived on the land. That was one of the reasons you were chosen for this in the beginning."

Jim tilted his head as understanding began to dawn. "You knew that this was going to come apart, didn't you? That you'd be relocating the SAC apes to the wild?"

"It was inevitable. We have spent the last ten years building a facility in anticipation of this very moment. Some of our less-successful apes have already been relocated there."

"Less-successful?"

"As in every scientific endeavor, we followed a learning curve." Smithwick shrugged. "Unlike some of our competitors in the biotechnology business, we took responsibility for our mistakes, gave them a place to live out their lives."

"Mistakes?"

"Call them what you will."

"And where is this place?"

"Equatorial Guinea."

Jim crossed his arms and blinked. "Where?"

"Between Gabon and Cameroon. Immediately north of the

equator on the west coast of Africa. It's a small place with an absolutely deplorable government. Ideal actually."

"You mean corrupt," Jim said, rubbing the back of his neck.

"Dr. Dutton, you will not speak of this with anyone, understood? I am serious about that. A breach of my trust might goad me to ask my associate"—he pointed an index finger at the door and lifted an eyebrow—"to interview your lovely assistant to see what you might have told her."

"I get the point," Jim said. "So, you covered all the bases? Either I play along or you hurt people I love. If I don't make waves, you reward me with . . . what?"

"Whatever you want, assuming it doesn't compromise our long-term objectives." Smithwick made a subtle gesture with his hands. "The story is going to break, of that there is no doubt. We will delay it as long as possible, but in the end there will be a media debacle. Years from now, after all is said and done, you may do as you will with your knowledge. We suspect that you will continue to protect Umber and her kin. No matter what, your career shall have been made. By that time the apes will be established."

Jim's shoulder muscles contracted, as though his body understood something in those words that his mind did not. "Genetically altered apes."

"That's right. Just like your Umber."

"Why are you doing this, Smithwick? It must have cost you billions—"

"For the apes, of course . . . and, as is usual, to make a profit for the company." Smithwick looked up. "It did cost us billions. And now, perhaps, realizing that, you can understand that Umber and her kin are most unique. Over the years, we have been filing patents to certain biological and genetic breakthroughs. The timing is so critical on these things. Our competitors are watching every move we make. File too many patents, and they will understand the direction of our research.

Suffice it to say that we do not yet have a patent on Umber and her kind. We didn't want to tip our hand too soon. Augmented apes and the spin-off biotech are worth billions to SAC. Don't you think that would necessitate a great deal of care in the treatment of our wards?"

"Uh-huh, and this bullshit about doing it 'for the apes'?"

"Jim, if they're not as smart as we are, they're doomed to extinction. Deep down in your heart you know that, don't you?" A pause. "So. Are you in?"

Jim closed his eyes, searching for alternatives. The only viable strategy was to survive long enough to make certain his family was safe, then figure out how to turn the tables on them.

"Of course I'm in, Smithwick. Do you think I'm a fool?"

"I think you're a very intelligent man."

"Sure you do," Jim said bitterly.

Melody Hinsinger gave Vernon Shanks a frightened look as she indicated the burlap sack on the stainless steel dissection table. "That is it," she told him, a tremor in her voice. "I found it in the Alpha Group territory. I called you first thing, Vernon. I thought you'd want to take the first look."

Shanks wrinkled his nose at the smell. He stepped across the lab to the table and carefully pulled back the grimy cloth. With one hand he flicked on the overhead lights and bent closer, wincing at the stench. The rotting specimen couldn't be mistaken. He was staring at a primate's arm, the flesh swollen and half consumed by insects, many of which still speckled the brown meat where the insecticide had killed them.

"Is it one of the Alpha Group?" Melody asked plaintively.

Shanks continued his examination and froze when his gaze fell on the hands. "No, it's not."

"How can you be so sure?" Melody asked.

Shanks reached for one of the scalpels in the tray and used the keen point to scrape at one of the fingers. Through the hardened blood and fluids, a silver gleam caught the light. "Apes don't wear jewelry. No, Melody, this is a human arm."

She didn't react, as if his words hadn't quite made an impact. "Human? I don't understand."

Shanks backed away and took a deep breath. "I don't either. Is anyone missing? Are all of the staff accounted for?"

She nodded, then added, "At least, I think so."

"And where, exactly, was this found?"

Melody's lips had pursed. "I came across it in the forest, Vern. Close to the canal, just down the slope from the Alpha Group's village. You know, we're still searching for Sky Eyes. And you know, the funny thing is, we had walked that area before. We just couldn't have missed something like this."

"Find out if anyone is missing. This"—he indicated the arm—"has been out there for a while. In the meantime, I want crews to crisscross that area again. Look for signs of leopards, and . . . and, I don't know. But I want that area searched, and I want Sky Eyes found. Right now."

Getting Mark White to the Kensington hotel had taken all of Valerie's skill, and half the resources of the Triple N London bureau. First, they had to persuade him that yes, Triple N could protect a source. Second, they had determined that he had an aunt in Plymouth who could reasonably be suspected of having a medical emergency. A reporter was picked from the Triple N pool and sent to Plymouth with a complicated computer that plugged into the aunt's telephone jack.

Only after the arrangement had been made and tested did

Mark White finally seem to believe he might really stand a chance of getting away with it.

Valerie inspected the plush suite they had rented for him at their hotel. She looked into the bedroom where White lay on the bed, fully clothed and sound asleep. He was young, in his twenties. Soft brown hair curled over his pale forehead. He had an upturned nose. He needed a shave, but all in all he looked like a nice kid.

Valerie checked her watch. Almost eight.

She stretched her tired back. Her tan tweed skirt and white silk shirt had looked great when she'd first put them on twenty-six hours ago. Now they appeared made of wrinkles.

At a soft knock, she opened the door. Roberto gave her a puffy-eyed stare. He glanced at Myles, flopped loose-limbed on the chaise. "We still got the kid?"

"He's been asleep since two A.M."

"Did you get any sleep?"

"A couple of hours." She shifted and stretched. "Let's call room service for breakfast. As soon as they get here, we'll eat, get the subject in a good mood, and wring our young Mr. White dry." Valerie tucked blond hair behind her ears and gave him a wary smile.

Roberto picked up the phone and ordered four big English breakfasts while Valerie went in to wake Mark White.

After the emptied breakfast dishes had been placed in the hallway Valerie indicated the piles of paper on the table. "All right, Mark, can you help us sort through this? Start at the top. What's SAC up to, and why all the secrecy?"

Myles surreptitiously used his toe to flick the switch on the recorder under the table.

Mark White stepped over to the table and stared down at the piles of documents. "You mean you don't understand? I thought I gave you everything you'd need. It's so apparent. Even a child could see it."

"See what?" Valerie demanded, stepping forward.

"This!" He picked up the photocopied picture of the ape. "This is what they're creating . . . have created!"

"It's a monkey!" Roberto threw his hands up.

Mark White tossed the photo down. "No, it's not. I've seen them. They're a hell of a lot smarter than you are."

Roberto's brows lifted.

Valerie said, "What do you mean, smarter?"

"Just what I damned well said. Smarter! They ought to be. They're born with human brains!"

For the moment, Valerie could only stare. She could almost hear her heart beat in the long moment that followed. One by one, White met their startled eyes. Finally, it was Roberto who broke the silence: *"Madre de Dios."*

Mark corrected himself, "I should have said that some of them have been born with human brains, the later animals. The early experiments . . . well, they made mistakes, produced monstrous things that had to be destroyed."

"This is a new program?" Myles asked, recovering. "Something they've just started?"

"No. It's been going on for years."

"Where are the apes?" Valerie grabbed up the photo, looking closely at the image. Sure, it was a photocopy of a photograph, a little blurry, but looking closely, she could see the outline of the skull. Those physical anthropology classes, taken so long ago, now stood her in good stead. "The rounded frontal bone, the width of the parietals, that's what we're seeing here, isn't it?"

White shrugged. "That I can't tell you. I'm a genetics technician. I just run the PCR."

"What's PCR?" Roberto asked.

"Polymerase chain reaction." White crossed his arms. "It's a machine that makes copies of DNA segments. It does it quickly, and well."

Valerie tried to rally her thoughts. "Help me get this straight. They take a human gene, copy it in the PCR, and insert it on the ape's chromosome?"

"Right."

"So how do they know which gene? In a human there are over one hundred thousand different genes encoded on hundreds of thousands of miles of DNA. We're talking about billions of base pairs, right?"

"Right." White still watched her skeptically. "But each chromosome has its own distinctive topography, if you will. Different bands that show up under electrophoresis."

"Electrophoresis?" Roberto asked.

"It's a way of exposing genetic material to an electromagnetic field," Valerie explained. "The field separates different genes. It's kind of like sorting metal filings on a piece of paper with a magnet." To White she said, "Okay, so you've got a chromosome, say number 12, then what? How do you know where you are on the chromosome?"

White glanced at Roberto. "Think of DNA as a long line of beads. The entire code for the thing is made of four colored beads, right? Adenine bonds to thymine, guanine to cytosine. White only bonds to blue, red only bonds to green. So we look for certain patterns of code. When we find them, we use specific enzymes to cut the DNA molecule in a given place. Since the cut is restricted to that location, we call it a restriction enzyme. With a restriction enzyme, we can map the chromosome down to even smaller segments. Then we use something called an 'alu.' It's a repetitive code that shows up over and over in human and chimp DNA. With that, we can count the repetitions and move even closer to a target site on a chromosome."

"But how do you know what a given section of DNA does?" Myles was rubbing his jaw, frowning, his bushy eyebrows drawn together.

"By the proteins that segment makes," White responded. "The

entire world has been mapping the human genome since the mid-1980s. The database is huge. SAC has ninety-five percent of the human genome in their big Cray supercomputers."

Perspiration had matted Mark's soft brown hair to his forehead and temples. Beads glistened on his upturned nose. He spread his arms and asked, "Do you understand?"

Valerie rubbed the back of her neck. "I'm starting to. Take me back to the chimps. How do you know what genes to insert? How do you make a chimp grow a bigger brain? We know human DNA, that I'll grant, but chimpanzees, that's a whole different species."

"Is it?" White gave a sober look. "We share almost ninety-nine percent of a bonobo's DNA."

"What's a bonobo?" Roberto asked.

"Pygmy chimp," Valerie responded. "*Pan paniscus.* It's a separate species from the common chimp you're familiar with. It's also rare, and only comes from the central Democratic Republic of Congo." She gestured. "But get back to the story, Mark. How do you tell what you're going to remove from the chimp and replace with human DNA?"

"By hybridization."

Everything began to fit into place. "I see."

"See what?" Myles demanded. "I don't understand a bit of this! What the hell is hybridization?"

Valerie lifted a calming hand, smiling knowingly at Mark White. "So, they heat the DNA to separate the two strands." She glanced at Roberto. "Think of it like this. At a certain temperature, the two strings of beads separate from each other, like unzipping a zipper. So, the lab tech takes a half a zipper of human DNA and a half of chimp DNA and lays them side by side. When the temperature is lowered, they zip together again. But the fit isn't perfect. Some of the beads don't find their opposite color. That's hybridization, the way you identify the genes that differ between humans and chimpanzees."

Roberto had a glimmering, but Myles was still looking lost. Valerie shook her head. "Damn, that's still a huge undertaking. How do you deal with the difference in chromosomes? Humans have twenty-three pairs. Apes have twenty-four."

White grinned, respect in his brown eyes for the first time. "At some point in human evolution, two of the chromosomes were joined, merged into the modern human chromosome number 2. It's not a problem. SAC isn't trying to breed a human-ape cross, so they don't need to worry about it. They are keeping the species separate, just building a better ape. The baseline genetic material remains the same."

"How long have you been working at SAC?" Myles asked.

"Three years. Since I graduated." Mark walked over to the desk and poured a cup of coffee from the pot left over from breakfast.

"And you just figured all of this out?" Myles gestured at the stacks of paper.

"No, I didn't figure it out." White seemed to stiffen again. "It's what I do. I'm a genetic engineer. SAC pays me very well. I get to do something I'm good at. What I'm learning now will take care of me for the rest of my life, whether I work for SAC or for someone else. I've been on the cutting edge."

"Then why break silence now?" Myles asked.

Mark sipped at his coffee, a frown incising his pale forehead. "Because something's gone wrong. Godmoore, Johnson, and the others are nervous. I think the whole thing is about to come crashing down around their ears. When the world learns of this, some people are going to be very upset."

At that moment, the phone rang. Valerie watched Mark tense, swallow hard, and look pleadingly at each of them.

"If it's ringing here, it's for you. Patched through your aunt's house in Plymouth." Valerie indicated the phone.

White's hand trembled as he picked it up, saying, "Yes?" He listened for a moment, his color draining. "Oh, why, she's better, sir. We thought it might have been a stroke, but the doctor's not so sure." After another pause he said, "Tell Dr. Johnson that I left the results on my clipboard. I'd planned to hand that to him right off this morning." A pause. "No, sir. It was a surprise to me, too, sir." He clamped his jaw, listening. "Tomorrow morning, sir. I don't think it will take longer." Voice dropping, he said, "Yes, sir. Thank you, sir. I'll be sure and tell her." Then he carefully placed the handset in its cradle.

Valerie had seen similar expressions when men were declared guilty in a court of law. She considered the phone with narrowed eyes. SAC, it seemed, did indeed check up on its employees.

Fourteen

An hour after the African sunset, Mitu Bagawli placed his updated field notebook to one side. He yawned and reached over from his bunk, slipped his hand through the mosquito netting, and turned the knob on the lantern until it closed off the fuel. He lay back and stared up at the cramped cabin's tin ceiling. The mosquito netting made a gauzy tent that yellowed with the dying light. Mitu prayed that the bug spray had done its job. Last night, he had no more than fallen asleep when a big yellow and black spider had fallen smack onto the center of his chest.

In the six months that he had worked at Compound C, he had come to accept cobras, green mambas, gigantic centipedes, and the other forest fauna as regulars. Spiders, however, played upon some deep-seated fear that went back to his childhood, and the time he had managed to trap himself under Grandfather Magama's house. The darkness had terrified him. Crawling blindly around in the cramped space under the floor joists, spiderwebs had draped his face and he had felt the creatures skittering across his skin. His panicked screams had brought rescue, but changed his life forever.

The lantern hissed as the mantles dimmed. Shadows lengthened along the walls, playing over the worktable piled with his notes, the emergency radio, and the small food locker.

Compound C couldn't be called much more than a collection of shacks, but Mitu hadn't come here for the amenities.

He watched the last of the light fade until only a glow remained. The stink of the extinguished lantern intensified with the darkness, and the forest noises seemed to grow louder.

Mitu cocked his head, listening to the roar of the night insects. Out there in the trees his apes lay curled on their sides, asleep in their nests. The strange group of chimps that had chased them three days ago had vanished. He had searched for them for days but had found nothing. He should probably have reported it, but he had been working on an article—a follow-up to the last one he'd co-authored with Shanks for *Nature*. But this time it would be his work alone.

They had achieved so much here. His apes had lived almost their entire lives in metal cages. No one would believe how much they'd changed. Now those laboratory animals survived on their own in the forest. They lived free, located food, and mated. Most of the animals seemed to have overcome the scars inflicted while in captivity.

And I helped.

He smiled up into the darkness. Fruit bats chittered outside, prowling the compound on fluttering wings for overlooked tidbits.

The stifling heat pressed down on him. He actually thought about moving his bed outside, then discarded the idea as too much trouble. He'd think about it tomorrow since it involved rehanging the mosquito netting. And the thin walls of the shack did provide some protection from the local wildlife.

At this time the night before, the spider had come plummeting down from above. The memory left him unnerved, waiting for something.

"Oh, great," he muttered. "I'll never get to sleep now."

The night sounds seemed closer, the chirping, buzzing, and clicking of the insects amplified by his fear. The soft dripping of water, condensed from the tin roof, added to his unease.

"Stop it, Mitu." He growled, tossed onto his side, and punched up his pillow, vaguely noting it had started to smell like mildew. Foolishness, that's all this was. He'd have been in more danger at his parents' house in Nairobi, with its gangs and crime.

He didn't remember drifting off, but the click of the metal latch on the door brought him bolt upright, gasping.

Mitu blinked, rubbed his face, and listened as the rusting hinges on the door complained. Through the netting, he could see the brighter night outlined by the door frame. Black shapes wavered there.

"Who is it?" he called, his frantic fingers slipping over his flashlight. He gripped it and thumbed the switch. At first, all he could see was a blaze of white, his eyes blinded by the reflection off the mosquito netting.

"Get out!" He scrambled up on his bed. "I . . . I'm armed! I'll shoot!" he lied, but in his fright, he couldn't think of anything else to say.

A dark hand ripped the thin netting away as if it had been paper, and Mitu saw eyes shining in his flashlight beam. Soft pant-hoots filled the shack.

Mitu shrieked. "Dear God, what's happening? Don't hurt me!"

In panic, he leaped for the door. He made four steps before the apes leaped upon him, clinging to his back and legs. They knocked him to the ground. He could smell them, feel their hairy flesh against his.

"What do you want?" he cried.

He kicked out, flailing his fists, and heard a shriek of rage. In that instant, the flashlight beam in his hand illuminated an ape, a big male. Mitu couldn't believe the hatred in its strained smile. And then their eyes locked. In that short moment of disbelief Mitu stared into the most startling blue eyes.

A machete glinted, dreamlike, suspended above the male's head. It hung for an eternity, a silvery silhouette against the shadow-cast tin roof.

When it arced down, splitting the flashlight beam, a scream of terror ripped from Mitu's throat.

High in the crown, perched on terminal branches of the great tree, he raised the human's head toward the sky. Insect wings whispered in the air around him. The forest had hushed, as though in wary anticipation.

He lowered the head and studied the human's wide, staring eyes. With a finger, he poked them, still slightly surprised they didn't blink in response. The sense of power filled him, and he screamed in defiance of the world.

Then he propped the head in a Y *of the highest branch, signing: "Go, human. Tell her. Tell her to come back to me."*

The Bronco lights illuminated Dana's Toyota when Jim pulled into his driveway at ten-thirty. He breathed a sigh of relief, having driven by her apartment in town as well as the social sciences building on his way home. He parked beside the Toyota and just sat there, allowing the silence of the night to seep into his tired soul. The yellow glow of the porch light beckoned him: a refuge after the traumatic day. For the first time, it seemed an insignificant beacon.

The question he had been asking himself all night repeated: *Did I do the right thing?*

He had taken Smithwick's deal, but it made his gut crawl, as if he'd done something unclean.

If it was the only way, Jimbo, why do you feel so shitty about it?

The urge to hurt something—to retrieve his rifle, drive to the Marriott, and shoot Smithwick and Parnell—vied with the desire to lean his forehead against the steering wheel and sob.

Instead, he set the security system and walked across the frosted grass to the porch. It took two stabs with his key before he opened the lock.

Dana sat at the table in the dining room, a textbook open before her. She had unbraided her hair, and it streamed down in glossy waves. Brett and Umber were wrapped in each other's arms, sound asleep on the living room couch, blond hair mixing with ink black. He stopped short, staring down at them.

"Well?" Dana whispered as she looked up from her text.

"It's bad," Jim told her. He walked into the kitchen and withdrew a bottle of Guinness from the refrigerator. He gestured, and she nodded, so he popped a second one for her. He slumped down into one of the dining room chairs.

She gave him a measuring look. "I didn't want to be alone. Something about that Parnell. He sent shivers down my back, like when I was a little girl and Mother told me the Witiko was watching through my bedroom window."

"The Witiko. He's the mythical Cree Indian monster, isn't he? Has a heart of ice? A filthy cannibal?"

"That's him." Dana gave him a grim look.

He took a swallow of the rich stout. "They're taking Umber away. She's scheduled to be flown out on Friday."

She barely managed to strangle the cry of outrage. "We've got to stop this!"

"Dana, listen to me. Sending Parnell wasn't a lark on their part. He's the enforcer, the stick, if you get my meaning. Smithwick gave me the carrot after you left."

"My God, Jim, what kind of people are these?"

"Witikos. Every one of them. But . . ." Jim said. "I've worked out the details with Smithwick. I'm going with Umber, at least for the short term. You're taking over for me here. Someone has to cover my classes. And, after you hear what sort of outfit you're dealing with, if you still want to, you can be in charge of the new ape."

"New ape?" Her brown eyes reflected wariness.

"Your ape, Dana. The lab will continue to function. You will be the co-director. Salary starts at forty thousand a year. You get a two-thousand-dollar-a-year raise from there on out, provided you finish your Ph.D. within two years."

"Provided I sell them my soul?"

"If you're here, and they threaten you, you can always run for the border and disappear into the reserve backcounty. Secondly, I'll be coming back to the States every couple of months. I'll be able to advise you on what to do, on how dangerous this really is."

Dana's dark eyes bored into him. "Jim, where are they sending you?"

He told her, "Some sort of jungle compound in a place called Equatorial Guinea. It's in Africa. That's all I know."

"Why Africa?"

He glanced at Umber, her head resting on Brett's. "They've got some silly notion that Umber can be reintroduced to the wild."

"That's crazy!"

"Yeah, well, that's why I have to go with her. If anyone can get her through this, it's me."

"And Brett?"

"She's going to have to live with her granddad on the ranch." He rubbed the bridge of his nose, anticipating one hell of a headache. "It's going to be the toughest on her."

"But . . . Africa? That's so . . . far . . ." Dana leaned back.

"It's that, or Umber will be tranquilized, boxed up in a crate on Friday, and shipped out. Our grant will be canceled, and the moving company will clean out the lab next week." He met her eyes. "Dana, I had to make a decision. I don't know if I did the right thing, but I took the best option I had."

She gave him a weak smile. "I told you I was behind you one hundred percent. Nothing's changed."

For a long time they sat silently, hearing only the hum of the refrigerator.

"When are you going to tell them?" Dana asked, indicating Brett and Umber.

"Tomorrow. That will be soon enough." He rose and walked over to crouch down in front of the sofa. His two girls looked so peaceful, content in each other's arms. Jim shook Umber's elbow. "Hey, you guys. It's the middle of the night. Come on. Wake up, give me a big hug, and go on to bed."

"Wheep," Umber muttered and unlaced herself from Brett. She wrapped Jim in her long muscular arms.

He hugged her, then prodded her for the stairs. Umber climbed her pole, swung onto the landing, and vanished down the hall to her room.

Jim took Brett in his arms, holding her tightly. "Good night, angel," he said as he kissed her hair. "See you in the morning."

"Love you, Dad." Brett yawned and stumbled to her feet.

Jim stared after them long after they'd disappeared.

"You look like hell, Jim Dutton." Dana came to stand beside him, looking up the stairs.

"Yeah, well, you ought to feel what it's like on the inside."

Instinctively, he walked to the phone. In the directory, he found the number for the Marriott and dialed it. "Mr. Parnell's room, please."

He waited as the hotel operator rang, once, twice, three times, then four. At seven rings, the operator broke in and asked if he'd like to leave a message.

"No, thank you." Jim hung up and glanced out the window at the darkness beyond. "He's out there, somewhere. Your Witiko man."

"I haven't had that reaction to a man in a long time," Dana said, her dark eyes vacant as she stared out into the night.

Jim's hair began to prickle. He made a decision. "Dana, you're staying here until we know that the Witiko man is gone for good. I don't want you to leave my side."

Dana nodded.

Jim ran a hand through his hair. Under his breath, he whispered, "The Witiko man. God, what have I gotten my family into?"

Umber lies on her side on the couch in front of the fireplace. Orange light flickers through her black hair. Jim sits on the opposite side of the couch, watching the fire, yet not. He is dressed in his Brown Palace Hotel robe. She heard him walk down the stairs an hour ago, climbed from her blanket nest, and followed him. He hugged Umber for a while, but they have not signed a word to each other.

Prickles run along Umber's long arms. The insects of fear are eating away at her insides, and she cannot stop them.

The world outside is quiet. No owls hoot. Not even wind dares to breathe. Everyone is afraid.

Umber turns and blinks at Jim.

The lines in his forehead are deep and crooked.

A log breaks in the fire and bursts into flame, hissing and spitting.

Shadows slither from the dark corners and shoot across the ceiling, tongues flicking, golden tails flashing.

Umber shivers suddenly—and the insects inside her scurry on their clawed feet. When she was little, Jim had hidden rubber snakes on bottles under the kitchen sink, and in the bath-room, and on the rifle. On anything he did not want Umber to touch. They had terrified her. And then she'd seen her first rattlesnake in the backyard. It had hissed and struck at her.

Umber's eyes widen as the shadows dart toward her. She slaps at one.

Jim says, "Umber? Are you all right?" His face glows yellow in the firelight.

Umber makes a V with her first two fingers, points toward her eyes, then turns the fingers toward the ghost snakes.

Jim searches the ceiling and floor. "No, I don't see them. What do you see?"

Umber sits up. She makes the slithering serpent sign with her right hand and points to all the places in the darkness where they move. Her lungs have stopped breathing.

"Snakes?" Jim says, and his brows lower.

Umber holds her two fists in front of her chest and flicks them open and closed quickly, signing: *"Many! Many!"*

Jim puts an arm around her shoulders and pulls her close. He smells of soap and coffee.

"Well," he sighs, "I'd like to tell you there are no snakes in the world, Umber, but I met two today."

Umber cocks her head, not understanding. Something is wrong. The words are locked behind Jim's teeth, trying to get out, but he won't let them. It scares Umber.

Jim leans over and kisses Umber on top of the head. "Don't worry about the snakes. I won't let them hurt you tonight. You're safe."

She signs: "Insects inside."

"Are they?" He hugs Umber and smiles, and she can breathe again. Her lungs fill with warm air.

Jim rises and pulls the glass doors closed across the front of the fireplace. As the flames crawl into the crevices of the logs to sleep, the snakes vanish.

Umber looks around, searching for them, for the cracks where they must hide, but they are gone.

Jim reaches out a hand to Umber. "Come on, Umber. We both need to sleep. I'm going to figure a way out of this. I promise." He smiles.

But it is not a happy smile. She knows this smile: the same one he gave her when she was in bed with pneumonia, worried and afraid.

Umber slides off the couch and walks toward him with her hand out. The insects are waiting, hiding in the shadows cast by the now silent snakes.

When his fingers close around hers, the world changes.

The room is no longer alive with snakes. Everything glows, the couch, the table, Jim's bearded face.

As they climb the stairs together, Umber yawns and signs: "Love you."

Jim squeezes her hand harder. "I love you, too, Umber."

Fifteen

Valerie settled on the bed in her London hotel room and piled pillows behind her. Then she picked up the phone and dialed the number. She had slept for three hours, then showered. Her blond hair still hung damply around her face.

The line clicked and Joan Faulkner's nasal voice said, "Station manager's office. How may I help you?"

"Hello, Joan. This is Valerie Radin for Murray."

"What is this concerning, please."

"It's a damn update on a story, Joan. Let me talk to Murray."

"One moment, please."

Valerie could imagine her pinched look as she glared disdainfully at the phone. She waited for nearly three minutes before Murray said, "Hello. Val? That you?"

"Hi, Murray. God, listen, you've got to do something with the tarantula lady. If I have to listen to her alabaster bullshit again, I'm going to walk in there and kick her tight ass."

"She's protective of my time, Val. My last line of defense against a hard and cruel world."

"Don't give me that crock, Murray. If I'm calling, it's with an update, not to file a paternity suit, all right?"

"I'll tell her. What have you got?"

"I think it's going to be pure solid wondrous gold. What tipped you that this would be so big?"

"A silly hunch." He paused. "And the knowledge that your old boyfriend is up to his nose in it."

"What old boyfriend? Which one?"

"The father of your daughter." Murray paused. "Okay, I'm a schmuck, but I thought you might have been out for blood, so I stacked the deck a little if I needed to put you back in line." A pause. "Val? Do I owe you an apology?"

"I'm not sure yet. I have to think about it for a while."

"Well, if I do, let me know. Under the circumstances, I'll hope your mention of a paternity suit happened to be coincidentally timed bad humor."

Valerie squinted up at the chandelier, wondering what he'd do if she said it wasn't. "It was."

"Right. So, tell me what you've got."

"Jesus Christ, Murray," she said as the pieces began to fall into place, "are you telling me Jim's working with a SAC ape? One of these augmented jobs?"

"I don't know what it is, but he's working with it. We got a weird tip that wound its way through the system. Some primatologist in San Diego talked to a reporter who was dating an anthropologist who was telling him about this ape blowing the top off the learning curve—it wasn't a normal animal. Then, Myles reports that he's got a source inside SAC, something about apes. I did a little checking and got a hit on Jim Dutton's name. If it's about to break on both sides of the ocean, and you might be a loose cannon, well, my gut said go with it."

"Murray?"

"Yeah?"

She sighed. "You're a son of a bitch."

"And you're a master of understatement. Thanks. So. How good is this?"

"We've got the source on ice. We spent all day picking his

brain. Myles just FedExed a copy of the tape to you. It'll be on your desk tomorrow morning. They're fiddling with ape DNA, implanting human genes. In essence, they're making them more human, and less apelike."

"Why?"

"We don't know that yet, but how does this grab you? They're growing apes with human brains."

"Holy shit!"

"That's right, pal. But since we're talking about guts, I think there's something more here. What if, with the proper spin, SAC could make this work for them? You know, research for the greater human benefit, a cure for Alzheimer's, who knows? Like I said, there's something else at work here, something I don't understand that involves a lot of money."

"How much?"

"Over two hundred million pounds that don't show up on their financial statements—you know, the ones they send to stockholders."

"Wow! Okay, so what are you doing about it?"

"We're sending our snitch back to work tomorrow morning with instructions to grab anything he can lay his hot little hands on. When we get another batch of documents, and tie some loose ends together, I'm going in to do a live interview. Oh, and if it gets sticky, we've promised the source anonymity."

Murray grumbled to himself and said, "Val, I think I'd better issue that apology. I'll back it up by saying whatever you need, you've got an open account on this end."

"Thanks, Murray. Um, just one thing. I don't know what Jim's into with his ape, but could you keep him out of it? Do that, and we're square."

Why on earth did you say that, bitch?

"You've got it." She heard papers rustling. "How about a Shanna Bartlett? You know anything about her?"

"Nope."

"She's got one of these SAC apes. Maybe we'll send a crew by tomorrow and see what they turn up. If nothing else, it'll be B roll, or file tape for your piece."

"Sure, Murray." She flipped through her own notes. "You might want to put research to work on Equatorial Guinea, and something called IAR. We think that means International Ape Rescue, some sort of private foundation sponsored by SAC. That's where they've been dumping the money for the last ten years."

"Equatorial where?"

"Guinea. It's an old Spanish colony. Part of the country is on an island called Bioko, the capital is Malabo. The rest of the country is a tiny little square between Gabon and Cameroon. It's got a really bloody history of coups and civil wars, and from what we can determine with preliminary research, most of the country is for sale. Given the bundle of dough SAC has dropped there in the last ten years, they own it, and President Basala. They've also got their hooks into some guy called Don Amando. He's something called the 'Chief of Special Security' in what functions for the Equatoguinean Ministry of the Interior."

"We'll start digging. See what we can pry out of State. Need anything else?"

"Not that I can think of."

"All right. Keep me informed."

She hung up and stared thoughtfully at the ceiling. "You're not really in the middle of this shit, are you, Jim? Tell me you're just on the periphery. One of the scientists they're using to maximize profits." And Brett, was she involved, too?

Out of impulse, Valerie rolled over and pulled the photograph from her purse. Brett's face stared up at her, laughter on her lips.

Was that why she'd pulled Murray off Jim, because of Brett?

Did she still have some obscure urge to protect the daughter she'd never known?

"You silly bitch, you'll never admit you've got regrets, will you?" She studied the photograph, remembering the day she'd driven up from Denver, found the junior high school, and waited as she had so many times before. Even across the distance, she'd recognized her daughter, seen the younger copy of herself, and taken a whole roll of photos.

Two years ago, she'd been stunned to discover Brett in a cast, and had taken an extra two days off to ferret out the reason she'd had a broken arm. Sports, of all things.

Once she'd followed Brett and Jim to the El Burrito restaurant, surprised that it still survived after so many years. Wearing sunglasses and a scarf, she had seated herself in the booth behind them. She'd hung on every word, listening to talk about English class, and book reports, and departmental politics, and Granddad's first buffalo calf crop.

After all these years, how could the longings of her womb still claim so much of her heart? Spying on Jim and Brett that way was probably pathological in some obscure psychiatric sense.

"Valerie, my dear, you're just a sentimental psychotic at heart." She inspected the photograph yet again, asking, *Is there anything of me in her, beyond just her looks?*

The hard part was that she'd never know.

Brett blinked her eyes open when Umber bounced on her bed and squeaked her good morning call.

"God, go away and let me sleep."

Umber poked a stiff finger into Brett's ribs.

In reply, Brett threw a pillow, which Umber artfully ducked. The pillow sailed over and knocked one of Brett's perfume bottles off of her dresser. The glass shattered when it hit the floor.

"Damn." Brett sat up and shook her head, her blond hair hanging over her blue eyes in a tangled mess. "Don't step in it."

Umber gave her head that chimp shake that looked more like a shudder, then crinkled her nose at the rising scent of roses and musk and signed: "Smell big stink."

"Yeah, well. Each to her own stink."

Brett slipped out from under the blankets, found her slippers in the clutter on her closet floor, then retrieved the box of facial tissues and mopped up as much of the mess as she could. Wincing and holding her nose, she dropped the sopping tissues in her trash can and inspected the floor. "If you walk right in the middle, there are no glass splinters."

"Sharp. Cut bad," Umber signed emphatically.

"Watch your feet. Don't come in here until I sweep it good."

She retrieved her pillow, inspected it for glass fragments, and sailed it back to her rumpled bed. On the way out, she patted the full-length DiCaprio poster and followed Umber to the bathroom, yawning and rubbing a knuckle in her tired eyes. As Umber used the toilet, Brett brushed her teeth. They traded positions after Umber flushed.

"I don't want to go to school today," Brett moaned. "I've got an algebra test. I hate algebra."

"Going to be bad day," Umber signed, her toothbrush hanging in her mouth.

"How do you know that?"

"Monster came last night. Terrible." And with that Umber resumed her brushing and spit into the sink.

"Bad dreams, huh? Mine haven't been so great either." Brett stood and flushed. "I keep getting chased down back alleys by gangs of men. It's one of those 'you-can't-escape' kind of dreams."

Umber grunted in assent and dried her mouth on her towel. She reached out and put a hand on Brett's shoulders as they stared into the mirror. With her other hand, she signed: "Brett okay. Umber okay."

Brett met her eyes in the mirror, hugged her, and said, "Yeah. It's just going to be a little hard, that's all. But, hey, it can't last forever, right?"

"Wheep," Umber said and patted Brett tenderly. She checked herself one last time and slipped out the door. Brett showered and dressed for school. When she pulled her drapes back to check the day, she saw Dana's Toyota in the drive; its windows and hood were frosted as thickly as the Bronco's.

Dana had spent the night? A slow smile spread as Brett shot out the door, charged down the hallway, and took the stairs three at a time. She pulled her white sweater down over her jeans and headed for the kitchen.

Dana and Jim sat at the table, morning sunlight slanting through the big window behind them.

"Hi, guys." Brett tried to keep her voice neutral. "So, uh, Dana spent the night, huh?"

Her dad looked up from the papers on the table. "Good morning, Brett. There's hot chocolate made."

She had expected embarrassment, maybe an uncomfortable avoiding of the eyes, not this weird anxiety. Somewhat cowed, she stepped sideways into the kitchen and poured the hot chocolate from the pan. The coffeemaker was gurgling and steaming, so she poured Umber a cup, knowing she'd be down shortly.

The cups balanced carefully, she walked around the breakfast bar to the table, glancing suspiciously from Dana to her dad. Neither one looked the way Brett expected them to if they'd just made mad passionate love.

"So, what's up?" she asked.

"We've got things to talk about," Jim told her seriously. "I had visitors yesterday, Brett. Visitors from . . ."

At that point, Umber appeared wearing a lime green sweatshirt, her blue wristwatch, and canary yellow pants. She leaped from the landing to the climbing pole, dropping down the ladder of branches with her usual fluid grace. She hit the floor with a bounce, saw her cup steaming on the table, and trundled across the rug to pull out her chair. Her black face and hair glittered in the golden rays coming through the window.

Her hands below the table, out of her father's sight, Brett made the hand signs for "Dana, Dad, together last night."

Umber stopped short, her brown eyes fixing on Jim, and then Dana, reading the tension in their postures and expressions.

Jim resettled himself on his chair and reached out to cradle his coffee cup with both hands. He frowned, then said, "This is bad news, Brett. Prepare yourself."

"Yeah, so," Brett said flippantly. "Dana, does this mean I'm supposed to start thinking of you as Mom instead of just Dad's lab slave?"

Umber hooted.

But instead of a quick comeback, her father gave her a somber glance, one out of character for him. "Brettany, what are we talking about?"

"You mean, you and Dana . . ." And suddenly the cold knowledge that she'd made a mistake washed through her.

Through an uneasy blush, Dana said seriously, "Brett, we've had the rug pulled out from under us."

"As I was saying," Jim continued, fixing his hard gaze on Brett, "we had a visit last night from Brian Smithwick and his, uh, associate. SAC is concerned about Umber."

Under the table, Brett reached for Umber's hand, clutching it tightly. "What's wrong, Dad?"

Jim looked at Umber. "They want to move Umber to a reserve in central Africa where she won't be subject to as much interference from the press."

Umber's lips parted, her hair prickling and standing on end.

"Well they can't!" Brett cried. "Tell them no! Umber's staying with us!"

His steady gaze remained on Umber. "You've got to understand, Umber, you belong to them. I can't stop them. I would if I could, but if I fight them, they will hurt us. All of us. Me, you, Dana, and Brett. Do you understand?"

Umber began to wilt, her head drooping, shoulders bowing. Brett was on her feet, wrapping her arms around Umber's shoulders, tears blinding her eyes. "They're not taking you away. They're not. I won't let them!"

In the blur she didn't see her father step around the table to fold them into his arms. It seemed like an eternity that they stood in a huddle, holding one another. Brett finally blinked the tears away, sniffed, and stared up into Dana's tearstained face.

"They're not taking her," Brett said.

"We can't stop them," Dana insisted wearily. "We've been trying to think of a way all night. They've got us over a barrel, Brett. They didn't leave any loopholes we can use, and then, even if they did, they made it so that we wouldn't dare."

Umber twisted around to look up, giving Jim a pleading look. Jim lifted Umber into his arms and hugged her to his chest. "We have to be smart. This is going to hurt all of us, but it can't be helped, just endured."

Umber leaned out, her hairy hands forming the signs: "Umber not leave Jim and Brett."

"You won't have to leave me," he told her. "I'm going with you. You and I, we'll deal with this together."

Brett looked up suddenly. "We're going with Umber? Where? To Africa?" She used a napkin to blow her nose.

Jim tightened his hold on Umber. "Umber and I are going to Africa. You're staying here, Brett. You've got a choice. Dana and I discussed it this morning. You can live here, at the house, with Dana, or you can go up to the ranch and live with Grand-dad while Umber and I are gone."

Brett could only gape, stunned beyond response. Her soul drained out of her body, leaving only an empty husk. Her jaw was trembling when she managed to say, "No. I'm going."

"Brett," Jim said hollowly, "I can't take you. It's too danger-ous, and I've made the deal. They won't hurt you so long as Umber and I fulfill our part of the agreement."

"Dad, how can you let them do this to us?"

It was as if she'd stabbed a knife into his heart. "I did the best I could, Brett. I don't think it's good enough, either, but at least I bought us some time."

"Brett," Dana said, taking her hand. "I'm staying here to run the lab and take care of the house. SAC is sending another bonobo. I'm going to need help with her. I want you to help me."

Brett shook her head, staring defiantly into her father's mis-erable eyes. "You can't leave me. I'm going with Umber. That's all there is to it."

Jim said, "No, you're not. I won't take a chance on losing you, or having you hurt. I love you. Umber loves you. We'll do better if we know you're here, safe with Dana."

God, it was real. They were really going to take Umber away. This wasn't a joke. The ashen expression on her father's face wasn't a put-on. A sick feeling churned in her stomach. In a blind rush, she fled. Her chair clattered across the floor as she threw it out of her way. As it was, she barely made it to the bathroom before she threw up. The aftertaste of chocolate lay sour on her tongue.

Her belly heaved again. The spasm left her weak and trem-bling. No wonder Umber had been dreaming about monsters, and she'd been chased down blind alleys all night. She could only stare into the murky toilet water and wish she were dead.

Sixteen

Let me talk to her." Dana tilted her head in the direction Brett had fled.

Jim nodded. How, in the name of God, had it all gone so wrong so quickly? "Go."

Dana crossed the floor. The door to the downstairs bathroom opened off the rear of the dining room. Dana eased it open and peeked in before entering.

Jim cuddled Umber in his arms. She'd started whining, a keening high-pitched sound he'd never heard before. "Umber, it's all right. Don't worry. Come on, let's go sit on the couch and talk this through."

As he lowered himself to the soft cushions, he pried her wiry arms from around him, then held her hands. Umber's chest heaved with panicked breaths.

"I'm going with you, Umber. I won't leave you, do you understand?"

She pulled her right hand away to ask: "Why, Jim? Umber good girl."

"You've been perfect. I'm sorry, Umber. I should have seen this coming. I always knew that they could take you back, but I didn't believe it would happen. Now . . ." He exhaled hard.

Umber signed. "Umber scared."

"I am, too, Umber. But at least we'll be together."

"Brett come?"

"No." He shook his head. "No, she has to stay here. Dana has to look after the lab, and Brett has to help her. Besides, Brett has to go to school, Umber."

Umber's moist brown eyes filled with pain. "How far Africa?"

"It's a long way. I've shown you the map of Africa? That's where we're going. To a place on the west coast. It's close to the equator. They have other apes there. Chimps, and some bonobos." Or at least he hoped so.

Umber signed: "Why apes there?"

Jim leaned back into the cushions. "I don't know. They're doing something. Like they did with you. They're making apes smarter. Smithwick says they're doing it for the apes. Maybe that's true. But they've spent a lot of money, and are willing to spend a lot more. I guess we'll find out when we get to Africa."

"Umber has insects in stomach."

"I know, Umber. I feel the same way."

Umber crawled into his lap and buried her face in the crook of his neck. Jim could feel her trembling as her fingers twined in his sweatshirt. "Umber, listen to me. There is a way to win this. It's a very slim chance." He signed as he talked, emphasizing his words. "We have to go to Africa, see what the situation is. Then, if we are very smart, and very clever, we will find a way to come home. But you and I have to make SAC think we are working with them. It's a trick, do you see? We have to be smarter than the SAC people."

Umber's black fingers formed the word "How?"

"I don't know yet." Jim rubbed her arm comfortingly. "But I need you to help me. We can't win by threats, or fighting. From now on, we have to do everything they tell us, and do it with a smile. Understand?"

She lifted her head and stuck her lower lip out, exposing her stubby canine teeth. She signed: "When?"

"They want us to leave on Friday. That's four days from now. In the meantime, we stay together, all of us."

"Brett go to school today?"

"No. For one thing, we may not get to see her for months, so we need to spend all the time together that we can." He looked out through the windows at the morning beyond. Crows sailed through the blue sky. "And besides, Parnell is out there, somewhere. Smithwick might say he's under control, but I doubt it."

"Who?"

"A bad man that Brian Smithwick brought with him. You remember Smithwick?"

Umber made a "whoo" sound and nodded.

She sucked her lower lip for a while, as if deep in thought, then reached up with a long arm and pulled Jim's head down to kiss his cheek. When she released him, she signed: "Umber will go."

Jim kissed Umber's forehead. "I knew you would. You're a smart girl."

He rose and walked to the telephone. The phone book was still open to last night's listing for the Marriott, and he pressed in the numbers.

The hotel operator answered and Jim was transferred immediately.

"Smithwick here."

"Hello, Brian, this is Jim Dutton."

"Ah, Dr. Dutton. I trust you've had a good morning?"

"I've had better." Jim glanced at Umber, who had propped herself on the back of the couch to watch him. He told Smithwick what his family had decided.

"And your ape, Dr. Dutton? Have you explained matters to her?"

"Umber is willing to participate in your program provided that I accompany her, and that I don't leave without her consent."

"That will be most satisfactory." Smithwick sounded pleased. "I would like to meet with you and Ms. Marks at your laboratory today. We have some other things to discuss, arrangements to be made and materials to be gathered. Noon?"

"We'll be there." Jim hesitated. "But if I see Parnell, the deal is off. Do you get my drift? I want him out of the country, and as far away from my people as possible. Umber and I will cooperate only on those terms."

"He will be gone within the hour, Dr. Dutton." Smithwick actually sounded relieved. "I'm sure his services would be best put to use elsewhere."

"I'll see you at noon."

Jim hung up the phone and turned. Brett and Dana stood at the bathroom door. Brett's face looked red and swollen. Jim asked, "Are you all right, Brett?"

"No, I—I've got an algebra test. I think I missed the bus."

"You're not going to school this week, Brett. I'll call the principal."

Brett bit her lip. "Dad. It's . . . it's okay. We'll figure out a way of getting Umber back." He saw the determination in her blue eyes. "I'll do whatever I have to to help."

Brian Smithwick loosened his tie as he strode up the hallway in the Marriott. The day had gone perfectly. He had dispatched the loathsome Doug Parnell to Denver to pull wings off flies, boff a prostitute, or do whatever he did during his off time. The meeting at the lab had been slightly hostile, but nevertheless productive. He had given Dutton the materials list for packing and briefed both him and the ape about the flight and preparations for relocation. He had sent in the visa information for SAC to dispatch to Malabo for President Basala's personal signature.

Dana Marks had impressed him as a very intelligent young woman. She had actually spotted the shortcomings of the contract and signed only with the stipulation that it be mutually renewable yearly, a point that Smithwick had felt comfortable enough with.

Umber had gazed at him with dark sad eyes, but she'd pitched into the process of locating reports with a facility that surprised Smithwick. By the end of the day, he'd actually begun to think of Umber less as a project ape than as another colleague. What a remarkable subject she was. But for her bonobo form and features, she was incredibly human.

In his room, the red message light was flashing. When he pushed the replay button, Godmoore's starchy voice asked him to call no matter what the hour.

Smithwick punched in the number and waited for the overseas connection. Godmoore answered.

"Smithwick, sir. I just finished dinner and returned to my room."

"How is the Dutton situation?"

"Satisfactory, sir. He'll do whatever we ask him to provided that his assistant and daughter are left alone. He's definitely unhappy, but he doesn't feel he has any choice. He will accompany Umber to the preserve. Of course, once he's there, he's entirely under our control."

"How comfortable are you with the situation?"

"Very, sir."

"Comfortable enough to catch a flight to Texas in the morning?"

"Texas?" Smithwick considered the state to be one of the last bastions of primitivism in the world. "For what reason, sir?"

"I believe we may be faced with another situation needing

containment. I have a report from Mr. Parnell that a news crew arrived at Dr. Shanna Bartlett's door. I'm not certain what transpired. The recordings were a little slurred."

"I see, sir."

Godmoore gave him the flight details and there was a pause. "Oh, and you might want to take Mr. Parnell with you. On occasion, Dr. Bartlett has given us cause for concern. Mr. Parnell seems to have a peculiar way with women, don't you agree?"

Smithwick winced. "Sir, if I could suggest, I'd say we should keep him away from Dr. Bartlett. If she feels threatened by Parnell, I don't know but that it might backfire on us."

Godmoore paused, considering. "Brian, I can't take the chance. Take him with you. It's up to you to control him. He works for us. We pay him. He will bloody well follow your orders, or we will find someone else who will." He paused. "Geoffrey is already at Compound D. If he should contact you, say nothing about this. Dan Aberly has already been briefed on the situation. A fax will be awaiting you at your hotel in Austin. Your schedule for the next several weeks. Ring me up if you have anything to report. I'll be at the office for a couple of days."

"Yes, sir." Smithwick laid the handset on the cradle. For a long moment he stared at emptiness. Withdrawing all of the cross-fostered apes? Why? And he was to withdraw Kivu next? He shook his head. Shanna Bartlett had always been an enigma to him. With Jim Dutton, there had been a sense of balance. He fit into Umber's life, and she fit into his life. Shanna Bartlett was obsessed with Kivu. He had even suspected that the link between Kivu and Bartlett was somehow unhealthy. Their high degree of mutual interdependence frightened him. The idea of Bartlett and Parnell frightened him even more, he . . .

The phone rang, jarring him out of his thoughts. "Smithwick."

"Dr. Smithwick." The voice sounded young, oddly familiar.

"Who is this, please?"

"My name is Brettany Radin Dutton. I'm Dr. Dutton's daughter. I was at the lab all afternoon."

"Yes, that's right. How may I help you?" He remembered her indeed, a startlingly pretty young girl who had watched him with the most intense blue eyes. That scathing look had almost unsettled him—or would have had she not been just a lanky girl.

"I am going to Africa with my father."

Smithwick sighed. "My dear, I think you had better discuss it with Dr. Dutton. I—"

"I am going to Africa with Umber and my father, Dr. Smithwick. And you are going to see to it."

"Oh?" He laughed softly. "And why might that be?"

"Does the number 1-800-NNN-NEWS mean anything to you?"

"The toll-free number for Triple N." He smiled. "Do you really believe they would jump on an anonymous tip of a thirteen-year-old girl?"

"I think so, Dr. Smithwick. My mother's name is Valerie Radin. I'd imagine even you've heard of her, probably seen her on television a time or two."

Smithwick stopped stone cold. His mind compared the two faces, and he felt himself pale. The girl was a virtual carbon copy of Valerie Radin. Was this information in the Dutton file? Surely it must have been there. SAC's internal investigations division was quite thorough. How had he missed it? He said, "Uh . . . have you talked to your mother recently?"

"No, sir. But if I don't go to Africa with Umber and my father, I will. I have some really interesting things to tell her about Smyth-Archer Chemists and the kind of apes they're making."

"Ah. Yes. I see."

"Good. I understand that you used a threat to get Dad and Dana to do what you wanted. So, I guess you can understand how a threat works. Dad says that you added a sweetener to

the deal. I'll do the same. Umber is my sister. She needs me.
And so does my dad. I'll help make sure that Umber and Dad
do their best for you. And I'm better off in Africa than dead
or molested by the Witiko man, don't you think?"

"The what? The who?"

"The Witiko man, the one who scared Dana so badly. You
might be tempted to send him after me. If anything happened
to me, I don't think Umber, Dad, or Dana would be quite as
cooperative, do you?"

Smithwick stared at the wall. She meant Parnell, of course.

"Dr. Smithwick? Are you still there?"

"Yes," he said as he slumped down on the bed. "Very well,
young lady. I shall process your entrance visa to Equatorial
Guinea. You do have a passport, I take it."

"I do."

"I'm afraid you shall have to convince your father you are
going, however. And be assured, young lady, I shall tell him
exactly what you told me."

"Deal. It's a pleasure doing business with you, Dr. Smithwick. Call if you need anything." She hung up.

"Bloody hell." Smithwick shook his head and threw his gray
coat on the bed. "God help us if she ever grows up to be president."

Umber sits outside on the dead lawn. Starlight silvers the grass
and the orange fur of the cat she holds in her lap. Her name
is Stray. That's what Jim calls her.

Umber reaches into the pocket of her white CSU sweatshirt,
draws out a piece of meat she saved from dinner, and feeds
the cat. Stray chews and swallows, then purrs softly.

Umber lifts the index finger of her right hand, slips it between the first two fingers of her left hand, and pulls it away

fast. She repeats the sign over and over: "Run away, run away, run away."

Stray doesn't seem to feel the fear that eats at the base of Umber's throat. The cat kneads Umber's purple sweatpants with her claws and blinks sleepily.

Umber strokes the orange fur with long black fingers. Brett's window is dark. And Jim's. The SAC people are going to take her away from her home.

She picks up Stray and holds the cat against her chest. The purring feels like an earthquake inside her. Umber concentrates on the rumble. The cold air and starlight. Stray's sleepy eyes.

Her heart is shaking apart. It hurts when it beats. The insects are feeding on her. She can feel their sharp mouths in her soul.

Umber lifts her hand in front of Stray's face and signs: "Stray O-K?"

Stray looks at Umber's hands and flicks her tail.

Umber peers deeply into Stray's eyes. She sees loneliness and hunger.

She arranges Stray in her lap and pokes ever so gently at Stray's insides, feeling her ribs and shoulders, her backbone.

Umber is lonely, too, and afraid. Yet her bones are gone. The fear has clawed them to pieces. She can barely walk on her rubbery legs.

She curls on her side in the grass, staring up at the shining stars and dark mountains; she holds the cat protectively against her stomach.

She signs: "All O-K, Stray. Sleep."

Umber lets out a breath, standing guard, protecting Stray from the claws that walk in the bones.

Seventeen

Valerie studied her notes as Myles drove her and Roberto to a meeting with Godmoore. The night before, Mark White had met them outside The Corked Sow and delivered a new cache of documents. The picture was starting to come into focus, but the *why* of it all eluded her.

"I'm still surprised Godmoore granted an interview," Myles said.

"He must know about the Triple N crew that landed on that lady's doorstep in Texas," Roberto said, shaking his head.

"Some lady," Myles replied. "She threatened them with a meat cleaver."

Valerie glanced out at the rolling farmland filled with grazing sheep and horses—picturesque England at its best. "How long did I sleep?"

Myles told her, "We just passed through Billingshurst. We'll be there soon."

Valerie pulled her compact from her purse and deftly checked her appearance. From long practice, she knew just what touch-up was necessary for the camera. Brushing her hair to a glossy sheen, she pinned it back professionally and watched as they slowed and took a right onto a graveled road.

A decorative sign made of metal and granite announced: SMYTH-ARCHER CHEMISTS SUSSEX RESEARCH DIVISION. No more than a tenth of a mile down the manicured lane they encountered a high chain-link fence topped with razor wire. A glass-fronted white guard shack sat in the middle of the road. The uniformed security officer leaned out as Myles lowered his window. "Help you, sir?"

"We're the Triple N news crew. We have a ten o'clock appointment with Dr. Godmoore."

The guard checked his watch. "You're about an hour early, I'd say."

Myles jerked a thumb toward the rear where the camera and light cases were stacked in their boxes behind the hatch. "We need an hour to set up the lights, attach the mikes, adjust the sound, that sort of thing."

The guard hesitated, craned his neck to study the aluminum-bound cases, then grudgingly nodded. "Main building. Straight ahead. I'll call and tell them to expect you."

As Myles started down the lane he said, "I don't guess that they get a lot of media. When I telephoned for an interview, they sounded surprised and a bit ruffled." Myles shrugged. "Said they'd call back. Took them two hours to make the decision. If we're right, and there's something here, it was probably two hours of panicked scrambling, hurried board meetings, and ad hoc strategy sessions. I feinted and told them we were doing a series on genetic engineering, a cutting-edge sort of piece, about where the new technology is taking us. Vague enough, but close enough to the mark that they can't cry foul later."

"They'll cry it anyway," Roberto promised. "They always do."

Myles parked them straight in front of the large stressed-concrete building. The walls had been tastefully impregnated with dark flint from Kent, and tall narrow windows set in aluminum frames, like medieval arrow slits, lay between the slabs.

The tiled lobby, with couches, potted plants, and white paneling, looked normal enough. A wood veneer desk, like some huge canted clam, seemed to guard the doorway that led to the interior. A receptionist had half risen from behind its rounded contours when a black-haired young man in a brown suit came through the glass door. His expression looked strained, reminding Valerie of a teenager suddenly given more authority than he knew how to handle.

"I'm Kevin Clark, Dr. Godmoore's secretary."

As Valerie extended her hand, Myles bulled through the doorway with a crate. Roberto was hot on his heels, the camera perched on his shoulder.

"Hello, Mr. Clark, I'm Valerie Radin. This is Roberto Naez, my cameraman, and Myles Edwards is our associate producer."

"Righto, pleased to meet you." Myles shook the young man's hand. "Where would you like us to set up? We'd really like to get some footage of the apes, too."

Clark wet his lips, apparently stunned. He handed each of them guest badges and ushered them through the security doors. They wound through long hallways, past rather ordinary-looking offices, well furnished with computers, potted plants, and bookshelves drooping with softbound publications.

Finally Clark opened a door to a conference room and said: "We'll do the interview here."

"Hey, man." Roberto looked around, his camera mimicking his movements. "There's nothing here, you know? You don't have something more, well, visually appealing? You know how this is going to look? Sterile. Can't we do better than a generic corporate conference room?"

Clark looked completely confused. "But, well . . ."

"A laboratory?" Valerie suggested. "An active background, like we were standing at the heart of the research. Or someplace with the apes behind us. Give the viewer a feeling of being there as the actual science is being conducted."

"That's restricted."

"Mr. Clark, this entire building is restricted." Valerie pointed to her badge. "That's why we have these. Look, Kevin, we're not here to record your procedures, but to tape an interview with the man who heads your leading-edge research. The best place for that is right where that research is conducted."

She saw the sweat that started to glisten where his scalp met his black hair. He finally said, "I'll have to get permission," and beat a hasty retreat, calling, "Wait here, please," over his shoulder.

They waited for less than three minutes before Richard Godmoore himself stepped into the room. He wore a tailored black silk suit worth at least three thousand dollars. Valerie figured him for mid-fifties. His limp brown hair had started to thin and gray. He had a long, pale face, with a sharply pointed nose. He walked up to her and said, "What is it that you want, exactly?"

"Hello, Dr. Godmoore, I'm Valerie Radin from—"

"I know who you are. What do you want?"

Despite his imperious tone, anxiety seethed behind his eyes. She had interviewed many desperate men—terrorists, murderers. Something had scared Godmoore to the point of making an otherwise ordinary man dangerous.

From gut instinct, she straightforwardly said, "You're fooling around with ape genetics and the human genome. We don't have all the details yet, but we know you're making apes more human. What we don't know is why you would want to do that. The trail runs from London to Equatorial Guinea and clear back to Austin, Texas. A little more digging, and maybe we'll find lots of other trails."

"Then go dig. You'll do as you wish with the information." His stiff face didn't give, but the lines at the corners of his brown eyes pinched. Desperate he might be, but he obviously still believed he had an edge, some control over the situation.

"But, Dr. Godmoore, what if you had a reason for spending all this money and investing in this much effort? That's the thing about this whole story that intrigues me." She leaned against the table and studied him thoughtfully. "I usually find someone lining his pockets in a way that people wouldn't approve of. But in this case, the scent is a little different. You're making smart apes, and maybe the patents on the genetics will pay off long term? Or maybe your goal is to create a ruckus to land better research grants? Why would you be building smarter apes to take to a backwater toilet like Equatorial Guinea?"

She caught the faintest tic at the corner of his wide mouth. "Ms. Radin, we've broken no laws, violated no agreements. What we do with our money is up to us. What you will find in Equatorial Guinea is an ape refuge for research animals that would otherwise have been destroyed. We built that compound for the apes, Ms. Radin. They have a place to live now. Not in some filthy little wire cage, but in a rain forest. We did it because it was right, and I don't give a damn whether you believe that or not."

"What if we wanted to go and see this refuge?" Valerie asked tentatively.

"Be my guest. Accommodations are a bit crude, and you will have to bring your own provisions. Go see what you will. There will be no restrictions on your movements, or on what you may film."

Valerie cocked her head mistrustfully. "And what about the augmented apes, like the one in Texas?"

"What about them? They belong to us. We've taken special care of them, had them raised in the finest of environments. As I believe you know, Dr. Bartlett dismissed your Triple N newspeople and ordered them from her property. She has a right to her privacy."

Valerie narrowed her eyes. "Let me get this straight. Would

it be correct to say that these apes are being genetically engineered to have human brains? Is that the kind of performance we're talking about?"

"We don't know the parameters of augmented intelligence yet. The data are incomplete."

"But you didn't deny it."

"We don't have the data," he insisted.

"Isn't this playing God with another species?" Valerie asked. "I don't think religious leaders are going to be cheering over your success."

"This is no more playing God than chopping off a boxer's tail, or trimming a Doberman's ears." He lifted his chin as if his collar were too tight. "Ms. Radin, humans alter gene frequencies in given populations all the time, whether it's for a cow that gives more milk, or for a better-tempered bull. No one complains about that."

"So, from that logic, you're saying you *do* have a purpose in breeding these apes for certain traits."

Godmoore gave her a cold smile. "We are interested in intelligence, Ms. Radin."

"So am I, but I haven't spent two hundred million pounds and some change on a project that doesn't show up on the annual financial reports. Would you care to comment—"

"That will be enough! I have no idea where you obtained that ludicrous figure. I do *not* discuss Smyth-Archer finances with the press. Kevin will show you to the door." His face had blanched, the tic quivering at the corner of his lip.

"What about Equatorial Guinea?" Valerie called after him.

"Go there yourself and see, Ms. Radin. Good day. Have a pleasant drive back to wherever you came from." He disappeared down the hallway.

Roberto laughed silently, shaking his head.

Valerie lifted an eyebrow as Kevin Clark nervously stepped

inside. His green eyes gone huge, he said, "If you will follow me."

"Can we see the apes?" Valerie asked.

"Oh, I don't think so, no," Clark replied, waving them forward. "Please, follow me."

Five minutes later, they were outside, loading crates into the back of the Holden wagon. "How'd we do?" Valerie asked under her breath as she leaned next to Roberto.

"Me and John Wayne. Shot him from the hip. The camera angle will be interesting, but I think I got it all."

As she closed the hatch she clapped him on the hand.

Only when they'd passed the guard shack did Myles say, "Now that was one cool cucumber, right up to the question about the two hundred million quid."

"Yes. You just watch, we'll roll him in the end," Valerie promised. But down deep, she shivered. The invitation to the SAC compound in Africa had been just too easy. Why? What the hell was Richard Godmoore hiding?

How had they known about the money? Fear trembled Richard Godmoore's very soul as he walked away from the meeting with the reporters. Now, as the fear faded, bitter anger rose in its place. *How dare they come here? Attempt to beard me in my own den!*

"Damn you, Geoffrey," he muttered under his breath as he passed the long row of offices on the top floor and entered his office. Once ensconced behind his massive teakwood desk, he searched his drawer for the aspirin he knew he'd need and tried to think out all of the angles. If he could just hold it together for another two months! If he could just get through the stockholders' meeting, file the patents, cover the misuse of company funds. Then he could make it all work.

Godmoore settled back into his padded leather chair, swiveled to the phone, and put in a call to Don Amando in Equatorial Guinea. For the right price, Don Amando would make Ms. Valerie Radin disappear, just another poor victim of his country's political instability.

Rain pattered off Vernon Shanks's military-style poncho and stippled the puddles that dotted the red mud. He stared out at the green fortress of rain forest. The pungent odor of vegetation and flowers mixed with decomposing organic material taunted his nostrils. The red mud gave way to trampled grass and then rose into the nearly vertical wall of leaves, vines, and creepers, all slick with rain.

Worry ate him like a thing alive. He could hear the distant shouts as members of the search party scattered about, calling Mitu Bagawli's name.

Shanks lifted his pocket radio and keyed the mike. "Find anything?"

After a burst of static, Meggan O'Neil's Irish voice answered, "Nothing, Vern. It's odd, too. The apes should be coming in for provisions—it's the right time of day—but they aren't. Maybe Mitu is with them, wherever they are."

He looked back at the trashed field cabin. "If so, he didn't take his field pack, or his notebook, and he should have called in to let us know he was going into the bush."

"I'll call if we find anything."

"Be careful out there," he warned, trying to keep the concern out of his voice. For the last month he and Meggan had been sleeping together. While it wasn't any secret—not on a project like this—he still didn't want to sound overly protective.

Where the hell had Mitu disappeared to? He had been exemplary; he seemed to have a second sight when it came to problems shared by the reintroduced apes. Bagawli had been the man who had finally broken the parasite problem. The apes had been losing hair, growing thinner and ever susceptible to more diseases, and their stools had been riddled with worms. Bagawli had suggested that while wild apes knew the pharmaceutical plants to eat to control parasites, the reintroduced animals, only trained in foodstuffs, did not. At Bagawli's suggestion, they had treated the fruit at the provisioning ground with a wormicide and the apes had recovered. As a result, SAC teams in northern Gabon had started conducting field trials to determine what the wild chimp populations there ate to prevent worms. As soon as the data were in, SAC would be analyzing the plants for potential pharmaceuticals, and they would be teaching their reintroduced animals to eat them in the wild.

Shanks turned and walked back to the four squat cabins that made up the Compound C research station. He heard an approaching engine and turned as one of the preserve Kawasakis drove into the compound clearing.

"Hello, Shelly," he greeted. "Still no sign of Bagawli. I've got teams out working the ridgelines and flats."

Shelly nodded. "Very good, Vernon."

She would be an attractive woman if she didn't insist upon adopting that hard-as-nails manner. She had no personal life that he knew about, although rumor hinted that she had a child somewhere.

"You said the cabin had been ransacked by apes?" She stepped up on the porch and pushed the door open; he followed her inside.

"Yes."

She studied the shredded mosquito netting, the overturned table and scattered notebooks. The little cooler had been opened, and the radio lay on the floor.

"Why do you think it was apes? It might have been a leopard."

"That would be a handy explanation, but it doesn't seem to fit. Some things, like Bagawli's flashlight, his machete, his pocket radio, and his alarm clock, are missing. That suggests they were carried off."

"Robbery?" she asked. "Over the last couple of months things have been reported missing. We suspect some of the locals. Don Amando has the Equatoguinean police investigating a local Fang named Masala. Rumor says he's fencing preserve tools on the black market."

Vernon pointed at the radio. "Why would a robber leave that? It's the most expensive piece of equipment here."

She grunted noncommittally and stepped around the toppled chair. With the toe of her boot, she rocked the broken lantern where it lay in dried red stains. "Bagawli's blood?"

"Unknown. It is my fervent hope that one of the apes stepped on the broken lantern glass and cut himself. There's blood outside, too, in the nesting area where the apes usually sleep."

She gave him an irritated stare. "Vernon, this is Compound C. These are rehabilitated lab chimpanzees, not augmented animals. Even if they did attack a human, they would have beaten him, bitten him, and left him. Besides, we've monitored each of these animals, not only in the lab, but in Compound B before they were moved up here. None of them was particularly violent. Oh, Rasper is aggressive, but not against humans. Further, Mitu Bagawli is a trained primate ethologist. He wouldn't have provoked them to do this. And had some of the males been enraged, Bagawli knew how to act submissive to defuse their wrath. We have an entire universe of possible explanations for this event."

Shanks gazed down at the blood on the floor and took a deep breath. "Shelly—"

Coldly, she said, "I will take this up with Dr. Godmoore, but for the time being, the official policy is that Mitu Bagawli is missing. We do not suspect foul play, and expect that he has his own reasons for his unannounced absence."

"Shelly, you're starting to sound ridiculous. We found body parts over in—"

She stiffened. "That *is* the policy."

"Do you want to take any precautions?"

"Against what?" she said in a tone that dared him to disagree.

Shanks threw up his hands. "The Alpha Group hasn't been located yet, Shelly!"

McDougal's eyebrow lifted. "So you think they flew over here, murdered Bagawli, and committed this mayhem? If they didn't fly, Vernon, how could they cross the canal? You and I both know that apes are deathly afraid of water. The maintenance crews went through two weeks ago and trimmed the forest back. The apes *can't* cross. That's all there is to it."

Shanks folded his arms. "The fact remains, they're missing, and now so are Bagawli and the Compound C apes."

"Coincidence," McDougal assured him.

From the shelter of the high branches, he watched the humans. A slow smile spread across his thin lips as he listened to their frantic calls. Humans, it turned out, weren't as smart as he had always thought. He raised his bloody machete and gestured at the rest of his band, meeting their hooded gazes.

"Come." He cocked his head, listening for her voice. "We have other worlds to search."

Eighteen

Doug Parnell slowed and turned the rented Pontiac Bonneville off of County Route 12. He had been preoccupied over the last couple of days. Dana Marks filtered through his imagination every time he closed his eyes. Now, as he drove a tight-jawed Brian Smithwick through the central Texas afternoon, she lingered at the edge of his consciousness, her large dark eyes staring into his. Parnell accelerated down a dirt lane that led between picturesque live oaks to a locked gate. The chain and padlock looked spanking new.

Parnell brought the car to a stop and glanced at Smithwick. "What now?"

"Can you attend to that? We know that Dr. Bartlett's classes are on Monday, Wednesday, and Friday. Since she wasn't at her laboratory, we must assume she is here."

Parnell grinned. "With pleasure, sir." He pulled the release for the trunk, opened his door, and stepped around to the rear of the vehicle. He unzipped a heavy canvas bag before removing a small set of lock picks. Walking to the gate, he found nothing more complicated than a Master lock. Under his nimble fingers, it resisted for no more than thirty seconds before he clicked the last of the tumblers open.

Ten seconds later, he was back in the Bonneville, driving them toward an old farmhouse: a frame bungalow, with a peaked roof. Brown shingles covered the walls, and the house had a cedar-shake roof. A stone fireplace dominated the east wall, and a low, drooping porch gave it a quaint and rustic look. Late-blooming pansies nodded in planters made from whiskey barrels cut in half. An older model Toyota Land Cruiser stood to the side, halfway between the house and an open-faced tool-shed in which a rusty John Deere tractor, a hay rake, and riding lawnmower could be seen. Behind that, against the foot of the hill, an old windmill rattled and clanked, spilling water into a stone tank.

As Parnell reached for his door handle, a tall blond woman stepped out onto the porch. She had dazzling brown eyes and the body of a Greek goddess.

"My God," Parnell drawled, "that's Dr. Bartlett?"

"That's her," Smithwick said evenly. "We don't want a scene, Doug. That's not the point. I remind you, you follow my orders. We're here to ensure Dr. Bartlett's compliance, nothing more."

Bartlett shouted from the porch, "Doesn't a padlock mean anything to you people? I'm calling the sheriff. I've had it!"

"Dr. Bartlett?" Smithwick called. "Don't you remember me?"

She stopped short, shading her eyes with the flat of her hand. "Brian Smithwick?"

"Yes, it's me."

He got out of the car, and Parnell followed.

Parnell took inventory. Her high breasts filled her blue denim shirt. Sunlight glittered in her pale blond hair. She wore sandals and snug jeans that hugged a thin waist and emphasized her long legs.

"Shanna, I'm sorry to just drop in on you, but we've grown concerned." Smithwick smiled. "My associate, Doug Parnell."

When her eyes met Parnell's he got the usual thrill watching her squirm under his predatory gaze. What was it about that vulnerable look that excited him so? He could see right inside her, see her wilt down away from him. He ran his tongue along his barely parted lips. She went pale and stepped back.

That's right, baby. Come on, tell old Smithwick you don't want to play ball.

He'd hoped for this with Dutton and his gorgeous black-haired assistant, but Dutton had given in. Maybe here there was a different opportunity. He knew women, knew what made them tick. *Baby, you and me are going to play a little game, have us a little fun.*

"Shanna, could we talk?" Smithwick said, his voice soothing, apparently reading her reaction to Parnell.

She forced herself to look only into Smithwick's eyes. "What's . . . what's wrong?"

"A news crew was here two days ago. What did they want?"

"They wanted to see Kivu. I sent them away. Brian, I don't want anyone here. It's bad enough that Kivu and I have to go into the lab three times a week."

"Is there a problem with that? Anything we could help you with?"

"No." She shook her head, too quickly, still avoiding Parnell's eyes.

"How is Kivu? Can we see him?" Parnell asked, stepping forward.

She shot a quick glance Parnell's way, then her back firmed. "Brian, what's this about?"

"Some of the data you've been sending back has confused our analysts. Kivu's performance seems to have dropped off considerably."

"If your people can't deal with raw data, that's not my problem. Just what in particular are they concerned about?"

"We think that Kivu should be doing better than your reports indicate." Smithwick frowned. "You wouldn't be . . . well, excluding certain data, would you?"

"Kivu's fine," she said deliberately. "I don't want him disturbed."

"Dr. Bartlett, do I have to remind you Kivu is our ape? He belongs to SAC. Part of your contract stipulated that we could visit anytime we wanted, to monitor his progress."

Parnell watched the interplay with interest. God, she was a beauty. He knew the type, trying to put on airs, make herself look tougher than she really was. The neat thing about that kind of woman was that when they broke, they completely fell apart. His blood began to race in anticipation. He'd had women like that before. That final moment, when they caved in, was wondrous. Something happened that reflected in their eyes, the way the defiance just snapped, and behind it there was . . . nothing. Only disintegration. Just one time, that moment of disintegration had come when he was raping a woman, and it had brought a climax he'd never experienced before or since.

"I could do that with you," he whispered under his breath, not quite loud enough for her to understand.

She shot him an alarmed look, her eyes hardening, yes, almost glazing. To push her, Parnell grinned and shifted his leg forward, tucking his thumbs into his belt, mocking her.

"Dr. Bartlett? You aren't going to make this difficult for us, are you?" Smithwick asked, oblivious. "We just want to see Kivu and discuss some things."

"I think you should go." Her voice sounded strained, her eyes narrowing as she watched Parnell.

"Shanna, please." Smithwick stepped up to her. "If you make this difficult, we'll have to—"

"Are you threatening me?" She whirled, color rising in her pale face. "You don't threaten me, Brian. If you do, you'll wish you'd never left London!"

Smithwick held up his hands. "Let's back up a step, shall

we? Kivu belongs to Smyth-Archer Chemists. If you wish to ignore the stipulations of the contract, our people will be here first thing Monday morning to remove him. Do you understand?"

Parnell grinned again. Time to push just a little further. "I'll step inside, Brian, and see if he's there." And before either could react he pushed by Bartlett, strode through the door and into a large living room.

A big leather couch stood against the back wall. A television with VCR and a stack of videos filled one corner. Paintings—modern art—hung on the walls. The bright colors looked garish, the composition bold and expressive. A thick Mexican wool rug covered the pine floor. On his right, the fireplace maw gaped, sooty and black. Pokers, a stack of wood, and newspapers lay on the hearth. To his left stood an upright piano. A hallway led back toward what looked like a kitchen glassed with French windows.

As he had anticipated, Shanna Bartlett charged in after him. She did exactly what he had hoped she would. She grabbed him by the shoulder.

He whirled, pinned her arm behind her, and pulled her right up close so he could stare into those wondrous brown eyes. "Doc, you don't want to go grabbing me that way. I know I'm a hunk, but you've got to wait your turn."

For a moment, her eyes lost focus, then the craziness filled them as she struggled to break free of his grip. "You . . . you piece of filth!"

"Doug!" Smithwick warned as he rushed in. "Leave her alone."

"It's okay, Brian." Parnell grinned disarmingly as he let Bartlett loose. "She grabbed me first. I have that effect on women, ain't that right, sweetie?"

Smithwick gave Parnell a hard look and turned to Bartlett. "Please, Shanna, we want to work with you. Do you realize what you're doing? That we can take everything away? Your grant, Kivu, everything."

"No way, you bastard!" She had locked her burning gaze on Parnell, her body rigid. He liked that look. It sent a shiver of excitement through every cell in his body.

Parnell laughed. "She ain't gonna be good and dance to our tune, Brian. If she's this high-handed with us, why there's no telling what she's done to Kivu. I'd better go have a look."

"Doug, for God's sake, back off," Smithwick cried, but it was too late; as he knew she would, Bartlett threw herself on Parnell's back before he made two steps toward the hallway that led to the rear.

Parnell stepped agilely to the side, ducked a shoulder, and neatly slipped an arm around her waist. This time he muscled her to him, lifting a thigh to block the kick she aimed at his balls. He slipped his other hand around her, and when his hand cupped her breast, she suddenly ceased struggling, and tensed, as though every muscle had frozen.

"So," he whispered into her ear. "You been to this rodeo before, baby?"

"Doug!" Smithwick cried, hurrying across the room. "I'm ordering you! Let go of her! This is all coming apart! It's not supposed to work this way!"

"Brian, go on outside," Parnell said evenly. "She's not going to help us, are you, Shanna?"

She barely jerked her head, then burst into another fit of kicking, biting, and thrashing.

"See, Brian?" As he spoke, Parnell worked his hand between the buttons of her shirt, sliding his fingers under her bra. In a cooing voice, he said, "No, me and Shanna are going to lay down here on the couch and discuss this. Then, when we're done, Brian, we'll be a whole lot more flexible. That's a good word, isn't it, Shanna?"

But she wasn't listening; instead, a strangled, frightened sound seemed to be stuck in her throat. Ignoring Smithwick, Parnell lifted the woman and threw her on the couch. He pinned her there, looking down into her frantic eyes. "How's this going to be, Shanna? Easy or hard?" And in that instant, he saw it, that wonderful split second when her resistance began to give way to despair. With one hand, he reached down, ripping the snap of her Levi's open, running the zipper down to drive his hand past her panties, across her tawny pubic hair, to prod at her vulva.

God, yes! Watch her go! Lights out, baby. You're mine now, all . . .

Brian shouted, "Stop! Stop this instant!" He pulled impotently at Parnell's shoulder.

Doug laughed and started to rise when something black came bolting from the hallway. It screamed in a high-pitched rage.

Parnell tore his eyes from Shanna Bartlett's in time to see the ape fling Smithwick bodily into the piano. Then the raging black beast was on him, battering him with hard hands, biting at Parnell's face, arms, and neck.

Parnell screamed and struck out, only to have the animal jerk him violently away. Parnell crashed to the floor, and the ape was on him. Piercing shrieks added to Parnell's fright as the ape landed full on his chest, driving the breath from his lungs. A dark blur swung down and hammered his head against the floor.

Yellow-white light flashed behind Parnell's eyes. Pain sheared through his head as the animal bit his face. He actually felt one of the ape's teeth sliding along his cheekbone. Disoriented, Parnell rolled, got to his feet, and charged headlong into the fireplace, tucking himself into the hollow; soft ash puffed up around him.

The ape battered his unprotected back, then turned away. Looking under his arm, Parnell saw Smithwick staggering forward, shouting, "No!"

The ape lunged for Smithwick.

Parnell's right hand instinctively reached for the butt of the pistol under his coat. He shook his head to clear his vision, and centered the sights on the ape's back. Smithwick let out a shrill cry as the animal threw him to the floor and ripped a chunk of flesh from his shoulder with its teeth.

In that frozen instant, it struck Parnell that the ape was wearing blue Levi's. Think of it, he was shooting down an ape in blue Levi's.

A woman's panicked scream rent the air.

He pulled the trigger.

Nineteen

Umber is anxious, her stomach unsettled. As the Bronco takes the exit off of Interstate 25, Brett nervously fingers the seat belt strap that crosses her chest. Umber sits in the backseat beside her, wearing purple pants, moccasins, and an oversized white CSU Rams sweatshirt. Brett stares vacantly out the window at the farmland sliding past. Her black jeans and red wool sweater shine in the sunlight. She has pulled her blond hair back and clipped it at the nape of her neck.

Preoccupied, Jim drives with one hand on the wheel. Dana sits in the passenger seat, lost in her own thoughts. The rear of the Bronco is piled to the roof with suitcases, crates, and equipment, including most of Umber's belongings. Her computer sits on the floorboard in front of her. Even her bow and arrows ride atop the Bronco, packed in a PVC tube.

Umber has been trying to be brave, but sadness lives in her soft brown eyes as she gazes out at the world. She has been talking to herself a lot, signing when she thinks no one is watching. Umber had been packing her buffalo hand puppet, a toy she'd had since she was three years old. Umber had slipped the toy over her left hand and moved it around, as if the buffalo were galloping forward. With the other hand Umber had hit the back of her fisted right hand on the floor, the sign for "darn," or "damn," and pulled her lips tightly over her teeth, displaying frustration. Then she'd taken the puppet from her hand, tucked it into her suitcase, and curled on her side on the floor. She'd placed her fingertips below her eyes, drawing them slowly down her face in the sign for "sad." She'd repeated the sign several times before Brett had walked into the room and hugged her.

As they pull up to a stop sign, Brett leans over and asks, "Are you okay?"

Umber looks at her, then signs: "Insects are inside. Umber is worried."

"Yeah, me, too." Brett grins. "But I'd have done anything to keep from taking that algebra test."

"Brett comes with Jim and Umber. All okay." Umber flashes her teeth, trying to be brave. "Adventure in Africa."

"Yeah, we'll probably be eaten by cannibals."

Jim turns west on the airport road. Last night he carefully trimmed his dark brown hair and beard. Umber has never seen his beard this short; two inches of hair curved around his chin. Ordinarily she would have thought he looked good, except for his eyes. They have taken on a cut-crystal sharpness, as if he has his own insects eating away his insides.

Thinking about cannibals, Umber juts her lower jaw out and chides: "Brett too skinny. Cannibals like *fat* girls."

Brett balls a fist and smacks Umber in the shoulder. Umber shrieks and swings a backhand at Brett, who ducks just in the nick of time.

"What's going on back there?" Jim calls, looking at Brett through the rearview mirror.

"Umber started it." Brett crosses her arms over her chest and pouts.

Umber indignantly signs: "Brett hit first."

"Well, cut it out," he orders and glares at Brett.

Umber crouches down into her seat as they follow the road around the terminal and through the tall chain-link fence with its entrance to the private portion of the airfield. Umber glances at Brett and signs, "Sorry. Umber sorry."

Brett's lips quirk for an instant, then she grins slyly, before pointing. "Look, that must be it."

Umber cranes her neck, staring at the sleek white jet that rests on the tarmac. A fuel truck is parked beside it, hoses and lines running to the wing tanks like fat umbilicals.

Umber looks at Brett and thumps her fingers against her chest, her way of saying that her heart has started to beat fast. Brett nods in agreement. They are really leaving. Tonight Umber will not sleep in her safe bed.

"Well," Jim says, "let's get on with it."

At that moment a man walks out from behind the fuel truck and starts toward them. Around forty, he stands over six feet tall and has salt-and-pepper hair. Umber studies the man. His long narrow face reminds Umber of that actor who played Zefram Cochrane in the *Star Trek* movie.

"That's Dan Aberly," Jim says. "It's been five years, but I'd recognize him anywhere."

Umber nods as she remembers.

"Well," Dana says, "we should start unpacking." She pulls her blue sweater down over her jeans, and her long braid swings in time to her movements as she opens her door.

Jim steps out. Umber unbuckles her seat belt and waits for Dana to pull the seat forward. Umber's moccasined feet land on the hard asphalt and she walks around the front of the Bronco.

"Good to see you, Dr. Dutton." Aberly shakes Jim's hand, then turns his gaze on Umber, and she stops short. Her hair begins to prickle around the collar and cuffs of her sweatshirt.

"Umber? Hello," Aberly says, stepping forward, his eyes full of curiosity. "I'm Dan Aberly. I'm here to make sure your trip is happy and safe." He reaches out, offering his hand.

Umber hesitates, fighting the instinctive fear response she usually feels toward strangers. She signs: "Good to meet you."

"I assure you, Umber," he says, speaking with an English accent, "the pleasure is indeed mine. You have exceeded my expectations."

Umber grunts at that, not sure what to make of it, then she shakes his hand and quickly pulls back at the cool dry feel of his skin.

Jim introduces Dana, and Aberly holds out his hand to her, saying, "Dr. Marks, the pleasure is mine."

"Not quite a Ph.D.," she tells him.

Brett stands awkwardly, her chin up. Finally, her father says, "Oh, and this is my daughter, Brettany."

Dan reaches for Brett's hand. "I've heard a great deal about you, young woman," he says, an amused smile on his lips. "Brian Smithwick is afraid you might become president someday."

Brett shakes his hand and gives him a practiced smile. "Yeah, well, he *should* be." She has actually joked with Umber that the moment she waltzes into the White House she'll give the assassins in the CIA their first target.

Aberly releases her hand and straightens. "Dr. Dutton, Brian told me that you thought Umber could travel without sedatives. Is that still your recommendation?"

Jim glances at the jet, then at Umber. "What about it? Would you like a tranquilizer?"

Umber rolls her lips, shooting a glance at the plane. She asks: "Will Brett take?"

"No." Brett crosses her arms. "I've flown before. There's nothing to it."

Aberly crouches, placing himself on Umber's level, looking honestly into her eyes, something she isn't used to with strangers. She backs up a step. "Umber, could I make a suggestion?"

"Wheep." The insects are crawling.

"Could you take some sedative? This is your first flight, and it will help to relax you. Then, if you want, on the next leg we can try it without. Does that make sense? The sedative comes in fruit juice. I won't try to stick you with any needles."

Umber rocks back and forth on her feet, her nervous glance straying to the big white airplane, and then up at Jim.

Jim smiles confidently down at her. "Why don't we both drink some, Umber? I could use the sleep."

The insects ease in her gut. She nods and says, "Wheep."

"Good. Then I'll go and fetch us a couple of glasses of fruit juice."

Two men in overalls duck under the rounded belly of the plane, walking forward. Each has earmuffs around his neck and pads on his knees. One man pulls a small notebook from an oversized pocket. "Dr. Dutton, according to the sheet here, we're supposed to load some scientific equipment."

"This way." Jim leads them to the back of the Bronco, swings the tire out of the way, and opens the back. He and Dana start placing bags and boxes on the tarmac.

Umber flashes signs at Brett: "You think Umber needs sleep drink?"

"No." Brett sticks her hands in her pocket, looking worldly while the wind teases her long blond hair. "Flying's cool. Nothing to it."

"Jim is drinking."

"Maybe flying bothers his stomach." Brett glances back to where her dad and Dana stand talking. "So, you scared? I mean, going to Africa and all?" Brett keeps shooting uncertain glances at her father.

Umber frowns, stares at the ground for a long moment, then

shrugs and reaches for Brett's hand, which she gently holds against her black cheek.

Brett scratches the back of Umber's neck. "Yeah. I'm glad to have you, too, Umber."

Aberly arrives with two cans of juice. "Here's one for you, Umber. You'd best drink it now so it has time to take effect."

Umber takes the cool can, sniffs it, and smells orange juice. She glances suspiciously at Aberly and signs: "You still think okay?"

He smiles at her. "Oh, yes. I promise. It will just keep you from panicking if the airplane hits any rough air."

Umber tilts the can back and gulps the sweet fluid down. She hands the can to Aberly and waits, wondering if the stuff will kill the insects inside. She can't feel them dying.

Brett pokes her in the ribs. "Come on. Let's go see the plane." Umber allows Brett to lead her to the stairs.

Umber has seen pictures of the inside of these fancy planes in magazines and on television. The reality is even better. The door to the cockpit is open, and two pilots are bent over clipboards, fooling with papers and checking gauges. Umber starts to enter the cockpit but Brett jerks her backward.

"Not in the cockpit, silly. You touch the wrong button in there and we'll crash and die." Brett gives her a serious blue-eyed stare.

Umber looks into the little bathroom and studies the first of the plushly padded seats; she props herself on the seat backs, and hangs in midair, dangling her legs.

"Hey, quit that," Brett chides, slapping her with the back of her hand. "You're twelve. Try to act mature."

Umber shoots a glance over her shoulder and grins before bouncing into a seat and peering out one of the oval windows at the wing. Jim and Dana are below. The pile of baggage has just about vanished as the workmen carry it off.

Umber vaults over the seat back and pushes off each row of

seats to the rear. There she finds two foldout couches with seat belts. She flops onto one and stretches out. Brett follows her, checking it out. Umber rolls off and steps to the rear to find a small aluminum kitchen and closed aluminum cabinets. She can hear thumpings in the rear of the jet as the last bags are loaded.

Umber turns and signs: "Neat airplane."

"Awesome," Brett replies. "And it's just for us. No other passengers."

Jim and Dana duck into the cabin, Jim calling, "You two haven't demolished the plane, have you?"

"No, Dad," Brett responds, that frustrated sound in her voice.

Umber calls out, "Whuh!" She realizes that the insects have disappeared. She is feeling fine for the first time in days. Her nerves are unusually placid.

"All right, come on up here." Jim turns, unable to stand upright in the restriction of the cabin. To Dana he says, "I guess this is it."

"Yeah," Dana answers wistfully. Then she squeezes past Jim and holds her arms out. "Kids, I came to say good-bye."

Umber rushes forward, flinging herself into Dana's arms. An unexpected whimper forms in her throat as she clings tightly.

"It's all right, Umber," Dana says and kisses her ear. "Jim and Brett will take good care of you." Her voice seems to catch. "Just remember that I love you. Be good."

"Umber loves Dana. Love you. Bye." Umber's oddly heavy hands form the signs, even though Dana can't see them behind her back.

Next Dana hugs Brett, bending down to search her eyes. "Be good, kid. Remember the things we talked about. Take care of your dad for me, okay?"

"Yeah. I will."

"And keep an open mind. You're going to see a lot of strange things. Some of it is going to be wonderful, and some of it will upset you. It's just a different face of the world. Most of all, be smart." She lays a hand on Brett's shoulder. "I'll miss you."

"I'll miss you, too."

Dana turns, takes Jim's hand, and tears fill her eyes. "Be careful."

"We will," Jim says. "Take care of yourself."

She turns and hurries down the stairs. Jim stands for a moment, sadness in his eyes.

Umber reaches out and takes Jim's hand. When she has his attention, she signs: "You drink juice? Okay?"

Jim smiles down into Umber's concerned eyes. "I drank it. Did you?"

Umber nods, not sure she believes him. Oddly, she doesn't care.

"Well, let's find seats, shall we?"

Jim seats himself across from Umber, saying under his breath, "God, I miss her already."

"So, Dad, you going to marry Dana?" Brett asks, plunking herself in the seat behind Jim and hanging over his chair back.

He turns, looking at her inquisitively. "Do you think I should?"

"I don't know." Brett looks away self-consciously.

Umber half climbs onto Jim's lap, looking out the window at the Bronco where it stands beside the fence. Dana waits there, leaning against the hood of the truck.

At the doorway, Aberly calls out, "Dr. Dutton? Do you need anything else?"

"No. We're as ready as we'll ever be. You're sure we can't just unload and go home?"

Aberly smiles. "You have your passports? All the documents you need?"

"In my pack," Jim replies.

The stairs fold up into the door. Aberly sticks his head into the cockpit and speaks for several seconds to the pilots, then walks back to the first line of seats. As the engines begin to whine, he says, "I guess I'm your flight attendant for this trip. You're riding in the Smyth-Archer Gulfstream III. We'll be taking off soon. Please keep your seat belts fastened until we hear from the pilot. After we're under way, feel free to use the water closet. We have a small kitchen in the rear. Nothing fancy, but you can make sandwiches. I believe we've got some microwave pizzas in the cooler."

Umber grins at that, feeling a deep-seated lethargy settling into her bones.

"We'll be landing in New Jersey, just outside of New York City, refueling, and flying on to the Azores. Once refueled, we'll cross western Africa, just clip the Gulf of Guinea, and then continue into the SAC ape preserve in Río Muni."

"Río Muni?" Brett asks.

"That's what we call the mainland portion of Equatorial Guinea." Aberly clasps his hands together. "Now, since you will be staying at the IAR compound for a while, you'll be exposed to the local flora and fauna. I have an entire battery of inoculations to give each of you."

"Vaccinations for what?" Jim asks.

"Yellow fever, malaria, dengue, tuberculosis. That sort of thing."

Brett catches Umber's look of distaste. She says, "I thought you told Umber no needles? She hates them. Says they remind her of rattlesnakes."

Umber lifts her index fingers to the top of her open mouth, making the "fang" sign for rattlesnake, then shakes her head violently and huffs. Her neck feels loose.

Jim looks at Brett, then at Umber, his blue eyes stern. "Give it up. You're both going to have shots. If you think rattlesnakes are bad, you'll like dengue fever even less."

Aberly adds: "I'll see to the vaccinations when we're airborne. Any questions?"

"Tell me about the IAR compound," Jim says as he sinks back into his chair and folds his hands in his lap.

"We've created a six-hundred-square-mile preserve in southeastern Río Muni. The main compound, what we call Compound A, is a dormitory, a small shop and cafeteria, a tiny hospital where we treat apes and people, the computer building, and the administration building. That's where our communications center is. We have our own water system and a small electricity generating station."

"If there's a Compound A, is there a B?" Brett asks. Umber is having trouble thinking.

"There are three compounds," Aberly tells Brett. "Compounds B and C are remote science stations, little more than cabins in clearings cut out of the jungle. That's where our behavioral scientists go to study the apes in the wild."

"Like Gombe, and Wamba?" Jim asks.

"Yes, Dr. Dutton. Compound B is where our most recent inductees are relocated after adaptation and acclimatization. When they've adjusted to fending for themselves, we move them to Compound C, where they are more or less in a wild state."

"What keeps someone from Compound C from going back to Compound B?" Brett asks.

"Water." Aberly lifts an eyebrow. "Umber, do you like to swim?"

Umber makes a face, signing: "Umber swim like rock."

Aberly laughs at that. "Apes have a denser body than humans. They don't have the subcutaneous fat that people have. That's why you sink, Umber. And that's what keeps the apes from changing compounds. We've cut canals between the different areas. By that means we can keep bonobos separated from chimps, chimps from gorillas, and so forth."

"Then your facility is for multiple species?"

"Oh, yes." Aberly nods. "The only apes we don't deal with at IAR are gibbons and orangutans. First, they haven't been utilized as much for research, so we don't have large populations to be repopulated to the wild. And second, as you know, they're Asian animals. If we need to do something for them, we'll build a facility in Borneo."

The whine begins to build and Umber and Brett bend to the window, seeing the men walking away with the blocks that stopped the wheels.

"I suppose we'd best buckle up." Aberly walks over. "Umber, can you use your seat belt?"

Umber digs out the strap and buckle with thick fingers and fastens them over her lap. Aberly checks the tightness and says, "Look up at me. Let me see your eyes."

Umber obediently stares into his eyes.

"How do you feel?"

Umber answers, "Good."

Brett cranes her neck around. As the whine increases to a roar, Umber just sits, staring around the cabin.

"Bye, Dana," Brett calls, waving from her window as the big jet moves. Umber strains to keep watching the red and brown Bronco. Dana still stands by the front fender, waving. When Umber tries to wave, her hand seems slightly out of synch with her movements.

They roll past large metal hangars and lines of airplanes, each with the wings tied down. Over the intercom, the pilot recites final takeoff instructions to the four of them, and Aberly takes the seat immediately behind Umber. Umber can hear him working with a metal case. When she cranes her neck, she sees that he has taken a compact dart pistol from its case and is filling a syringe from a little glass bottle.

"What's that?" Jim asks from across the aisle.

"Just a precaution that I don't think I'm going to have to use," Aberly replies. "I'm hoping that on the next takeoff, Umber doesn't need a tranquilizer." Aberly looks straight into Umber's eyes again, saying, "I think you're going to remake the world, Umber. In fact, we've bet on that."

Umber doesn't answer, she just turns back and looks out the window. The plane stops, rocking slightly. The whining roar builds, the cabin shaking, then the jet lurches forward and it's as though a mighty hand is shoving her back into the seat.

She grips the armrests and watches as the land flashes past, the airplane shaking itself like a big dog. Then the floor seems to slant up, and she hears a thump. Outside her window, the ground drops away and she rises, shooting into the sky.

A long "Wheeep!" escapes Umber's throat. She lifts her hands and signs: "Umber flies like bird."

Brett laughs at the look on her face. Umber stares in amazement as the big plane banks, and the ground becomes smaller and smaller, houses, fields, and roads shrinking in her view.

As the plane turns eastward, the mountains disappear, and they cross Interstate 25, climbing ever higher.

Umber signs, "Bye, home. Bye."

Twenty

Three hours into the flight, an endless bank of clouds obscured the ground. Jim used the opportunity to raid the compact galley, fixing himself a ham and cheddar sandwich.

Either it was the tranquilizer or the sleepless nights, but Umber was out like the proverbial light, her head canted to one side, her mouth opened just enough to produce a burring snore. Dan Aberly sat behind her, his briefcase open on the seat beside him as he attended to paperwork.

Jim settled himself in the seat beside Brett. She was watching the clouds drift slowly past below, a vacant stare in her tired eyes.

"How you doing?"

"Am I too old to say, 'Are we there yet?'"

Jim smiled. "You are." He enjoyed a bite of the sandwich, then said, "When I sat down you had a horrible look on your face."

Brett frowned at him. "We're really doing this. Going to Africa. It's finally sort of sinking in, you know? I was just thinking, by the time we all get home, if we get home, everything's going to be changed. Basketball season will be long gone. It's like, wow, my whole life's on hold. No school, no sports, no movies, no TV, no phone calls to Susan, or Ginger, or Trish, or any of my friends." She shook her head.

He looked into her eyes. "It's not too late, Brett. We're landing in New Jersey to refuel. We could have Dan book you a flight back to Denver. Dana could pick you up."

Brett looked down at her hands. "No, Dad. No matter what, I want to go with you and Umber. It's where I belong. You know what I mean?"

"Yes, but I worry about taking you along on this trip. I still think it's a bad idea." He took another bite of sandwich, now barely tasting it as he chewed.

"Then why did you give in?"

"Because Brian said you'd be safe. And Dana thought it would be good for you to go. She said that if you didn't go, you might resent it for the rest of your life." He took another bite. "You know, there's something to say for growing up like Dana did. All those hard times taught her a lot about life. Things I've forgotten over the last twenty years."

"Like what?"

He put his arm around her and hugged her. "Like sometimes you have to take risks to understand just how precious your life is."

Brett glanced over at Aberly. "I don't trust him, or any of these SAC guys. How do you trust people that bug your truck and your phones? And did you see that dart pistol when we took off? It's like he didn't trust Umber not to go nuts."

"Just a precaution," Jim said around another bite of ham and cheese. "Would you want a berserk animal loose inside an airplane?"

Brett considered it and asked, "So, what's the difference? She's still an ape, right, even if they've added human genes. What makes them willing to treat her differently?"

Jim swallowed and said, "A couple of things. Umber's brain has more cortex, what we call gray matter. We know that the frontal lobe of the brain gives us social skills and helps us to overcome emotional reactions. Umber's frontal cortex is a great deal larger than that of other apes." He paused and looked over at Umber. "And in a very real sense, Umber is a human. She's been raised as a human, and with her augmented brain, she acts like one."

"So how," Brett lowered her voice even more, "is she supposed to become an ape again?"

"I don't think she can." Jim glanced sidelong at Aberly. "In fact, just between you and me, I'm betting on it."

Brett studied him thoughtfully. "Is there something you're not telling me?"

"There's a lot I'm not telling you. But it's for your own good."

Brett slumped in her seat and pressed her knees against the seat back in front of her. Gruffly, she folded her arms. "Right, Dad. You told me that when I was six and wanted to know what the dogs were doing climbing on each other's backs."

Jim finished his sandwich and wiped the crumbs from his hands onto the floor. "I told you eventually, didn't I?"

"Yeah, I was like twelve, Dad. I'd forgotten the question."

Jim glanced at Aberly, making sure he was still absorbed in his work, then he turned toward Brett and lowered his voice until it was barely audible. "Okay, listen. Whatever SAC's long-term goal, the only hope we have is that enculturated, socialized apes—like Umber—aren't any more suited to SAC's needs than humans are."

"And if she isn't suited for their needs?" Brett sounded hopeful for the first time.

"Then we're there, on the spot, to offer to take Umber home with us. We'll promise to accept responsibility for her care and to continue to collect data on her. That way SAC gets at least a little long-term gain, and maybe, just maybe, we have some leverage for bargaining."

Brett's frown deepened as she considered. "What about Dana and the ape she's getting?"

"Same thing. If their experiment with Umber doesn't work, maybe they won't be interested in keeping such a stranglehold on Dana's animal. When Dana's option to renew comes up next year, we can renegotiate."

After a long silence, Brett gave him a cool look with her level blue eyes. "All right, so we're going off to Africa, and maybe we'll be eaten by cannibals—"

"African cannibals are highly overrated. A person is more likely to be captured by revolutionaries."

"Right, whatever, I just thought . . ."

"Do we need to have some kind of father-daughter talk, Brettany?"

"I don't know. I was watching the way Dana was looking at you. Thinking, that's all. I mean, leaving her behind and stuff. It's like a major change in my life. I just got to thinking about Mom, that's all. You still love her, don't you?"

Jim instinctively stiffened. "That was a long time ago."

Brett's serious eyes narrowed. "Is that why you never brought women home? You were staying true to Mom?"

After thirteen years of skillfully avoiding this conversation, for once he had nowhere to go. Meeting Brett's sober blue eyes, he took a deep breath and said, "To tell you the truth, I don't know. Maybe. I really loved your mother, Brett."

What an understatement. He had thought she was the most exciting, beautiful woman in the world. When he'd looked into those blue eyes of hers, he'd seen eternity. Never before or since had he met a woman who challenged and stimulated him the way Valerie had. Valerie had a presence. It was partly sexual, partly daring, and completely self-assured. When she entered a room, her manner announced, "Here I am, and you'd better take me seriously."

He looked over at Brett. She had turned her attention to the clouds. After a short while, she wet her lips nervously and looked back at him.

"What brought the two of you together?"

Jim pulled at his newly shortened beard. "I think it was the fact that I treated her as an equal. Half of the men were scared stiff of her, intimidated to their bones; the other half were drowning in so much lust that they came off as slobbering fools. What interested Val was someone who would look past her beauty and see the real her. The two things she despised in men were insecurity and being patronized by them."

"Why didn't you ever get married?"

Christ, how did he answer that? "Brett, she had different goals . . . wanted different things out of life than I did. I mean, look at what she does. Can you imagine Valerie Radin as a housewife in Fort Collins, Colorado? Can you see her at a faculty party, standing around with a drink in her hand discussing the price of eggs down at King Soopers?"

"But I thought love was supposed to overcome those things?"

"You've been reading too many novels. Love overcomes most things, but not all of them. Bit by bit, reality seeps in. Life has a way of leveling the peaks and valleys of passion." He stared into his memory, watching Valerie's expression change from love to the keen blade of resentment. "In the end, I did the one thing she couldn't help but hate. I tried to cage her so she couldn't escape." He looked at Brett. She was biting her lip. "That's why she left. It didn't have anything to do with you. She left to get away from me."

Images drifted through his memory: dancing at the Ramskeller in the student center; writing notes to each other during lectures; late evenings studying for exams. He remembered the first night they had made love, camped up at Chamber's Lake with a crackling fire, the breeze in the fir trees and fifteen billion sparkling stars overhead. Her hair had pooled on the sleeping bag, reflecting like spun gold in the firelight. Their first joining had been wild and tempestuous, the second passionate and frantic. By morning they had refined their union to a graceful undulation of artistic symmetry.

In the following months, they had seemed to grow together, thoughts, minds, bodies, and souls. The mating between them had been flawless, seamless, and so inevitable it might have been a law of nature that they become one. Only their dreams had remained separate, somehow inviolate. If one of his sperm hadn't found her egg, even those might have eventually fused.

Valerie's probing blue eyes stared at him across the gulf of time, measuring, evaluating. Brett had become the ultimate weapon they'd used against each other. Mutually assured destruction. It had worked with devastating effect.

"So, did you ask her to marry you?" Brett pressed.

"Ask?" He laughed. "I pleaded, begged, threw myself at her feet and sobbed." He ran a hand through his dark brown hair. "She said no, Brett."

"Stupid woman."

"Yeah?" he said and gazed into his daughter's bright blue eyes. "Why?"

"Because you're a hunk, Dad."

Jim smiled, said, "Come here," and pulled her over to kiss her forehead.

Vernon Shanks made it halfway through the morning reports before the problem of Mitu Bagawli's disappearance absorbed him totally. For long minutes, Vern stared absently at his office wall and worried. The blood on the cabin floor over in C had been Bagawli's. No doubt about it.

Shanks sipped absently at his cold coffee and glared at the manila folder in the file index to his right. He reached for it, unable to resist. Opening the cover, he stared at the photo reproduced there: A young chimpanzee stared back at him with bright blue eyes.

Fourteen pages of subject history reviewed Sky Eyes's placement in a foster home in Denmark. Excerpts of reports followed, some beginning with, "Subject shows unstable behavior, with violent outbursts," and others claiming, "Sky Eyes seems unusually destructive, having broken a drinking glass and used it to slice open upholstery in the living room."

Then after thirty months had come the death of little Karin Dinnesen. Shanks studied the photo of the blond girl. Her body had been found at the bottom of the steps, and Sky Eyes next to her, holding her hand, talking to her in sign language. Though only three, he had insisted that he had nothing to do with her death, and only wanted her to "wake up and play bird."

After withdrawal from the Dinnesen home, Sky Eyes had been bounced from one SAC facility to another. Despite his rages, Geoffrey had insisted that Sky Eyes be pampered, excused for making threats. Finally, Sky Eyes had been the first augmented ape released in Compound D.

Shanks hated Sky Eyes, and from the looks Sky Eyes gave Shanks, it was mutual.

After closing the file, Vernon stared absently at the wall, asking, "Where are you, you little bastard?"

The intercom interrupted his reverie. He stabbed the button with his thick finger. "Yes?"

"Melody here, sir. I'm on the FM by the canal below the Alphas' village. You might want to drive out here. We just found what looks like a human leg." She seemed to be nerving herself. "And, sir, it's propped up right in the middle of the trail. It's as if someone left it here for us to find."

"What did you think of the tape?" Valerie asked when Murray finally picked up his phone.

She sat cross-legged on her hotel bed with her back propped by pillows. Dressed in a tan sweater and brown pants, she felt truly comfortable for the first time in days. The night noises of London filtered up from the street and across the hotel room. Roberto sat in a chair, shooting her occasional questioning glances. The tape of the Godmoore interview had been transmitted via satellite to the Washington bureau.

"Val? I think it's one of the coolest snow jobs I've ever seen, and I'm damn glad we've got it. Another day, and you'd have been turned down cold."

"Oh?" Valerie cocked an eyebrow Roberto's way. His brows pulled together as he leaned forward. "Thanks for your boundless faith in me. Now, what's up? Why do you think SAC would have fed us the boot?"

"I'm faxing the preliminary report to your hotel. Things are picking up here. You remember sending us after the SAC ape in Texas? Shanna Bartlett's animal?"

"The last I heard, she got nasty with the crew we sent to do the interview."

"Bartlett's dead. So is a John Doe, found at the scene. The ape, a male called Kivu, is alive, barely, with a bullet hole in him. Some guy named Brian Smithwick, traveling on a U.K. passport, is in intensive care at a hospital in Austin. He's got several crushed ribs that poked holes into his right lung, a sprained neck—that's one step short of broken—and lacerations over his face, throat, hands, and arms. Smithwick isn't talking, but we know he's on SAC's payroll from his credit card number."

"Jesus," Valerie whispered.

"Smithwick and John Doe flew into Austin on Thursday,"

Murray continued. "They rented a car from Avis and drove out to Bartlett's. Something went haywire and bodies got broken and shot, or shot and broken, as the case may be. When it was over, Smithwick called an ambulance. At the mention of a shooting, the hospital called the sheriff's office. Smithwick kept the deputies from shooting the ape and got it sent to a vet clinic somewhere."

"What happened, Murray? Have you got any idea?"

"The deputies guessed that the participants might have had some sort of argument. The ape evidently attacked John Doe, or Smithwick, or both of them. John Doe pulled a gun and started shooting. One of the slugs caught the ape low in the back, and another caught Dr. Bartlett full in the face. The guy used a .357 Sig auto, so that, as they say, was that. We'll know more when the forensic report comes in, or at least we will if the judge doesn't seal the case."

"Jesus, Murray, you're telling me that a SAC ape killed one man and critically wounded another?"

"That's what it looks like, but remember, it's also possible the ape attacked in self-defense, or to defend Dr. Bartlett."

Valerie pondered that for a moment. "What else have you got?"

"Not much." He rustled some papers on his end.

"Anything, Murray, any little detail."

More paper rattled. "Wait, here's a note. You remember that news crew we sent out? The assigned reporter made a note here that while they were standing in the doorway, trying to get Bartlett to talk to them, the phone rang. Since Dr. Bartlett was arguing with our guy, she didn't pick up the phone. He heard the answering machine. It was someone named Tory calling to talk about Kivu. After they left our reporter thought maybe he was being scooped by someone else, so he checked around. None of the Torys he could find in the news business seemed to fit."

"Wait a minute. Tory . . ." Valerie wondered. She looked across at Roberto. "Hang tight, Murray. Let me check something. Taco, hand me that primatology textbook. Yeah, the one with the blue cover."

Roberto tossed the thick textbook onto the bed beside Valerie. "This is the latest thing on primatology. Came out this year. Let's see, index, bibliography." She flipped through the pages, running her fingernail down the list of referenced authors. She stopped short in the Ds. "Son of a bitch!"

"You got something, Val?" Roberto and Murray asked simultaneously.

"Tory Driggers. I'll be damned." Valerie chuckled. "Talk about old home week."

"You know her?" Murray asked.

"Yeah," Val said, suddenly uneasy. "Went to school with her. She was in the department when Jim and I were undergraduates." She scanned the long list of references. "And from the list of her publications, she's one of the leading primatologists in the country. Whoops, here's an article on bonobos and their close relation to humans. Looks like she's at Arizona University."

"Call her," Murray said. "If she's the Tory who tried to reach Bartlett, maybe she knows something." Then she heard him shout, "Joan? Pull up directories for professors at the University of Arizona."

Valerie took a deep breath, tension rising in her chest. "Murray, maybe you'd better ask our reporter who was at the scene—"

"I want *you* to call her. You're an old friend. Besides, you have a better handle on what this is all about. You might be able to pick up on something subtle that would blow right past anybody else."

Valerie bit her lip in the ensuing silence.

Then Murray said, "Okay, I've got her numbers at the University of Arizona and at home."

Valerie wrote the numbers as Murray dictated them, then repeated to make sure she'd gotten them right.

Murray said, "If it's seven-thirty here, it should be four-thirty in Tucson. See if you can catch her before she leaves. Val, this story is just breaking. She won't have heard about Bartlett. You'll be breaking it to her."

"Right. Murray, keep me—"

"Sure thing, Val. Don't waste time talking to me. Call Dr. Driggers and see where it takes you. Then, if you can get back to SAC, see what you can pry out of them. I'm faxing everything. Keep in touch."

The line went dead.

For a long moment, Valerie held the receiver to her ear, hearing the dial tone.

"So, what's up, Fuerta?" Roberto rose from his chair and stretched his back muscles.

"Damn it, Taco, I've got to call an old friend and tell her something I don't want to." She finally hung up the phone, taking a deep breath. "I'm starting to hate this story. It's getting closer and closer to things I don't want to deal with."

He lifted a dark eyebrow. "Want me to call the lady?"

Valerie rubbed her forehead, as if to stimulate her brain. "No, but thanks. I've got to shoot my own dogs."

With that she picked up the receiver, dialed the international access codes and Tory's number. As it rang, Valerie said, "She's probably skipped anyway. The Tory I remember was always the first one to FAC."

"What's FAC?"

"Friday afternoon club. You gather at the local club, drink, dance . . ." The line clicked as a woman said crisply, "Dr. Driggers."

Valerie's heart skipped as if a voice had just spoken to her from the grave.

Twenty-one

Sudden panic grabbed at the base of Valerie's throat. Then she managed, "Tory? Is that you?"

"Yes, it is. Fat, sassy, and ready to blow this joint. So, what can I help you with?"

Valerie took a deep breath. "Tory, this is Valerie Radin. I don't know if you'll remember . . ."

"Val! Hell yes! How have you been? Damn, it's been a long time."

"It sure has. How's the ape business? I see you've made quite a name for yourself in the field. Full professor I assume."

"I brought them too much grant money. They had to keep me in spite of their better judgment. You haven't done so badly yourself. I see you on the news every so often." And then her voice changed. "Uh, this isn't exactly a social call, is it?"

"No, I'm afraid not. Tory, how well do you know Shanna Bartlett?"

"Pretty well."

After it was apparent that Tory wouldn't say more, Valerie asked, "And her ape, Kivu? Are you familiar with him?"

"Valerie, where's this going?"

"Tory, do you think Kivu is capable of murder?"

"What? What kind of silly goddamned question is that? He's one of the smartest, gentlest apes I've ever known. That's nuts!"

"Tory, I have to break some bad news to you. Shanna's dead. She was killed this afternoon. The preliminary reports are that she was shot in the head. Kivu was also shot. He's alive, at a vet hospital. I don't have any other details."

"Shot? By whom?"

"We don't know that either, Tory. One man, currently listed as John Doe, was found dead at the scene, apparently killed by Kivu. Another man, a Dr. Brian Smithwick, was found injured there. He's in critical condition, apparently mauled by Kivu."

After a long silence, Valerie said, "Tory, are you there?"

"I'm here." She sounded sick to her stomach. Then she said, "Goddamn them."

"Goddamn who? Tory, what's going on?"

Another long pause, then: "Valerie, what's your interest in this? How come it was you who called to tell me this?"

"I thought you'd be the one with the answers."

"Bullshit, Val. Did Jim call you?"

She stiffened in spite of herself. "No, Tory, he didn't."

"Well, if you want answers, I've got some. Not all, but some. But you have to start first. Tell me how you got into this, and I'll fill in some of the blanks . . . off the record."

"All right, fair enough. I was assigned by Triple N to do a piece on Smyth-Archer Chemists. They're spending a lot of money in interesting places like Equatorial Guinea. They're doing some fascinating work with recombinant genetics, implanting human genes in apes. One of those apes is Kivu, who was given to Shanna Bartlett. Am I right so far?"

"Exactly right."

"And now we have this recent tragedy. The question is, why? What's going on?"

"Do you want truth, Val, or media hype? Where are you going with this?"

"I thought we had a deal. I told you what I had, you tell me what you have."

"Sure, up to a point. Just because I know you doesn't mean I trust you, Valerie."

"Do you want to explain that?"

"Sure. I don't trust you because I don't want to see some sensational scare story about berserk genetically engineered apes raping, killing, and plundering. Just out of curiosity, has anyone asked Kivu what happened?"

Valerie's gaze darted around the room. "Asked Kivu?"

"Damn right. He's fluent in American Sign Language, uses a voice-synthesizing keyboard, the whole bit. He can tell you exactly what happened, if anyone would think to ask."

Valerie stared sightlessly at Roberto. "What do you think happened, Tory? I mean it. I'll take this wherever the story goes."

"Your word?"

"I didn't get where I am by chasing ambulances. I did it by asking hard questions that made people rethink their policies. Yeah, you've got my word."

"All right, I think Smithwick showed up and tried to strong-arm Shanna. She always acted tough, put on an armored front, chip on her shoulder. You know the type? Hard as nails outside, brittle as cracked glass inside. Shanna and Kivu were close, maybe too close. She depended upon him for all of her psychological needs. They bonded like no two individuals I've ever seen. This is just a wild-assed guess, but I'd say that Smithwick applied pressure, and Shanna snapped. When she did, Kivu did just what you'd expect him to. He tried to protect her." Tory paused. "You said Kivu and Shanna were shot?"

"Yes."

"Shanna hated guns," Tory continued. "She wasn't wild about

Texas because everyone has a gun there. She came from Massachusetts where they ban guns. She'd never even have allowed
a gun in her house. If there was shooting going on, Smithwick
or this other man did it."

"Did you know Smithwick?"

"I met him at a couple of conferences."

"Was he a gun-packing type?"

"My guess is no."

"So John Doe was the muscle." Valerie frowned. "But what
were they trying to get her to do?"

"They were trying to get her to keep quiet about the way
SAC manages their apes. They wanted to muzzle her."

"Why did you call Shanna on Wednesday?"

A pause. "To warn her that Smithwick was in the neighbor-
hood. I got her answering machine. She never returned my
call."

"How did you know about Smithwick?"

"I don't think I should answer that," Tory said.

"Why not?"

"I promised someone."

"Tory, look, people are dead. This whole thing has just taken
on another dimension. I think you know that the first story to
break sets the tone for those that follow. Do you want that
rampaging ape story to land first? If you don't, then, please,
tell me why you wanted to warn Shanna Bartlett."

"Because Smithwick had just succeeded in putting a muzzle
on Jim."

"My Jim?"

"That's right. I flew up to Fort Collins to look at Umber—
Jim's SAC ape. Umber had blown the top off the learning
curve . . . acting more within human parameters than an ape
should. After I returned to Tucson, Jim called and ordered me
to destroy all the data he'd given me. He said that if I didn't,
SAC would take Umber away from him. It was a pretty melo-

dramatic phone call, about bugged phones and SAC knowing all kinds of things about him that they shouldn't."

"Like what?"

"Oh, for example, he told me that SAC had recorded a conversation we had at the Marriott bar. I thought he'd lost his mind."

"Tory, any good investigator can obtain information using a long-distance microphone. Journalists do it all the time. How did Jim react?"

"He was terrified. Valerie, Umber's as much his child as Brett is. Dear God, how would you feel if someone just came in and took away a beloved member of your family?"

Valerie hardened herself against the sudden pang in her heart. "Can SAC do that? Just take an ape away?"

"The animal belongs to them; they own it. The apes are property on loan for research. SAC can pull one anytime they want to. That's probably what they threatened Shanna with. That, and she didn't deal with men very well."

Valerie shook her head. "Damn it."

"What, Val?"

"You'll hear about it eventually, Tory, so I'd better tell you. I got your phone number because a Triple N news crew was at her house when you called on Wednesday. They heard you on the answering machine just before Shanna threw them out. But if SAC was monitoring phones, bugging houses, they'd have known we were there. That, coupled with your visiting Jim, might have made them panic."

"Panic about what? Augmented apes will be controversial, but we create new organisms all the time."

"You're a scientist, Tory. You see it from an anthropological perspective, not from T. H. Mits's point of view."

"Who?"

"The Honorable Man in the Streets. Aka John Q. Public. Lift

an ape up on the alabaster pillar with human beings? People won't like it."

"That's no skin off SAC's nose."

"It is when public reaction could affect corporate earnings, Tory. What happens if several billion dollars of SAC's stock drops by, say, fifty percent, because the public decides to boy-cott SAC products?"

"Some things start to make sense, that's what happens," Tory said slowly.

Valerie turned to Roberto, remembering Godmoore's ashen reaction to the money question, and whispered, "Get Myles on the phone, have him do a little digging, see who the major stockholders in SAC are."

Roberto nodded and trotted out the door.

"Tory, if anything comes up, call me. But in the meantime, I've got an idea. What are you doing this weekend?"

"Meeting my heartthrob in Yuma, why?"

"If I have a ticket waiting at the Tucson airport, can you fly to Austin? Is this thing important enough that you would go and see Kivu? Does he know you? Would he trust you?"

"I think so, yes. Wait a minute! Just fly off to Austin?"

"Do you want to be part of how this story develops? Or do you want to leave it to press hounds like me, who might get it wrong?"

"You always were a bitch, Val."

"Yeah, I know."

"I'll do it."

"Good."

A pause, and then Tory said, "Are you going to call Jim?"

She felt like a huge hand had just closed around her heart, squeezing. "No, Tory. I think I can get the story without pick-ing scabs off old wounds."

"He's doing well, you know. And Brett is a super kid. You'd

be proud of her." Tory hesitated. "I just thought you might like to know."

"Yeah, thanks, Tory." She squared her shoulders. "Stay right where you are. Our people will call you about travel arrangements in less than a half hour."

Valerie carefully settled the handset on the receiver. For what seemed an eternity she sat and stared at the blank TV screen across the room, rethinking the entire conversation.

"Dear God," she whispered. "I called him 'my Jim.' "

It took Richard Godmoore three tries to place the telephone handset on the golden cradle. In shock, he sat bolt upright in his leather chair. Shanna Bartlett lay in a morgue someplace in Texas, and beside her, Parnell was just as dead. Smithwick had just called from a hospital in Austin, and no one knew where Kivu was. Deputy sheriffs—still police no matter what they called themselves in Texas—were waiting to question Smithwick. And Kivu? What on earth had happened to him?

Reporters were bound to follow closely on the tail of the police. Godmoore turned toward the computer and fumbled his way to the directory. Then a cold realization washed over him; he had no one to call. Parnell had handled the United States for him. And Parnell was dead. For the moment, Richard Godmoore had no way of controlling the situation.

Angrily, he leaped to his feet, paced back and forth until his gaze lit on the photo of him, Geoffrey, and the little ape. He plucked it off of his desk, whirled, and threw it at the paneled wall across from him.

Hearing it crash, and the tinkle of splintering glass, he slumped, head in hands, as he fought for control. Time and space drained away. Only the widening gulf of futility remained within.

If this blossoms out of control, there will be questions at the stockholders' meeting. I'll lose it all. Fifty million pounds! It will evaporate like water in the Sahara.

"Damn you, Geoffrey! Damn you and your miserable little monkeys!"

Only then did he notice that when he had thrown the photograph of Geoffrey, it had impacted the wall amidst the pictures of his children, sending them all crashing down on the thick red carpet.

The Kawasaki splashed through puddles as Vernon Shanks drove it down toward the canal crossing. He shifted his six-foot frame uncomfortably. These vehicles weren't made for tall men. He clamped his heavy jaw and focused his brown eyes ahead. The lights bathed the narrow road in yellow and reflected from swarms of insects. They reminded him of snowflakes, but the illusion rapidly faded in the hot muggy night. His close-cropped black hair clung wetly to his skull.

Beside him, Meggan O'Neil slumped in the passenger seat, dirty, tired, and depressed after a long day of combing the ridges that ran through Compound C.

"Vern," her delicate Irish accent carried above the muffled engine.

"Yes?" He steered around one of the corners and surprised a duiker in the headlights. The animal froze for a moment and then bounded through a hole in the forest wall.

"It doesn't make sense. Bagawli didn't just vanish into thin air. I know him. He's not like that."

Shanks grunted. As much as he wanted to agree with Meggan, Shelly McDougal insisted that the official policy was that Mitu was missing. Further, she had sworn him and Melody to silence about the unidentified arm and leg they had located over in Compound D. Blood-typing those grisly finds proved they were from two different people—neither one of whom was Mitu Bagawli. Up to now, he had managed to get along with McDougal. She might have the personality of a badger, but he hadn't had any misgivings about her dedication to the project.

At three that afternoon they had located the Compound C chimpanzees at the extreme eastern end, high in the upper canopy. Something had terrified them to drive them that far. When they'd seen the Kawasakis, the chimps had climbed down, descending with their long black hair bristling while they glanced around nervously. Meggan's crew, in the process of taking a census of the animals, had discovered that two of the males, the alpha and gamma, were missing.

"Do you want my guess, Vern?" Meggan looked over at him. In the glow of the instrument panel, he could see her red hair and freckled face. Her green eyes shone darkly.

"Of course, darling." He tried to smile.

"I think we've been raided by poachers. Somehow they sneaked in past that hooligan Amando's soldiers. That's why they didn't take the radio. They were just after bush meat. Bagawli must have stumbled onto them, and they killed him."

Poachers? That's a real possibility. But where is Alpha Group? And who is scattering body parts around Compound D? Why are they doing it?

Aloud, he said, "I'll ask Shelly to have a word with Don Amando. He's already investigating one rumor. If they were poachers, Evinayong is the closest place to sell the meat." He paused. "But, Meg, you must do me a favor. Keep this to yourself. You know how the cafeteria generates rumors. Since you're close to me, everyone is going to be pressuring you for information. Just tell them the truth, that it's under investigation."

She rubbed her arms, looking out at the trees illuminated in the headlights. "It's just so frightening. To think that despite all of our efforts people can still sneak in here."

Vernon slapped the steering wheel, hating himself for lying to the woman he loved. "You know, we're going to look very foolish if we declare a state of siege, batten down the hatches, and Bagawli comes walking out of the bush a few days from now, babbling on about the alpha and gamma males going off for a weeklong homosexual liaison, aren't we?"

"God, I hope you're right," Meg agreed.

Yes, I wish I was, too.

They rounded the last bend on the steep descent to the Compound C bridge. As the lights played across the raised drawbridge, Vernon thought he saw something leap for the shadows on the far side.

He pulled up beside the control box, removed the key hanging from its ring on the knob that worked the lights, and inserted the key to activate the box.

As they watched, the bridge slowly lowered on its counterbalancers. A length of vine hung loose, draping down toward the water, then one end fell free. "That just figures," Vernon muttered. "The crews came through here a week ago. How could they miss a vine that thick?"

As the bridge dropped into place, he drove forward, the Kawasaki rumbling over the aluminum and wooden structure.

"If it is poachers," Meg stated, "they simply must be captured, Vern. We can't have them think they can come here, kill our apes, and then get away. If one bunch does, another will be tempted to try."

Vern frowned as he drove onto the solid ground of Compound B and looked over his shoulder. The weight of the vehicle had tripped the trigger that raised the bridge back into position, effectively separating Compounds B and C.

He accelerated down the narrow track. Poachers certainly made more sense than his deepest worry, that the Alpha Group had somehow escaped from Compound D. But if the work crews weren't policing the vines . . .

He braked to a halt.

"What's wrong?" Meggan reached over to place her hand on his leg.

"Oh, that damned vine." He slipped the Kawasaki into reverse, backing down the road. "I'm tired, Meg. Too much on my mind. Not thinking well. I should have just stopped, chopped the thing loose, and been done with it. I don't know what's wrong with me."

"I do," she said teasingly. "You're thinking just like me, looking forward to a hot shower, a warm meal, and a little lovemaking before we both fall sound asleep."

He grinned. "I'll hold you to that."

Shanks stopped the Kawasaki on the bridge approach, set the brake, and stepped out. Night sounds pulsed in the heavy air. He could hear something splash in the water below. From the toolbox, he took an electric lamp and one of the machetes. Then he walked onto the planks, shining his light up along the railing where he'd seen the vine trailing.

Perplexed, he leaned over the side and shone the beam downward, searching the murky water. Several meters out, a crocodile's eyes caught the light and reflected. A swarm of insects gathered, whirling like dervishes in the light.

For the first time since he'd come to the project, he realized just how lonely it could be out in the bush. He had a radio, of course, but even if he called for an emergency, it would take them twenty minutes to arrive. The wall of leaves on either side of him suddenly became ominous, threatening.

"Did you get the vine?" Meggan called.

"No. I don't see it now. I'd swear that was a vine."

"Or maybe just a long snake." She sounded like she was trying to convince herself.

"A long snake," he agreed, not believing it for an instant. He had seen a vine, and it had been . . .

"Vern!" Meggan called, her voice anxious. "What is that? To your left!"

He turned and saw nothing. He backed to the Kawasaki. "What? Where?"

"In the trees. Over there." She pointed. "I saw something move at the edge of the light."

He shone his lamp over the area. The leaves still rustled.

"Did you see what it was? Another duiker, perhaps?"

"I—I don't know."

Vernon's spine tingled. The feeling of being watched by unseen eyes ate at his subconscious.

"Let's go," Meggan said uneasily. "I don't know what it is, but I just feel . . ."

"Yes, all right."

Rather than take the time to stow the machete and light, he tossed them in the back, settled into the driver's seat, slipped the Kawasaki into gear, and raced the throttle as he sped them up the road.

He watched the lights disappear as the man and woman raced away. He had recognized Shanks, seen him reach out, insert the key. He knew about keys, had seen them used in the cage locks. As the others in his small band gathered around him, he coiled the thick vine they had used for the perilous crossing into this new world.

A key . . . a key was all it took to bridge the worlds.

The Gulfstream climbed into the evening sky and turned east over New York City. Umber had refused a sedative and watched from her seat. Her only reaction had been a low squeal as the g forces pushed her back into the cushions. As the jet gained altitude, Brett and Umber hovered at the windows, watching the magical lights of the city recede below them.

They had changed pilots for the long flight over the Atlantic to the Azores. During the interim, Aberly had dispatched some reports and received several faxes.

Jim had been studying him for about an hour. Something had changed. Aberly looked like a man who had a lot of bad news on his mind. His long face had tightened, and beads of sweat glistened on his narrow pointed nose. His normally easy-going eyes lacked focus, locked on some internal disturbance.

Jim unbuckled his seat belt and bent over Brett's seat. In the dim cabin lighting, her red sweater looked orange. Blond hair tumbled around her pretty face. "How are you feeling?"

She rubbed her arms where Aberly had injected her with multiple vaccinations. "Not so hot, Dad. I feel like I did two overtimes against the varsity squad."

He placed a hand on her forehead. "You're running a fever. About one hundred and one Fahrenheit, if I were to make a fatherly guess. Why don't you go back and sack out on the couch. There's not much to see but black ocean down there anyway. If you sleep it off, you'll recover faster."

She nodded.

Jim looked at Umber. Her purple pants and white sweatshirt had grown a thousand wrinkles. "Are you ready to sleep, too?"

"Wheep," she said and looked up at him with soft brown eyes. She signed: "Feel sick. Think shots for people. Not bonobos."

Jim smiled. "I think they make all primates a little ill, Umber. And you can get just as sick from African diseases as people can. The next stop is eight hours away. Why don't you and Brett both try to sleep."

Brett rose and made her way toward the rear. Umber slipped out of her seat and followed, gripping the chair arms to steady herself as she passed. Her black hair glittered with her movements. Jim went back, spread blankets over them, and strapped them in. "If you need anything, I'll be right up front."

"Night, Dad," Brett said wearily as she curled on her side.

"Good night, angel. Sleep well."

Umber touched a hand to her mouth, then drew it down over her face, fingers spread, signing, "Good sleep." Then she yawned, exposing her pink tongue and stubby teeth, and rolled on her side to stare at Brett.

He knelt beside Umber and kissed her forehead. "Everything's going to be all right."

She blinked slowly and nodded.

Jim turned off the lights and made his way forward to where Aberly sat, bent over his papers.

"How are we doing, Dan?" Jim settled across from him and smoothed his hands over the creases in his gray Levi's.

"I've sent in the medical certifications," Aberly said and wiped the sweat from his nose and forehead. "Your visas are being processed in Malabo, the capital city, as we speak. When we land at the compound, they'll have both the visas and IHCs ready for you."

"IHCs?" Jim asked.

"International health certificates. You'll want to stop by the clinic and receive boosters. The nice thing is, you're getting the best battery Smyth-Archer has ever devised. Some, like the magnumefloquine, are hot off the drawing board. In most people, it acts as a malarial vaccine rather than just suppressing the symptoms."

"Lucky us." In a low voice, he said, "Dan, I've known you for years. You helped me put Umber's health plan together. Level with me. Why all the strong-arm tactics? What's really happening here? This idea of returning Umber to the wild is ludicrous. Umber could no more go back to being a wild ape than Brett could go live in a jungle."

Aberly frowned down at the papers spread out in front of him. "Yesterday, Jim, I would have agreed with you. Today, I'm not so sure but that it might be her only chance for survival."

"What are you talking about?"

Aberly wet his lips. The nostrils of his narrow nose flared. "I received a fax back at Newark. You remember Shanna Bartlett? Well, apparently Kivu killed a man and hurt Brian Smithwick rather badly. They say he'll live, but he's pretty broken up."

Jim sat forward. "Parnell? Is that who was killed?"

"I believe so, yes. I never met the man, but I heard Brian say that he didn't particularly care for him."

"Dana, my lab assistant, called him the Witiko man. That's the name of the Cree Indian cannibal monster that prowls out in the snow and kills innocent people. Parnell . . . he had a thing for women. If he's dead, I would guess he made a very bad mistake. He probably got aggressive with Shanna and she freaked."

Aberly leaned back. "You seem to know Dr. Bartlett fairly well. Is that what she would have done?"

"I think so."

Dan frowned, hesitated, and purposelessly riffled his papers. "She's dead. Shot in the head. Apparently by Parnell."

"What's the matter with you people?" Jim punched the seat back ahead of him. "Why would you use a man like Parnell? Couldn't you just be honest with us, tell us what's happening? What are you so afraid of?"

Aberly absently chewed on the end of his pen, then said, "We're taking some very calculated risks, Jim. The vast majority of people won't understand what we're doing. If this backfires, it could seriously damage SAC, have a terrible impact on profits, perhaps ruin the company. A lot of people would be hurt. Smyth-Archer is more than just the ape project, but Geoff doesn't seem to see that. We've got to be very careful, and now, if Kivu really killed Parnell, the whole thing is about to explode onto the front pages." He met Jim's eyes. "We may have to evacuate all the SAC apes."

"All?" Jim asked, recalling that Smithwick had told him there were five or six. "How many are there?"

"About twenty. Spread here and there around the world. Umber and Kivu are the most advanced. We were hoping they would mate one day."

Jim massaged his forehead, trying to make sense of it all. "Those pills you send each month for Umber. They're estrogen inhibitors, aren't they?"

"Very good, Jim. How did you figure that out?"

"Umber is twelve. She should be reaching sexual maturity. When that happens, a female bonobo's vulva swells until it's as large as a grapefruit. Umber's has remained undeveloped."

Aberly leaned back on one elbow, twiddling his pen between his fingers. "We wanted Umber's youth extended because of her brain. We didn't want hormones to interfere with her natural socialization. You're familiar with Lucy, the chimp raised by Maurice Temerlin? She began to crave human males, even masturbated over *Playgirl* magazines. Um, you haven't noticed behavior like that and forgotten to include it in your reports, have you?"

Jim shrugged. "Let's put it this way, one scientist to another: primates explore their sexuality. That goes for humans as well as bonobos. Father though I might be, I don't have any clue as to what sexual explorations might be going on under either Brett's or Umber's covers at night."

"No *Playgirl* magazines?"

"No, but Brett's too sophisticated for that. She reads novels. She likes Nora Roberts, and there's some explicit stuff in those books. I assume if Brett knows about birds, then Umber knows about bees. Neither one of them spends a great deal of time talking to me about it."

"So. Tell me the truth, Jim." Aberly studied him soberly. "Is Umber an ape, or a human?"

"She's a person." Jim hesitated. "Though she's never really been given the opportunity to find out if she can function in human society. She can't go into a restaurant with us because of health codes. She can't go into public buildings because they don't allow animals. Brett and Ginger have taken Umber to the movies with them, dressed her up as a human girl and bought her a ticket."

He paused. "We had a little talk after that escapade. Otherwise, Umber functions perfectly around the house. She does chores, cooks, does dishes, and just about anything but clean her room." He opened his hands. "As to what her limits are, I have no idea, and I've lived with her for years."

"We've never had the chance to test a bonobo in human society," Aberly said and ran a hand through his salt-and-pepper hair. "Social restrictions are rather boorish, aren't they?"

"Is that what this is all about? Making apes that can function in human society? Why would you want to do that, Dan? To make slaves out of them like in *Planet of the Apes*?"

"Actually, we're a bit more optimistic than that."

"What does that mean?"

"I can't tell you everything, Jim. I'm not authorized to—"

"Did Shanna know? Or perhaps Kivu?" Jim glared, knowing it gave his blue eyes an inhuman sparkle.

Aberly recoiled a little and said, "Jim, I—"

Jim didn't let him finish. He rose and walked toward the rear of the plane, dropping down in a seat where he could watch Brett and Umber. He rubbed his tired eyes. Kivu had killed Parnell? Shanna was dead?

He leaned his head back against the seat and stared at the white ceiling. Dear God, what awaited them in Africa?

Twenty-two

The secretary's formal English accent grated on Valerie's nerves: "I'm sorry, Ms. Radin, but Dr. Godmoore isn't taking interviews from any parties at the present time."

Valerie glanced across her hotel suite to where Myles Edwards watched her over a table piled high with mounds of reports, documents, and books. Through the window behind him, she could see the streetlights gleaming in the darkness. Myles's silvered hair and bushy gray eyebrows glinted as he leaned forward expectantly.

Valerie rolled her eyes to indicate the status of the call. "I don't think you understand, ma'am, a man and woman have been killed, another man, one of your employees, is hospitalized. A SAC ape is involved. Doesn't Dr. Godmoore think some official response from Smyth-Archer is in order?"

"I'm sorry, Ms. Radin," the stiff voice informed her. "We have no official reaction to those charges. They are currently under investigation."

"And that's it?"

"Yes, Ms. Radin. If anything changes, Smyth-Archer will be prompt in its response."

"Right. Thank you for being so forthcoming."

At the click, Valerie slammed the phone down. "Go to hell, bitch. Now I'm really pissed."

She leaned her head back and rubbed her temples. "How's Roberto doing with that piece for Murray?"

Myles checked his watch. "He should be about done with the editing. It'll run tonight on satellite feed."

"Good." They had broken down the footage taken at Smyth-Archer and mixed it with footage the Triple N news crew had taken at Shanna Bartlett's farmhouse outside of Austin. The photos supplied by Mark White were included as Valerie's voice-over outlined what they knew about the SAC apes and the deaths in Texas. In response, they had Godmoore's image, captured by Roberto's camera in the Smyth-Archer conference room. They had Valerie's questions, and Godmoore's responses. When the piece aired, the proverbial shit was going to hit the fan.

"What did you turn up today?"

Myles faced the table. "SAC has spent nearly two hundred and fifty million pounds on their ape compound in Equatorial Guinea."

"And no one has asked questions?"

"Though SAC is a publicly held company, stockholders of any major pharmaceutical company know that new drugs require huge investments in research and development. No one expects all of their projects to pay off immediately."

Valerie dropped the sheet onto the table. "I still don't get it. How on earth can half-human chimpanzees make them billions? And why do they have a compound in Equatorial Guinea? Why not somewhere civilized and closer to home? This isn't freak entertainment. People aren't going to pay a fortune to go see chimpanzees in the jungle, no matter how smart they are."

"Most especially, they're not going to Equatorial Guinea. It's the poorest country in Africa. Half of it, including the capital, is on an island called Bioko in the Gulf of Guinea. The other half, Río Muni, is on the mainland, sandwiched between Gabon and Cameroon. In the seventies a dictator named Macias Nguema killed or exiled half of the population and destroyed the economy."

"Which was based on?" Valerie crossed her arms.

"Cocoa from Bioko."

Valerie shuffled through the papers, picking out a photocopy of a map. "This is it?"

"That is the IAR ape compound." Myles indicated a winding channel leading up from what was called the Mitemele River. It was marked "Controlled Water Access." Other channels wound around like interconnecting snakes, each labeled "Containment Canals."

"I wonder just what they are trying to contain?"

"Well, as you can see, you've got Compounds A, B, C, and D. Each is separated from the other by water. One landing strip is in Compound A, and another, smaller one is in D."

Valerie returned to her study of the map. "What do you think is going on?"

"I think they've got their own little playground in the middle of deepest, darkest Africa." Myles pulled at his chin, staring down thoughtfully. "Most interesting."

"And at a couple million pounds sterling, most expensive." She thumped the map with her index finger. "Tell me, Myles, if you were running a wildlife preserve for apes in a backwater like Equatorial Guinea, how much do you think it would cost? What's the budget for other preserves?"

"Surely not more than several hundred thousand a year, I'd suspect." Myles lifted a bushy gray eyebrow. "When do we go?"

"*Me*, Myles. Remember when you were worried that I'd take all the credit for this? There are two stories here. One is in Africa, the other is here."

"Doing what?" he objected.

"Following the money, laddio. Godmoore flinched when we

brought up the money. Something's rotten here, and I suspect Dickie Godmoore's up to his eyebrows in it. It's the kind of digging you're good at. I don't do as well ferreting out slick accountants as I do picking leeches off my ankles." She looked up. "Any word on my special luggage yet?"

"Be in tomorrow. Just what kind of special luggage are we talking about?"

"Survival gear. I've put it together over the years. Solar battery chargers, a satellite phone system, medical kit, water purification kit, emergency flares, that sort of thing. Everything looks appropriately battered and aged so it passes customs without raising eyebrows." She struggled to memorize the map of the IAR preserve.

"I've taken the liberty of doing some checking, Val. It's one thing to say you're going, quite another to get there."

She looked up. "It's just Africa, for heaven's sake. As of today's news, we're between wars."

"Yes, well, it's also Equatorial Guinea," Myles said. "The travel office ran into a mess trying to book you through Malabo. It will take almost a week if you go that way."

"What about chartering an airplane in Cameroon?" She pointed to the map. "There's a landing strip right there."

Myles gave her a sheepish glance. "I hadn't thought of that."

"Uh-huh, and that's why you're staying here to follow the money trail." She gave him a smile. "Trust me, Myles, Taco and me, we're good at this."

"What if SAC has reneged on their invitation?"

She gave him a bland look. "Who's going to tell them we're coming? Not me, and I doubt . . ."

The phone rang. Valerie stepped across and picked it up. "Radin."

"Valerie? It's Tory. I'm in Austin. I'm having a little trouble with your reporter here."

Valerie sat on the edge of her bed. "What kind of trouble?"

"Well, I'm at the vet's clinic in a jerkwater place called Smith's Corners. I'm calling on my credit card from their phone. Look, I've got the receptionist here, and she's willing to release Kivu to me if I pay the bill. The Hays County sheriff's deputy who dropped him off didn't leave any instructions. I guess they just figured that Kivu would be here when they got around to picking him up."

"Jesus. Have you talked to him? Can he travel?"

"He's in a full body cast, Val. He's heavily sedated, but keeps signing over and over, 'Help, help,' and 'Kivu hurt.'" She paused. "The bullet broke his back—severed his spinal cord. His legs are paralyzed. He'll never walk again."

Valerie's eyes hardened, feeling that instinctive human compassion for an animal in pain, and anger at the person who had hurt him. "So, what do you need from me?"

"Tell your damn reporter to let me do this. I'll pay, Val. Out of my own pocket. I can't leave him here like this. When he comes to, he's going to start looking for Shanna, and when he finds out she's dead . . . well, he's going to need a friend."

"Is it medically sound to remove him from the vet's?"

"He's immobilized. It should be safe. They resected his colon and intestine where the bullet tore through. This vet might be good at preg testing cows and spaying cats, but an ape is out of his ballpark. Kivu needs better treatment than he's getting here. He's on an intravenous diet, but I'd say yes, as long as he's kept quiet, we can move him."

"Put the Triple N reporter on the phone."

She listened as voices muttered, and then a crisp voice said, "Valerie? Matt Johnson here. Listen, I can't—"

"Pay the bill, Matt. Get that ape out of there."

"Jesus Christ, Valerie, he's a witness in a murder investigation. Hell, he's a suspect! What are you talking about?"

"Do it. Now. Before that receptionist gets nervous and changes her mind or calls the sheriff. Get Kivu out of there and then do whatever Tory tells you to. Do you understand?"

"What if the sheriff comes after him? We could be arrested!"

Val thought for a minute. "Is Slim Harriman still in Austin?"

"Are you kidding? He's the most notorious lawyer in the state."

"Call him. Tell him he's got a new client. Tell him I sent you, and that I'm calling in old favors. Got that?"

"Christ, Valerie, you've lost your mind. Maybe you're willing to risk your career at Triple N, but I'm not!"

"That's entirely possible . . . but I just gave you the story of your life, Matt. Greatness and a shot at the Peabody Awards involves a little risk." She let that sink in. "So, tell me, what's it worth to run an in-depth interview with the first nonhuman witness in a murder investigation? Especially one that's about to go international?"

He paused, and she could hear him take a deep breath. "Okay, my credit card's out. Where do I take him?"

"Wherever Tory tells you to. You've got a witness to care for and keep healthy. Slim Harriman will tell you how to keep Kivu on ice."

"Got it. Here's Tory back."

Valerie heard the phone change hands and Tory said: "Whatever you did sure lit a fire under his butt."

"Tory, keep Kivu healthy. Do whatever you have to. Call anyone you need to. I told Matt to hire Slim Harriman. He's a lawyer. Kivu is going to need him."

"A lawyer? For Kivu?"

Valerie stared blindly at the chandelier above her. It cast multicolored sparkles on the ceiling. "It's the logical next step, Tory. Think about it. I'm going to be traveling for a few days. If you need anything, here's Murray Stanton's personal number in Washington." She gave it to Tory, then added, "He'll see to it that you get what you need. Wherever you end up, leave your number with him."

There was a pause. "Val, why are you doing this? Just for the story? I don't want Kivu jumping through the hoops of a media circus. He's too ill for that."

Valerie smiled wearily. "Tory, step back and think. The moment that those people died in that farmhouse, Kivu was cast front and center. He's already condemned one way or another. The story here, the one I'm writing, is what is Kivu? Is he a wild animal who killed a man? Or is he a person who was forced to protect his best friend with the only means at his disposal? That Hays County deputy just gave Kivu the biggest break he's going to get in his entire life. If you can get him out of there, set him up someplace safe, and under the legal protection of an attorney, he's made the first step toward individual rights. Do you follow me?"

"You bet your ass I do! We're out of here."

The line went dead. Valerie slowly replaced the phone, looking up at Myles. "You know, there are times when you own the story, and others when the story owns you."

"You look worried."

She nodded slowly. "This whole thing is avalanching, and the problem with an avalanche is that when you finally stop rolling, you're usually buried alive."

Twenty-three

Below, dark blue water spreads in every direction, but when she cranes her head and looks forward, Umber can see a green coast separated from the water by a thin line of surf and white beach.

Africa. Her earliest memories are of Jim showing her pictures of Africa. Far below, the land of her ancestors unfolds.

She softly grunts "Whuh" in greeting.

The pilot calls over the intercom for them to fasten their seat belts and stow all gear for landing. Umber's computer keyboard synthesizer still lies under the seat in front of her, but she leans forward to check it anyway.

The jet's attitude changes, as if it is leaning back into the wind. The high whine of motors accompanies the change in the roar as the flaps lower. The jet wiggles and pitches slightly. Each time it drops suddenly, her stomach tickles and her heart leaps into her throat.

"You okay?" Brett asks.

She shoots Brett a fear-grin.

"Yeah," Brett agrees, looking a little pale herself. "I hate landings the worst."

"I've been in and out of this strip for years," Aberly says from behind Umber. "It's nothing to worry about."

"Wheep," Umber replies bravely but digs her fingers into the armrest. Despite her fear, the descent fascinates her. She watches the shoreline pass beneath, catching a brief glimpse of crashing waves, sand, and then a green carpet of treetops. It does look like carpet, all humped and irregular, as if a giant finger might push it down and find the feel spongy.

To the north, she can see lines cut through the endless forest and a place where an inlet sticks into the coastline like a thumb. She bends around in the seat and signs: "What that?"

Aberly follows her glance and says, "Cabo Dos Puntas. The two towns on either side of the inlet are Bolando and Mbini. Jim, from your side you should be able to see the Del Muni estuary. The little town on the north shore is Acalayong, and then, across the river, is Cogo. The big river we cross is the Mitemele."

Umber watches the land continue to rise, piling up like green ice cream on a plate. She gestures for Aberly's attention and points at the mountain that rises majestically on the left.

"That's Monte Mitra. It's the highest point in Río Muni, about three thousand five hundred feet."

"Looks like rough country," Jim says. "Odd, I didn't think it would be this mountainous so close to the coast."

"Africa," Aberly tells him, "rises out of the sea like a giant plateau. That's one of the reasons the Europeans came here last. With the waterfalls, they couldn't navigate the rivers. It took railroads to make the exploitation of the interior possible."

Umber stares at the huge bulk of the mountain as they fly past. Looking down at the rumpled ridges, she sees sunlight reflecting off water in the drainage bottoms. They cross over a wide valley. In the bottom lies a twisting serpent of a river, its water brown, torn white here and there by rocks, rapids, and low falls. In the floodplain Umber can see clearings, some with blue smoke rising. She signs: "People."

The jet whines again, louder this time, and the nose lifts. The floor thumps under her feet.

Brett says, "Gear's down."

Umber presses her nose against the window; the trees move by faster and faster. Umber curls her toes as the jet banks in a steep turn, then levels out.

The treetops pass by even with her window, and a flat lane of grass flashes underneath as the trees give way. No matter that she'd sworn to be brave, a single screech breaks from her throat as the big jet drops, touches the ground, and settles. Then Umber freezes as the brakes throw her forward and a mighty roar comes from the engines. The plane shakes and flexes around her, then rolls gracefully into a turn and seems to creep across the tarmac toward a two-story metal building with a curved roof.

People stand behind tractors and machinery. Most are black-skinned, watching with expressionless faces. They wear cotton pants and shirts. All of them have hats.

The jet shudders one last time and stops.

Umber blinks, swallows hard, and shakes her head. *I'm here. Africa.*

A voice seeps from the roof above Umber. "This is the pilot. Welcome to Río Muni. The local time is one-forty P.M. and the temperature is a nice balmy thirty degrees Celsius, eighty-six Fahrenheit." The voice then tells Dr. Aberly they are free to disembark.

Umber grabs her voice synthesizer from under the seat and hugs it close. It seems an eternity before Aberly turns the latch and unlocks the door. As it opens, the stairs fold out.

Jim grabs Umber's arm, forcing her to tear her gaze from the stairs and look up at him. "Brett, Umber, you stay close, hear me? I don't want you wandering off."

"Wheep," Umber agrees. She follows Aberly onto the stairs, and the air hits her, pressing down, warm and moist like a hug in a hot shower. By the time she steps down onto the cement, she is grimacing, her lower lip thrust out in discomfort. "Hot," she signs to Brett as she steps off the plane.

"Yeah, whew! And smell. Have you ever smelled anything like that?" Brett's blond hair gleams in the sunlight.

Umber flares her nostrils at the pungent odor. Forest, that is what she smells. Damp, humid forest. This is air that her ancestors had breathed. With curious detachment, she searches inside herself, seeking . . . What? Some thread to the past, to a heritage that she barely understands?

"Africa," Jim says with awe in his voice. "I've always wanted to do this. To come here, set foot on her soil."

"Is the whole continent a sauna?" Brett asks, rubbing her fingers together. "Feel this. I'm slimy already."

A little red Kawasaki Mule arrives, its engine puttering. It has a canvas top, seats for four, and the windshield is folded down in front. The black driver smiles at Jim, then gives Umber a reserved inspection, studying her purple pants, moccasins, and white CSU Rams sweatshirt.

"Looks more like a golf cart than a jeep," Jim notes.

Aberly tucks his thumbs into his belt. "These things take less gasoline and maintenance than a four-wheel-drive does. They do better in the mud, too." He gestures for them to climb in. The rear seat is just wide enough to hold Brett, Jim, and Umber side by side. Aberly takes the passenger seat.

The Kawasaki pulls out in a wide turn, and Umber looks back at the sleek white jet that has brought her to this hot place with its pungent odors and strange people.

She signs: "Bye, airplane. Fly home safe."

They round a stack of tall fuel barrels, and then the corner of the big metal hangar cuts off her view. They follow a dirt track down a narrow lane. Tall, vibrantly green grass grows right up to the edge of the roadway, and half a stone's pitch beyond, the forest rises in a high, green wall.

Umber has always imagined the rain forest to be a quiet place, but over the engine she can hear it, full of birdsong and the buzzing and churring of insects, as if the wall of green pulses and vibrates. She sees flowers, thousands of them, and in all colors. Leaning her head out into the wind and filling her nose, she discovers that the sweetness in the forest's pungency comes from flowers. Brightly colored butterflies and moths flutter and dance on the warm air. Looking up at the sky, she can see insect wings glittering against the sunlight.

Half to herself, she signs: "Alive. This world is all alive."

"It looks like you cut this right out of the jungle," Jim remarks as the Mule rocks down the red dirt road.

"Oh, we did. One word of warning: Don't go wading about in the grass and don't walk around barefoot."

"As hot as it is here, who needs shoes?" Brett asks.

"Have you ever had worms, Brett?"

She scowls. "Like for fishing?"

"No, like internal parasites. The larvae are microscopic and live in the soil. They attach to the skin on your feet, eat their way through, and circulate in your bloodstream. They eat through the intestinal wall, mate, and lay their eggs inside you. They eventually pass out onto the ground in your feces, thereby starting the entire cycle over again."

"Gross." Brett makes a face. "Okay, so I'll wear shoes."

"And another thing," Aberly adds. "There are clothes dryers in the north end of the dormitory. Use them. We have women who come in each evening to do ironing. Do not leave wet clothes hanging up to dry."

"Why is that?" Jim asks.

"The tumba fly is one of the delightful locals here. The female lays her eggs on damp cloth. If they aren't scalded, either by the clothes dryer or steamed by a hot iron, the larvae will hatch and burrow under your skin. Treatment is easy. Vaseline kills them, and they can be popped out like a pimple, but don't let them go."

Brett says sourly, "Anything else?"

"Yes, no swimming. Not only do we have crocodiles, but poisonous snakes like water. Most importantly, organisms that cause what is called onchocerciasis, or 'river blindness,' and bilharzia, or schistosomiasis, are found in the rivers here. River blindness is just that, an infection that makes you go blind. Bilharzia is a fluke, a little worm that eats through your skin. If you're lucky, it migrates through your veins to your intestines and lays its eggs there. If you're unlucky, they end up in your heart, liver, or spleen. We'll check you periodically, because we can cure schisto." One by one, Aberly meets their eyes. "Listen, all of you, Umber, you, too. If you feel ill at any time, go immediately to the hospital." He winked at Umber. "We're set up specifically to treat humans or apes. We take health very seriously here, and most things we can fix or cure."

Jim asks Aberly, "Do they have Guinea worm here?"

"We do. Short-timers usually aren't exposed."

Umber leans forward and signs: "What worm?"

"A parasite that lives in the body," Jim replies, watching Brett. "I saw it in an anthropological film once. It can be over six feet long. When it finally breaks through the skin, the only way to get it out is to wind it out on a stick, pulling it an inch or so a day. It can take months to winch that little beauty out of a person's body."

Brett turns uneasy eyes toward the green wall they pass. "Okay. I get it."

Umber fixes her attention on the lush grass, wary now. With the list of ailments Aberly has recounted, she is starting to yearn for Fort Collins, in far-off Colorado. At home, she just has to watch for rattlesnakes in summer, ticks in spring, and slap occasional mosquitoes.

A hand-painted sign announcing "Compound A" hangs from a tall chain-link fence topped by thick coils of razor wire that remind Umber of a shining caterpillar.

The buildings within the enclosure have been constructed of prestressed concrete. Large and square, with tin roofs, they are laid out on either side of the graveled street, three on one side, four on the other. Each one has a small sign in front denoting its purpose. The largest is the dormitory, the smallest is the administration building with its radio towers and microwave and satellite dishes. Big floodlights look down on the compound from high poles, and still more sprout from each building corner. People are walking along the paths, most waving as the Kawasaki Mule purrs past. Umber waves back, noting that the human population seems evenly mixed between whites and blacks.

The next thing to catch her attention is the grass, mown short to the fence, and again just beyond, right up to the green cliff of jungle. Why would anyone mow between the fence and the jungle?

"Jeez, Dad," Brett says. "It looks like a prison."

Umber turns to study the buildings as they pass them. All of the windows have thick wire mesh screens.

Jim's blue eyes narrow as he looks at the fence line. "That's pretty new construction, isn't it? In this climate you must have to work hard to keep the plants from growing up through the chain link. Especially all the vines and creepers."

Aberly nods. "I suppose I should have prepared you a little better." He gestures out beyond the fence. "That's raw rain forest out there. We've got leopards, snakes, forest buffalo, apes— as you'd no doubt guess—crocs, and monkeys. The chain link is to stop the things that walk; the razor wire stymies the climbers. The crawlers, well, you'll have to keep your eyes open for them. We do have a curfew, and you should know the gates are locked at sundown. If you do get caught out after dark, don't panic. We have a twenty-four-hour security team here. Show up at the main gate, raise a ruckus, and someone will let you in."

The Kawasaki pulls up in front of the last, and largest, of the buildings. The dormitory stands three stories tall, long, with rows of windows peeking out of the gray-cast concrete walls. Umber smells the cafeteria across the street, a two-story building from which the sound of fans can be heard over the noise of the forest.

Wide cement walkways connect all of the buildings. Good, she won't have to walk in the grass where worms and insects can get her. She glances down, thankful for her moccasins.

"If you need it"—Aberly points at the square concrete building painted white—"that's our hospital. We have four regular physicians on staff as well as visiting specialists in tropical diseases. Half of the facility is dedicated to humans, and half to ape medicine."

"Pretty impressive." Jim prods Umber to get out. She slips over the side and glances down curiously at the hard-packed pavement lest any crawling things try to get her.

"Come, I'll show you your quarters." Aberly leads them down the walk, opens one of the metal double doors, and ushers them into a lobby. The room is complete with couches, tables, reading lights, and a big-screen TV, the sound off, but definitely Triple N from the format. One entire wall has been covered with corkboard, from which are hung photos of animals, pictures of sunsets on white beaches, and mist sifting through green trees. Another part, designated "Bullet'N'Board," is cluttered with colored bits of paper that Umber recognizes as notes.

She sniffs, signing: "What smell?"

"Bug bomb," Aberly replies. "Being in the bush has its challenges. We had a technician step into the shower a week ago, and, well, she was unaware that a rather large tarantula was in with her. Do you know what a tarantula is, Umber?"

"Ugly spider," she signs.

Aberly nods soberly, studying her. Then, as if by effort, he remembers what he was about. "Oh, as I was saying, this is the social area. Over in the corner is a satellite phone link. Feel free to use it whenever. It's about five dollars a minute to the United States."

"Bugged like my phone at home?" Jim asks mildly, his eyes on Aberly.

"I beg your pardon?" To Umber's way of thinking, Aberly seems completely oblivious. But then, maybe he doesn't think an ape would know what "bugging" meant.

They follow Aberly through another set of double doors and into a long hallway. "Looks like a motel," Brett decides, glancing down the corridor at the featureless brown doors with numbers on them.

"Quite right. This floor is for individuals. Each room has four beds and a shared bath." He pushes through the fire doors and takes the stairs to the second floor. Again the hallway is lined with doors. "Separate quarters here. One bed, one bath."

Umber and Brett glance at each other as they continue up the stairs in Aberly's wake. Brett signs: "I'll bet I can beat you up and down these stairs."

Umber grins, looking at the way the metal railing is constructed. She shakes her head, already planning how she will outfox Brett's longer legs.

Aberly pushes through the third-floor doors and into another hallway. He stops at the second door on the left and gestures them inside. Umber charges forward. A bed sits against one wall with a recliner against another. Each faces the small television in the corner. A screened window looks out at the forest beyond. A desk, with chair, has been placed in another corner. A small nook contains closets and a little refrigerator.

Umber points at the gauzy white fabric that hangs in folds from the roof. "What that?"

"Mosquito netting, silly," Brett tells her. "You drape it around the bed at night. You saw *Out of Africa*."

A door leads to a bathroom that includes a toilet, tub and shower, sink, and mirror. Another door on the opposite side leads out to another room furnished similarly to the first.

Aberly walks to the mesh-covered window and says, "We thought these rooms would best suit your needs. At least for the first few weeks until Umber begins to acclimate. From there, we'll evaluate her progress and make the appropriate adjustments."

Umber turns to Aberly. She signs: "Umber wants go home with Brett and Jim."

Aberly raises his hands, then lets them drop. "It's not my decision." His troubled gaze goes from one to the other of them. "But consider this: Smyth-Archer Chemists has invested incredible sums in this project. Everything you see here. Not to mention the extensive research that culminated in Umber and the others like her. A great deal is riding on the success of this project."

Umber tilts her head to the side and looks at Aberly, completely puzzled. Brett stands next to her, frowning.

"Uh-huh." Beneath his beard, Jim's jaw grinds. "Godmoore didn't spend millions on a lark. He didn't do it for any academic jingoism like 'learning more about what it means to be human.' He's not the curious kind. I think he could not care less about solving the 'mysteries of life.' I picture him as a bottom-line man, interested in profits."

Aberly sighs. "He's the quintessential administrator. It's not Godmoore, Jim. It's Geoff."

"Who? Geoffrey Smyth-Archer?" Jim looks startled.

Aberly rubs the back of his neck. "Mr. Smyth-Archer owns sixty-eight percent of the voting stock in Smyth-Archer Chemists. He's the man who tells us what to do." Aberly looks around uncomfortably and lowers his voice. "Look, I just work here. I don't have anything to do with the decisions that are made. My job is strictly to see to the animals' health, to determine which medical procedures are suited to both species and which are not. Some of the spin-off has led to better medical procedures for humans. The rumor is that the entire ape experimentation project is Geoffrey's. He started it. Dickie Godmoore administers the everyday workings and the whispers are that, privately, he's terrified of what we're doing. Godmoore scrapes every bit of information out of the system, frantically looking for spin-offs that will be profitable. Any shred of data that will help justify the project, or create commercial returns. The word is that Godmoore runs everything with an iron fist because he's afraid that if it gets out—what we're doing I mean—it will create a public relations nightmare. And since Godmoore owns about ten percent of the voting stock, and another ten percent in common shares, he doesn't want it to get out that we've created a new species by mixing humans and apes; it could bring unwanted scrutiny."

"If it's so controversial and costly, why do it at all?" Jim asks.

Aberly looks utterly surprised. "Why, for the apes, of course! You mean to tell me that you are unaware of Geoffrey Smyth-Archer's mission? From the latest surveys we've conducted, they will be extinct in another twenty years. Humans are hunting them for meat, selling body parts on the black market, but most importantly, we're logging off the forest they live in and planting it in farms to feed billions of humans."

Jim's eyes glint. "And you think you can change that?"

"We *have* changed it," Aberly tells them levelly. "That's what this is all about. If we're destroying the habitat that apes need to survive, we need to readapt the ape to our human-centered environment."

Jim props his hands on his hips and paces to the window to frown out at the compound. "I feel like I just fell through the looking glass."

Twenty-four

Meggan O'Neil pulled her red hair into a tight knot at the nape of her neck and wound a rubber band around it. Wearing it loose in hot muggy weather like this would have been torture, especially with the tropical sun beating down on the soil of Compound B.

Behind her, the big Volvo grunted and coughed, a puff of black diesel smoke rising as the engine sawed to life.

"Hey, Miss Meggan," called the driver, Bitu. He had a moony face, with skin the color of time-aged mahogany. He pulled the dual-wheel truck around from the pile of plantains, sugarcane, and pineapples he had just dropped on the provision ground. "You need an'thing else, you call, yes?"

"I'll call, yes," she shouted over the roar of the truck. Bitu gave her a wide grin, and the heavy truck roared and whined across Compound B.

She watched it pass through the narrow opening in the forest wall. As the noise faded away, only the forest sounds surrounded the clearing with its four little cabins.

Meggan turned, looking toward the towering trees. As she knew they would, the chimpanzees appeared one by one from the forest. The alpha male, followed by his subordinates, led the way, and then some of the older females emerged. Meggan had always enjoyed watching this moment, it soothed something primal in her soul. The chimps had a rolling, ambling knuckle-walk. Their black hair caught the sunlight, glistening and long. They radiated a sleek power.

She squinted in the bright light, counting, "Four, five, six . . . eight, ten, thirteen . . . sixteen, nineteen . . ." as the apes continued to stream out of the forest.

The big males had reached the line of fruit and squatted down to pick up their favorite treat, a plantain for one, or sugarcane for another. Immediately, squabbles broke out, screaming and arm waving sufficing to drive the subordinates beyond the radius of personal space deemed proper by the dominants.

". . . twenty-three, twenty-four . . ." Meggan frowned. "Wait, there he is. There's T-Rex. Twenty-five. All present and accounted for."

Meggan shaded her eyes, watching T-Rex as he stopped just short of the treeline. He looked around uneasily, rocking back and forth on his stiff arms. He had been one of the first apes brought here. After nearly ten years, he still hadn't graduated from Compound B. Meggan had come to realize, as others had before her, that he never would.

"Poor old nut," Meggan said to herself. She turned, looking at the line of stainless steel cages. Side by side, they rested on stilts forty centimeters above the ground. Most of them included blankets. The doors had easily manipulated latches. The third from the end belonged to T-Rex. He slept there every night, as he had for years. For him, the cage meant sanctuary. Meggan had read the report of the time a previous researcher had packed up the cages and trucked them off in an attempt to make T-Rex leave. He had wandered out of the forest at dusk and stopped short, bewildered. In blind panic, he had run to the spot where the cages had been. Huddling down on the precise location of his old cage, he had spent the night rocking back and forth, whimpering and picking at himself. By the next morning, he was nearly catatonic. And remained that way for days, even after his beloved cage had been returned.

"Dearest Father in Heaven," Meggan said to herself. "We've done some terrible things to them."

She thought back to the first ape she had seen in Dublin. One look into those intelligent brown eyes and she had been hooked. Primatology had become her life and passion.

Meggan reviewed her preparations for the new ape scheduled to arrive today. It was her job to teach new apes how to readapt to the wild. She'd successfully done it with these twenty-five. An animal twice as smart should learn twice as fast.

She thought about Bagawli, still missing, and was suddenly uneasy. His disappearance had spawned new rules that said no one was to stay alone in Compounds B or C. Yet here she was, alone. She'd sent her assistant off to Compound A for badly needed insecticide, but he would return within the hour, and she figured no one would be the wiser.

At the edge of the headlights last night, she would have sworn she'd seen an ape standing. Not a chimpanzee, but one of the augmented animals.

Except that was patently absurd. She had been on the project for two years, and only in the last month had she even learned about the existence of Compound D. Vernon had finally admitted that it existed, and that augmented apes were indeed living there, but under exceptional security. And even then, he'd only told her since she was being placed in charge of the American ape's reintroduction.

From the porch of the cabin, she again surveyed the clearing. The apes had cleaned up the provisions before retiring to the forest to nap, digest, and attend to their grooming.

She rubbed her arms, feeling lonely. An eerie silence had descended. Even the ever present racket made by the insects seemed muted.

"It's just your nerves, Meggan," she told herself, then slapped her hands to her sides. "Come now, lass, you're a big girl."

On impulse, she turned and walked along the line of cages where they lay in the shadowed protection of the ramada.

In the trees, the shriek of a mustached cephus monkey split the air.

Meggan turned, gazing intently at the green wall, then she ran for the place where her apes had disappeared.

The cephus's screams grew more shrill.

She had heard a cephus make that sound before, usually when they were being hunted. True, a monkey might have happened upon a snake, or an eagle had made a grab for him, but if there was a chance that her apes were being hunted by poachers, she had to see the men with her own eyes, or they'd never be brought to justice.

A cacophony of wild screams broke from behind the screen of leaves. Meggan pounded along, running toward the sound, then slowed as the ape voices changed. Their excitement turned to fear.

She could hear the tearing of leaves, the lashing of branches, as the chimps fled directly toward her.

Meggan began to backpedal, never taking her eyes from the forest. She had retreated halfway to the cabin when the first of the females burst from the green wall—a young mother racing with her infant clinging to her breast.

They poured out in a flood, bristling, running in panic. They charged past Meggan and into the clearing beyond. The biggest males brought up the rear. They slowed to whirl around and scream at the forest before rushing by her.

"Lord God!" Meggan called. "What is it?"

The last of the males broke from the forest, springing as fast as he could for the safety of the far trees.

Meggan stared in disbelief. In her two years, she had never seen such a thing. One high-pitched voice still shrieked, as if tormented by devils. Meggan could hear his terrified voice marking his progress through the forest, past the bedding sites, but he seemed to be running in circles, as though pursued.

T-Rex, winded, his hair on end, lunged from the trees with his mouth hanging open, his eyes glazed. He ran headlong, diving like a madman into his cage and huddling there with his head covered.

The forest had gone silent again. Not even the birds dared to sing. Meggan glanced at T-Rex, then she walked carefully toward the cage. "T-Rex? Are you all right? T-Rex?"

She stopped short at the sight of him. Every muscle trembled. A whimper sounded with each breath from his laboring lungs. He was rocking back and forth, his face hidden in his hands.

"T-Rex?" Meggan called again. "Are you all right?"

When she stepped closer, he cried out and clawed madly at the bottom of his cage, as if to dig a hole to hide himself.

"T-Rex, you know me. I'm not going to hurt you. I . . ."

From the corner of her eye, she caught movement. She spun, searching the trees to her left. Branches swayed.

Meggan slowly rose to her feet. She shouted, "Who's there?"

Ordinarily her yell would have brought a roar from the forest. Startled birds should have chirped and burst into flight. Apes should be howling . . .

But nothing dared to breathe.

Meggan backed toward the cabin. She could sense someone, something, watching from behind the screen of leaves.

Her heart thundered. She turned and ran as hard as she could for the cabin door.

Valerie and Roberto glanced around at the brightly lit international terminal at Charles de Gaulle airport.

"That way," he said and pointed to the signs directing passengers to their gates.

By the time they made it through the check-in and security, down the jetway, and to their seats on the A310, they barely had time to buckle in. Valerie immediately pulled out the maps of the IAR preserve.

"Looks like rough country," Roberto noted, leaning over to study the map. "Curious. Why do you think they have one landing strip at Compound A, and another at Compound D? Why not just build one strip and truck the stuff?"

"Got me. It's just one little mystery after another, isn't it?" She rubbed her eyes as people shuffled past toward the rear of the plane. Most were African, some dressed in traditional garb.

"Worried about something?" Roberto asked.

"Just thinking about Jim. He's going to know that I'm involved in this. Hell, Tory's probably already told him. That, or he's going to see the piece on SAC." She sipped her wine and curled the edge of the map with her thumb. "What's he going to think? What's Brett going to think? Should I have called him first, asked for his side of this?"

Roberto leaned back, silent, his dark brown eyes passive.

Valerie shook her head. "You know, I've sure made a mess out of my life."

"I don't know, man, it got you into first class." He looked around. "Of course, we're going first class right to the middle of the jungle, but, hey, it beats driving a tractor and spraying insecticide on orange groves."

"I was just trying to figure out why no matter how hard I work at enjoying life, I'm always unsatisfied. Like there's something missing."

"What?"

The stewardess was saying in French that people needed to be seated and buckled in before they could leave the gate. Valerie shuffled her papers, placing them in the briefcase and stowing it beneath the seat in front of her.

Roberto checked his seat belt and leaned back, gently saying, "You got a lot of thorns, Fuerta. Kind of like a cactus. You think it's part of the job. Only one tough bitch can break a story in a war zone with dead people lying around. You think you gotta be tough, 'cause that's the character you've made for yourself. That's Valerie Radin, armor-plated reporter. If you doubt it, all you need to do is watch that Valerie Radin on the news that night, and there she is, standing in the middle of blood and gore and inhumanity. She's so cool, analytical in the face of chaos, a rational voice speaking from the darkness of the pit."

"Is that so bad?" But her heart had begun to pound.

"The thing that scares you more than anything"—Roberto steepled his fingers like a priest—"is that someone might find out you're soft on the inside. Hell, you're afraid *you'll* find out you're soft on the inside." He met her eyes, and she saw kindness in those dark depths. "And you know, if you ever do, it'll be okay, Val."

"Go to hell, Taco."

"I thought you wanted me to go to Africa?"

"Maybe it's the same thing."

As the big airbus whined to life, Valerie turned to look out the window. This time, she'd finish the job, tell the story, and then she could take some time, go someplace quiet, and wrestle with her inner demons.

The big jet shivered and started forward, rolling across the expansion joints in the tarmac. She had been to Africa before: Rwanda, covering the aftermath of genocide; Burundi, doing more of the same; Southern Sudan, documenting the Arab slave trade and their constant efforts to kick the black population out, or at least exterminate them. And then she'd done that last interview with Moammar Qaddafi, her skin crawling as she looked into his arrogant eyes and read his real thoughts about her.

Africa had always been bad news. Why did she think it would be any different this time?

Brett let out a cry of dismay as she started down the stairs, taking them three at a time in long jumps, only to see Umber vault over the handrail and drop like a rock.

"Hey!" her dad yelled from above. "You two stop that! Brett, Umber, do you hear me?"

But by then Brett's running shoes hit the second-floor landing. She pushed off the wall to make the turn, risking neck and limb to dash down the stairs. It was no use. Umber had already swung down, dropped to the tile floor, and beaten her to the door.

"Umber! You cheated!" she cried as she charged down the last set of stairs and hit the crash bar that opened to the lobby. Umber wheezed in high-pitched laughter as they shoved each other. She wore an orange tank top, blue shorts, and beaded moccasins that Dana had made for her.

Suddenly Umber's smile faded.

"What's wrong?" Brett asked, pulling her white T-shirt down over her lightweight brown cotton shorts.

Umber lifted a long finger and pointed at the large-screen TV.

Brett turned. "Holy shit."

Tory Driggers stood on the steps of an official-looking building, wearing a black suit, her face stiff. Reporters surrounded her. Beside her, a tall man in a tan suit and white cowboy hat gave the cameras a crooked grin.

Brett walked over, found a remote control on one of the tables, and pressed the volume button.

"... are doing this. The fact remains that Kivu is currently undergoing surgery for his back," Tory said. "We are hoping that he will have some function, but the prognosis is bad."

Jim burst through the door behind them. He wore a green T-shirt, khaki shorts, and hiking boots. "Brett, Umber, damn it! You don't *ever* run down those stairs like that again! You hear me? If you . . ."

Brett waved him down as the man in the white hat said in a long Texas drawl, "Look folks, if the sheriff decides to charge my client with murder, then, of course, he will surrender himself and take his chances in a court of law. As of today, that just hasn't happened. And, to tell you the truth, I don't think it's going to."

A rash of frantic questions sounded like meaningless babble. The tall Texan raised both hands to wave them down. "Y'all listen up, now. We've got an identification on the dead man. His name was Wayne Morrison. He traveled to Austin under an assumed name: Doug Parnell. Morrison's got a record so long you could lasso a hog in the next county with it. Theft, racketeering, three separate assault charges, attempted rape, attempted murder, and to top it all off, a dishonorable discharge from the Marine Corps." He grinned. "You tell me, folks, what was a guy like that doing out at Dr. Bartlett's?"

The image switched to a reporter looking steadfastly into the screen, a redbrick courthouse in the background. "In further developments, we attempted to interview the sheriff of San Marcos County. However, his response to each of our questions was: 'No comment.' "

Shifting his microphone, the reporter continued, "So the story continues to unwind. The bonobo chimp, Kivu, has not been charged as of this report. As you saw, Kivu's attorney, Slim Harriman, doesn't think it likely. It looks like the case is becoming ever more convoluted. Reporting from Austin, this is Matt Johnson, Triple N News."

"Thank you, Matt. We'll be keeping up with developments

on your end." The brown-haired news anchor shifted his gaze to the camera. "The story about Kivu doesn't stop in Texas. Instead, it takes another bizarre twist half a world away. The following special report has been compiled by Triple N correspondent Valerie Radin, in London."

Brett stood rooted, the remote frozen in her hand, as Valerie's image appeared before a backdrop of rolling English farmland. Her blond hair looked beautiful against her dark blue suit.

"Good evening, this is Valerie Radin, Triple N News, on assignment south of London. What you see behind me is deceiving, for here, in the peaceful farm country of Sussex, lies one of the largest of Smyth-Archer Chemists' research complexes."

The shot changed to a concrete sign, declaring: SMYTH-ARCHER CHEMISTS, SUSSEX UNIT. Then Brett saw a tall fence, a guardhouse, and a huge building something like the one she was now in.

"This is the main building of the Sussex research facility," Valerie's voice continued. "We came here to investigate what we thought were wild stories about unusual genetic experiments. Specifically, we came to clear up allegations that Smyth-Archer Chemists has been creating a new kind of creature."

The picture switched to a large-headed bonobo very much like Umber.

"Kivu," Jim said in a hushed voice.

". . . This is the creature we've come to Sussex to find," Valerie's voice continued. "It is an ape known to science as a bonobo." The image changed again, Brett recognizing an average male bonobo, with its lower forehead and smaller skull. "Compare the two," Valerie commanded, and then by TV magic they were overlaid.

"As you can see, the ape Smyth-Archer Chemists has supposedly produced has dramatically different characteristics." The picture switched to Valerie's serious face. "It has been alleged that geneticists at Smyth-Archer Chemists have been replacing bonobo genes with those taken from the animal's closest cousin . . ." A pause. "Us. Human beings."

Valerie frowned. "We came here, to Sussex, to the Smyth-Archer Chemists facility, to ask Dr. Richard Godmoore about these animals. The following footage contains Dr. Godmoore's remarks to us. It should be stated that this was shot prior to the tragedy in Texas."

Brett had never seen Dr. Godmoore before, but he looked normal enough, although his face seemed a little stiff, but that could have been from the unusual camera angle.

Valerie seemed to rankle at Godmoore's arrogant answers to her questions; Brett knew that posture from a thousand interviews.

"Son of a bitch," her dad whispered behind her.

Brett glanced at his glittering eyes, then turned to Umber. Her black hair had started to bristle, and her mouth had frozen in a fear-grin.

"This is no more playing God than chopping off a boxer's tail, or trimming a Doberman's ears." Godmoore seemed to be staring down his nose at Valerie. "Ms. Radin, humans alter gene frequencies in given populations all the time, whether it's for a cow that gives more milk, or for a better-tempered bull. No one complains about that."

"So, from that logic, you're saying you *do* have a purpose in breeding these apes for certain traits."

Godmoore gave her a cold smile. "We are interested in intelligence, Ms. Radin."

The footage ended and Valerie's face appeared again. "Shortly after this, the interview was terminated. The question isn't what Smyth-Archer Chemists has done. They admit to that. The question now is, what are these creatures? Who are they?"

She took a half step and looked directly into the camera. "Through the study of anthropology the gap between ape and man has narrowed over the last fifty years. We have discovered that very little separates our species. Now those boundaries have been blurred even more. Some will cry foul and declare Kivu and his kind monsters. Others will shy away, afraid of what they cannot understand, and demand the immediate destruction of these intelligent beings. People like Dr. Tory Driggers will extend a hand of friendship. If there is any tragedy in this, it has fallen squarely on young Kivu's shoulders. Today, ladies and gentlemen, the world has changed. Human beings are no longer alone. The question is, how will we deal with our new situation? In fear and ignorance, in pride and arrogance? Or will we employ that rarest of all commodities: true intelligence?" She paused. "Valerie Radin, reporting from Sussex, England."

Brett flung the remote onto one of the couches and wrapped her arms around Umber. "Are you okay?"

Umber pointed to herself, then stuck the thumb of her right hand under her chin and brought it forward quickly—meaning "Umber not"—and made the sign for "monster," hanging her open hands alongside her head and snarling while her hands bobbed up and down.

"She didn't say that you were a monster," Jim said. "I thought she was going to trash us, and then, in that last instant, she may have saved Kivu." He folded his arms across his green T-shirt. "In fact, I'd say she did a pretty good job for a reporter. Come on, girls, let's think this thing through. Kivu's got an attorney. Slim Harriman. He's pretty famous. And Tory's in the middle of it. How on earth did she get to Austin from Tucson?"

Umber gazed up at Jim with moist brown eyes. She signed: "Tory help Kivu?"

"Yes," Jim said. "Of course she will."

Brett added, "Aunt Tory is nobody's fool, Umber. Kivu has the best friend he could ever have."

Her dad smoothed his dark brown beard as he stared at the TV, and murmured, "She must have called her."

"Called who?" Brett asked.

Umber wrapped her long arms around Brett and leaned her head on Brett's shoulder. Those strong arms reassured Brett in this suddenly uncertain world.

"Valerie. She called Tory," Jim said. "It has to be."

"Huh? Why?"

Jim gestured to the TV. "She said she did that interview before Kivu killed Parnell, or Morrison, or whatever his name was. Valerie was sniffing around this before it blew up. Maybe that's *why* it blew up."

Umber touched the right side of her forehead, pulled the hand away and formed it into a Y—the three middle fingers down on the palm with the thumb and little finger extended: "Why?"

"She was getting close, Smyth-Archer panicked." Jim waved at the lobby. "And here we are in Africa."

"So it's Mom's fault?" Brett's stomach muscles tightened.

Jim gave her a level look. "No, Brett. Your mother is good at what she does." He looked back at the big TV screen, where Triple N showed automobiles and houses being washed away in California. "That piece cut right through the sensationalism. I'd give half a year's pay to talk to Tory right now."

"So, call her." Brett indicated the phone Aberly had pointed out to them earlier.

"Not on your life. SAC would be listening."

No one moved. Brett and Umber held each other, Jim stood, head down, hands on his hips. The television silently exhibited a sleek new automobile.

Umber touched the middle of her chest, moved the hand down a short distance, then made the sign for "now."

"Yeah, I'm hungry, too." Brett forced the worry away and reached out. "You coming, Dad? Let's see what the chow line's like in this place."

Twenty-five

Jim led them out into the warm, humid air. It seemed to rush over him, pressing down like a weight. The smell, pungent and sweetly aromatic, filled his nostrils.

He held Brett's hand on one side and Umber's on the other. He had forced himself and the kids to nap, but his sleep had been troubled, plagued by images of Umber, lost in the forest, screaming in fear.

"How do we play along?" he asked himself as they walked down the cement sidewalk, crossed the gravel-packed street, and headed for the hulking building marked "Cafeteria."

"Play along?" Brett asked.

He picked his words very carefully. "Look, we've got to make them think it might work. Reintroducing Umber to the wild. Understand? If we openly fight them, they can hurt us."

Umber made the sign for "hurt," followed by "how?"

"They can send Brett and me home. Keep you here, alone, Umber."

"So, what do we do, Dad?" Brett asked as she brushed long blond hair behind her ears.

"We learn," Jim said firmly. "We try to learn everything we can. Everything they want us to learn."

"Right. Awesome. And I thought algebra was bad."

Two men and a woman stepped out of the administration building and walked toward them. Jim recognized Dan Aberly and muttered, "On deck, guys. Smile and be friendly."

"Jim," Aberly greeted, looking nervous as he walked up with the others. The armpits of his white shirt were damp, and his salt-and-pepper hair stuck to his forehead. "I want you to meet Dr. Shelly McDougal, she runs the preserve. And this is Dr. Vernon Shanks, her number two."

"Nice to meet you." Jim shook hands with the woman, who met his gaze levelly. Her medium-length graying hair was clipped back in a severe ponytail. Through her black-rimmed glasses she gave him a look that would brook no nonsense.

"Dr. Dutton," Shanks greeted, offering a big hand. "Good to meet you. We've been anticipating your arrival with Umber." He turned warm brown eyes on Umber. "And you are Umber. Welcome to IAR."

He offered his hand, and Umber reached out, taking it in a firm grip. McDougal's mouth tightened as she took in Umber's laser blue shorts, neon orange tank top, the bright blue wristwatch, and red and blue beaded moccasins.

"This is my daughter, Brett," Jim introduced.

"Welcome to Africa," Shelly McDougal said, her voice heavy with a Scottish brogue. "It's not often that we have young people come to visit."

Offering her hand, Brett met McDougal's hard eyes with a defiant stare—one Jim knew well, and often dreaded—and said, "I'm not here to visit, Dr. McDougal. I'm here to assist Umber's transition to the wild and learn all I can about IAR."

McDougal hesitated, fingered her chin, then nodded. "Is that so, Miss Dutton? Then we shall see that you are given all the challenge you desire."

With forced joviality, Aberly said, "We were just on the way to the cafeteria to meet the lot of you. Dr. McDougal will ultimately be responsible for Umber's reintroduction program, but Dr. Shanks is the immediate supervisor."

Jim shot McDougal a measuring glance. "I take it that Umber is welcome in your food services area?"

"Of course," McDougal answered formally. "We're familiar with her record, Dr. Dutton. It will be interesting to have her at our table." She stepped toward the cafeteria. "Shall we go and eat? I've heard that tonight's fare is chicken, cassava, yams, and a local root called malanga. I hope you like spicy food. The word 'bland' isn't in the local Fang vocabulary."

"If it's spicy, Umber will fall in love with it," Jim said. "She's quite a cook herself. Perhaps, if you have a kitchen, we could treat you to one of Umber's culinary creations." Jim smiled.

"Perhaps, Dr. Dutton, but I'm thinking you'll be occupied by more serious concerns." McDougal dismissed him with a look, then walked on ahead, taking the lead.

Jim narrowed an eye at her back. He knew that look. They'd just met, and already Shelly McDougal disapproved of him, and, more importantly, of Umber.

Brett was wary of Dr. McDougal: her precise way of speaking, the way she held herself so formally, and the lack of any spark of humor in her speech or expression.

As they walked toward the entrance, Umber touched her fingertips to her lips twice, used her index finger to tap her right ear, and ended by touching her lips again and placing the back of her right hand against the palm of her left.

"The food sounds good, huh?" Brett translated. "Well, if it's as spicy as they say, you're going to be in seventh heaven here."

Umber grinned and nodded. She held the door as they passed into the air-conditioned foyer.

Brett glanced toward McDougal and signed to Umber: "Let's show them you're no animal."

"Wheep!" Umber gave her a playful jab with an elbow.

"This is the ground floor." Dr. McDougal indicated the two aluminum-framed glass doors that led into the cafeteria. "The first floor"—she indicated stairs leading up—"contains a small shop where you can find necessities. We have a simple credit system here. Your account will be billed. Deductions will be made directly from your monthly wages."

Brett's eyes followed the tiled stairs up, wondering just what a store in central Africa might be like. She and Umber would check it out first thing.

Aberly and Shanks pushed the cafeteria doors open and Brett followed them in.

Umber sniffed happily.

"God," Brett whispered, "how long has it been since we've eaten a real meal?"

"About half a world," Jim said.

The cafeteria looked just like every other institutional eatery in the Western world. Native Africans scooped food from stainless steel tubs and handed it over the glass top. Behind them, the stoves, ovens, and large walk-in refrigerator could be seen.

The kitchen staff's reaction to Umber fascinated Brett. They refused to look Umber in the eyes, as if her very presence made them uncomfortable. Brett took it upon herself to interpret Umber's hand signs and said, "She'll have that stuff. What is it?"

"Girl, dat cassava," the woman said, glancing uneasily at Umber.

"We'll try it."

"The cafeteria is open from six in the morning to ten at night," McDougal said as they walked over to the long tables and settled themselves in the uncomfortable gray plastic chairs. "That doesn't mean you can eat at any time. Breakfast is finished at half ten. Dinner is served from half eleven until two. Supper will be available from half four to nine. Special meals, takeout, and field meals can be ordered in advance."

McDougal and Shanks watched Umber settle herself in her chair, place her napkin in her lap, and organize her silverware. Brett stifled a grin; Umber was showing off.

Umber looked up at McDougal and signed: "Pass salt, please."

McDougal scowled at Umber's hands. The same with Shanks. Nothing.

Umber tucked in her lower lip, tilted her black head, and signed to Brett: "They don't talk?"

Brett signed back: "What can I say? They're ignorant," and said aloud, "Dr. McDougal? Umber asked you to pass the salt, please." She gave McDougal a silky smile, secretly gleeful that they had an edge here. At least so long as Aberly, who knew signs, didn't catch on.

People were beginning to trickle in, most talking shop in that manner Brett had grown used to when hanging around with her father. Lots of glances came their way as the cafeteria filled.

To Brett's absolute delight, Umber ate with grace, taking small bites, a glint of superiority in her knowing brown eyes.

"What exactly is the protocol for us?" Jim asked, chewing as he waggled his fork for emphasis. "How is this project supposed to work?"

"We will begin tomorrow with orientation," McDougal said in her brogue. "Dr. Shanks will take you around, show you the compounds, laboratories, and whatnot. Once you've familiarized yourselves with the preserve, Umber will begin survival training, learning what to eat and what not to eat. Most of that training will be in the field at Compound B."

Umber stopped eating to listen more carefully. She signed: "How do I dress? What tools will I need?"

Jim translated, and Brett watched the surprised looks. Shanks sat back in his chair, his black brows lifted.

"Well, Umber, you won't need to dress at all," Aberly said uncertainly, and ran a hand through his salt-and-pepper hair. "And we'll teach you how to make any tools you'll need in the wild."

Umber's lips twitched in what Brett knew from long experience was sarcastic humor. She used her fork to spear a mouthful of baked plantains and, as she chewed, signed: "Dr. Shanks go naked, too?"

Brett giggled and shot a wry look at her father. Aberly appeared completely confused. To his credit, Jim translated the question in deadpan terms.

"You must understand, Umber." Dr. McDougal leaned forward, her expression unforgiving. "We're here to see to it that you relearn the wild. There will be no clothes in the forest. You must make do with what nature gave you. Relearn the skills of your ancestors."

The thick lines in Umber's black forehead deepened. She carefully placed her fork at the side of her plate, lifted her cup of orange juice, and sipped it. After she dabbed at her lips with her napkin, her hands danced in signs.

Jim translated, "Umber says, 'I am a cross between a human and a bonobo, yes? Who are my ancestors?'" Jim paused while she continued, then added, "Umber will go naked if other humans do."

Umber followed the translation with a questioning "Wheep?"

The table had gone silent, Umber's unwavering gaze locked with Dr. McDougal's. Aberly and Shanks, both stunned, sat frozen in place, Shanks with a spoon halfway to his mouth.

"Now, that's a real good point," Brett said. "How about it, Dr. McDougal? I'm game, are you?"

"Brett," Jim warned, "that's enough."

"Just trying to help, Dad. We could learn a lot, you know. Umber and me are both about the same age."

"We're getting away from the point," McDougal declared, fire in her eyes.

Umber placed the middle finger of her right hand on the back of her left wrist, then dragged it down to the fingertips, making the sign for "naked," while she shook her head in that vehement chimp shake that looked a little like an epileptic fit.

"Umber," Jim said, reading McDougal's growing displeasure. "Perhaps we could discuss this."

"No, Dad," Brett said softly. "You know I'm with you one hundred percent, but this is serious. I mean, think about it. How did you feel when I just said I'd go out into the forest naked? Why is it different for me than it is for Umber? She—"

"Because Umber's a bonobo," McDougal interrupted, enunciating each syllable. "She is *our* bonobo, and she will go naked. That is the end of this discussion."

Aberly tugged at the collar of his white shirt and fidgeted in his seat. "I think, Dr. McDougal, that we've a point to consider here. Umber is not a bonobo. She's a highly intelligent being capable of thinking for herself. As such, I firmly believe we should be willing to rethink our research design at any time that it becomes apparent it may not suit our long-term needs."

McDougal lifted an eyebrow as she turned her attention to Aberly. "Dan, let's be candid. That is not how science is done."

"With all respect, Shelly, Umber is not a 'specimen' in the classical sense. We're talking about *behavioral* science here, not physical science. With Umber, we're in uncharted waters. She's intelligent, rational, and self-aware. The point is, if Umber isn't comfortable, and if she isn't a willing participant, we will certainly fail. I suggest that we consider her feelings. Any other action will significantly bias our chances of success."

McDougal leaned back, ordering her plates, silverware, and glass, each action methodical, as if putting her world in its precise place. When she looked up, her thin lips were pressed to-gether. The glare she gave each of them made Brett's throat constrict.

"Very well, Umber may go dressed if she wishes, but I think there had better not be many more changes from the research design we decided upon." With that she stood and picked up her tray. "Good day, gentlemen." She barely jerked a nod at Brett and Umber. "I think you all have some work to do."

She walked away with her back stiff. She only nodded in re-sponse to the greetings from the tables she passed.

"Wow," Brett whispered, "she could work for the SS."

"Brett, there are times when you have the social skills of a bulldozer." Jim looked at Aberly and Shanks. "She takes her job seriously, doesn't she?"

"Cut her some slack," Aberly said, relaxing a little. "She's got a tough job here. A great deal of responsibility. When God-moore picked her to run this place, it was little more than an idea and a pin stuck into a map. A lot of people thought she'd fall flat on her face."

"She built this preserve out of sheer willpower," Shanks added, his brown eyes narrowed. "She works twelve hours a day, gives one hundred and twenty percent, and expects the same from those under her authority."

Jim leaned his elbows on the table. "But that's just it, isn't it? I mean, Umber's not really under her authority."

This time, it was Shanks who leaned forward. "Dr. Dutton, please understand. If she makes the decision, you and your daughter will be out of here on the next plane. On this proj-ect, Dr. McDougal's word is law."

"And," Brett asked, "if Umber doesn't want to cooperate after we're gone?"

Shanks's gaze bored into Brett. "Let's be honest, shall we? There is no way we are going to destroy an animal that we've invested as much in as we have in Umber." He turned to Umber.

"The fact is, Umber, if you don't cooperate, Dr. McDougal will consider your reintroduction a failure."

"Then what?" Brett pressed, sensing the first possibility Dad's plan might work.

"Shelly is not a behavioral scientist, but a geneticist. She could not care less if Umber adapts to the wild. What interests her most is if Umber is fertile. If Umber can't be reintroduced to the wild, I assure you, Shelly will place her in a contained environment, artificially inseminate her, and use Umber for breeding experiments," Shanks replied evenly.

Umber slashed her right index finger across her left palm, sharply asking, "What is that?"

"It means they'll put you in a cage and keep you knocked up," Brett said angrily. "So I guess we're all going to go learn how to live in the forest." She swallowed hard.

Shanks replied, "I'm glad that you see the wisdom in that, young lady."

Umber signed: "At least we wear clothes."

Brett said, "Yeah. For now."

Twenty-six

The name of the hotel was the Casa de Huespedes. The two rooms Valerie had booked for the night featured squeaky bedsprings, dubiously stained mattresses, and abundant life-forms. Of course, the rub was that it was the only hotel in Evinayong.

"What a trip," Valerie said as she looked at the roaches skittering across the floor.

Roberto nodded grimly. "You can say that again."

She and Roberto had landed in Douala, Cameroon, cleared customs, and gone in search of a charter flight to the SAC preserve. It should have been a piece of cake, but flying into Equatorial Guinea, it turned out, was more like hardtack. The bush pilots would only take them to Malabo, the capital city on Bioko Island, across the Bight of Biafra; or they would fly to Bata, the largest city on the mainland coast of Río Muni. No pilot, for any amount of money, was willing to fly into a private airstrip anywhere in Equatoguinean territory. It wasn't worth the probable confiscation of their aircraft, the exorbitant fines, or the jail time.

Undaunted, Valerie had declared, "All right, we'll do it the hard way. We'll go by road. Give me the map, let's see how to do this."

Valerie had bought two tickets on Unitair to the Cameroon capital of Yaounde. Her press credentials, along with a brassy show of force, levered them through customs, to a taxi, and off to the Gare Routiere du Centre. There, she hired a bush taxi. The road south was a combination of patched pavement, deep potholes filled with muddy water, and slithery mud. The driver literally pounded his way down the road, the Peugeot whining, growling, and howling. Because of a broken spring, the right rear wheel rubbed on the fender well each time they hit a dip. The only thing that would have made the trip any more harrowing would have been snipers and land mines.

They finally crossed the border into Equatorial Guinea and, in Ebibiyin, hired another bush taxi that promised only to take them as far as Aconibe. But when Valerie offered another five thousand *cefas,* the driver decided he could make it as far as Evinayong.

So they had ended up here, at the Casa de Huespedes.

"Dinner?" Valerie asked Roberto, reaching into one of the cases and holding up plastic trays.

"Hey, you're my hero, Fuerta. I got just the right table. Nice scenic view of the street."

They ended up eating MREs—military "meals ready to eat"— on the sagging front steps of the hotel as rain cascaded onto the tin roof overhead and battered the red dirt street in front of them.

Evinayong, Valerie decided, had the potential to be a pleasant place in another two or three hundred years. For the present, it consisted of a collection of shacks on a mountaintop. Chickens, pigs, and dogs loitered on the streets, apparently heedless of the warm rain. Here and there a dilapidated truck or van sat rusting in the moist air, drawn here to die in peace. The rutted streets were dirt, and the only electricity in town

came from private generators. The one commodity that Evinayong had in plenty—along with the rest of Equatorial Guinea—
was bars.

Even as that thought crossed her mind, two men stepped
out of the beer joint on the opposite corner, bowed their heads
against the rain, and plodded stalwartly toward the hotel
awning.

Both were Fang, as Valerie had come to recognize the locals.
One wore a green shirt that looked military. The other was
dressed in white cotton and wore faded blue pants. His feet
were shod in sandals and he walked with a definite limp.

"Umbolahnee," Valerie greeted, having picked up that little
bit of Fang during the day.

"Ahmbolahnee." They held each other to keep from staggering.

"Nice night," Roberto greeted, then added, *"Es un buena noche."*

"Si. Es un gran' noche," the soldier said. Then, in the pidgin
English of the region, he added, "You want go to project?"

Roberto nodded. "We work for TV."

"Yes." The soldier smiled. "Triple N. Number one. I see it
in Bata when I go for army. My name Bembe. This, how you
say, brother-brother?"

"Cousin," Roberto guessed. *"Primo?"*

"Yaa. *Si.* He named Masala," Bembe supplied. "He has heard
that you go to the project. That you do a story there."

Masala's mouth opened, showing rotted front teeth. His red-
rimmed black eyes kept drifting.

"Take it wherever it will go," Valerie murmured. She kept
her head lowered, allowing Roberto to do the talking. This was
Africa. In the backcountry, women ran things, but men were
the negotiators. From the corner of her eye, she watched the
two men. Bembe seemed all right, the happy-go-lucky sort.
Masala, however, had haunted eyes. Something had broken him.

"This man," Bembe indicated Masala, "used to work at project. He want to know, maybe you go to see demons?"

"Demons?" Roberto smiled. "You've got demons out at the project?"

"Bad demons." Bembe nodded. "This man, he say if you buy him a bottle of good rum, he will tell you the story."

Roberto reached into his back pocket. "Bembe, I'll buy if Masala stays here and starts the story while you fetch the hooch."

Bembe took the five hundred *cefa* note and sprinted across the street.

As Masala cleared his throat, Valerie eased her pen and notebook from her purse. Her hand paused long enough to turn on the small tape recorder there. Beyond them, out in the street, rain continued to pour from the dark gray clouds.

The story lasted a long time, as long as the bottle of rum. As the night settled, generators chugged to life here and there around the village. Masala talked on, his voice soft. When the pidgin failed, Roberto used Spanish, getting the gist of it.

Masala said, "I want you to tell this story so that people know that I am not crazy. Tell people so that they know that this project is evil, breeding these demons that kill people."

"Who did they kill?" Roberto asked solicitously.

"The demons killed Ntogo." Masala's eyes seemed to lose focus. "With his own arrow. They drove it into his side. Ngasala and I, we bent down to help him, to see if we could save him. And from the night, one of the demon apes jumped on my back. He pulled me down, and I lost the light I was carrying. One of the apes picked it up. They beat me, but Ngasala was escaping, so they chased him with the light. I think they believed they had killed me."

Masala blinked, wavering as the alcohol addled his balance. "For a moment, I lay there in the darkness, frightened so badly I couldn't move. Then I heard Ngasala's shotgun. *Bang!*" He paused, frowning. "I crawled away. It was down a steep hill." He rubbed his face, shaking his head.

Go ahead," Roberto prompted. "Then what happened?"

"I saw it. Ngasala had killed one of the females. He cut the infant from her, probably hoping it would live and he could sell it. The demon apes attacked him. I watched. They used machetes, like a man would . . . and they cut him apart, screaming and chopping at him, until Ngasala was in pieces."

He went silent, staring through the alcoholic haze into the terrible past.

"How did you get away?" Roberto asked in a soft voice.

"We were next to the canal. I could hear the water. It was just through the leaves. I dragged myself to it. If I could get to the water, maybe I could find the cayuco. I was scared." He nodded drunkenly. "That's when I saw him."

"Saw who?" Roberto prodded.

"The demon ape." Masala looked up. "I could see him clearly. One of the others was holding the light as the demon ape picked up Ngasala's head. Cut off, you know. And he lifted it, looked into Ngasala's dead eyes, and bit into his face. I saw the demon ape's eyes. They were blue. Like a white man's. Like this woman's sitting beside you."

The only sound came from the pattering of rain on the roof over their heads.

Masala lifted the nearly empty bottle to his lips, sloshing the liquor as he swallowed. Wiping his mouth, he added, "Only a devil ape would have eyes like that. Tell them. That is all."

Roberto offered up another note, which Masala folded into his fingers, and together he and Bembe staggered off into the darkness. The generators had been turned off. The town was mostly dark.

"What do you think?" Roberto asked. "A blue-eyed demon?"

"Killer apes?" She shook her head. "Maybe we need to re-think what Kivu did in Texas."

Jim had always been a morning person, but on this first full day in Africa, he would much rather have fallen back in bed and slept. Seven A.M. in Equatorial Guinea was eleven P.M. at home in Colorado. According to his biorhythms, he should have just been falling into alpha sleep.

Instead, he faced the start of a new day. The fork clinked as he placed it on his plate and rotated his shoulders. He'd dressed in cool clothing, a lightweight tan T-shirt, khaki shorts, and hiking boots. The heavily mineralized water had given his dark brown hair and beard a copper sheen.

Brett slumped in her chair, picking at the last of her eggs. Umber's eyes had fastened vacantly on her plate, but her ears, in their shiny black bed of hair, twitched as if with annoyance.

"Come on, guys, time to go." Jim tossed back the last of his coffee.

Umber yawned, picked up her tray, and followed Brett to the dish return. She and Brett had had a terrible time waking up. They had barely managed to make it out of the shower, get dressed, and stumble over to the cafeteria for breakfast.

Jim checked his watch and pointed to Umber's keyboard pack, forgotten beside her chair. Umber lifted her head to follow his hand. "I don't think you want to lose that."

She said, "Wheep," and hurried over to retrieve the voice synthesizer, her long arms swinging at her sides. Jim held the door for Brett and the lagging Umber. Then they walked out to await Dr. Shanks's arrival. The wet heat folded around them like a steaming towel.

Today, as a way of making a special statement, Umber had chosen a white T-shirt Jim had brought her from an American Association of Physical Anthropology meeting, one from France Casting that had drawings of human, chimpanzee, gorilla, and baboon skulls. She wore baggy green cotton pants with bright red polka dots, and moccasins. She caressed her voice synthesizer. That piece of technology might make Shanks and McDougal understand how ludicrous the "reintroduction" idea was.

Brett had settled for a white T-shirt and ordinary jeans, which Jim thought she would regret in the wet heat. She had braided her long blond hair and carried a small daypack over one shoulder. He'd helped her pack notebooks, pens, and several bottles of juice.

"Come on, Shanks." Jim glanced down at his watch. "It's a quarter after seven. Shanks said he'd be here on the dot."

Brett shivered with revulsion and looked up at Jim. "What kind of breakfast was that, Dad? That gray stuff. It reminded me of grade school paste with ginger and peppers in it."

Umber tapped her keyboard, and a tinny mechanical voice said, "Umber—thought—it—was—good."

Jim smiled and gazed out at the forest, where hundreds of birds sang simultaneously, creating a cacophonous symphony. "I think that's what they call malanga. I didn't think much of it, either, but I could really come to like baked plantain for breakfast."

One of the Kawasaki Mules came put-putting down the graveled road. Umber stuck out her chin and pursed her lips as if ready to admonish the woman driving the vehicle for being late. Jim had just about decided it wasn't their ride when the machine pulled to a stop before them.

"Dr. Dutton?" A young woman, her fine red hair pulled back into a bun, sat behind the wheel. She wore a canvas bush hat, and other standard khaki jungle wear. In contrast to the image of a rough-and-ready field scientist, she wore bobbing gold earrings.

"I'm Meggan O'Neil." Her voice was filled with Irish. "I work for Dr. Shanks. He sends his regrets, but something came up. He's detained in the office. Since I'll be working with you directly, he thought we could do a drive-about and see the compounds."

"Good to meet you," Jim said, extending a hand. She smiled, and he decided he liked her. "Please call me Jim. This, of course, is Umber, and my other daughter, Brett."

"My pleasure." She nodded to Brett, then her attention fixed on Umber, as if mesmerized. "Hop in and we'll be off."

Umber climbed into the rear, next to Brett, took her keyboard out of her pack, and held it in her lap. Brett glanced suspiciously at Meggan, rolled her eyes, and shrugged.

Jim gave Brett a questioning look as he settled into the front passenger seat. He saw Umber sign to Brett: "What's wrong?"

The Kawasaki started forward.

Brett signed back: "Don't you think it's odd that Shanks didn't show this morning?"

Jim turned to Meggan and gave her a pleasant smile, asking, "Are you fluent in the sign language the apes use?"

Meggan steered around a curve and answered, "I'm afraid not. I've never had the time to pick it up. My work has been with the laboratory apes." Then she added expectantly, "But I'm looking forward to learning."

Jim draped an arm over the seat back where Meggan couldn't see and signed, "Okay. Talk," winking at Brett. Aloud, he said, "As I remember it, the airport and the road to Evinayong are back the other way."

"Quite right." Meggan nodded. "Today we'll take a drive over to Compound B, and then to Compound C. That way you'll have an idea of how the preserve is laid out, and a notion of where you'll be working."

As they rolled toward the compound fence, Jim noticed the two soldiers in green military uniforms with rifles slung over their backs. Had they been there yesterday and he hadn't noticed? Were they keeping something in? Or something out?

Jim swiveled to look at Umber. Her black bonobo face and

serene brown eyes gave the appearance of animal innocence, but he had seen her defend herself. She'd been four years old, sitting in the front yard making mud castles with Brett, when a big dog had trotted up and barked at them. Before Jim could get outside, Brett had screamed and run. The dog leaped to chase after her, and Umber's response had been immediate and ferocious; she'd run in front of the dog, blocking its path to Brett, and when the dog tried to veer around her, Umber had leaped on its back, riding it like a bucking bronc while she shredded its ears with her teeth. The mutilated dog finally managed to fling Umber off and took off like a shot, yelping down the road, but Umber had not considered the battle over. She'd raced after it, screaming and throwing sticks and rocks. Jim had sprinted two hundred yards before he'd caught up with Umber.

The soldiers waved as the Kawasaki rolled past.

Jim looked over at Meggan. "Are soldiers routine here?"

Meggan returned the wave and said, "They've been here as long as I have."

"How long is that?"

"I've worked here a little over two years now. I came to finish some research on primate food resources on the *mesetas,* the top of the mountain ridge."

"Isn't that Spanish?" Brett asked.

"That's the official language, although in this area, the natives speak the Okak dialect of Fang," Meggan said. "Okak Fang are mostly found south of the Mbini River. The Ntumu Fang are north of it."

"You're from Ireland?" Jim asked. "What part?"

"I was raised in Dublin. A rich aunt paid my tuition and I attended Boston College for my bachelor's degree. Then I went off to Cambridge and received my master's. My field was originally nutrition, and I was interested in what the human stomach was really adapted for. That led me to ape diet, and I did several papers on the development of the gut."

"Americans use junk food and beer to develop their guts," Brett announced.

Umber pant-hooted at that, and even Meggan laughed as she drove them out around another puddle.

Jim watched Umber pull her shoulder in to avoid the grass. If Umber wasn't going to allow the grass to touch her, her first lesson in foraging was going to be worth watching.

Umber typed on her keyboard, "What will Umber eat in jungle?"

"We'll show you. You'd be surprised what's out there. We'll just adjust your diet slowly." She looked back at Umber. "You've had bad diarrhea?"

"Yeah," Brett chimed in before Umber could answer. "She drank half a bottle of dish soap when she was a baby. Had the squirts for a week after that. It would have gagged a maggot."

Umber smacked Brett with the back of her hand, and Brett punched her back. "I can still remember the smell! Yuck!"

"Can you tell they're sisters?" Jim asked mildly.

Meggan nodded. "That I can."

She steered the Kawasaki around a corner and the road started down a steep grade.

"This is a series of switchbacks that drop us down to the canal," Meggan explained as she descended the steep grade, honking the horn before rounding the blind corners. "You always want to honk," she told them. "It avoids the surprise of meeting a provision truck coming from the other way."

"I see," Jim replied, trying to imagine how far they'd descended. He guessed two hundred feet. The last curve brought them to a bridge abutment. The central span of the bridge was raised high, its end sticking up toward the cloudy sky. Beyond it lay an expanse of brown water, the surface broken by rings created by insects and minnows.

Meggan took a key ring from the headlight knob. "The drawbridge is controlled by this key." She inserted it into a plastic electrical box. "The system is powered by solar panels and batteries." The drawbridge lowered, the whine of electric motors barely audible over the idle of the engine.

Meggan withdrew the key and accelerated as the bridge settled in place. Umber leaned out, staring down at the murky water. Her pink lips pulled back, and Jim knew her skin must be crawling.

"This is one of the dividing canals Dan Aberly told me about?" Jim asked as the Mule rumbled across the aluminum and wooden bridge, which began to rise automatically after they had crossed.

"It is. We have a barge crew that floats around the canals and cuts out the vegetation. It's a constant job, but we don't want apes crossing boundaries." She returned the key to the headlight knob. "You're not to take a key from its vehicle. That is one of the cardinal rules."

The tinny voice of Umber's keyboard asked, "How—many—apes—are—here?"

"Three hundred and seventy-eight at last census." Meggan drove forward. "That includes the chimpanzees who were living here when the preserve was built as well as the ones we've repatriated to the wild. They were mostly laboratory apes, poor things."

"But not augmented animals like Umber?" Jim asked.

"No." She rounded a curve, and the thick canopy left them in complete shadow. The scent changed, too, more like damp moss than trees. Umber leaned her head back and stared up at the green roof. Monkeys screamed and leaped from branch to branch.

Umber's long black fingers danced over the keyboard, and the machine said: "This—is—like—TV—show."

Brett, glancing nervously upward, said, "Yeah, it's *The X-Files*."

The Kawasaki began to labor. Only looking back did Jim realize just how much they had started to climb. The Mule growled and lurched as they made their way up the rutted trail.

"It's a little rougher here." Jim grasped the roll bar to stabilize himself.

"You'll see why in another couple hundred meters." Meggan's expression had turned grim, but she kept the throttle down and they finally cleared the crest.

Meggan pulled off at a wide spot just beyond the crest. "Come on. This is one of our observation research towers. The view is spectacular." She locked the bridge key in the little glove box and stepped out.

Brett and Umber came rolling out after her, each staring suspiciously at the ground.

"I take it you have an observation station here?" Jim asked.

"Several," Meggan said. "Some of our animals wear radio locators. From the treetops we can triangulate." She started for a hole hacked in the leaves. "This way."

Umber stopped to stare at the pruned ends of the stems.

"It's rain forest, Umber," Jim told her. "Things grow fast here. This is the richest environment on earth." He batted at the insects hovering around him. "Come on, let's go see what's inside." He smiled at her. "This reintroduction notion of theirs may be crazy, but it's still exciting to be here, don't you think?"

Umber looked up at him, her dark brown eyes concerned. She patted his hand and made the signs for "not like" and pointed to the forest.

"Why?" Jim asked.

Umber wrinkled her black nose and pointed at her breast, making the signs for "bad feeling."

"Dad? Umber? Come on!" Brett called from inside the curtain of leaves.

Umber runs back to the Kawasaki for her keyboard. When she ducks through the hole, tall dark shadows lean over her. She draws something of the forest into her with each breath: wet leaves and dirt, flowers. The birdcalls, shrieks of monkeys, and churring of insects grows louder, pressing down from all sides.

"Not what you expected, is it?" Meggan asks, shoving red hair away from her face.

"No," Jim answers. "It reminds me of a cathedral."

Umber walks forward. The leaves under her feet are soft, springy. She walks without a sound here. Roots, like knotted snakes, crawl across the ground, and thick tree trunks rise and rise into a high green ceiling.

Eyes watch. All around her. Eyes she can't see but knows are there. She holds her keyboard against her chest to keep her heart from swelling through her ribs.

All of these sights and sounds are stars falling inside her. She can feel them hitting her bones. White and hot.

"Umber?" Brett's hand brings Umber back. "What's the matter with you? That's the second time I called you."

Umber blinks into Brett's blue eyes. She tucks her keyboard under one arm, then moves her right middle finger upward on her chest, signing, "Feel it?"

"Feel what?"

Umber points to her eye, then her heart.

"God?" Brett follows Umber's glance up toward the canopy. "Uh, you mean that kind of spooky sense of being watched?"

Umber nods.

"Yeah, well, there's definitely a presence here. I'd call it the eyes outside, though. Lots of them."

"Hey. You two coming?" Jim calls. "Or do you want to get eaten by a lion?"

Umber turns and sees that Jim and Meggan are far ahead, following a trail in the leaves.

"Come on," Brett says. "I'll race you, but watch out for the roots, they'll trip you in nothing flat."

Brett leaps a root and runs. Umber catches up with her, Jim, and Meggan at the base of a huge tree. A stairway curls up the tree like a vine.

Meggan starts up, her boots thumping on the wooden steps. "This is our own invention," she calls back. "We needed a way to keep track of the apes. These stairways screw into the tree itself. We seal the screws with a special tar so the insects can't gain a foothold and harm the tree."

"What about growth?" Jim asks.

"The little gaps are expansion joints," she answers. "So the tree can continue to grow."

Umber sets her keyboard down at the base of the tree and turns to Brett, signing, "Race now?"

"Not on your life." But Brett leaps for the stairs, her blond braid swinging.

Umber bounds up behind her.

As Umber climbs, ferns, moss, and vines dangle through the lowest branches, swaying in yellowish green freckles of light. She climbs higher, into flowers, and sunlight, and finally out onto a wooden floor.

Her breath catches in her throat. She can see very far. The land is lumpy and clothed in green.

"Wow!" Brett says. "Awesome! Look!"

Umber follows Brett's finger to a canyon. A white waterfall tumbles down, while mist rises in ghostly patterns.

The sky is not the deep blue of her home. The sun seems whiter. The clouds are not piles of whipped cream, but walls of gray.

"This is absolutely magnificent," Jim says. "Why didn't I bring my camera?"

"'Tis a pretty place," Meggan agrees. "We like to come up here whenever we can. There's a trail down the road a ways that leads to the waterfall. The water's safe. You can actually swim there." She grins. "If you see a piece of cloth at the trailhead, don't go down. It means it's"—she shoots an uncertain glance at Brett—"well, occupied, if you catch my meaning."

"Lovers, huh?" Brett says.

Birds flit through the air around Umber, feathers splashing yellow, red, and blue. Umber hoots softly. Vines twine around the floor planks and hand railing.

"What kind of trees are these?" Brett asks.

"Lots of kinds," Meggan replies. "This is an okume. The scientific name is *Aukoumea kleinia.* In this forest alone we've more than one hundred and forty species of hardwoods, including African walnut. The tall tree next to us is one of the mahogany family; we've cataloged more than forty different mahogany species alone."

Umber tries to catch a bright blue butterfly that flutters around her head, unafraid of the bug spray she used that morning.

Meggan leans back against the railing and crosses her arms. "The trees here at the top differ from the ones down the slope, which differ from the ones in the valley. Down below, by the stream, you'll find wild pig and chevrotain antelopes. The duikers, a sort of antelope, inhabit the slopes. The larger antelopes like the bongo live on the ridge crests. Each species is specialized. Even the monkeys. We've started to realize that different species of monkeys utilize different kinds of trees. We call each of these units 'biotopes.'"

Umber walks over and looks down at the big leaves. Insects on cellophane wings glitter. The sounds of the forest amaze her. Were they made by a bug, or a bird? How different. At home the forests are peaceful, especially in the winter when the snow clothes the trees. On cold nights, after people go to sleep, Umber used to step out and listen to that silence.

Does the forest here ever sleep? Does it listen?

In the tree below them, something gives off a loud shriek, and Umber jumps.

"What was that?" Brett says, leaning over the railing.

"One of the colobus monkeys," Meggan replies. "They are leaf eaters. Sometimes they squabble."

"Colobus monkeys." Jim looks happy. "That's what chimpanzees hunt. A prey species."

Umber purses her lips and makes the signs for "pizza," "fruit salad," and "much better."

Brett laughs and translates for Meggan.

"In Equatorial Guinea," Meggan says, "they call monkey 'bush meat.' You can find it in the villages."

"Bush meat?" Brett asks. "The villagers eat monkeys? Yuck!"

"You've never been hungry, Brett," Jim says. "People living in the backcountry don't have King Soopers or Safeway to run to. When your belly is empty, you'd be surprised what you'll eat."

Brett curls a lip. "Monkey? Never!"

Meggan looks at her watch. "We're running short on time. Come on, we'd better get down and on to Compound B. We want to be there by feeding time. It should be most interesting."

Everyone climbs down. Umber waits. She keeps looking, and listening. The baby fireflies in her chest flutter wildly, as if trying to warn her about something.

"Umber!" Brett calls from below.

Umber charges down the spiral staircase. Around her, birds chirp and insects whir. She hears the colobus monkey shriek again. The light grows dimmer as she gets closer to the ground.

When she reaches the bottom, she runs for Jim and Brett.

"Eeep!" she cries suddenly, turns, and races back toward the base of the tree for her keyboard.

She stops, staring.

"Umber?" Jim calls.

Frantically, Umber searches back and forth. Right here, it was here. She bends down. There, against the root, she sees a light scratch where the keyboard sat.

"Umber?" Jim asks, walking up behind her. "What's wrong?"

She signs, "Keyboard gone."

"Where did you leave it?"

She points to the spot on the ground.

Jim crouches. "Are you sure you left it here?"

She nods.

Meggan and Brett backtrack, and Jim stands.

Umber signs to Brett, "Took keyboard! Took keyboard!"

Brett's brows pull together. "Somebody klepped your keyboard? Out here?"

Jim shakes his head and studies the ground. "Too bad this leaf mat doesn't take a track."

"Is something wrong?" Meggan asks, walking up.

"Umber set her keyboard here before she climbed the tree. Now it's missing." Jim peers at the tall shadows. "Do you have a lot of trouble with theft here?"

"Not usually." But Meggan's arm muscles suddenly bunch, and she stares around uneasily. "Come on. We'd better be going."

"Keyboard!" Umber signs and stamps her feet. "My keyboard!"

"We'll get you another one," Jim says. "Come on. And, who knows, maybe this one will turn up."

Umber follows them back, ducks through the hole in the leaves. The sun hurts her eyes, as much as needles hurt in the doctor's office. She climbs into the Kawasaki.

"We'll find your keyboard," Brett soothes, taking Umber's hand.

Umber hangs her head. She makes the signs for "Without keyboard can't talk to these . . ." She pauses, taps her right index finger on her forehead, touches her thumb and little finger together, then flicks her thumb off the finger.

Brett sighs and whispers, "Yeah, they are nitwits, aren't they?"

As Meggan drives away, Umber rests on her knees and turns

around in the seat. The world goes backward. She squints. There, in the shadows, eyes shine. As they drive farther away, he leans out from the leaves. But Umber blinks, and he is gone.

The Kawasaki bumps over a root. Umber cocks her head, thinks about it, and touches Jim's shoulder.

"What is it, Umber?" Jim looks back.

Umber signs: "What apes have blue eyes?"

Twenty-seven

As the Kawasaki wound its way through the emerald canyon cut in the towering forest, Jim considered Umber's question. Some apes were born with blue eyes that turned brown within days, but Umber insisted that she'd seen a full-sized animal.

"If it was one of the compound workers, Umber's keyboard will turn up," Meggan insisted. "Word will get around. It always does."

"The thief will be disciplined. Kicked off the project. Most take their back wages and head for Bata, the big city over on the coast. When they've drunk away their last *cefa*, they come skulking back, heads down, asking for their jobs and promising that they'll never touch anything that's not theirs again."

"And they're rehired?" Jim asked.

Meggan smiled humorlessly, red hair fluttering over her eyes. "No. We have a one-chance policy. To forgive would become an incentive to repeat behavior. The few thieves we've had are in Evinayong." She downshifted for an incredibly steep section of road. Jim smiled uncomfortably and braced a hand on the dash. His stomach muscles clenched as the Kawasaki growled and crawled its way down the rocky grade.

Meggan continued, "The deal that Smyth-Archer brokered

with the Equatoguinean government was that we'd lease and manage the preserve, that the native people already living within the boundaries would be given jobs. Average income in the bush is about two hundred and fifty pounds a year. We pay them an even thousand and provide all health, board, and food."

"That's a pretty fair deal." Jim nodded. In America that would be like handing someone on welfare a hundred grand a year, plus housing, food, and health care. "I take it that you don't have a lot of turnover in employees."

"More than you'd think. Many just don't like the work. They'd rather be subsistence farming in the bush than living here. But over the years the numbers have leveled off. The malcontents have left, for the most part. The people here are actually learning. Miracle that that is."

"Miracle?" Jim asked, surprised by what sounded like a politically incorrect statement.

Meggan eased the Kawasaki through a little brook that ran across the road, the water seeming to appear out of the leaves and then run right back into them. "They had a dictator in the 1970s. A fellow named Macias Nguema who came to power just after independence. He killed or exiled half of the population, destroyed the economy, and bankrupted the country. Equatorial Guinea has never recovered. The people lost their schools, their roads, and their plantations. The ones who survived lived in the bush. Our workers are the generation that followed, the one that grew up in the ruins. The men drink because their fathers drank. They can't read, because their fathers didn't read." She shook her head. "The one thing that coming here has taught me is just how fragile civilization is. You can lose it all in one generation."

The compassion in her voice made Jim revise his opinion about Meggan's earlier comment.

She crept through a rocky section, the Kawasaki lurching from side to side.

"I'm sorry Dr. Shanks couldn't come with us today," Jim said, changing the subject. "It didn't have to do with that Triple N news report, did it?"

Meggan glanced at him. "Heard that, did you?"

"It was tough to miss. Everyone in the dormitory was listening by the time we got back after supper."

" 'Twill cause us some problems, I'm sure." Meggan licked her lips. "I think they were trying to assess damage control. I know that Vernon was on the comsat with the Sussex division. Maybe I'll hear more tonight."

Meggan drove them through a dip and out into a clearing. Here, the grass had been beaten flat. A series of small cabins stood in a line ahead of them. To the left, several roofed ramada-like structures protected rows of stainless steel cages. Solar panels perched like blue wings atop tall poles.

"Compound B," Meggan said as she drove up to the first cabin. Sixteen feet long and twenty feet wide, the cabin had two windows on either side of the front door. She shut off the engine and carefully removed the key. "Always take the Mule keys with you in the compound. If you don't, and a chimp happens to take one, you'll never see it again."

"I thought the bridge key always stayed in the vehicle," Brett reminded.

"The *bridge* key does, locked in the compartment." Meggan tapped the small glove box. "Let's go in and meet Bradley Cummings, my assistant."

She led the way as they entered the cabin. Stuffed bookshelves and file cabinets lined the walls. In the rear, a young man with sandy hair, thoughtful green eyes, and a round face looked up from a laptop computer. Spread on the table before him were a stack of papers, several field notebooks, and a can of insect repellent. Meggan introduced Bradley.

Cummings smiled, said, "Hello, everyone," then walked around the table, hunched down before Umber, and said gently,

"Well, hello there." He made a point of keeping his head half turned, eyes lowered.

"Don't be afraid," Brett said to Brad, crouching beside him. "Umber's friendly. Shake hands."

Umber stepped forward, offering her hand. Cummings took it reluctantly, still avoiding her eyes. "Here, among the chimpanzees, it's good manners to never look an unfamiliar ape in the eyes," he said. "That communicates threat. So does a smile. An upright posture indicates a challenge being made."

Jim smiled in appreciation of Brad's knowledge. "But Umber is human, Bradley. She thinks just like you do."

Cummings looked up into Umber's eyes and smiled.

"I can vouch for Umber," Meggan said. "She's remarkable." Meggan walked over to the screened window to the left of the door. "I don't see any of the apes in. We're coming up on feeding, aren't we?"

"Something set them off again earlier," Cummings said, running a hand through his tousled sandy hair. "I didn't see what, but T-Rex bolted into his cage and covered his head with his blanket. Maybe whatever frightened them when you were here alone yesterday is back. We might have a leopard prowling around." He glanced uncertainly at Jim.

"Are leopards often a problem?" Jim asked, his old hunter's instinct piqued. What would it be like to hunt leopards out in that cavernous forest? How would he track anything across that leaf mat?

Umber walked over to the window just right of the door and peered out at the compound. She was making soft sounds.

"We get them on occasion." Meggan walked back to the table.

Brett had discovered a flat, odd-looking bat propped just inside the door. She picked it up and tested the heft. Jim could see the gleam in her softball player's eyes.

"Bradley," she said. "What is this?"

"Oh, that's a cricket bat. A few of us get together on Saturdays for an informal test." He grinned as he watched Brett lift the bat and test her grip. "Not bad. Have you played before?"

"No, but I've played a lot of softball and baseball."

"The principle's the same."

Bradley extended a hand to the bat. "Keep it for a while, if you like. And if you're still interested on Saturday, meet me in the cafeteria at eight o'clock sharp."

"Really?" Brett said, her mouth open. "You'll let me play?"

Bradley smiled. "Of course. We're all coed here."

Jim lifted his brows. Brett might not have as hard a time fitting in here as he'd thought. A ball team would truly be good for her. She'd meet people and be a part of things while he was trying to figure out how to get them home again.

"Wheep," Umber said, and her long arm flung out, pointing.

Jim stepped over, following her finger. There, at the forest edge, several black forms came shambling out of the leaves.

"Here are your apes." Jim placed his hands on Umber's soft muscular shoulders and watched them come. "Marvelous," he whispered. His heart skipped, a sudden surge of warmth in his veins. This was a dream come true! Just like the films, but here, he was seeing it live. In Africa. With real chimpanzees!

Brett ran over and crowded up next to him. "Awesome, Dad!"

"Better go and dump a load of food," Meggan said. "Oh, and Brad, keep an eye out. Something stole Umber's keyboard. If it turns up here, we'll know the culprit was one of ours."

Bradley stopped short. "That reminds me. You know, we locked up before we left last night. It looked like someone hacked at the padlock. The metal was nicked and the wood around it has been marred, as if with an ax or machete."

Meggan turned suddenly, and Jim's skin prickled at the expression on her freckled face. She didn't seem to be breathing. It lasted only a few seconds, then she smiled nervously, shoved red hair away from her eyes, and said, "I'll tell security. Meanwhile, go and feed."

"On my way." Cummings patted Brett's head as he passed by, and stepped out.

Meggan turned to Jim. "I was planning on driving you on over to Compound C, but would you like to stay for the feeding?"

"You bet your life," he said. "What do we do?"

"Follow me." Meggan led the way through the door and toward the cages. She said, "Don't look them in the eye if they come close. Don't run. Hold your ground, but act submissive. Hunch your shoulders, and by all means, keep yourself lower than they are. The final cardinal rule is, don't smile. Remember what Bradley said. Everything we think of as normal—walking forward, smiling, meeting their eyes—is an aggressive act in the chimp world."

"I knew that," Brett said airily. She gripped the bat with both hands, as if she'd just stepped up to the plate, and fell in behind Jim, swinging it back and forth.

"But would you have remembered?" Jim asked. "Knowing is one thing. Instinct is something else."

"Yeah, Dad." Brett watched as the apes continued to emerge from the forest. Unlike Umber, they knuckle-walked, their rolling gait balanced on long arms.

"What do you think, Umber?" Brett asked. "Do they look familiar?"

Umber lifted the first two fingers of her right hand to her eyes, brought the palm of her right hand down onto the back of her left hand—"see on"—and made the letters for TV.

"Magical," Jim whispered. "There is something wondrous about seeing a subject that you've taught, or worked with in zoos, come alive in its real environment." He turned to Meggan, who stood beside them, arms crossed as she watched the apes. "They're all chimps?"

She nodded. "Yes, these are all laboratory animals. They weren't born here, Dr. Dutton. They were born in cages all over the world. Because of the environment they were raised in, many of these animals are mentally stunted. They'll never leave the compound because they're not smart enough or emotionally stable enough to make it on their own. This is the cream of the crop right here. Many of the others are out hiding in the forest. When the dominant individuals are finished feeding, they'll come in one by one and scavenge the leavings."

"Why?" Brett asked.

"Because they don't have social skills." Meggan gestured to the side, pointing out a big solitary male. "We call him T-Rex. He's a burly guy, and when you make him mad, he goes completely berserk. He won't allow anyone near him." She pointed to a steel cage that stood behind the cabin. "T-Rex sleeps there. He was raised in a cage, by himself. It scarred him for life."

Umber tugged on Jim's sleeve, signed, and he translated, "Umber wants to know 'scarred how?'"

Meggan shook her head. "I can't really say. He developed abnormally. He can't function in any social situation. Not even the most rudimentary. I think he's quite mad, actually."

Meggan turned at the sound of a motor and Bradley appeared driving a small Toyota truck, the back heaped with plantains. He drove in a wide arc, the hydraulic system moaning as the bed tilted up and plantains slid off.

Just like feeding cattle on the ranch in the wintertime. Jim smiled at the similarity. And, like cattle, the apes came at a gallop, each stopping and sitting as they grabbed up the plantains and bit off the ends, chewing happily.

T-Rex remained to one side, watching, rocking nervously on his hands and feet.

Umber stepped toward the chimps, her hands moving, signing to herself the way humans talked to themselves in moments of excitement.

"Dad, look, a baby!" Brett used the cricket bat to point at a female, her infant hugged to her chest. The round-faced baby had big ears and a pink face.

"That must make you feel good," Jim said to Meggan.

She smiled. "It does at that. She's Molly, short for Molly Maguire, if you know your Irish history." Meggan shooed a fly. "She was one of the apes we were worried about. A complete misfit at first. Then, when she had the little one, it was as if the experience reordered her mind and she fit right in."

"How long do they stay here?" Jim watched as the line spaced out, some of the big males bunching together. "Dan said Compound B was the first stop."

"That's right. When they've learned enough of the wild foods, we pack them up and transport them to Compound C. We take as many animals as possible in one group at one time, since we don't want to disrupt the social structure of their band. At Compound C, we decrease the feed supplement and keep an eye on them. Sometimes that means a researcher has to go out in the bush with them on 'a follow,' just to keep track of how they are doing."

"Had much success?" Jim asked.

"That depends, Dr. Dutton, on the individual apes. The ones that aren't right psychologically, like T-Rex there, will never be able to fend for themselves. Some of the others, who weren't too badly damaged, reintroduce without much trouble. The normal ones are intelligent, adaptable, and flexible creatures."

The chimps continued to emerge from the trees and filter along the line of plantains, eating. Molly, Jim noticed, wasn't the only mother. "What about their social structure?"

Meggan gave her apes a knowing squint as she studied them. "Just what you'd expect of chimpanzees. Male-dominated, but without the sophistication of chimps in the wild. Here, leadership is more fluid; alliances shift rapidly. That is one of the things we've been trying to deal with. If we had a formal leader who could build a solid alliance, it would help group stability. As it is, the chimps are always wary, uncertain as to who is in charge."

"But you had a wild population in the compound when you started, didn't you?"

"We did. They control the land over on the other side of the mountain. This country here was mostly shot out by the local Fang. Part of coming here was to relocate the animals, another was to keep some of the resident population alive. Chimpanzee gene pools are shrinking all over Africa. I hope you have enough genetics training in your background to know just how significant that would be for the species."

"I do. Once a genotype is lost, it's gone forever."

One of the males walked over and screamed at one of the young mothers. She barked back, hair bristling, but dutifully gave way, holding her infant the entire time so as to keep her body between the infant and the aggressive male.

"Have you seen infanticide?" Jim asked.

"Infanticide!" Brett cried, turning. "Among chimps? I thought we were the only species to do that sort of thing."

"Here, infanticide only happens when a high-ranking male is displaced, killed, or driven from the group." Meggan studied Brett's reaction. "We think the male that steps into that alpha position kills his predecessor's offspring to bring the females back into estrus. Then he impregnates them, and they raise his offspring. If you understand natural selection, Brett, you can see where doing so has selective advantages."

"Gross," she said. "Bonobos are more civilized than chimps."

Umber uttered a low, strained, "Wheep," and lifted her hands to make the sign for "monster."

"I've forgotten my notebook," Meggan said and started back toward the cabin. "I won't be a minute."

"Can I come with you?" Jim asked. "I have a thousand questions."

"Of course, Dr. Dutton."

Meggan started forward, and Jim ran to catch up, leaving the girls behind. He asked, "Just what, exactly, are you planning for Umber? How is this supposed to work? Dr. Shanks was a little vague on that yesterday."

She gave him an uncertain look. "I'm not really sure yet, Dr. Dutton. Until I met Umber, I was thinking we'd treat her like all the rest. Leave her here, caged nightly and hand-fed. Then, one of my assistants would work with her. Take her out into the forest on a leash, show her the things she can eat and those she can't. At the same time, we would supplement here in the compound." She gestured at the line of feeding chimpanzees. "Many of the individuals in this group are about to be transported over to Compound C, maybe within the month. Then, we'd have introduced Umber to the new group coming in. She would learn with them, forge new social links, and finally help build that society. Then, in another year, they, too, would be shipped over to C."

"And?" Jim lifted an eyebrow, aware that he was at least getting an honest response from Meggan.

"Well, Dr. Dutton, I didn't expect a bonobo in a skull-decorated T-shirt and polka dot pants, carrying a computer and acting like a tourist." She shook her head. "Of course, I read the biographies on animals like Lucy and Washo, Bruno and Booee. Kanzi, too. But I didn't expect Umber to be so . . ."

Jim smiled. "American?"

"Yes, that's it." Meggan frowned. "This is going to be a bit difficult, I think. You're not in favor of this, I'm told."

"No more so than if I'd been told I had to make Brett go through it." Jim kicked at a banana peel. "I have no choice. SAC owns Umber. Her training will be voluntary, or compelled. Either way, it's going to happen, so I choose to cooperate." He took a deep breath. "If I do, it might make it easier on Umber."

Meggan stuck her hands in the back pockets of her brown

shorts and stared thoughtfully at the line of chimpanzees. In her soft Irish voice, she said, "It's not so bad, Dr. Dutton. I've come to like it here. Sometimes, I can't imagine being anywhere else. The land grows on you and so does the climate."

He stopped and turned to face her. "But, Meggan, we both know that you can go home and spend Christmas with your family. You're here because you want to be. If you decide to leave, you can. I'm betting that if I told you you were going to have to spend the rest of your life in the bush, no showers, no hotel rooms, no nice dinners in Bata or Evinayong, you'd change your mind in a hurry."

The corners of her eyes drew down, and she stepped silently into her cabin.

Twenty-eight

A mixture of fascination, intrigue, disgust, and pity whirled around inside Brett like a cyclone. These were Umber's kin, of sorts. Chimpanzees, not bonobos, to be sure, but still kin.

The feeding apes squatted on the dirt, smearing themselves with their food, pushing and shoving as they hooted at one another, or shrieked, or charged to browbeat their way through to the plantains.

What do I feel for them? The question seemed to stumble and fall, mired in her conflicting emotions. She had dreamed of this day, a mild sort of fantasy for late at night on the way to sleep back in her Fort Collins bed. She'd thought she might be the Jane Goodall of the twenty-first century, but here, faced with real chimps, she couldn't imagine spending her life working with them.

They want Umber to breed with these things? That notion seemed to stick sideways in her head. How on earth would Umber do it? Brett had seen pictures of chimps mating in Goodall's books, and in De Waal's book on bonobos. It didn't look appealing, especially when faced with one of these animals in the flesh.

"What do you think of them?" Brett asked as she laid a hand on Umber's shoulder. The sun had warmed the soft black hair.

Umber laid her hand, palm down, under her chin and wiggled her fingers, signing, "filthy," then "black bugs." She bared her teeth in distaste.

Brett studied the chimps. One of the babies had climbed up on his mother's shoulders, perching there while she finished eating. "But, Umber, you don't even know any of them yet."

Umber shook her head with bonobo flair and signed: "Ignorant. Don't talk." And to make her point, Umber tried to mimic chimpanzee pant-hoots and screams with her high-pitched bonobo voice. The only reaction she got was an intent stare from the closest chimps, who seemed curious, yet not curious enough to leave their meals.

"Yeah, well, I don't need to remind you, you didn't exactly fit in in Fort Collins, either," Brett said with a smile and tipped the cricket bat over her shoulder, watching Meggan and her father talk on the porch.

Umber elbowed Brett, and she turned back.

T-Rex had circled, his gaze on Umber.

She signed, "Look. Ugly. Stupid."

"Hey, lighten up. Meggan told us he was hurt. Locked in a cage. Come on, Umber. It was people that made him that way." She paused, inspecting T-Rex, watching his awkward swaying as he sidled closer to them. His eyes locked with Brett's and he jolted, as if electrically shocked. His lips pulled back to show stained teeth. It made his freckled face look worse. "But you're right. He sure is butt ugly."

T-Rex's hair bristled as he grabbed up a broken branch, squealed, and started forward, dragging his branch, slapping the ground with it.

Umber "whuffed!" and ran, but Brett stood watching, fascinated.

T-Rex lifted the branch over his head, and fear tingled up

from Brett's belly, rising to the top of her head. She started to back up.

T-Rex threw the branch down and charged like a freight train, screaming. Brett let out a cry. T-Rex hit her like a block of granite, knocking the bat from her hands and flattening her to the ground. Brett shrieked, *"Dad!"* just as she saw a black form fly over her head.

Umber crashed into T-Rex and slammed him to the ground. Screaming in a high-pitched voice, Umber clamped her hands around T-Rex's throat and shook him.

Brett scrambled away on her hands and knees, watching T-Rex thrash beneath Umber, and realized just how strong he was. *She caught him off guard, but he's stronger than Umber. He's going to throw her off and kill her!*

T-Rex had freed his arms, grabbed handfuls of Umber's shirt, and ripped it apart. As the cloth tore, Umber tightened her grip and savagely bit the side of his face. Her cries echoed across the forest.

Brett yelled, "Umber, let him go! He'll kill you!"

Umber didn't seem to be able to let go, probably out of fear that then he really would kill her. T-Rex solved the matter by simply flinging Umber off of him as if she were a rag doll. Umber's body thumped hard as she rolled.

T-Rex locked eyes with Brett, and the glazed madness reflected there paralyzed her. He bowled Brett over again, driving her down onto the ground. With one swipe, he batted her clawing hands away as though they were willowy wands. Yellow snapping teeth snagged a mouthful of Brett's T-shirt, and he pulled back, the material stretching.

Brett felt an impact through T-Rex's body, heard the hollow thump, followed by a pained grunt. T-Rex wavered. From the edge of her vision she saw Umber rise high, the cricket bat clutched in her hands.

Umber hammered him again, this time in the small of the

back. T-Rex rolled away across the grass, and Umber shrieked after him, slamming his legs and head with the bat. Desperate to escape, he charged off toward his cage, screaming.

Brett cried, "Umber, that's enough!" and got on her knees. Umber stopped short, and Brett saw that the chimps had gathered around them. She whispered, "Holy shit."

"Brett, don't move!" her father yelled as he came charging forward. Bradley was struggling to hold him back, shouting something.

The excited males bounced on their hands and feet, hair bristling black and shiny. They watched Brett with a weird light in their eyes, something she'd never seen before, and it frightened her. All it would take would be one wrong move, and they'd charge.

Brett started to stand, but Umber pushed her down, muttering a soft, warning "whuh."

Brett whispered, "Jeez, what should we do?"

In answer, Umber tightened her grip on the bat.

Meggan called: "Umber, Brett, back up slowly for the cabin. Do you hear me? *Slowly!*"

Brett got her feet beneath her, instinctively mimicking Umber's hunched stance. They backed away from the closing circle. Jim tore from Brad's and Meggan's grasp and ran toward his girls. The chimps broke and ran, retreating amidst loud hoots.

Jim got one arm around Brett, while Umber took his hand, her other one hefting the bat. Together they backed to the cabin, where Meggan and Brad waited.

"My God," Jim said as he set Brett on the ground and smoothed her hair back, checking her head and neck for injuries. "You could have been killed! What did you do?"

Brett could feel him shaking. He was pale, his legs wobbly, but so were her own.

"I . . . God, Dad, I don't know." Brett panted for air. "We were talking. Umber and me. And he was sneaking closer and closer to us. You know, like he was curious. Then, I looked at him, and he just ran at me."

Jim said, "Damn it, Brett. I told you not to look them in the eyes!"

She swallowed convulsively, wincing with guilt.

Umber handed the bat to Brett and tugged Jim's arm. Her pink lips worked as she put a finger beside Brett's blue eyes, tapped Brett's temple, and signed: "Scared ugly chimp."

Brett said, "You think my eyes scared him? Because they're blue?"

Jim glanced uneasily at the cage where T-Rex had buried himself under the ragged old blankets. "That could just be coincidence."

"Is everyone all right?" Meggan asked. Her face had flushed. "Brett, please, let me look you over. Did he bite you? If so, we'll need to treat it."

Brett poked her fingers through the holes in her T-shirt. Her blond hair lay in tangles where the braid had come loose. "No. I just hit the ground hard. But nothing worse than sliding into third base."

"Umber?" Jim asked and bent down, looking at Umber's shredded shirt. "Did he hurt you?"

Umber gave her head a hard shake. She pointed at T-Rex, made a fist with the thumb out, and touched the thumb to her chin. Then she turned the wrist to her left, and lifted her hand so that her thumb rested on the right side of her chin. She drew the thumb forward and ended with what non–ASL speakers would call a "thumbs-up" sign.

Jim chuckled in spite of himself and bowed his head.

"What's she saying?" Meggan asked.

Jim said, "Umber doesn't think T-Rex is going to be feeling so hot tomorrow. Maybe you'd better check on him."

"Yes, I will. But for now I think we had better get you back to the dormitory for fresh clothes. This is enough excitement for one day."

Brett ran her fingers down the polished wood of the cricket bat. Now that she and Umber were safe, jubilation was coursing through her veins. "Hey, Dad, I want one just like this," she said. "For when I become president."

He frowned at her. "You think there are big ugly chimps in the White House?"

Brett gave him a deadpan stare.

Jim nodded. "Okay. Right. But don't call me until after they've counted the electoral votes."

"Sure, Dad. If that's the way you want it."

"What can I tell you?" Don Amando shrugged. "Somehow she got a visa and permit with the vice president's signature on it. But Ms. Radin has not landed in either Malabo, or Bata on the mainland. Could it be that she is traveling by land?"

Godmoore watched him on the communications monitor, the round-faced African again smoothly shrugging. "She struck me as the kind of woman who would fly." Godmoore pressed his fingers against his temples. Another headache began to build behind his eyes.

"Don't know what to tell you, man," Don Amando said. "But, if you want me to issue an alert, close the borders, I can do that."

Godmoore clenched a fist. "Over the years, a great deal of money has been placed in your account, Don Amando. We have never been less than generous. Now, when I have urgent need of—"

Don Amando raised a hand. "Hey, man. This woman, she's going to your project, no?" He grinned, exposing a row of straight teeth. "Hey, look. I send a couple of my 'special' troops over there. So, like, Ms. Radin, she get off a plane in Malabo, or Bata, we got her. She show up in your project, your Dr. Mc-Dougal tells my sergeant, and he arrest her, bring her to me."

"You are sure that won't compromise the SAC preserve?"

"No problem, man." Don Amando leaned back, inspecting his fingernails. "Maybe she have visa trouble? Maybe press permit not in order? Who knows? Maybe her airplane disappears on the flight back to Malabo?" His grin returned. "Maybe Ms. Radin and her cameraman end up under the roots of cocoa tree, huh? You know, fertilizer?"

Godmoore sighed. "I'll see to it that she's allowed through the preserve gate. Your people can pick her up there." He paused. "Don Amando, please don't disappoint me."

Amando watched him with thoughtful eyes. "Not a problem. My sergeant and a couple of his men will leave tonight."

For some reason, the rains were holding off that day, and late-afternoon sunlight slanted through occasional holes in the clouds. Meggan parked the Kawasaki Mule at the trailhead and shut off the engine. She looked fondly over at Vernon Shanks, then locked the bridge key in its compartment. "All right, I've told you my adventure, what happened to you?" she asked.

Shanks reached into the back and grabbed up the canvas travel bag. He walked around the front of the Mule and hung a brightly colored piece of cloth on the pointed stick at the trailhead. Holding hands, they descended into the forest's cavernous shadows.

As they picked their way over the thick roots, he said, "The news piece from Texas was like a bomb. Godmoore's alternately furious, anxious, or frightened."

"Godmoore? Frightened?" Meggan laughed. "I can't imagine."

"You don't know the man, luv. He's afraid this whole thing

is going to come apart. It's the augmented apes that have him concerned. We can justify everything else. It's just that everything is piling up: the Dutton ape arriving here; the trouble in Texas; Alpha Group still missing; and some other things. On top of that, I find out today that that Triple N reporter, Radin, is supposedly on her way here. Shelly ordered me to tell security to pass her, and to have her report to me. Then I'm to inform Shelly immediately, and she'll handle it. Something about visa irregularities."

"And how did Shelly react to all this? She's Godmoore's soul mate when it comes to Little Hitler complexes."

"Like you'd expect: stoic, thoughtful, and bleeding tough." Shanks shook his head. "Shelly believes it will all pass."

"Will it?" Meggan asked. "I told you about the Dutton ape at the compound today. Vernon, she's not an ape. Oh, to be sure, she looks like an ape. But you didn't see her standing there, that cricket bat in her hand like a chieftain's shillelagh. And she didn't use the bat the way an ape would. Not only that, but her use of language is human."

"You've known about the augmented apes for a time now, Meg."

"But this is the first time I've been around one." She steeled herself and continued, "Vern, look, I know the project has decided to reintroduce Umber to the wild, but I don't think it's such a good idea. I think, if we pursue this, we're going to have a disaster on our hands, one way or another."

As the roar of the water grew louder, they picked their way down a steep slope, stepping on roots and rocks. Vernon helped her through a particularly steep spot. The rushing of the water was louder now. The late-afternoon light shone through patches in the canopy above. "It was your first day. Umber's, too. You will work it out."

"Maybe I ought to form the question this way: *Should* we be doing this?" Meggan asked rhetorically. She took the lead where the trail narrowed and stepped through a gap hacked in the brush at the stream's edge. "Vern, every day I deal with apes who were misused by human beings. The last time this was tried, it was with the Temerlin ape, Lucy. Remember? She was killed by poachers because she thought all humans were friends. She walked right up to her murderers with her arms out."

They stepped from boulder to boulder, each water-rounded and polished. Turning a bend, they came upon the waterfall. Streamers cascaded down for nearly two hundred feet to hiss into a clear pool. Mist rose on the hot air, adding to the humidity. On a section of rocky beach, Vernon dropped the bag and pulled his shirt over his head.

"Faith," Meggan said. "After today, I needed to come here." She peeled her dirty white shirt off, unhooked her bra, and sat down to unlace her hiking boots. "What do you think of Dutton?"

"I like him." Vernon kicked his shoes off and undid his trousers. When he'd stepped out of them, he took off his Rolex, setting it atop his shirt. He smiled as Meg peeled out of her shorts and panties. What was it about watching a woman undress that excited a man so? One by one, she removed her gold earrings and placed them on one of the rocks.

She reached for his hand and they waded out into the warm water. Vernon dove when they reached thigh depth, and Meg followed. She surfaced, blew, and wrung out her red hair. "I like him, too," she added. "And he really cares for his ape. Umber is like a daughter to him. You should have seen him. I couldn't tell which daughter he was more worried about."

"Meg." Vernon paddled over to her. "We've got to make this work. Godmoore as much as ordered it."

She splashed, settled on her back, and tried to float. The water soothed her, but Vernon could tell it didn't lessen the worry chewing about the edges of her consciousness. "If we do, Vernon, I'm afraid we might destroy them all."

"We've got our marching orders." His voice was muffled through the water.

She sat up. "Something odd happened today. At the lookout tree. Umber left her computer at the foot of the tree. When we came down, it was gone. Stolen."

"One of the workers?"

"I don't know." Meg frowned. "Umber said something that didn't make sense. She said that she'd seen a blue-eyed ape. That T-Rex went berserk because he looked into Brett's big blue eyes . . ."

Shanks came bolt upright out of the water, fear surging like fire through his veins.

"Vernon? What's wrong?"

"A blue-eyed ape?"

"Yes. Now surely we're not talking fairies and leprechauns here."

"At the lookout tree?"

"Aye." Meg cocked her head. "Vernon, you're not going to tell me we've blue-eyed apes here."

"No," he said seriously. "At least we're not supposed to have them in Compound B. Come on, we're leaving."

"Vernon, you're daft. We just got here. I'm going to soak, and then I'd planned on dragging you over to the beach."

"Meg." He sloshed toward the shallows. "I'm serious. The lookout tree isn't that far . . ."

She twisted around in the water, rising to her feet. She had decided she knew exactly how to change his mind about leaving. Something about the effect a female hand had on a man when it wrapped around his male parts. She'd used that tactic on him before when he thought he was in a rush. She slogged toward him.

He was standing stock-still, water dripping off his lean body, his attention fixed on the shore. The rigid way he stood made her stop.

For the moment, her mind failed to register. Immediately, she thought that Umber had followed them, but there were two, then three, and finally a fourth. None of these apes wore clothing, but each carried a rust-stained machete.

The big male had piercing blue eyes. No. No, they were insane eyes. Wild. Enraged. He made a sign with his hands.

"Dear God in heaven," Meggan whispered. "Where did they come from?"

"I think we're in trouble," Vernon whispered. "Bad trouble."

The apes flashed their hands at each other and uttered high-pitched birdlike chirps.

Then the blue-eyed male made a clear gesture for Meg and Vernon to leave the pond.

Shanks wet his lips and whispered, "Listen to me, Meg, I want you to run. If I don't make it to the trailhead, get the hell out of here. Get back to Shelly, and tell her *the Alpha Group has escaped from Compound D.* Got that?"

"Yes, but what—"

"Run!" Vernon shoved her toward the opposite side of the pool and bulled through the water toward the waiting apes.

The apes broke into a frenzy, running around wildly, flinging rocks and branches, squealing.

Meggan dashed through the knee-deep water, heading for the trail that would take her to the Kawasaki.

Vernon screamed.

Panicked, she cried, "Vernon!" The water dragged at her feet as she spun around.

They leaped for her, two of them, knocking her back.

Meggan writhed against the hairy hands that shoved her under the water. Through the shining veil, she could see the apes hooting. Then, the image flickering in the wash of the waves, one raised a rusted brown machete high. Meggan was rising, her head just breaking water as it slashed downward.

Twenty-nine

As Jim chewed a chicken thigh at the cafeteria table, he studied his girls and the other diners lingering over their supper trays. The topic of everyone's conversation was the meaning of the Triple N newscast, and the apparent concern of the administrators.

People trickled by the table, introducing themselves, all obviously interested in Umber. Jim couldn't remember half of their names; only Dr. Marcus Yamasaki stood out, partly because Jim knew he needed to be on a first-name basis with the preserve's senior medical man—especially if his girls were going to go around picking fights with burly male chimps.

"Well." Jim washed the spicy chicken down with a gulp of coffee. The brew was locally grown, called "robusta," and bitter. "This has been quite a first day. If you hadn't latched onto that bat, Brett, you might not be sitting here right now."

Umber grunted an assent and patted Brett on the shoulder. Umber had ruefully discarded her mangled skull T-shirt for a bright yellow one that prominently stated: "Ski Vail," just the sort of thing for a tropical rain forest. Umber's long fingers signed: "Nasty ugly animal."

Jim rubbed his face. "Now you understand just how dangerous these apes are." Foreboding twisted Jim's gut, upsetting his digestion. "Let's talk about our game plan. Meggan said that tomorrow we're going back to Compound B and Umber is going to start learning plants. We're all going to do it. Together. What Umber tries, Brett, you and I will try."

"And then what?" Brett asked.

"Once we prove that Umber isn't capable of going back to the wild, then we'll make a counterproposal," Jim insisted. "We offer to take Umber home and continue the research on her development and education." He took a deep breath. "But I want you to prepare yourselves. There might be a catch."

"What catch?" Brett said through a mouthful of chicken. Her blue eyes glittered.

"Umber might have to have a baby."

Umber made the signs for "Umber won't," then pressed the first two fingers of her right hand into the palm of her left hand and twisted. She finished that with a final "whew!" to make her point.

Jim gave her a level stare. "That was crude, Umber. Who taught you to use that word like that?" He blinked and slowly turned to pin Brett with steely eyes.

"Oh, be real, Dad," Brett said as she gnawed the last meat from the chicken leg. "I didn't teach her the F word, did I?"

Jim sat back in his chair and pulled his coffee cup toward him. He stared at Brett until she got nervous and said, "Okay, Dad, I'm sorry, all right? I won't teach her anything else useful."

He shoved his plate away. "I'll believe it when I see it. Anyway, there are other ways to get pregnant than . . ." He put the first two fingers of his right hand into his left palm and twisted. "Do you remember Shanks talking about artificial insemination?"

Brett cried, "What do they think Umber is? A goddamned cow!"

He lowered his brows, meeting Brett's violent blue eyes with his own. "Yes. They do. What are you going to do about it? Let's hear it. What's the way out of this?"

Brett threw down her chicken leg and said, "I don't know, but it's not *right!*"

"No, it's not. But our first priority is getting Umber home. If Umber has to have a child to do that, she'll have a child. At least she'll have it with us, and not in some cage somewhere."

Umber's lips curled into a pout, and she lowered her hands to finger the edge of the table.

"I'm sorry, Umber." Jim's heart ached at her expression. "But you have to hear the truth. They've invested heavily in your genetics. They're going to want to see if you can reproduce."

"It's goddamned slavery," Brett said and folded her arms over her chest.

Jim tossed off the last of his coffee. He could see depression settling over Umber like a black blanket. "Hey, guys, we're not licked yet. We'll get through this. Show some faith in the old man, okay?"

Umber made a soft sound and hung her head.

Jim said gently, "Are you all right?"

Her fingers formed the letters N-O.

"She doesn't want to have babies, Dad!" Brett thumped the table. "And she doesn't want to go slum with the street gangs in the forest!"

The black hairs on Umber's upper lip quivered. She signed, "Something bad in forest."

"Got that right," Brett agreed.

"Your blue-eyed ape?" Jim asked. "Probably just the shadows playing tricks on you. Meggan's never heard of a blue-eyed ape, and she knows them all."

Umber's fingers made the letters N-O again. Then she repeated them.

He lifted his hands. "Look, kids, for the time being, we have to pretend we're cooperating."

"There are cobras, leopards, and green mambas out there, Dad." Brett leaned forward in her chair and gave Jim a hard stare. "I want to go home."

Umber gazed at Jim imploringly.

"Soon, Umber. I'm really trying. You know that, don't you?"

She nodded, but pointed to herself, heaved a sigh, and made the sign for "scared, scared."

Jim reached across the table to take Umber's warm hand. "Everything's frightening when it's new and strange. Maybe we'll have Meggan take us on a long hike, or a camping trip. Something to give us an idea of what it's like to live with the forest."

Then he rose from his chair, and Brett and Umber gathered their trays and followed him to the dishwasher conveyor belt. As they filed out, they waved to some of their new acquaintances. Umber was talking to herself, signing: "Don't want to walk in forest. Bad. Bad chimp there."

They stepped out into the warm, muggy evening and saw a muddy Toyota Land Cruiser whining its way down the hard-packed dirt road. The vehicle rattled to a stop about fifty feet from the cafeteria.

The rear doors were tied closed with a rope to accommodate oversized luggage. Jim could see mud-spattered cases protruding. The black driver was peering wide-eyed at the SAC compound as if he'd just driven into hell. The passenger door opened, and a mustached white man in mud-splotched khaki stepped out, wincing and stretching his back. He leaned his seat forward and helped a blond woman to the ground. She, too, was dressed in khaki, her clothes crusted with red mud. They walked around to the rear, untied the rope, and lifted out the heavy cases.

The woman counted out bills to pay the driver. The Fang man nodded, smiled, then pocketed the money, took out a gasoline can, and dumped it into the fuel filler. After closing the rear, he ran back for the driver's seat. The worn starter motor groaned and screeched before the Toyota coughed to life. He cut a tight turn, waved, and hurried back the way he'd come. A plume of blue smoke rose from the tailpipe.

"Now that," Jim said, "looks like the end of a really tough trip." He started down the walk, holding Umber's hand in his. Brett followed along behind, casting curious glances at the pair as they took stock of their baggage. To Jim, they looked like newcomers. The man saw Jim, poked his companion, and pointed. The woman glanced at Jim and Umber, grabbed up a case, and started in their direction, calling, "Excuse me. Sir, a moment please?"

Jim hesitated, something clicking deep in his memory. He stopped short, blood rushing in his veins. He knew that purposeful stride, that set of the shoulders. He shook his head. No, it was absurd. A trick played by his imagination.

Then her familiar blue eyes met his and widened in shocked surprise. Her steps faltered.

Dear God, she was still beautiful. Perfect cheekbones, full lips, straight nose, and lapis eyes. The spitting image of Brett. Jim's heart pounded, and the world seemed to drift. He'd dreamed this moment, but it had been in the United States, in a setting he controlled. Now, all he could feel was a desperate need to turn and run.

He stood there, separated from her by no more than five feet. The years began to peel back, leaving the wound raw in Jim's soul.

He found his voice. "Hello, Valerie. I didn't expect to see you here."

It took her two tries before she managed, "J-Jim."

"It's been a long time." He could feel the heat rising in his face. He fidgeted and realized that Umber was trying to tug her hand from his crushing grip.

Jim let her go and turned. Brett might have been made of

wood. Her eyes were wide, her lips parted, her blanched expression a mask of fear and disbelief.

He put a steadying hand on Brett's back. "Valerie," he said, "I'd like you to meet your daughter. Brettany, this is your mother."

Thirty

Jim saw the color drain from Valerie's face as she stared at her daughter. Scared, scared stiff.

"Hello," Brett barely whispered. She looked like she might be sick.

"Hello, Brett." Valerie swallowed hard and tried to smile, then looked down at Umber, struggling to keep her expression under control. "And who is this?"

Umber signed that she was Brett's sister and walked forward, extending her hand to Valerie.

Jim said, "This is Umber, Valerie."

Valerie reached out and tentatively shook Umber's hand, the action forced and unnatural.

"Hey, Fuerta," the man called, walking up behind Valerie with a hard-sided case hanging from his hand. "Do we want background now, before they throw us out, or take a chance . . ." He slowed, seeing Valerie's rigid posture, then looked at Brett, and startled recognition filled his eyes. He muttered, *"Madre de Dios."*

The man's voice seemed to penetrate Valerie's shock. She straightened, arching her back, recovering the poise that Jim remembered so well.

"Well," she said, "this is a surprise."

The little voice inside Jim's head said, *Excuse yourself, take your daughters, and leave her the way she left you.*

She seemed to read his mind, as she always had. She took a step backward, and he could see that she was shaking. "Jim, I—I know . . ."

"No, Valerie, you don't." He walked forward, took her in his arms, and hugged her close. The stiffness in her body melted, and her arms tightened around his waist.

He hadn't expected to feel his heart swell as if it would burst through his ribs. "God, it's good to see you," he said. "What on earth are you doing here?"

Like the Valerie of old, she bounced back fast; her misty eyes cleared. She gave him that familiar devilish smile. "Following the story." She turned and stepped away from him. "Jim, this is my cameraman, Roberto Naez." Then she turned to Brett, standing, ashen-faced, and clutching Umber's hand in a death grip. "And Roberto—this is Brett."

Roberto shook hands all around. When he offered his hand to Brett, she barely took it, her unfocused gaze on her mother. Brettany had never looked so unsure of herself.

Umber, too, just stared.

"Well," Jim said with a smile, "why don't we all go inside and . . . and talk. Val, I thought you were in England."

She nodded. "Richard Godmoore told us to come visit the preserve. Jim, what the hell is going on here?" She looked at Umber. "What's with these augmented apes? Is he like Kivu?"

Umber shook her head so hard her ears flapped.

"She," Jim corrected. "Umber is a she."

"I'm sorry, Umber." Valerie seemed positively contrite, and doing everything she could to keep from meeting Brett's intense gaze.

Things were turning awkward. He could see Valerie's panic growing and said, "Have you eaten? Where are you staying?"

Valerie shrugged and glanced uneasily at Roberto. "We just got here. The driver said he had to get back before the rains. That if he didn't, he'd lose his truck in a stream crossing." She slapped at the mud on her khaki trousers. "If this is a drought, I'd hate to see it flood. But more to the point, we had MREs about sixty mud holes back. That would have been about noon. I haven't any idea where we're staying. The guards at the gate told us to see someone named Shanks immediately."

Jim turned. "Brett, would you and Umber please go back to the cafeteria and get Valerie and Roberto a couple of box dinners? Then maybe you could help carry their things up to our room."

"Our room?" Brett turned anxiety-bright eyes on him.

"Well, we can't just leave their cases sitting in the street. And Lord alone knows where Dr. Shanks is. He'd have left the administration building by now. We'll run him down later and find out where Valerie and Roberto are supposed to stay."

"Jim, I don't think you want to do that," Valerie said, placing a hand on his arm. It sent a warm tingle through him. "We may not be the most welcome of guests here. It could cost you."

She was right, of course. He already had a dicey relationship with SAC, but some part of his soul wanted to protect her the way it had all those years ago. "Val, what's your angle here? Whose side are you on? Are you here for the apes, or against them?"

She said, "What's the truth, Jim? That's my angle. Who did what to whom. That's what I want to know." An elegant eyebrow lifted. "Even if it means bringing your SAC friends to the mat."

Brett's face had become a mask of conflicting emotions.

Roberto seemed to sense it; he stepped up and placed a friendly hand on Brett's shoulder. "Hey, I'll go with you. You can show me how this place works, and I can grab the heavy crates, huh?" He gently led Brett back toward the door, with Umber still clutching her hand.

When they were out of hearing, Valerie seemed to shrink, looking suddenly older, frail. "God, I made a mess of that."

Jim shrugged. "Not as bad as you think. Just to set the tone for this discussion, I don't blame you for anything, Val. You did what you had to do. I stood behind you then, and I do now. All right?"

She tipped her head toward Brett's retreating back. "But she doesn't."

"She watches you on TV every night, and I'm sure she repeats a mantra of 'what ifs.' You'll have to make your own way with Brett."

Valerie smoothed blond hair away from her beautiful face. "Jim, back there. I saw it in your eyes. You wanted to hurt me, but you hugged me instead. Why?"

He sighed and looked up at the tropical sky. "Oh, a lot of reasons. Over the years I've thought us up and down, in and out, and back and forth. I've dwelt on all the things I did wrong. Thirteen years ago I tried to trap you, and I shouldn't have. I've always regretted it. So, I hugged you. My way of apologizing." He gave her a sidelong look and smiled. "I also did it because down deep I really wanted to."

"God, Jim," she said sadly. "You always were a saint." Then her face fell. "Does she hate me?"

"No," he replied and shoved his hands into his shorts pockets. "It's much worse than that. I think she loves you clear down to the bottom of her soul."

Terror returned to her eyes.

Brett walked in a daze. A thousand dreams spun over most of her life had just been shredded in the grinding jaws of reality. *That was her. It was really her!*

That image of her father stepping into Valerie's arms, hugging her to him, and the tears springing out of Valerie's eyes . . . Real, all of it was real, and yet unreal. The Valerie of dreams was the steely-eyed reporter from the TV. Not this mud-smeared woman in wrinkled bush clothing. And the real Valerie wouldn't have stared at Brett with that look of fear. She would have marched up, taken her measure, and said, "You've done well for yourself, kid."

As they pushed through the door into the foyer, Umber signed: "All right, Brett?"

"Yeah, I'm all right." She straight-armed the cafeteria door, bursting into the room, unsure whether she wanted to break down and cry or throw things and scream. But the man was following just behind them, adding to the straitjacket that seemed to suffocate her.

She walked up to the glass counter with its railing and waved until she got one of the cooks' attention. "We'd like two box lunches, please. Lots of chicken." She pointed. "And could you drown it in that red sauce?" When he poured a spoonful over the chicken, Brett said, "Oh, more than that. Maybe another spoonful. That's right."

Umber cast her a glance and signed: "Careful."

Brett signed back: "SHUT UP." Aloud, she said, "And some of that cassava and malanga. Oh, and some yams, too, please."

When they had the boxes, Brett directed Umber to grab four cans of soda. The guy that ran the computer charged the meals to the Dutton account, and Roberto took one of the boxes.

Just doing something had eased Brett's staggering emotions. As they left the cafeteria, she glanced around and didn't see her parents anywhere. Brett looked at Roberto. "So, are you, like, married to my mother?"

Roberto shook his head. "No, chica. That would take a braver man than me. And I'm not her boyfriend either, okay?" He laughed. "What a reunion! I have to hand it to you, in all these years, I've never seen her so close to breaking down and crying."

"She did cry," Brett insisted. "When Dad hugged her."

"Yeah, she did." He cocked his head. "You know, your dad is just all right. Took a lot of class and guts to meet her that way." He peered down at Brett. "And how about you? I been wondering about you for a lot of years, wondering what you were like."

"How did you know about me?" Brett asked. Umber squeezed Brett's hand, and she glanced down into those soft brown eyes. "Stop it," she hissed, "I'm all right." And she was, she discovered.

"She talks a lot about you," Roberto said. "So, over the years I been wondering if you were like her."

"Yeah? What do you think?"

He grinned and tucked his box lunch under his arm. "I think you're a lot like her. Strong, smart, and savvy. *Muy machisma.*"

"Is that right?" Brett glanced at Umber to see how she was taking it. Umber's oversolicitous gaze was nearly liquid with worry.

"That's right." Roberto chuckled.

It was the way Roberto moved, half dancing as he talked, the sparkle in his brown eyes, that broke down Brett's defenses. She decided Roberto was probably all right.

They stopped at four heavy crates. Brett placed the box lunch on one and lifted, grunting as she picked it up. "Might be two trips."

Umber hoisted the biggest one easily. Maybe she felt better showing off like that after T-Rex had manhandled her.

They crossed to the dormitory, climbed the stairs, and opened the room door. Brett could hear the subdued voices of her mother and father in the adjoining room. *Mother and father.* Startled, she realized that she had never used those words in that combination before. Her belly tightened again.

"Come on," she said to Umber, "let's go get the last of the cases. After your keyboard, we don't know what might get stolen around here."

To her surprise, Roberto followed her back through the door. "Umber and me, we can get the last two."

"Naw." Roberto waved her away. "One is deceptively heavy."

Umber made a muscle, showed a row of white teeth, and signed: "We beat up ugly chimp today. Can carry box." Brett laughed at that, partly in relief.

"Umber," Roberto said, "you're gonna have to teach me that sign language. You do that, and I'll teach you border Mexican. *Que no?*"

"Wheep!"

"That's yes," Brett translated. "And now she's saying that even asking to learn makes you smarter than a lot of these SAC people."

Umber grinned up at Roberto and took his hand.

Roberto squeezed her long black fingers, studying them with an awed curiosity, as if fascinated by their feel. People started drifting out of the cafeteria, scientists mostly. Roberto watched them, apparently in no hurry. He patted Umber's hand and sat down on one of the boxes, watching the sky change. "Ah, evening on the equator."

"Don't you want to get these things up to the room?" Brett indicated the boxes.

"Nope." He patted the other box next to him. "Sit, Fuertita. You, too, Umber. Look up at the sky, listen to the sounds of the forest. Enjoy a moment of peace."

Brett and Umber clambered onto the box, looking curiously at each other. Brett said, "Yeah, okay. You're stalling. I know why."

"Yeah, man." Roberto grinned. "You see, I figure it like this. Your dad and Val, they got about thirteen years to smooth out"—he made a flattening motion with his two hands—"be-

tween them, right? Why don't we just give them a while before we go barge in on them with all kinds of rush?"

Brett slapped a mosquito. "You taking your malaria drugs,
Roberto?"

"Yeah, but I've already had it. Laid me out for a solid month
in Bangladesh." He stood, fished out a key from his pants, and
opened one of the trunks. Brett craned her neck to see all kinds
of odd-looking gear, some with digital readouts, coils of cables,
and funny-looking flashlights.

Roberto found a spray can, popped off the lid, and sprayed
his arms, and then Brett's. "Bug spray. Umber, you want some?"

"Wheep." She extended her arms and allowed Roberto to
shoot the fine mist onto her.

"She doesn't usually like strangers," Brett said and watched
Umber's fingers moving.

"What did she say?" Roberto replaced the bug spray and re-
seated himself on the crate.

Brett cocked her head. "She said she likes you. That you
take horrible pictures."

"Oh, man," he said, dejected, "and she doesn't even know
me."

Umber slapped Brett's leg, and Brett laughed. "Uh, sorry,
Roberto. I guess I didn't translate that very well. Umber meant
that you take pictures of horrible things, like wars and plagues
and stuff." Brett studied Umber's hands and translated for
Roberto, "Umber wants to know if you have bad dreams later?"

"Yeah, I do. Nobody's ever asked me that before." He gave
Umber a careful inspection. "You're cool, Umber. I think I'm
going to like you. How do I say that in signs?" He offered his
hands, and to Brett's amazement, it was Umber who helped
him form the right gestures.

"Awesome!" Roberto grinned. Out in the forest one of the
night birds uttered a low whistling shriek. "Well, maybe we

better lug this stuff up, huh? You'd hurt your mom's feelings if you stayed away too long."

"Hurt *her*? She never even sent me a card!"

Umber shifted nervously, suddenly very interested in the palms of her hands.

Roberto kicked at the packed dirt. "Yeah, I know. I guess you just scare the living shit outta her, Fuertita."

"What's that mean, Fooerteeta?"

"It's Mexican. Means tough little girl." He grinned, his teeth shining under the bandido mustache. "Sometime, after you decide that you don't want to kill her, ask her about that picture she's got in her purse. And remember, Brett, someday you're gonna face something that really scares you, too."

With that, he stood, lifted one of the heavy aluminum-bound crates, and threw it over his shoulder. "Come on, amigas, let's go see how the grown-ups are doing."

Brett took one handle of the last crate while Umber took the other. As they struggled toward the dormitory, Brett wondered, *How could she be scared of me?*

Thirty-one

Inside the locked administration building, Shelly McDougal strode purposefully for the communications room with its computers, monitors, and consoles. She was due to communicate with Godmoore at 19:00 hours.

While Shelly was a tolerably good scientist, her true passion was to be in charge. Eventually, when the ape project was finally revealed to the world, the cameras would be coming to her. She would be the one in the spotlight.

Now, however, the entire venture was somehow going astray. Rumors were starting to circulate about the missing Mitu Bagawli, Alpha Group over in D, and the arrival of the famous Triple N news reporter. That very afternoon, ten minutes after Shanks disappeared to boff his Irish dolly, a shaken Hinsinger had called to report that yet another leg had been found—this one from an ape.

McDougal seated herself in front of the monitor and pressed the key that would connect her with far-off Sussex.

Godmoore's face formed on the monitor. Instead of the usual coldly precise stare, haggard and hooded eyes met hers. The impression was that he hadn't slept in days.

"What is your situation?" he asked without preamble.

She gave her report carefully and concisely. When she finished, Godmoore frowned. "Have you seen the evening news?"

"No, sir."

"Triple N has obtained a detailed map of the ape preserve." His lip quivered, and he said, "Compound D was plainly visible."

"Such a leak did *not* come from *my* people. I—"

"Yes, yes. I know you would never have let this happen." The faintest trace of ironic humor vanished. "No, the leak came from here. Don't worry, I'll discover who. In the meantime, I have finally managed to convince Geoffrey to fly down there. His ETA is around 21:50 hours this evening. I want you to meet him. Give Geoffrey a project, some problem to keep him occupied and away from the cameras. Do you understand? I can't allow him to be interviewed. God alone knows what that lunatic would say to the press."

McDougal's lips twitched.

Godmoore continued, "Don Amando is sending a team to pick up the Radin woman and her cameraman. I want their extraction handled discreetly. She's to be arrested and removed without incident." He paused, voice dropping. "Is that *understood*?"

It took a moment for his meaning to sink in. Shelly started, suddenly aware of the beaded perspiration on his pale skin, visible even on the monitor. "Aye," she whispered softly, her heart beginning to pound.

"And I want this situation in Compound D eradicated, neatly, cleanly, and quickly. When the world descends on our little ape preserve, I want them to discover only one thing: dedicated SAC personnel working to habituate abused apes to the forest. See to it personally, or I'll find someone who can."

"What if something should—"

"*Use whatever means are necessary.* I don't have the luxury of holding your hand, Shelly. Don Amando will provide any backup you need." He leaned forward and lowered his voice. "If you are not up to this, tell me now."

Shelly McDougal sat frozen. Violent and bloody visions formed behind her unfocused blue eyes. As if in a trance, she said, "I'm up to it, Richard."

"And wait 'til you meet Dr. McDougal," Jim said to Valerie as they walked down the long white dormitory hall in search of Vernon Shanks. "Shelly is a real tyrannosaurus. She never goes off duty."

He had offered the shower, and both Valerie and Roberto had gratefully taken the opportunity. Now, Valerie looked professional and refreshed.

"Excuse me," Jim called as a young man stepped out of one of the ground-floor apartments. "We're looking for Dr. Shanks."

The young man looked at Valerie and smiled slightly, as if he knew her. "Come to think of it, I saw him take off in one of the Mules with Meg at about five."

"How about Dr. Aberly?"

"He flew out on the plane yesterday, bound for Sussex."

Jim considered seeking out Shelly McDougal, then checked his watch and decided against it. "Val, it's almost nine. Tell you what. We'll chase Shanks down in the morning. Why don't you and Roberto take the kids' room." He paused, flushed at the implications, and added, "Or he, uh . . . I mean, I assume . . ."

She laughed nervously, and he caught himself marveling at the smooth lines of her throat. When she met his eyes, he thought he'd drown in those cool blue depths. That was one of the best things about Valerie, the color of her eyes, almost a cerulean.

"Jim, Roberto and I have slept on airplanes, in buses, in trucks, in foxholes, in bunkers, in waiting rooms, and just about everywhere else. He's my best friend . . . not my lover." She gestured with a graceful hand. "Hell, he knows every single one of my sins, shortcomings, faults, and failures. The wonder of it is that he still works with me of his own free will."

"I wasn't prying." He tried to backtrack as he started up the corridor. "I thought you might want to spend time with your daughter."

"Oh . . ." she said softly. "No, I—I think Taco and I can share a room. It might be better that way. For now."

"Scared of Brett?"

"Did you see that look she gave me while I was devouring dinner? I've seen murderers give their executioners kinder looks while they were being strapped into the electric chair. Hey, speaking of dinner, that was pretty good. Do they normally drown chicken in that much hot sauce?"

Jim grimaced at the white linoleum floor. "Actually, I think Brett and Umber did that to you. You were supposed to gag, grab your throat, and run screaming for the bathroom sink. Believe me, you made points by not even breaking a sweat."

Valerie stopped on the stairs. She lifted her hand, studied the palm with a frown, then gently placed it on Jim's arm. "I'm not very good at this, but somehow I have to figure out a way to let you know that you've done all right with her. She's a good kid. Smart."

He looked down at her slender tanned fingers, knowing it must be hard for her to touch him after the way she'd treated him the last time they'd seen each other. He patted her hand and leaned back against the railing. "I think it's been an accident of convenience that I haven't throttled her yet. When she gets into one of her moods, she'll make trouble in the most innovative and ingenious ways."

Two frown lines formed above Valerie's eyes. "She and Umber, God, they're like sisters."

"They *are* sisters." He resumed the climb.

"Jim, about these SAC apes." Valerie followed a step behind him. "Is Umber typical? I mean, I've seen film of Kivu, but I wasn't expecting such unique behavior."

"You mean human."

"Yes. Is Kivu as good as Umber at dealing with people?"

He stopped her on the third-floor landing, glancing back down the steps to ensure they were alone. He braced his hands on the railing. "How much have you talked to Tory?"

"Just on the phone. I put her onto Kivu, set her up with our regional reporter."

He considered picking his words, and then opted for the unvarnished truth. "Val, Shanna Bartlett wasn't what you'd call psychologically stable. I can't tell you what kind of reaction you'll get out of Kivu if you stress him out. I don't even know what Umber will do if she's pushed too far. Christ, she and Brett got in a fight with a psyched-out male chimp today. He attacked them, and they beat the hell out of him. We're in uncharted waters here, dealing with creatures who are just reaching an age where their true potential is starting to manifest itself."

"Jim, Kivu *killed* a man."

"I know. I saw your report." He wet his lips, remembering the sound of Parnell's voice when he'd suggested that Jim might not want to see anything bad happen to Dana or Brett. His grip tightened on the railing. "The guy Kivu killed, Parnell, you'd have killed him yourself if you'd seen the way he looked at your daughter. The guy was a psychopath. I'm convinced he threatened Shanna sexually, and Kivu took him."

Jim smoothed his beard and glanced uncertainly at Valerie. "Quid pro quo. How come you're mixed up in this? Is it because of me?"

"Yes, though I didn't know it at the time. In the past few years I've been trying to use my position in journalism to help victims. Mostly, I've done well. From what I could figure out,

Kivu seemed like a victim." She turned hard blue eyes on him. "You tell me, is he?"

"I don't know Kivu, Val. But Umber is a victim. She wants to be home with the people she loves. Instead she's here in a preposterous 'reintroduction to the wild' program." He balled his fists, then sighed. "Come on, let's go kick the girls out of their room."

Valerie led the way down the hall. Jim followed, acutely conscious of the sway of her hips, her straight posture, and the way the lights gleamed in her hair. She'd weathered the years well. She still had the ability to mesmerize him.

Jim shook his head. *One problem at a time.*

At breakfast, some of the staff dropped by the table to introduce themselves to the famous Valerie Radin.

When Jim took his tray to the conveyor belt, a white-coated Dr. Yamasaki just happened to meet him there. He jerked his head toward Valerie. "What does she want here?"

"She's doing a story on the apes, Marcus. This is just a suggestion, of course, but if she got a little cooperation from you, and everybody else, she could probably turn this thing around for us." Jim turned toward Valerie. She sat at the table, allowing Umber to form her hand into the fingers-from-lips sign to say "thank you."

Yamasaki nodded. "I see what you mean."

Jim checked his watch. "I've got half an hour to find her a room and make it to my rendezvous with Meggan."

Yamasaki gave him a startled look. "Meggan? She and Shanks are still out in the bush. They went for a drive and didn't make it back last night. They normally have breakfast with the department heads. They probably spent the night in one of the cabins up at B. I'm sure if they'd had trouble, they would have radioed in."

"Yeah, Meggan will probably meet me on time." Jim nodded and walked back to the table, seating himself.

Umber lifted her head, and her brows wiggled in a frown. For today's adventure she wore a red T-shirt, purple shorts, and moccasins. She signed, "What's wrong?"

"Probably nothing. Meggan and Shanks weren't in the compound last night."

He glanced at Brett. She'd been quiet all morning, carefully avoiding Valerie's eyes, her expression dour. Her face looked almost as white as her tank top. After yesterday's battle, she'd chosen to wear jeans again—probably to protect herself in case another ape decided to roll her through the brush. "Come on, guys, let's go over to administration and make sure that Val and Roberto get a room."

Jim led the way out of the building. Dark rain clouds drifted across the skies, and the air had a heavy feel.

Inside the administration building door, a young black woman seated behind a polished aluminum desk told them, "Dr. McDougal is in conference on the satellite link and can't be disturbed."

"Well, who can assign rooms? Miss Radin and Mr. Naez need a place to sleep."

Reluctantly, she pulled a loose-leaf binder from her desk. "I'll assign them a suite on the third floor, but be aware that no assignment is final until approved by Dr. McDougal."

"Of course," Valerie said. "Thank you."

The woman searched her drawer until she found the right keys, then handed them to Valerie.

As they stepped out the door, Jim saw Brett grit her teeth, as if enduring something painful.

Valerie checked the suite. The place had a foldout couch, a TV, two stuffed chairs, a desk, and a wet bar. The bedroom was furnished with a dresser, chair, and one double bed. The bathroom consisted of a sink, toilet, and tub with shower.

"Not bad," Roberto declared as he, Jim, Brett, and Umber carried the last of the travel cases into the room.

Valerie lugged the heaviest of her cases into the bedroom. To her surprise Umber picked up one end. When they settled it at the foot of the bed, Val placed her fingers to her lips and signed: "Thank you."

Umber's teeth flashed in a smile as her hand opened in the palm-up "you're welcome" gesture.

Valerie pulled out her daypack and slung it over her shoulder. She cocked her head, meeting Umber's curious eyes. "How about starting with you, Umber? Can we do that? Follow you through a day here?"

"Wheep." Umber reached out, taking her hand, and led her out into the other room. Umber looked at Jim and her hands entered a graceful dance.

"Sure," Jim said. "I guess." He checked his watch. "Our ride should pick us up in five minutes."

"What's happening?" Roberto asked, sorting through his camera case. Brett was sticking unnaturally close to him, peering over his shoulder. Several times that morning, Valerie had caught Brett giving her a surreptitious scrutiny and seen the hurt and confusion in her eyes. It might have been a knife in her heart.

"Hey, Taco, you're not keeping up on your studies. We're doing 'a day in the life' piece on Umber. Grab your stuff. We're burning daylight."

Valerie grinned at Jim. As she stepped out into the hall, she heard Brett ask, "Why does she call you 'Taco'?"

"It's short for 'taco vendor,' an ethnic slur," Roberto explained as he followed along behind. "Terrible revenge from the time I called her a 'Nordic nitwit.'"

They trooped out into the muggy morning, and Jim checked his watch again. He had definitely dressed for the field, wearing brown cotton trousers, hiking boots, a tan bush shirt complete with epaulettes, and finally, a battered old gray cowboy hat. The hat gave his bearded face a rugged look as he squinted up at the sky and said, "It's going to rain today."

"This is supposed to be the start of the wet season," Valerie agreed. "Where's your ride?"

"Dr. Yamasaki said that Meggan and Dr. Shanks didn't come back last night, but I'm sure they'll assign someone else to meet us. Maybe Meggan's assistant, Bradley."

Valerie looked at Roberto and raised an eyebrow. They'd heard the words "I'm sure they'll . . ." in a hundred different backwater countries and knew what it meant. She adjusted her pack over her shoulder. "Motor pool?"

"Motor pool," Roberto agreed.

Jim gave her a mild look. "Motor pool?"

"The motor pool's over behind the storage building and across from the generator." Valerie started off. "That's where they keep half of the vehicles. The other half are at the landing strip."

"How do you know that?" Jim caught up and walked beside her. "You just got here."

"It's on the map."

"Map? What map?"

"The preserve maps. One of which is in my pack. We also have documents boxed up back in the room."

"Maps? Documents?" Jim was looking truly interested. "Where on earth did you find them?"

"Hey, cut me some slack. I'm an investigative reporter, for God's sake."

"Can I see them?"

"I'll consider it. So be nice to me today."

They rounded the corner of the concrete storage building where a brown steel Quonset stood. The large garage door was raised, and inside a row of Kawasakis were lined up against one wall. The place smelled of grease, fuel, and rubber. Two men, both native Fang dressed in coveralls, got to their feet as Valerie strode up to them. Both stared uneasily between her and Umber, who had come to stand beside her.

"*Umbohlahnee.* We need a vehicle," she announced and fished her press pass from her pocket. The document was official, with the national palm tree seal on it. Val pointed to the signatures. "It's all been cleared. Dr. Dutton here needs to take Umber up to Compound B."

The man gave her a smile, pointing to the nearest Kawasaki. "Gas is good. Battery is good."

Jim came up behind Valerie, asking, "How about the bridge keys?"

"Oh, yaa." The mechanic stepped to a second vehicle and plucked the keys off the light switch.

Valerie asked, "Bridge keys?"

"I'll explain later." Jim took the keys. "Let's go."

Valerie took the passenger seat while Roberto and the girls piled in the back. Jim turned the key, and they lurched forward.

Jim glanced at Valerie. "We're going to be in hot water for taking the Mule."

"You work for SAC, don't you? What can they say? You've changed, Jimbo. You used to take risks without a second thought."

Valerie took the opportunity to turn in the seat and smile at her daughter . . . *her daughter.* The words soothed a deep wound. But Brett didn't meet her eyes. She had a sullen look on her young face.

Val tried not to feel. Instead she focused on the road ahead.

Jim drove them out of the compound, and Valerie looked up at the fence. "Looks like a prison."

"You're not the only one to make that connection." The Mule splashed through a puddle. "They told us the jungle starts right there on the other side of the fence. Lions and tigers and bears, that sort of thing."

Valerie swiveled in her seat to study the two soldiers who loitered outside the gate with slung AK rifles. The men watched them with stony eyes.

As they entered the dense forest, trees rose ten stories over their heads. The road cut seemed like a narrow canyon. Valerie said, "So, this road goes to Compounds B and C? How do you get to D?"

"D?" Jim gave her a wary look from under the brim of his battered old Rand hat. "What's D?"

Valerie pulled her pack up from where she'd placed it on the floorboard and withdrew the map they had made from the materials provided by Mark White. This one was reduced, and she had taken the special care to have it laminated in clear plastic. Jim slowed, his interest piqued.

"All right," Val said, her fingernail running along the wavy line. "This is the road in from Evinayong. And right here, on the preserve border, is a military checkpoint."

"Military?" Jim asked.

"Like the guys we just passed at the gate. They provide the security. They weren't about to let us in until I pulled the press pass and photo permits. And here's Compound A." She tapped the dots. "This is the road to Compound B; from there, a road winds around the side of the mountain to Compound C, but there's only a trail marked from there over to D, which, as you can see, has its own landing field."

Jim glanced back and forth as he followed the road. "Dan Aberly never mentioned any Compound D. No one has."

They drove in silence for a time, then Jim pulled up at the

canal, used the key, and lowered the bridge. "Apes can't swim," Jim explained. "This whole preserve appears to be designed to keep different groups of apes separated."

They drove across the bridge and started the ascent. Umber hooted and pointed at a wide spot at the crest of the hill. Valerie watched her make a sign that whisked the first two fingers of each hand away from her lips and asked, "What did Umber say?"

"She said 'Thief there,'" Brett told her. "Someone stole her voice synthesizer keyboard at the lookout tree that's down the trail."

Valerie felt the first tendrils of hope. Those were the first words Brett had spoken to her all day.

They made another of the steep climbs, and the road dropped down a precipitous grade. Valerie saw it first, and pointed. "Look, a Mule."

The Kawasaki sat to the side of another wide spot. Jim slowed, pulling up behind the vehicle.

"What happened?" Brett asked slowly.

The seat cushions had been pulled out and shredded. Something sharp had punctured the canvas top, leaving gaping rips in the fabric. The fold-down windshield in the front had been smashed out, glass spilled like crushed ice over the ground and interior.

"Doesn't look like it crashed," Roberto said. He immediately had his camera up and rolling.

Jim killed the engine, and Valerie saw his handsome face go serious. "Let's go check on this."

Valerie examined the sharp gashes in the Mule's paint; they resembled ax marks. Other dents looked like damage from a baseball bat. Broken pieces of branches, many with red paint, scattered the area around the vehicle.

Umber made a soft sound as she walked around the Mule.

Valerie asked, "Something out there?"

Umber nodded and made a quick series of signs.

Brett translated, "She says she feels trouble."

Jim walked over to the destroyed Mule and slapped the marred dash where the locking compartment had been pried open. "Keys are gone."

Valerie glanced sidelong at Roberto and caught his little nod. The old premonition started to gnaw at her, the one that insisted that something bad was going to happen. As Brett stepped over to peer into a gap in the leaves, Valerie said, "Jim, maybe we should take the girls back. I don't—"

"Hey, Dad, there's a trail here!" Brett took off at a run.

"Brett!" Jim called. "Wait!"

He took off after her, running hard.

Valerie's heart sank. Unlike the SAS crash, this time it was her daughter and Jim who had just disappeared into a break in the leaves.

"Come on, Taco," Valerie said. "There's safety in numbers."

Thirty-two

She found Jim and Brett a short distance down the trail, examining the narrow path through the shadowed forest. The way the old beat-up cowboy hat sat on Jim's head, the narrowing of his eyes as he studied the ground, made the years vanish. She remembered him high in the Wyoming Rockies, bent over a different forest trail. Her first hunting trip with him. She'd watched admiringly as he'd read the earth with a practiced eye.

Jim said, "Two sets of booted feet went this way. They didn't come back."

Umber was flashing her hands, Brett translating, "Meggan and Dr. Shanks?"

"Maybe." Jim straightened. "Valerie, grab the first aid kit from the Mule. They may be down there. Could be snakebite, a fall, who knows." He turned to Brett. "You wait here with Umber."

"You're going down there?" Brett asked worriedly.

"If you were hurt wouldn't you want to be rescued?" Jim reached out and mussed her hair. The smile that passed between Brett and her father brought an ache to Valerie's heart.

"Sure I would, but did it ever occur to you that maybe they

got hurt because they were out here alone. Umber and I aren't staying up here by ourselves, Dad. We're going with you."

"That's my girl," Valerie said softly. Brett met her gaze this time.

Jim said, "Okay, you're right. Come on."

He stopped periodically to squint at the places where leaves had been scuffed from the trail. "Peculiar," he said softly. "They walked down, but something else walked back on top of their tracks."

Valerie bent over to peer at the faint marks.

Jim pointed. "See where the front part of the boot sole left a crisp imprint? But here, on the back, it's crushed, rounded. Something soft pressed the damp soil down. The soil consistency is just wet enough to take a Vibram boot track, but not enough to take an impression of what walked here later."

Brett said, "Umber isn't making tracks in her moccasins, Dad."

Umber stared down at her own feet.

Jim straightened, pushing his hat brim back with one finger as he looked down the steep trail. "No, she's not."

They made their way carefully. "Waterfall," Jim said, identifying the roar first. "Wait, didn't Meggan tell us about this place?"

"Yeah, Dad. Skinny-dipping. Remember?" Brett asked.

They clambered down one last steep spot and out into a clear stream bottom where mist blew through the trees in eerie beauty. Picking their way across the rocks, they rounded the bend.

"Good God," Valerie whispered. "It's beautiful." She stared up at falling water, coming down in gauzy sheets, white against the wet black rock. The pool below was clear and inviting.

Jim shook his head, standing beside her. "Looks like paradise to me, Valerie."

"Better than Chamber's Lake," she agreed, and saw his expression change, his eyes oddly vulnerable and pained. In that instant, she could see down into his soul. Gentle, loving, and wounded.

You never forgot, did you? She tried to think of something to say, but her mind had gone blank. As if it had been yesterday, she could recall the stars, the flickering of the campfire, and their bodies sharing warmth in that zipped-together sleeping bag.

"Long time ago," Jim whispered. He wiped his hands on his brown pants and waded to the rocky shore, looking around, then picked up a gold earring. "Meggan's. She was wearing it yesterday."

Valerie took it. "Real gold, not plate. Not the sort of thing a woman would leave behind."

"Shanks wouldn't have left this, either," Jim added as he picked up a Rolex from where it had slipped down between the rounded stones.

Roberto tiptoed across the rocks to Valerie's side and panned the area with his camera, taking shots of the waterfall, the vine-covered cliff, and the overhanging trees. When he lowered the camera, he followed Valerie's gaze to where Brett and Umber moved their hands through the intimate dance of sign language.

Valerie said in a low voice, "I wish I knew what they were saying."

"You can learn, Fuerta. At least make the effort. I think she'd appreciate that."

"She hates me."

"Naw. She's just scared. Like you. You got to take your time, Val. Earn her trust."

Jim stepped into the plants that grew at the edge of the rocky little beach. "Got something." He fished around in the greenery for the pair of panties, then shouted, "Meggan? Dr. Shanks?"

"They're not going to hear much over the waterfall," said Valerie.

Jim pushed deeper into the undergrowth. "Here's a sock. Just one."

Valerie climbed up after him, motioning Roberto to follow with the camera.

The dense forest edge thinned rapidly as they pushed and clambered through the vines, stems, leaves, and suckers. In the shadowed interior, the trees rose to blot out the sky.

"Look," Jim said and pointed. A ripped shirt lay on the spongy leaf mat.

Jim crouched, his brow furrowing. "Something struggled here." He looked up as Brett pushed her way through the vegetation, muttering to herself.

Valerie bent down beside Jim. "Explain this. Roberto, get what you can on film."

Jim pointed. "It's more than just the ripped shirt. See how the leaf mat is torn up? Something hit the ground here, hard. And here," his voice dropped, "you can see where someone reached out and clawed their fingers through the leaf mat."

"Jesus," she whispered. "I've seen that on battlefields."

Jim scanned the steep slope above them—a tangle of prop roots, vines, and packed vegetation—then followed the scuffed leaves along the contour of the hill. "Look down there. More bruised vegetation."

From here, inside the belt of greenery, Valerie could see where the stems and leaves had been crushed. "Looks like a body was dragged in, the way the stems are broken."

"We'll make an elk hunter out of you yet. But we don't know that it's a body." The lines around Jim's eyes had pulled tight. "There's probably some simple explanation."

"Yeah. I hope so. Maybe it's just the kind of work I do, the places I go."

"The company you keep," Brett said unexpectedly. She was looking around, owl-eyed, at the tangle of interlaced branches and the thickly clustered tree boles.

"You can't imagine," Valerie said. "Hey, Taco, tell her about the time—"

"Oh," Jim said in a small voice.

Valerie looked down the trail to see Jim lift a hiking boot with a stick.

He looked directly at Valerie. "Meggan's," he said.

"Dad, maybe they walked up the trail barefoot," Brett said. "That would explain the tracks that were smashed."

"Yes," Jim said absently, his eyes scanning the shadows. "It would, but I don't think that's what happened, Brett."

"More drag marks here." Roberto pointed his hand, then his camera.

Jim climbed over roots and vines, then he stopped and reached down. He dabbed at a dark spot and said, "Blood."

"Big cat?" Valerie asked. "Leopards live in this country."

"Would a leopard take *two* people?"

They crossed the trail that they had taken down and followed the churned leaf mat for another sixty yards along the slope.

"Son of a bitch," Valerie said when Jim pulled up, staring straight ahead. "Roberto, you getting this?"

"Yeah."

She heard Brett's sudden intake of breath, and Umber's hoarse panting.

Valerie's eyes widened as she looked around. Old engrams kicked in, and she was on the alert for trip wires, for mines. Then she remembered they were on a wildlife preserve, and this was probably an animal kill.

He might have been asleep, propped between two thick roots, his back to the tree; but the head hung at an unnatural angle. Dark streaks ran down over his naked chest and shoulders. She bent down, lifting the loose weight of the man's head. The eyes had been poked out. His face was lacerated, as if slashed by a knife. "Roberto?"

"Right behind you, boss. I'm getting it."

When she moved his head, she could feel the grating. She tilted it to the side and saw the gaping cut in the back of his neck. Already the ants and beetles had found it.

She heard Jim step up behind her. "It's Vernon Shanks. Is he dead?"

"Very." She shook her head. "This isn't an animal kill, Jim. Someone whacked him with a machete."

"You sure?"

She nodded, and horrifying images flashed through her memory. "Just like the bodies we saw in Rwanda and Burundi." She took a deep breath. "All right, let's see what else there is. Roberto? You running with sound?"

"Yeah. We're on official record now."

Valerie carefully lifted the dead man's hands, holding them by the wrists. "We've got dirt under the fingernails where he probably clawed the ground. Contusions and hematoma are present on the arms. Parry marks are present on his forearms— he tried to block the blows. Both eyes have been poked out, and a sharp instrument cut laterally halfway through the back of his neck to partially sever the cervical vertebra and spinal cord."

She used a stick to pry his lips open. "His mouth is full of dirt." Her nose wrinkled. "Or maybe feces. From the smell, it's the latter."

Gripping his hair, she lifted. "I see what might be bite marks on his throat. That, or it could just be splotched with blood. The light's bad here."

She swallowed hard when she looked at his chest. "We've got a cut just below the sternum. The cut is lateral, roughly from nipple to nipple in width, and follows the anterior curvature of the rib cage. There's a lot of blood, and a little bit of tissue is extruded. I'd say something was pulled out."

She drew one of his legs to the side and winced. "His genitals have been mutilated. It looks like his penis was sawed off with a coarse blade, and the scrotum ripped open. I can't see either testicle."

She waved at a pesky fly and continued, "His legs are covered with dirt and blood. Anything else is going to have to be done in a forensic laboratory. You might get something from under the nails, and the mouth contents might be revealing."

She rose then, aware that Brett and Umber stood with their arms wrapped around each other, both staring wide-eyed at the corpse. Umber's upper lip was drawn back in a strained smile that Valerie remembered expressed terror in an ape. Brett looked like she was about to faint, or throw up, or both.

Valerie stepped over, placing a hand on Brett's shoulder. "Come on, you two. Let's walk over here, okay?"

She led them back along the trail to a thick root and sat them down. Her heart in her throat, she took one of Brett's hands in her own, and an electric tingle ran through her. "I know you don't see the likes of this at Blevins Junior High School. The important thing is that we've got it on tape. With a record, maybe we can figure out who did it. Sometimes we even bring them to justice."

Umber's hands did their artistic dance. It ended with a fish-like motion, and then she pointed at her eyes.

"God, Umber, I really wish I knew what you were saying."

"She says the blue-eyed ape did it." Brett looked at her, as if in judgment.

"A blue-eyed ape? Tell me about it."

Brett exhaled hard and seemed to be mustering the courage to speak to Valerie. She wiped her nervous hands on her blue jeans. "Umber's keyboard was stolen at the lookout tree. She thought she saw a blue-eyed ape, but nobody believes her."

Valerie considered. "Well, I don't know why not. If SAC can make people like Umber and Kivu, given the complexity of the brain, what's a little challenge like eye color?"

Umber said, "Wheep!"

Brett nodded absently, her eyes shifting uneasily in the direction of the corpse.

"Val?" Roberto called. "Come look at this."

She straightened. "Are you two going to be all right?"

"Wheep!" Umber tightened her grip on Brett's shoulder. Brett just nodded, but some of her spirit was returning.

Valerie clambered over the roots to where Jim and Roberto were looking up into the corpse tree. Thick green leaves blocked the light. "What have you got?"

"Looks like a pair of pants wadded up on a branch way up near the top." Roberto was looking through his camera, the lens zoomed.

"Where? And how in hell are we going to get up there to get it?" Valerie said.

Jim turned and extended a hand to his girls. "Umber? Can you do something for us?"

She came slowly, her worried brown eyes fixing on the dead man. Jim hugged her close for several moments, then pushed back and peered seriously into her eyes. "Umber, can you climb up there and get that pair of pants?"

She tilted her head back, looked at the tree, and nodded.

"Be careful," Valerie warned as Umber took off her moccasins. Umber led Jim around to the rear of the tree, away from the corpse, and let Jim boost her from the top of the prop roots to the lowest of the branches. Then she scuttled up with remarkable agility.

Umber needed no more than several minutes to swing out and pluck the pants loose. Even from the ground, Valerie heard Umber cry out in terror. Then she dropped the bundle, and it bounced from limb to limb before it smacked hard onto the ground.

"Umber? Are you all right?" Jim shouted as he ran to the spot at the base of the tree beneath Umber.

Umber sat on the branch, holding herself, whimpering.

"What the hell?" Roberto asked. "She's absolutely terrified."

"Dad?" Brett sat down and jerked off her running shoes. "Lift me up. I'm going to go get her."

"Brettany, you'll do no such thing," Jim said sternly. "You'll break your neck."

Valerie bent down, meeting Brett's eyes. "Are you sure you can climb that?"

"Hell yes," Brett replied. "When Dad's not home, Umber and me race up and down the climbing pole. And we've been up and down every tree out in back of the lab."

"I'll give you a boost up." Val took her hand.

"Valerie"—Jim placed a hand on her arm—"don't buck me on this."

Valerie squared her shoulders. "You gonna give me a hand, Jimbo? Umber's stuck up there and my daughter's going to get her down." Then she took Brett's foot and boosted her to the branch. Heart in her throat, Valerie stepped back, watching Brett climb.

Jim sidled up next to her. "I hope to hell you know what you're doing."

"Yeah," she murmured through a tight throat, "me, too."

Brett didn't have Umber's agility, but she made steady progress. When she reached the branch to which Umber clung, she called out: "Umber? You okay?"

Umber piped, "Wheep," and scuttled across the branch, wrapping her arms around Brett and pointing across into another tree. Brett stared at it, tightening her grip on Umber.

Jim cupped his hands around his mouth. "What is it?"

"Dad, it's a . . . God, it's a piece of a person. It looks like a leg from here." Brett looked remarkably delicate and vulnerable. "We're coming down now, Dad."

"Take your time, Brett. For God's sake, be careful!" Jim shifted from foot to foot as they climbed, as if ready to leap out and catch them if they fell.

Valerie's mouth had gone dry. Umber lowered herself first, using her long arms, hands, and feet as she descended hand-over-hand down the lianas.

Brett was slower, relying on branches to support her. Valerie saw it the moment she lost her grip, slipped, and twisted. For an instant she was falling, but landed on a branch. Her feet slipped off, but she scrambled, got her arms around the thick limb, and hung there.

"Brett!" Jim cried, leaping to climb the tree himself.

Umber shrieked and scrambled back toward Brett.

"I'm all right!" Brett called as she managed to reach out with a foot, found purchase on a branch, and hesitated long enough to catch her breath.

Umber was halfway back up to help when Brett resumed her methodical descent.

Jim stepped to the ground again, but Valerie could see the veins pulsing in his throat.

Umber clambered down, signing to Jim as she rushed into his arms, hugging him frantically, trembling. Her hair puffed out where it stuck through her clothing.

He patted her and said, "It's okay. You were very brave. We all get scared on occasion."

Brett let Jim lift her down from the tree. "You scared the be-jesus out of me," he told her, kissing the top of her blond head.

"Piece of cake, Dad." She gave him a skeptical look and then glanced at Valerie.

On impulse, Valerie raised her hand, slapping Brett's in a high five. "Good job, kid."

A smile almost curled the corner of Brett's lip, then died as Roberto called, "Val? You'd better come see this."

Valerie climbed over the roots and leaves to where the pants had fallen. The first thing she noticed was the insects crawling around in the bloody cloth. Then she saw the hair, pale-looking in the gloomy light. Roberto had laid his camera aside, using a stick to part the clotted fabric. Through the gap Valerie saw not only hair, but a human ear. The lobe had been pierced, the place where a gold earring would have hung.

"Son of a bitch, it's someone's head." She recoiled, grimacing. "Brett? You and Umber are sure you saw a leg up there in that other tree?"

They both nodded in unison.

"Leopards hide kills in trees," Roberto reminded.

Valerie glanced at Jim, Brett, and Umber. "No leopard would put a woman's head in a pair of pants. Camera time, Taco." As he lifted the camera, Valerie pulled back the cloth, winced, and added: "And leopards don't decapitate women with machetes, either."

"Dear God, it's Meggan." Jim closed his eyes.

"You hanging in there, Jimbo?" Valerie asked.

He swallowed hard. In a shaken voice, he said, "Humans don't usually leave dismembered people out on the ends of branches, either."

"Well, who does?" Brett asked.

Heads swiveled, slowly, one at a time, until all eyes rested on Umber.

Thirty-three

Jim had never considered himself squeamish. A man who grew up on a ranch understood life's nastier little realities. He'd had blood on his hands many times, pulling newborn calves, gutting, skinning, and butchering the animals he'd killed for food. His training, first as a physical anthropologist and then as a primatologist, had included hours in the anatomy lab, dissecting human beings, apes, and, sometimes, forensic specimens. But he hadn't been prepared to look down into Meggan O'Neil's dead face—not twenty hours after he'd spent a day in her company.

Tight-jawed, he drove the Kawasaki Mule to an abrupt stop in front of the hospital building in Compound A. As he shut off the engine, he said, "Umber, Brett, I think you'd better go back to the room and wait for us there. Lock the door and stay put."

Umber signed yes, while Brett cried, "But, Dad, I—"

"*Now*, Brett!" He turned hard eyes on her, and Brett nodded.

Jim stepped out of the Mule. He had to nerve himself to reach for the stained fabric and lift it from the back of the Kawasaki. A crawling feeling settled in his gut as he strode up the walk with Valerie and Roberto following. He stiff-armed the door into the hospital reception room. A Fang woman sat

behind a desk, blank-eyed until her gaze fixed on the bloody
cloth hanging from Jim's right hand. He asked for directions
to Dr. Yamasaki's office.

She pointed down a hallway and said, "Turn right at the
end."

He could hear Valerie's and Roberto's quick steps as they
rounded the corner behind him.

"Marcus, we're going to have a little talk," Jim declared as
he led Val and Roberto into Dr. Yamasaki's office. Yamasaki
looked up from an open folder on his desk, surprise in his
mild brown eyes.

Fluorescent lights gave the whole place a white, sanitary
look, right up until Jim pushed aside a stack of papers and deposited the bloody pants and Meggan's severed head on the
desktop.

Yamasaki lurched to his feet, his gaze fixed on the gruesome
object. "What—"

"We just found Vernon Shanks and Meggan O'Neil. That's
the part of her we could bring back. Shanks is propped against
a tree. Meggan is scattered around here and there in the treetops. They were killed over in B, by the waterfall. Evidently
someone didn't like their afternoon tryst in the pool."

Yamasaki, for all of his medical training, appeared to be on
the verge of gagging. He hadn't yet nerved himself to pull back
the blood-blackened cloth. "I don't . . ." He swallowed hard,
even more appalled when one of the orange-backed beetles
came crawling out, wiggling its antennae.

Valerie signaled Roberto to shoot, and he lifted his camera
as she stepped forward.

"Tell us about the blue-eyed ape," Valerie said. "Come on,
Doctor. People are being murdered. Your Compounds B and C,
they're just cover, aren't they? The real action is over in Compound D. That's where you're making your special blue-eyed
apes, isn't it?"

Yamasaki seemed to wilt, his breathing growing more rapid. "Compound D?" He ground his teeth. "I never heard of it."

"Aren't you going to look?" Jim indicated the bundle. "It's pretty grisly. Umber brought it down out of an okema tree for us. If Umber and Brett could stand it, I think you can."

Yamasaki seemed to nerve himself. "Bring it," he said. "Not here. One of the labs. Follow me." He waved furiously. "And turn off that camera!"

Jim gently lifted the bundle and followed Yamasaki down tiled corridors. They passed a couple of institutional metal doors, then Yamasaki opened a door marked "Dissection" and led them in. A stainless steel autopsy table dominated the center of the room.

"There." Yamasaki pointed, then turned to one of the benches lining the room. He donned a white lab coat, placed a mask over his mouth, and slipped on rubber gloves. By the time he approached the table with its bundle, he seemed to have recovered his professional control. When he reached for the cloth, he had focused to the point that he wasn't even aware of Roberto, standing to the side, his camera on his shoulder, his eye to the viewfinder.

Yamasaki pulled the fabric away where it had dried to the flesh, lifted the head free, and turned it over to look at the face. "Good God." He reached for one of the overhead hoses and rinsed off the neck. "I'm guessing machete." Bloody water and wiggling insects ran down the drains. "I see a longitudinal cut mark here. I'd say her throat was cut first. Her head was chopped off later. Nothing else would explain the speckles of blood on her face. That fine spray comes from exhalation through a severed trachea."

Yamasaki looked up. "What about Shanks's body?"

Valerie described his wounds, the eyes poked out, the castration, then turned to Jim. "Sound familiar?"

Jim nodded, his voice steely. "Male chimpanzees do that to their rivals."

Valerie turned back to Yamasaki. "How long has the blue-eyed ape been missing from Compound D?"

Yamasaki stubbornly said, "I've never heard of Compound D!"

"Yeah," Valerie told him. "Right."

Jim cocked his jaw, glaring at Yamasaki. "Have there been other people missing?"

Yamasaki hesitated too long.

"How many?" Valerie asked.

Yamasaki shook his head. "Just one, a researcher in Compound C, but look, I can't talk to you people! If you have any questions, take them to Dr. McDougal."

Jim said, "Where is she? Here? Or gone? She seems to spend a lot of time on the comlink to Sussex. Odd, isn't it, that she never shows up for meals anymore?" Jim stepped closer, watching Yamasaki. "Come on, Marcus, she's up at D, isn't she? Trying to figure out what went wrong."

Yamasaki pleaded, "I've told you all I can. You've got to take it up with—"

"Yeah, yeah, take it up with McDougal." Jim threw his hands up. "All right. What about Shanks and the other pieces of Meggan?"

"You know where they are, Dr. Dutton. I'll call a tree crew." Yamasaki suddenly looked very tired.

"Oh, one other thing," Valerie said evenly. "Do you have a shotgun?"

From the window in the dormitory lobby, Brett watched the Kawasaki Mules follow one another, one by one, as Jim and

Valerie led the recovery party back to the lonely waterfall, and the gruesome remains.

"Damn, Umber, what have we gotten ourselves into?"

Umber draped an arm around Brett's shoulder and hugged her close. Her hairy fingers formed the words: "In dreams I will see Meggan again." Umber lowered her hand and closed her eyes.

The gray sky had an ominous look to it, as if heavy with rain, and flashes of lightning lit the cloud bellies. Seconds later, they heard the rumble of distant thunder.

"I want to go home," Brett said. "I want to go someplace where people don't get killed."

Umber leaned her head close and kissed Brett's cheek.

Brett slipped her arm around Umber's waist, grateful for the feel of her slim, muscular body. "I'm not as brave as I thought I was, Umber."

Umber swallowed hard, her hands making the signs for "Me either."

"I've got the creeps just being alone here in a nice safe building. Come on. We're going shopping."

Umber gave her a skeptical look, warning in her gentle brown eyes. Pulling her other hand back, she signed: "Jim said stay here."

"Yeah, well, 'here' included the whole compound. We need something to do to keep from thinking about . . . come on." Brett opened the door and led the way.

Outside of the air-conditioned dormitory, the air pressed down, laden with heat and moisture. Lightning flashed right over their heads, then, a moment later, thunder boomed. The forest looked darker now. Somewhere in those green depths, she could imagine that blue-eyed ape of Umber's, big, hairy, and blood-caked. He watched from the shadows.

Watched her.

Inside the cafeteria, the feeling of partial safety returned. She could see the familiar Fang kitchen help, apparently oblivious to the changes in their world.

Brett led Umber up the steps. They hadn't had time to explore the store. Glass doors at the top landing opened into a big room.

A plump Fang woman wearing a long red skirt looked up amiably from behind the counter. Her face changed when she noticed that Umber wasn't human. To her credit, she tried to master her shock as Brett led Umber down the aisle.

"That ape ain't gonna hurt nothing?" The woman stood, unsure.

"She'll be fine," Brett replied.

When they found hiking equipment, Brett picked out a camouflage daypack. Umber pointed at it questioningly.

"Yes, I'm buying this. And some other stuff. If we're going to be here, I want to be prepared."

Umber gave her a slightly frightened look, then reached for a bright purple daypack with lots of pockets.

Brett looked around. "One more thing . . . wait." She walked down the next aisle and reached up. "Here, catch. Just the thing."

Umber caught the machete and pulled the long blade from the scabbard. She tested the grip and grunted. "Wheep," she said softly as she cautiously slipped it into the sheath.

Brett was reaching for another machete when the clerk appeared and demanded, "Whach you doing there?"

"These are for our parents." Brett adopted her angelic face. "It's all right. The account name is Dr. Jim Dutton. He sent us here with a list."

The clerk's face clouded, then she vanished for her computer.

Brett lifted the machete. "I think I'm going to sleep with this under my pillow."

Umber bowed her head and answered, "Wheep."

Valerie used a screwdriver to lift the grate from the window. Hot wet air seemed to roll into her suite from the rain-slashed night beyond. Since the unsettling discoveries of the day, both she and Roberto had showered and dressed in clean clothes.

"We're just about there," Roberto said, glancing up from the equipment-packed travel case and handing her what looked like an aluminum umbrella. She stuck the length of it out the window, pointed it at the sky, and opened it. The contraption folded out into a small satellite dish.

"We're about fifty miles north of the equator," Roberto said. "I'd say clip it just about straight up and down, and maybe a degree to the south."

Valerie used a screw-on clamp to fix the antenna to the window frame and adjusted the antenna arms so the dish pointed skyward.

"Got a signal," Roberto told her. "From the meter I'd say about fifteen degrees west."

Valerie carefully twisted a dial on the antenna mount.

"Whoa, up. Back a half a degree. There, that's it." Roberto flicked a couple of switches, watching his meters. "Five by five."

Valerie lifted a standard-looking telephone handset from the case, tapped in the number, and waited.

"Hello, this is Murray."

"Hi, Murray. Guess who?"

"What have you got, Val?"

"Would you believe a blue-eyed ape running around the jungle whacking people's heads off with a machete? Another talking ape who likes psychedelic clothes; a mysterious compound back in the jungle that no one will admit exists; a missing administrator; an unknown number of missing people; and two dead bodies."

A pause. "You're not joking, are you?"

"Murray, my favorite ex-love, what if I told you I had almost all of the above on tape? Well, except for the mysterious compound and the blue-eyed ape. We're still working on that." Valerie watched the lightning flash. "It's dynamite, Murray. As soon as we've finished our little chat, we'll set up a link and download everything Roberto caught on camera. We're transmitting raw meat, Murray, so please, don't fool with it. I'm only sending it to you for safekeeping."

"Then what do I air?"

"I'm sending a three-minute spot for on-air. That's tagged on the end. You and Burney can do what you want with it. Oh, and if I disappear, or come out of this piss-pot country in a body bag, air it all, got that?"

"Right."

"What's the story on Kivu?" she asked.

"He's brought us up two points over CNN and the networks. The sheriff's declared Kivu a dangerous animal. He had the audacity to demand that Kivu be turned over to the animal shelter for euthanasia. Your buddy Slim filed for a court order. Apparently Kivu says this Morrison, aka Parnell, assaulted Dr. Bartlett and Kivu tried to save her life. Forensics came in with powder residue on Wayne Morrison's hand." Murray added more legal details and updated Valerie on what Myles had turned up in Sussex, then added that fifty million pounds had gone missing from the SAC budget. "Trail leads right to Geoffrey Smyth-Archer himself. Trick is, no one can find him. Your snitch in the factory thinks he's in Africa. Anyone seen him around?"

"No one has mentioned him."

"Okay, then beam me up what you've got."

She pushed the end button and glanced at Roberto. "You ready to do a SAC whack?"

"In the words of the Prophet"—he grinned—"'make my

day.'" Then his dexterous brown fingers danced over the keyboard. The light went green and he pushed the feed button, the camera running as it turned the digital images into microwaves and sent them skyward.

The phone jangled on Dana's bedside table.

"Hello?" She blinked at the morning grayness that streamed through the bedroom window.

"Dana? It's me."

"Jim!" She sat up, trying to clear the fog of sleep from her brain. "Where are you?"

"The SAC preserve in Africa."

Jim started launching questions at her and she was instantly awake. Back and forth, they updated each other on Kivu, the murders at the SAC preserve, on the amazing role Valerie was playing in the ape story, and the bond building between Valerie and Brett.

Dana took a deep breath. "Listen, you should also know that I released a tape. One with Umber and Brett working on the computer. It hit the local news last night, all the Colorado stations. I think it's going national today. I thought it would help. With all the talk about Kivu and murder, all of a sudden here's this angelic blond girl and Umber the ape laughing and spelling things on a computer." She winced. "Did I make a mistake releasing that video?"

"I don't think so," he said, but she could hear the worry in his voice.

Dana paused, then whispered, "Watch your ass, Jim."

"Tell me about it. This place makes black timber look like a sage flat in comparison. I wish I had my ought six."

"Want me to box it up and send it along with one of Umber's keyboards?"

Jim forced a laugh. "Don't worry about me. You're doing a great job keeping the home fires burning, and you've got lectures to prepare, right, Dr. Marks?" He sighed. "Listen, I've got to go. I'll call when I can."

"I'll be here."

"Bye, Dana."

The line went dead.

Dr. Shelly McDougal glanced up into Marcus Yamasaki's worried brown eyes. He had just autopsied bits and pieces of Meggan and Vernon.

"And the reporter filmed all of this?" McDougal asked.

"She was with Dutton when they found the bodies, Shelly." Marcus straightened, crossing his arms. "We've got a real problem here. This can't be covered up. The Alpha Group—"

"You have your instructions."

"Shelly, damn it! Stop worrying about damage control! What we have here isn't some poacher out in the bush! Do you want to take bets on what happened to Mitu? We've got to go out and hunt that twisted—"

"*You have your instructions!*" she thundered at him.

Marcus wilted, then said in despair, "Shelly, you've got to do something."

"Aye," she added stiffly. "I'm on my way to do it right now." She turned on her heel, struggling to order her mind. In the hallway, she caught sight of Sergeant Bonoficio, natty-looking in a khaki uniform with gold braid hanging from the epaulettes. He and his four men wore scarlet berets, polished boots, and each carried an immaculately maintained assault rifle from a shoulder sling.

When she met Bonoficio's flat black eyes, she nodded. "Sergeant, come. Let us find your reporter. I assume that you can carry an extra two passengers, besides the reporter, with you to Malabo?"

"Who?" Bonoficio asked flatly.

"Dr. James Dutton and his daughter."

"She young, this daughter?" Bonoficio's eyebrow lifted in interest.

"Aye."

Bonoficio glanced sidelong at the other soldiers. "No problem."

At the tone in his voice, Shelly's gut wrenched, and a sick feeling left her unsteady as she turned and started down the hallway.

Thirty-four

Umber cried out from somewhere far away . . .

Bang! Bang! Bang! The sounds pounded in rhythm with Brett's heart.

Brett jerked her eyes wide, bolted upright in bed, and stared around the room. Umber sat up beside her, kicked out from the blankets, and stumbled over to the door. Her black hair shone in the light streaming through the window.

The pounding came again. Brett reached up to rub her moist face. Safe. Safe here in her room with Umber.

Umber opened the door, and Brett looked up. "Dr. McDougal?"

"Hello, Brett," the woman said in her precise voice. The Scottish accent seemed to make it all the more formidable. "I must see your father."

Brett knotted a fist in her nightgown. Umber rocked back and forth. Brett got up, trying to banish her unease. "Uh, Dad's not here," Brett told the woman. "He'll be back tonight, I think."

"You think?" Dr. McDougal stood stiffly in the doorway. She wore a white blouse over a gray skirt that hung to just below the knees. Her hair was pulled back into that severe ponytail, and she looked with distaste at Brett through her black-framed glasses. Behind them, her blue eyes seemed particularly unforgiving.

"He and Valerie told me they'd be leaving early," Brett said. "He didn't know when they'd be back."

"I see, and where were they going?"

Brett frowned. "One of the compounds."

McDougal seemed to be thinking. "Well, security will find them. In the meantime, lass, you can start packing. You, your father, and his lady friend will be leaving today. We've a plane due at sixteen hundred. When it takes off at seventeen-thirty, we expect you to be aboard."

Umber clapped her hands together and hooted. She tromped up next to Brett and hugged her, signing: "Home! Home!"

Brett hugged Umber. "You bet we're going home! Get your stuff packed, Umber."

"Umber will not be going with you," Dr. McDougal stated, and her thin nostrils flared. "It is you, Brett, your father, and his journalist friends who are leaving. You will be flown from here to Malabo, and from there, well, that will be arranged. As to Umber"—she turned her hard blue eyes on Umber—"we will move her to Compound B as soon as you are gone. See to it that she's prepared. A vehicle will arrive here to pick you up at half four." She smiled humorlessly, as if amused by their speechless shock. "Oh, and do be ready. You've caused more than enough trouble for us already. I'd not look kindly on having to hold the plane for you."

She turned and vanished.

Brett stood by the bed, her mouth open. Umber closed the door and whimpered.

Brett ran for her, grabbing her around the shoulders. Umber's hands twined in Brett's nightgown, and she let out a long, low cry.

"They're not doing this," Brett promised as tears filled her eyes. "They're not!"

Umber lifted her head and looked up at Brett pleadingly. She slipped her right index finger between the middle fingers of her left hand, and pulled it out quickly. She repeated the gesture as she cried, her chest heaving.

Brett savagely rubbed the tears away. Run away. That's what Umber kept signing. *Run away!*

Brett ran to look out the window at the morning. Rain was falling. Mist filled the compound. "We've got to think. Once we're off their property, we're not under their control anymore, but where are we going to go?"

Umber slumped to the floor, dropped her head in her hands, and rocked. Soft, mournful sounds strained against her closed lips.

"Evinayong," Brett said firmly. "About thirty miles." She looked out at the downpour. "The rain ought to cover our tracks."

Umber gave Brett a worried look and made the sign for "Jim."

"We'll leave Dad a note. Tell him where we're going." Brett knelt, placed her hands on Umber's shoulders, and peered into her tormented eyes. "Look, this isn't going to be easy. But it's the only way. Hey, even if they physically manhandle Dad onto the plane, he'll know to find us in Evinayong. He'll be back for us, you can count on it. And there'll be a phone there. We can call Dana collect."

Umber wrapped her long arms around her midsection, as if hugging herself, and started rocking again.

"Don't worry," Brett said bluffly. "I've got a hundred and twenty bucks in my purse. Roberto said that a dollar is worth about two hundred and eighty *cefas*. Rooms cost about two thousand a night at a hotel. It'll hold us until Dad wires us more money."

Umber reached for Brett and drew her close, softly mouthing Brett's neck, as she'd done when she was a baby and frightened.

Brett looked out at the rain again and checked her watch. "Look, we're not going to make thirty miles today, but we can cover half of it if we hustle. If we hear a truck coming, we duck into the forest until it passes. If it's Dad, we jump out and wave him down. Piece of cake."

Umber signed, "Where we sleep tonight?"

"Rolled up in our ponchos." Brett looked at the pack she'd bought at the store, thankful as never before that she'd chosen a little bit of anything they might need. "But we're taking machetes, and you're taking your bow and arrow."

Umber chewed her lower lip and gazed up at Brett. She signed: "Wait for Jim."

"We don't have time!" Brett insisted, desperation in her voice. "Look, he said himself, SAC is calling the shots. And I'll die before I let them take you away from us."

The Kawasaki growled its way up a steep slope, rain pattering on the canvas top. Water ran like a stream down the road, and the Kawasaki's real value had become rapidly apparent. Where it couldn't get traction, the damn thing floated. Valerie rode in the passenger seat, casting glances at Jim.

He still had a rugged charisma. He had pulled his old cowboy hat down over his eyes against the rain. Deep lines etched his forehead, but the neatly trimmed beard gave him a distinguished look and accented his blue eyes. He concentrated on the road, one hand gripping the wheel as he peered through the drenched windshield. If only, if only . . . Such small words with such large meanings.

They rolled up to the bridge crossing and Jim braked. According to Valerie's map, this canal divided Compounds C and D.

Valerie looked down into the murky water below. As they

drove across the bridge, she said, "Welcome to Compound D. I wish we had your friend Yamasaki along. Maybe we could have refreshed his memory."

"It doesn't look particularly ominous," Jim noted. "You'd think they'd have big fences, or signs up, like in the movies."

Valerie checked her watch. "Eight o'clock. I'd say the girls ought to be getting up about now."

Jim rounded a bend in the road and climbed a ridge. "Neither one of them threw a fit when I told them to stay in the room today. It's amazing what a little abject horror can do for discipline," he said ruefully, gripping the wheel as they drove around a curve.

"Well," Valerie said, "leaving before daylight meant they didn't have time to wake up and reconsider."

Jim tapped the side of his head. "The trick is, always stay one step ahead of them. Otherwise, before you know it, you're wrapped around their little fingers and doing all kinds of things you don't want to do."

Valerie leaned back. "You made a pretty good father, Jim." She enjoyed his fleeting smile. "I wish I could have . . ."

"Why didn't you?" Jim shot her a neutral glance. "Was it my fault? Were you afraid I'd try to pressure you? I know I . . ." He glanced back at Roberto, who seemed to be uncommonly interested in the mud splashing out from the rear wheels. ". . . I made mistakes. Val, did I hurt you so badly you couldn't make yourself even talk to me?"

She fumbled with the map. "Do you always blame yourself when it comes to me?"

"Yes. I was young, and so in love with you I wasn't thinking straight. If I only could have gone back, done things . . ." His voice trailed off as they drove out into a clearing.

There, in the hip-deep grass, stood little huts of a kind Valerie had never seen before. "Jim, stop."

He braked and Valerie stepped out and pulled the hood of

her green poncho over her head. "Looks like some sort of abandoned village."

As Jim and Roberto stepped out, she started forward. Rain splashed from her hood. The place had a dreary look, the domed huts pathetic. In all of her travels, she'd never seen anything so crude.

She dropped down to stare into the first one. A clutter of sticks and piles of leaves filled the inside. Here and there, she could see where the sticks had been sharpened.

Jim knelt beside her. His voice went low. "Dear God."

"What? I mean, this isn't a Fang village. This hut's more like an upside-down bird's nest than—"

"It's a village," Jim said softly. "Just not one made by *Homo sapiens.*"

Valerie touched the grass wall. "You mean it's an ape village?"

Jim studied the pole frame construction, the roof and walls, and replied, "More like a hominid village. This is the sort of thing I've always imagined *Homo erectus* would have built."

"My God," Valerie whispered. "You think apes did this? Built these huts, used these sharpened sticks for tools?"

"Well," Roberto said from behind the eyepiece of his camera as he panned the village, "there are no apes here now. And it looks like it's been a while."

"Not so long." Jim stood, looking around. Rain spattered the shoulders of his denim shirt and old gray cowboy hat. "The clearing is still covered with grass. None of the trees or brush has started up yet. In this environment, that happens rapidly."

"Yeah," Valerie agreed, "like yesterday." She shook her head.

Jim bent down and picked up a bit of gnawed bone. "Humerus. From a monkey. Notice how the ends have been bitten off?"

Valerie took the bone, studying it. "So?"

"Chimps are hunters, we've known that for forty years, but

this . . . this is something different." He kicked around in the grass. "Fruit husks, all moldy. Stripped twigs. Here's another bone fragment. Looks like an innominate."

"Huh?" Roberto asked. As he leaned over, rain streamed from the top of his green hood.

"Hipbone," Jim replied. "Also a monkey." He walked over to the largest of the huts. "Let's see what's inside."

Valerie followed him, jumping sideways as a snake jetted off into the grass. There, planted in the ground, was another of the sharpened sticks. Atop it, an animal skull had been mounted, the sharpened end of the stick driven into the hole where the spinal cord emerged.

"Looks like some sort of small antelope." Roberto knelt, focusing the camera on it. "Like a standard of some sort. Maybe a trophy."

Jim ducked into the doorway. "If you like that, you'll love this."

Valerie slipped through the low opening. The walls, made of branches, leaves, and grass, obviously were water resistant, because only a few damp spots splotched the floor. This hut had three beds in it, made of grass and sticks.

Jim pointed at the walls and Valerie's gaze lifted. There, in a line about three feet off the ground, a row of skulls hung on projecting sticks. Monkey skulls. A finger had dabbed them with red color to create a dotted effect on the white bone.

"That looks like ritual treatment," Valerie said in awe.

Jim nodded. "It is ritual treatment." He smoothed his beard as he stared at the line of skulls. "So, the question is, were they taught to do this? Or did they invent religion on their own?"

Valerie looked around uneasily. "I'm worried about something leaping out of the grass so it can add my skull to the wall, and you're worried about the evolution of consciousness."

Jim picked up a rock from the floor and turned it over in

his hand. "Battered. It's a hammerstone." He picked up another, a thin wedge of stone. Looking at it closely, he said, "Amazing. SAC has done better than Sue Savage-Rumbaugh did with Kanzi. The SAC apes can make flakes. This is one of the pieces they used to sharpen those sticks."

"Right. Sure." Valerie took the thin bit of stone. "How do you know they sharpened a stick with this flake, Dutton?"

He gave her a deadpan stare. "Because that flake was laying in the middle of a pile of these." He picked up a thin wood-shaving.

Valerie smiled in spite of the tension. "Oh. Right."

Jim backed out into the rain. She followed him and straightened, looking around. Roberto immediately ducked inside, fiddling with his camera and the angle to see if he could get enough light to record the skulls, artifacts, and bedding.

"So, what does this mean?" Valerie asked.

Jim walked through the village, picking up bits of stone and wood. "It means that our blue-eyed ape isn't an ape."

"What?" She stopped and watched the rain splashing into the puddles around him.

"Bonobos, chimpanzees, gorillas, none of them behave this way." He clutched a bone in his hand. "Spiral fracture, Valerie. They broke this femur open. See, here's the impact point. You get a conical break. Kind of like a BB hitting glass. Then the fractures spiral out. That's what they used that hammerstone for, among other things." He crouched down and examined the white bone again and tilted his head curiously. "Skulls on sticks? Painted? And permanent structures?"

"If this whole SAC preserve is a teaching program—"

Jim tossed her the bone fragment. "No," he said, "this Compound D isn't for ordinary lab animals, Val. The creatures here are not chimps. They're a lot more intelligent and sophisticated. Like Umber. Like Kivu."

Valerie's eyes suddenly darted around. "You mean this Compound D is reserved specifically for augmented apes? I didn't think SAC had that many. At least our information suggested—"

"Godmoore told me they had five augmented apes. Aberly told me twenty. But . . ." His blue eyes took on a crystalline gleam. "I have a horrible feeling they meant twenty 'normal' augmented apes."

"What does that mean?" She could see the tension in his expression.

"It means that SAC was lying to us. Lying by omission. They had twenty apes that *could* be placed in human homes."

"So," Valerie said as her thoughts whirled. "You think that in the process of creating 'normal' augmented apes, they created some 'abnormal' augmented apes? Dear God." A shiver climbed her spine. "Is that what Compound D is? A big cage for the terrifying mistakes?"

Jim rose to his feet and his gaze went over the forest beyond the village, as if he expected to see something out there looking back. Barely audibly, he said, "I think so, yes."

Roberto ducked through the doorway. "It was pretty dark in there, but maybe I can do some tricks in the lab."

Neither Jim nor Valerie paid him any attention. Jim turned to Valerie and stared at her, unblinking; she could see the dark thoughts that coalesced behind his eyes.

She said, "The blue-eyed ape?"

"That's what I was thinking."

"Yeah, well," Roberto said as he walked up beside Val. "The Drs. Frankenstein who created the blue-eyed ape are over there somewhere." He pointed to where the clouds had packed against a green mountainside. "Let's go see if we can find our mysterious landing strip in the jungle."

Jim frowned at the ground as they walked back to the Kawasaki. "The data," he murmured. "The data must be phenomenal."

"What are you babbling about?" Valerie asked as she climbed into the Mule.

Jim sat for a moment in the driver's seat, eyes focused on infinity. "Human beings, we're Pleistocene hunters and gatherers, Val. No matter how we dress ourselves up, or what technology we use to insulate ourselves from the real world, we're still hardwired to be hunting and gathering animals. We crave fats, sweets, and salts. When we get mad, the brain floods our bodies with chemicals that would save our lives in the wild, but will burn us out in the office." He bowed his head and shook it as if to shake some sense into his brain. "This whole place is a laboratory on the development of not only culture, but also the *psychology* of culture. What is truly ape, and what is human?"

"Assuming they don't train the apes to do these things?"

"By God, I wish I knew." Jim thumped the steering wheel with the palm of his hand.

Valerie pointed at the key. "Why don't you turn that little metal flake, my Pleistocene hunter, start this thing up, and we'll utilize this technology the way we've been trained to and go find out."

Jim smiled, his eyes sparkling and alive. The Kawasaki roared to life.

As they splashed down the forest road, Valerie looked back. Painted skulls? Mounted on the walls? Why did trophies always have to be related to death? And what did it say about the beings who had built that place?

The Mule climbed a hill, its motor racing as trees flashed by. Valerie filled her lungs with the scents of flowers and damp earth.

Death rituals meant that somebody cared about the dead.

She looked back toward the village, wondering . . .

Brett walked ahead of Umber, the hood of her yellow raincoat up. To her relief no one seemed to give them a second glance. Umber kept her head down, her hood shielding her face. Anyone who looked out simply saw two people wearing packs as they strode down the muddy red road toward the gate.

At the gate soldiers huddled in one of the Kawasaki Mules, talking and smoking under the protection of the canvas top.

Brett glanced at Umber. "Well, here goes. Try not to hobble. Walk more human, and don't say or sign anything. Leave the talking to me."

Brett lifted a hand to the soldiers as they passed. The men waved back, returned to their conversation, and Brett and Umber walked right out the front gate.

When they entered the forest Brett put a hand to her heart and said, "I don't believe it. Why did they just let us walk out like that?"

Umber shrugged, resetting her purple pack on her shoulders. The curved bow shone, water slick, where it rested crosswise on the top of her pack. Her quiver hung down off her right shoulder. She signed: "Maybe only keep people out?"

"Got me." Brett glanced up at the forest that rose on either side of them. The flowers were still beautiful in their frames of murky black shadows.

Brett, this is not one of your better ideas. She shook off the notion. The fact was, if they didn't get away from SAC, Umber would be a prisoner here. "And while I've got breath in my body, that's not going to happen," she promised herself.

Umber looked at her and signed: "What?"

Brett waved the question away. "Talking to myself. Come on, let's make time."

Brett wanted to break into a ground-eating jog, but Umber, with her ape-shaped hips, just couldn't keep the pace. Nor did the pack on her shoulders help matters. The cold reality was that they would travel as rapidly as Umber could manage, and no faster.

Umber cast uncertain glances up at the green wall of forest. It seemed to press in on either side of the narrow ribbon of road.

Brett had the feeling that hidden eyes watched every move they made. "Remember, at the first sound of a motor, we dive into the leaves. We don't want them to catch us out in the open."

"Wheep."

"It'll be okay, Umber. We're going to make it." Brett chewed her lips. She was already hot, her clothing damp under the raincoat. "And someday, I'm going to find a way to make Shelly McDougal gag on her own vomit for forcing us to do this."

Umber signed: "She's scary."

"Yeah. What is it about her? She's like some sort of female tank. It's like she's got a Hitler complex. Roberto, now, if he'd been with us this morning, he'd have cut her down to size."

Umber's eyes were questioning. "Brett like Roberto?"

She made a face, but said, "Yeah, when he smiles at me, I want to melt. And he looks really mag in tight Levi's."

Umber's thin lips pulled back in a grin, and her chevron nose wrinkled.

"Don't give me that look," Brett said. Umber knew her too well. "All right," Brett admitted grudgingly. "So I might have a slight crush on him. What of it?"

Umber shook her head and wheezed in laughter.

Brett laughed, too. It helped her to ignore the sounds coming from the forest on either side of them. The usual noise had muted somewhat, the birds, insects, and beasts waiting out the rain, but the patter of drops on leaves, in puddles, and on their plastic coats added to the effect.

Umber signed: "What you think?"

"That I'll be seventeen in four years. That's old enough."

Umber broke into one of her "hee-haii" spells of laughter, and for a moment Brett didn't recognize the sound of the engine, then she and Umber stiffened at the same instant.

Umber signed: "Motor!" and leaped for the trees on the left, while Brett broke for the wall of leaves on the right. Brett tore desperately at them, fighting her way through. When she finally bulled her way in, she looked down. Her raincoat hung in yellow tatters, almost torn in half.

Brett could see Umber struggling to shrug out of the pack with its sideways bow. Rather than fight the leaves, Umber simply grabbed handfuls of the vines and climbed them, disappearing into the cover of the canopy.

As the roar of the engine grew louder, Brett flopped on her stomach, smelling the mud, water, and bruised leaves. It seemed to take an eternity, then the big Benz diesel lumbered past, tires sucking at the mud.

Brett let out a sigh and started to stand.

The vegetation rattled behind her.

She spun, searching the dense undergrowth.

No one. Not even a bird. She turned back to watch the Benz.

It rocked and splashed over the uneven road, spitting blue smoke.

The forest had gone silent. Brett listened until the roar of the diesel engine faded, then she put a hand on a limb and pulled herself to her knees. She leaned out of the hole she'd torn in the brush and saw the Benz disappear around a curve. Rain battered her yellow hood and streamed down in front of her eyes.

Brett crawled forward, watching the trees on the other side of the road, expecting to see Umber climbing . . .

Someone grabbed her from behind and dragged her back through the hole.

Before she could scream, a leathery black hand clapped over her mouth.

Then there were more hands, on her legs and arms, her sides and neck. Her pack was roughly torn from her shoulders, and someone brutally jerked her around.

He shoved his black face against Brett's, his nose touching hers, his bright blue eyes glittering.

Umber jumps down to the ground. She tugs up her yellow hood and looks down the road. The truck is gone, but she can still hear it growling.

She walks up onto the road. The rain and thunder gnash at each other, eating the truck's voice, but she can hear apes hooting out in the trees.

The places in her heart where the blood lives pulse and ache, feeling their tugs.

Umber hoots back, and the voices go away.

She shifts her pack and walks across the road. Mud squishes up around her moccasins.

When she reaches the hole Brett made in the vines and brush, she squats and peers inside.

Pieces of yellow plastic hang on the brush.

Umber touches one, stroking it, then sticks her hand through the brush and makes the sign for Brett's name. She makes it again and crawls out into dark, hunching shadows.

Umber maneuvers her pack through and stands up.

The trees lean over her, whining in dripping silence, their waving arms frozen motionless.

She lifts her hand and signs: "No. Can't run," then makes the sign for Brett's name again and draws a question mark in the air.

The ears of her soul hear the trees moan.

Umber rocks back and forth, searching the forest for Brett. The trees' voices glitter inside her like broken glass.

Umber can feel it. The eyes watching. But this time they are not alive. They are dead eyes underwater, and she can't breathe.

Ten steps ahead, she sees another strip of yellow plastic.

Where is Brett? Despite her fear, Umber runs as hard as she can.

Thirty-five

Heavy rain slashed at the Kawasaki's canvas top and battered the muddy road Jim drove down. Rather than the unused track Valerie's map indicated, a great number of vehicles had traveled up and down this section of road, many of them today.

Jim looked over at Valerie. She was slightly turned away from him, watching the water-slick leaves pass by. She looked marvelous. The delicate arch of the cheekbones, the smooth line of her jaw. It took an act of will to keep from reaching out to touch her.

The forest gave way abruptly and Jim braked to a stop at the edge of a huge concrete slab. The trees had been cut back here, the underbrush pruned, the grass mown.

"Runway," Valerie said, pointing a short distance to the right where the concrete gave way to landing lights. In front of them, Jim could see the black streaks left by tires.

"Not quite the dirt strip we expected, huh?" Roberto asked. "I thought we'd find a couple of DC3s pushed back under the trees with camouflage netting over the wings."

Jim steered around a hole in the concrete and said, "Let's see who's home, shall we?"

Roberto lifted his camera. "Rolling."

Jim accelerated across the runway. The buildings at the end of the ramp were shrouded by misty streamers of rain. As they drove closer, the lines firmed into rounded hangars. In front of them stood tractors, stacks of fifty-five-gallon fuel drums, and several vehicles. Jim headed for the largest of the hangars.

Jim pointed. "I don't think that's a DC3."

Valerie squinted at the big plane. "I don't either. Look at all the propellers. Roberto? What is it?"

"Antonov, I think," Roberto said. He panned it with the camera as they passed. Several Fang workers, dressed in coveralls, stopped what they were doing to watch them drive by. "An An-70, maybe. Made in the Ukraine. Hell of a good choice for Africa. I've heard they're cheap to operate, carry huge loads, and don't need much strip to lift off. They call those flower-petal props a 'propfan.' Supposed to be very efficient."

Jim frowned as he saw the next plane. "This one is easier. That's the Gulfstream that brought us here. Last time I saw it, it was on the other runway. Want to stop?" The Gulfstream was also nosed into a hangar. One of the engine nacelles was open and a mechanic stood on scaffolding, tinkering on the inside.

"What for? The action isn't going to be on the landing strip. It's going to be down that road." Valerie pointed to the road leading away, toward the forested slope.

The Kawasaki growled onward, and the forest closed in around them.

"I don't get it," Jim said. "Why not just run the whole thing out of Compound A? Why *two* landing strips?"

"Why indeed," Valerie said as she draped an arm over the seat back. "You've seen something of the other compounds, Jim. What kind of apes did you see? Any augmented ones?"

"No." He thought about that. "Are the others an open house for the world, while the real work goes on here?"

"Looks like we're about to find out," Roberto said as they approached a gate.

Jim drove through. There were no guards, no signs. On the other side, five large buildings, older-looking, the walls water-stained and mossy, stood in a circle surrounded by a chain-link fence topped with razor wire. Three Kawasakis sat in a row in the roundabout. No other roads radiated out from this compound. Only footpaths exited through small gates in the fence.

"End of the line," Valerie said.

"Looks like," Roberto agreed, his eye glued to his camera.

Jim leaned over the wheel, listening to the rain on the canvas roof. "Which way now?"

Valerie looked around, picked the newest-looking of the five buildings, and said, "There. That one has the most antennas and satellite dishes."

She climbed out, and Jim and Roberto followed her at a trot. It turned out to be a document storage facility.

The next building's cement exterior looked hard-used by the tropics, but the interior was a plush dormitory.

In the third building, they found professorial offices, right down to the family pictures and posters on the walls. Valerie leaned in and asked a woman who worked at a computer keyboard, "Where's Dr. Smyth-Archer?"

The woman looked up, blinked as if gathering her thoughts after the interruption, then pointed and said, "The lab next door, I think."

As they stepped out into the rain, Jim asked, "What on earth made you ask for him?"

"A hunch." Valerie had a determined look in her eye. "Murray said he wasn't in England. So, where else would he be? Look, Godmoore takes his orders from Smyth-Archer, right? This thing has to be our Geoffrey's baby. Or at least he's up to his neck in it. If he's here, then by God we're going to get to the bottom of all this."

"If he'll see us," Jim said, suspecting Smyth-Archer would run as hard and fast as he could if he saw Valerie.

"Oh, he'll see us," Valerie promised. "Trust me, Jimbo, I'll see him if I have to twist arms. Be on your toes, I'll be depending on you to decipher the bullshit they throw at us."

"Bullshit?" Jim asked. "What bullshit?"

"You'll know if we're being snowed on the science." Valerie stepped through glass doors into a white-tiled foyer. She stopped, gaze fixed on the security touch pad beside the white safety door that forbade further progress. Roberto said, "High-tech security, Fuerta."

Valerie smiled and replied, "Looks like we'll have to try the next best thing to high-tech." She lifted a fist and pounded on the door.

They waited.

Valerie knocked again, and moments later a young man in a white coat opened the door. Redheaded, he had a lean pale face and hazel eyes. In a thick Scottish brogue, he asked, "What's all this? Who are you?"

"We're here for our appointment with Dr. Smyth-Archer," Valerie said, offering a Triple N business card and introducing Jim and Roberto. "Surely Dr. McDougal informed you we were here." As the man was inspecting the card, Valerie stepped past him into the hallway. Roberto slipped through behind her, and Jim followed, admiring their style.

"But I . . ." The young technician's brow furrowed.

"It's all right," Valerie told him in a self-assured voice. "We understand that Dr. Smyth-Archer doesn't always inform everyone of his appointments. Um, if you could just direct us to where we could find him?"

"In the neonatal care unit, but, well, that's off-limits to visitors."

Valerie strode down the hallway. "That's this way?"

"Ma'am, ye mustn't just barge in!" The technician leaped to take the lead.

Valerie followed the half-panicked young man through a maze of corridors and past a plethora of doors marked ELEC-TROPHORESIS, COMPUTER ROOM, PCR, EMBRYO TRANSPLANT, IN VITRO MUTAGENESIS, MAPPING LAB, HUMAN-APE GENOME DATABASE, and the generic MEN and WOMEN. The chase ended before a door marked APE WING.

The tech led them into a dressing room. Benches lined the walls, and white coats hung from hooks. Boxes on either side of the door on the opposite end contained surgical masks and latex gloves.

"You'll have to wait here," the tech told them, holding out both hands as if that could stop them. "I'll go and get Dr. Smyth-Archer and he kin deal w' ye." The technician grabbed up one of the masks, tied it over his mouth, and pushed through the door.

Valerie was all set to continue her pursuit when Jim placed a hand on her shoulder. "Wait. Mask up first," he told her, grabbing one of the masks from the box.

"What? Why?" Valerie demanded.

"Health reasons. Do it." He took off his hat, left it on a counter, and tied the mask over his nose and mouth.

Valerie gave him a skeptical look but complied, removing her poncho and masking up. Roberto did the same. Jim put on latex gloves, indicating that Valerie do the same. To Roberto he said, "You're working the camera. That's all right, but touch nothing. Understand?"

"Okay, man." Roberto shrugged.

"Why all the latex?" Valerie demanded as Jim pushed the door open and they entered a long corridor. "What are they trying to protect us from?"

"It's not you they are trying to protect," Jim told her. "It's the apes. What you might experience as a minor sniffle can be deadly to these primates. Humans have been coadapting with rhinovirus and all the other common diseases for millennia, but apes have been safely isolated from endemic human diseases. Now you're bringing a whole host of potentially lethal microbes into their world."

Jim suddenly lost all train of thought. Each side of the corridor was walled in glass. To the left several levels of cages stood like an island in the middle of the room. Only two of the thirty cages were occupied by apes. Each appeared to be sleeping, or tranquilized.

On the right was a large nursery staffed by two human women in white lab coats, who played with a group of seven young apes. Even at a glance, Jim could tell they were augmented. No more than two or three years old, they already walked upright, colorful plastic toys in their hands. But for the thick black hair, the dark wrinkled faces, and apelike prognathism, they might have been human children at a preschool.

Past a room divider, Jim looked through the glass into a neonatal unit worthy of a major urban hospital. Each crib was backed against a wall. Complicated monitoring devices reflected heartbeats, respiration rates, body temperatures, and blood pressures. Some of the units had oxygen tents over the little beds.

The tech stood over one, talking to a tall, blue-eyed man who listened intently. The man was dressed like a surgeon in white cap, gown, and booties. Jim couldn't make out any of his features through the mask.

Valerie was reaching for the door when Jim called, "No, Val. Wait here."

"But I'm masked." She gave him an irritated look.

"Trust me." Jim nodded toward the room. "See how he's dressed? We're not. We'll wait here."

"Suits me," Roberto said, the viewfinder of his camera already pasted to his eye.

The tall man caught their movement from the corner of his

eye. He started, staring, meeting Jim's gaze through the transparency. Jim expected Geoffrey Smyth-Archer's reaction to this invasion of his sanctum sanctorum by the press to be anger, fear, or maybe irritation; instead, those dreamy blue eyes welled with curiosity. Smyth-Archer glanced back at the tech, said something, and the young technician turned, walked to the door, and let himself out.

Clearly irritated at seeing them in the hallway, the redheaded tech said, "Dr. Smyth-Archer will be wi' ye in a minute." He pushed past them and retreated down the hallway.

"Fascinating," Jim whispered. He walked past the neonatal unit and glanced into what was clearly a delivery unit. Next to it was a maternity ward with three nursing female apes and their bright-eyed young. Jim stopped, suddenly numb. "Val? Come see this."

She trotted by the delivery room. "What have you got?"

"Look at the female on the right. Wait, there, she's looking right at us. What do you see?"

"Son of a bitch! Roberto, zoom shot. That's right." Valerie swallowed hard.

Jim watched, a constriction in his chest. To his surprise, the blue-eyed bonobo cuddled her infant under her right breast and signed: "Who you?"

Jim hooked his right index finger over his left, then repeated the action, left over right, signing: *"Friend."*

He repeated the word.

The young mother smiled.

Jim's soul seemed to lift from his body.

Thirty-six

Brett stumbled and the two apes gripping her arms pulled her to her feet. They dragged her forward across a rocky section of trail, following their blue-eyed leader. Her yellow raincoat hung in shreds over her blue jeans and red T-shirt. Wet blond hair straggled around her cheeks. There were four of them, three big males and one female. They kept casting angry glances her way, grunting and baring their teeth. Rain glistened on the long blades of the machetes they carried.

Brett tripped and staggered forward. The male grasping her left arm chirped and jerked her against him. His pink lips quivered as he glared. Fetid breath puffed over her face.

She whispered, "No," and tensed, fighting the urge to throw up.

He shoved her away, and his long hairy fingers sank into her arm again. They dragged Brett to a mass of enormous prop roots that twisted over the ground and tangled with the lowest tree branches. Rain ran in streams down the black bark.

The male grunted to his companion, and they boosted Brett into the tree, forcing her to climb as fast as she could, clambering from handhold to handhold while they struck her legs and hooted at her. Shaking badly, she could barely force her limbs to comply.

She had always considered herself to be strong, especially for her age. But in the grip of the apes, she felt like a wet paper towel. They had an oddly pungent smell, like the garbage-eating bears she'd smelled in Yellowstone Park last summer. Sometimes their hands flashed in signs she only partly understood. The more she saw, the more she thought they'd developed some sort of shorthand version of ASL.

Brett hauled herself higher and higher into the canopy. Every time she lifted herself past a branch, her nose filled with the scent of damp, musty bark.

The leader, Blue Eyes, wore her backpack over his left shoulder. He leaped out onto a wet mat of interlinking branches and waddled across, Brett's machete propped over his shoulder. The female followed him, grunting softly.

"Oh, God," Brett moaned as one of the apes beneath her slapped her in the thigh with the side of his machete and pointed.

Brett scrambled out onto the interlinking branches and crawled across, staring down in horror as they crossed the heights. She couldn't swallow past the lump in her throat.

Ahead of her, Blue Eyes and the female yelped, leaped across a gap in the leafy trail, and swung from one branch to another through the next tree.

A sob rose in Brett's throat. She couldn't do that! The limbs were all shiny with rain. She reached the gap in the leaves and looked down. It was a hundred-foot drop.

The two males came up on either side of Brett and started kicking her and grunting with their teeth bared.

"I can't!" she cried. Tears flooded her eyes. "I'll slip and fall!"

Before the sound of the last word had died away, the apes had gripped her by the arms and lifted her like a sack of potatoes.

Brett writhed, trying to break their holds. "Let me go! Let me go!"

They threw her across the gap.

Brett screamed, grasped for the closest branch, praying, and caught it. She hung there, sobbing like a three-year-old.

The two males landed beside her, the branch shivering and swaying under the impact. Brett swallowed her fears and struggled to pull herself up onto the top of the branch. They swung up and hit her hard across the back, driving her after Blue Eyes and the female.

Brett hurried through the branches as quickly as she could.

Images of Meggan's severed head kept flashing through her mind. God, this couldn't be happening. It just couldn't!

Blue Eyes and the female climbed down the tree in front of Brett, and she followed, trying to prop her feet at the same time that she clawed at the branches above her.

She jumped down onto a fallen log, a forest giant that had toppled to span a steep-walled canyon fifty feet across and at least that far down. She tried to stand, and her legs folded. She would have fallen into the gully but for the quick reactions of a strong hairy hand.

As the ape held her there, he grunted to the leader. Blue Eyes turned.

The male with his hand twined in Brett's red shirt made the gestures for: "This is one? You sure?"

Blue Eyes signed: "Yes. Girl told me in dream."

Brett's mouth opened as hope shot through her. She understood! She could talk to them!

The male released Brett, and she collapsed onto the tree trunk, wondering who "Girl" was. The way he'd used the sign it was not "a" girl, but a name.

Blue Eyes stepped closer, his odd gaze on Brett.

She signed: "Don't kill me."

Blue Eyes wheezed in soft bonobo laughter and turned away,

beckoning the others. Brett cried out as the thick-skinned hands grabbed her up and shoved her across the improvised bridge.

"Get a grip, Brett," she whispered through gritted teeth. "You grew up with an ape. Your father's an anthropologist. If anyone can survive this, it's you."

Screwing up her courage, she scrambled across the moss-covered log. The forest was reclaiming the wood. Not only was the rotting bark loose, but moss and ferns grew on it. Vines wound around and up the splintered branches. A misstep would send her plunging into the depths. She forced herself to concentrate on her feet. Rain spattered down on her from the leaves overhead.

Crossing the chasm, they dropped, one by one, to the spongy forest floor and began climbing a steep ridge, pulling themselves up by roots and suckers.

She followed, but kept falling farther behind. Finally, one of the apes behind her cuffed her hard with the back of his hand.

Terrified, Brett threw her head back and shouted the first name that came to her: *"Umber!"*

The hard blow across her lower back sent a fiery tingle through Brett. Without willing it, her back arched and she cried out. The big male following her lifted his machete and shook it. If he decided to use the edge, she'd die right here, lost in the middle of the forest. Her father would never find her.

I have to stay alive for as long as I can. If she could live until night, maybe she could slip away under the cover of darkness. But slip away to where? She struggled to gather her thoughts. They had crossed two ridges, counting this one. In the gloomy depths of the forest, she had no idea what direction led back to the road.

Think! Think, or you're dead! What did a person do who was lost? Granddad's words echoed through her. "Walk downhill, girl. Follow the water, and eventually you'll find a person camped alongside it."

Would that work in Africa? She pulled herself up over a half-rotted log. Blue Eyes walked ahead of her, the young female in the lead. Behind Brett, the two burly brown-eyed males followed, watching her progress.

A snag caught in Brett's T-shirt, the fabric giving just enough to fling her backward. For a moment, she hung there, supported by the cloth, before it tore and she tumbled into the big ape's arms. He righted her, inspected her torn T-shirt, and ripped it from her body.

Brett stumbled backward, digging her heels into the slope to keep from falling. Amidst amused hee-haii hoots, her two captors ripped the T-shirt into rags and draped bits of it over their shoulders. The big male wheezed as he arranged the torn collar around his own neck.

Brett crossed her arms protectively over her bra and said, "You guys are worse than football players."

Blue Eyes grunted and turned back around. The big male wearing her red collar waved her on with his machete, and Brett scrambled up the slope on all fours.

The apes followed the crest of the ridge. Here, at least, a trail of sorts wove its way through the thick trees.

Within moments, they broke out onto one of the project roads, and Brett looked around. Rain beat on her head and shoulders.

As if he'd read her thoughts of escape, the big ape rammed a fist between her shoulder blades and knocked Brett to the ground.

"Cut it out! Asshole!" Brett staggered up, and the male used the tip of the machete to prod her down the road.

The female still led, but Blue Eyes stayed close behind her. On the flat muddy ground Brett's long legs ate at the distance that separated her from them.

She looked behind her, seeing the two males hurrying along side by side, swinging their machetes.

"Anything's better than this."

The road took a sharp bend ahead. Brett caught up with Blue Eyes and broke into a trot, matching his pace, aware of her shiny new machete clutched in one hand, and her backpack slapping on his shoulders. Ahead, the female loped along, panting. She started into the corner, and Brett dashed around Blue Eyes.

Putting on a burst of speed, she passed the female. Shrieks and excited hoots and yips broke out behind her.

"Yes!" she cried, charging down the long slope. Water ran in little rivulets. In the mud she could see the imprint of chevroned Kawasaki tires. Glancing over her shoulder, she saw the apes struggling to catch her, screaming in rage. She lengthened her stride, arms and legs pumping in the lashing rain.

"Run, Brett! Run like you've never run before!" The steep slope added to her momentum, leaving her at the verge of control. If she slipped, fell, she could still bound to her feet and flee with plenty of time.

But if you turn an ankle, you're dead meat. The notion took on a special relevance when she thought of Meggan O'Neil.

She reached another curve and shot a glance behind her. A bubble of laughter started up in her throat. Blessed God, they were gone! Had they given up already? Brett whooped.

"Hell. Easier than it ought to have been!" Now it would be an easy jog back to . . . where?

The implications of her predicament began to settle in. If she went running into Compound A, McDougal might just pack her up and send her off on an airplane to America, leaving Umber alone out on the Evinayong road, looking for Brett.

She slowed to make the tight corner where the road switchbacked. She'd been up and down the roads in Compound A, but had no idea which one she was on. The lush growth of forest right up to the edge of the road didn't provide much in the way of landmarks. One wall of green leaves looked pretty much like another.

The gray sky looked the same now as it had when she and Umber had left the compound, so a bearing off of the sun was out of the question. As to the distance she'd traveled with the apes, that, too, was beyond her. A mile? Three? Her time with them might have been an eternity.

Think, Brett! What are you going to do? If this road took her to Compound A, she couldn't let the SAC people catch her. No, she had to find Compound A, regain her bearings, and take the Evinayong road again so that she could find Umber.

God, poor Umber. She's all by herself out there, worried sick about me. She just couldn't leave Umber in this horrible place.

Brett was falling into her stride now, running easily, stretching out into her distance pace. On a good day, she could do five miles on the flats. This wasn't a good day, the roads were muddy, and she'd have to endure the uphill sections.

"You're just going to have to do it," she huffed. Desperation, it seemed, could be one hell of a motivator.

As she rounded a bend, screams broke out, the panicked calls of colobus monkeys. Brett's legs immediately reenergized. She shot ahead, leery of a misstep. Her running shoes made a slapping sound as they splashed through the wet red mud. Ahead was yet another of the switchbacks. Well, eventually she'd reach the bottom. Perhaps there she'd find a landmark to give her an idea of where she was.

Breath tore at the bottom of her throat. What if this was the road to Compound B, and the apes were between her and Compound A? They'd already ambushed her on the road once. Why wouldn't they just wait up there and grab her on the way back?

This thing was going from bad to worse.

Five minutes later, she rounded yet another of the switchbacks, and the road leveled out. Brett trotted around a gentle curve and there, in front of her, was one of the raised draw-bridges that separated the compounds.

"Son of a bitch!" She slowed, catching her breath as she stepped onto the bridge approach and looked up at the raised section. Walking over to the gray plastic box, she slammed it with the flat of her hand. It hardly jiggled, impervious to her blow.

She looked down at the murky brown water and shivered. Worms, river blindness, crocodiles and snakes, and God alone knew what else might be lurking down in that stuff.

"Well, at least I know where I am." She now faced the long run back to Compound A, back up that hill, past the apes lurking in ambush in the forest. She bowed her head and warm rain pattered on her soaked hair to trickle down her skin.

"Damn it!"

Could she sit here and wait until a SAC Kawasaki came by? No. Umber needed her. That was all that mattered.

The soft hoot brought her bolt upright. She tossed her wet blond hair back and spun around.

"No! Damn you! *No!*"

Blue Eyes and his band spread out across the bridge approach, blocking her exit.

Thirty-seven

"Dickie says I should have you all shot." Geoffrey Smyth-Archer stepped out of the neonatal unit and pulled down his surgical mask.

Valerie studied him. His handsome face had an innocent quality. If anything, he looked boyish, charming, and oddly vulnerable, the sort of combination that most women would find deadly. She wasn't completely immune to it herself.

"Dr. Smyth-Archer? I'm Valerie Radin, Triple N." She offered her gloved hand, and he took it, the handshake firm, unpatronizing, and professional. She introduced Roberto and Jim.

"Dr. Dutton," Smyth-Archer said. "I'm so pleased to meet you. I can't wait to hear about Umber. You've done a splendid job with her. We've been so happy with your progress. Really, she's one of our stars, you know."

"Really?" Jim asked. His dark brown hair and beard shone in the fluorescent light. Valerie caught herself comparing them: Smyth-Archer radiated a numinous quality, something abstract and celestial, while Jim had a solid magnetism, a secular reality, tempered and quenched. Divinity and the warrior hero, eye to eye.

"Oh, to be sure." Smyth-Archer clapped his hands together.

"Well, I really hadn't expected you here today. I have some tests to perform, but I suppose they can wait. Would you mind sharing tea with me? Does your schedule permit that?"

"We'd be delighted, Dr. Smyth-Archer." Valerie clamped a hand on his arm like a predator. She caught Roberto's eye. They had to make the most of this interview.

"Oh, please, please." Smyth-Archer waved. "I'm Geoffrey. Way too many syllables the other way, don't you think?"

"What are we seeing here?" Jim pointed to the glass-walled rooms that lined the hallway.

"Why, the breeding program, of course." Smyth-Archer indicated the line of wire cages. "On occasion we bring in some of the feral apes, and this is their short-term holding facility. I hate those bloody cages, but, well, to tell you the truth, the feral animals simply cannot be handled any other way. When they're confined, we keep them down so they don't become depressed. However, let me assure you, none is kept more than forty-eight hours."

"Forty-eight hours?" Valerie asked, aware of the change in his expression.

"Would you want to huddle in a little cage like that, Miss Radin?" He pinned her with his gentle blue eyes.

So, Geoffrey Smyth-Archer is the program's messiah, Valerie thought.

"Only under the most extreme circumstances should apes be confined." He gestured, the movement birdlike. "We, I mean, human beings, have treated them abysmally, you know. All in the name of science. Have you ever heard of an isolette? It's a tiny little cage like a cramped prison box. Some apes are forced to live their whole lives in such a space, two feet wide, three feet deep, and three feet tall." His blue eyes had a haunted glaze. "We have tried and executed humans for confining other humans to a space that small. Odd, isn't it, that we reward the scientists and institutions who treat their chimpanzees that way?"

His smile warmed when he looked at Jim. "Dr. Dutton, I can't thank you enough for taking such good care of Umber."

Jim propped his hands on his hips. His damp denim shirt stretched out over his broad shoulders. "Then why are you breaking up my family?"

"I don't understand." Smyth-Archer turned to him.

"I don't know what your long-term goal was with Umber, but she's part of my family. If the goal was to see just how much an augmented ape could be encultured through cross-fostering, I can tell you it worked. Umber is as American as my daughter, Brett. Umber wants to go home with her family."

Smyth-Archer frowned. "Is that a problem?"

Valerie asked, "Who runs this place, Geoffrey? You? Or Dr. Godmoore?"

Smyth-Archer blinked, as if confused by the question. "I take care of these apes. They are my responsibility."

Roberto surreptitiously edged forward, catching the exchange on film.

"But the day-to-day administration of Smyth-Archer Chemists, that's Dr. Godmoore's province, isn't it? Doesn't he see to the details?"

"Yes." Smyth-Archer smiled wistfully. "Dickie's very good at that."

Valerie said, "Are you aware that people are being killed, Dr. Smyth-Archer? That Kivu is being charged with murder? That the evidence seems to indicate that Dr. Shanks and his assistant, Meggan O'Neil, were murdered by one of your apes?"

He seemed genuinely stunned. "No. Well, I had heard that Kivu was in some sort of trouble, but not murder. He's not the type to do anything like that."

Jim's blue eyes narrowed. "Your goons are the ones who made him do it. By threatening Shanna Bartlett!"

"Goons?" Smyth-Archer glanced back and forth. "What are goons?"

"Enforcers," Valerie said softly and gestured for Jim to desist. He gave her a frustrated look. Valerie continued, "Let me explain," and she related in detail the tragedy in Texas.

Smyth-Archer took a step back. "This can't be. Is that why Dickie is so upset with you? Why are you making these things up about us?"

Jim stepped forward. "We're not making any of this up. You mean you really don't know what's going on in your own company?"

"No, Jim," Valerie said in a low voice. "He doesn't." She smiled then and changed her voice to a nonconfrontational tone. "Geoffrey, we're not here to make things up about you, or the apes. We're here to help, and everyone has tried to stop us from seeing you. Listen, you said something about tea? Let's go and talk. We'll tell you what we know, and you tell us what you know. Then, together, we'll figure out what the real truth is. Is that an equitable deal?"

He gave her a suspicious look, but his reserve melted under her winning smile. "Yes, Ms. Radin. I could do that."

"Good." She took his arm and led him back down the hallway. "We've been looking for the answer to one central question, and it's probably the question you'll be asked the most when the rest of the world finds out about you and your project apes. *Why* are you doing all this?"

He glanced down at her, honesty in his eyes. "Why, for the apes, of course. It's for them."

"We don't get it," Jim said from behind Valerie. "What's for them?"

"Oh." Smyth-Archer looked back over his shoulder. "Everything. All of this. Dr. Dutton, human beings have been exterminating them. Causing their extinction. Genocide is not too strong a word to use in this context. Humans have done terrible things, infected them with our diseases to watch how they die, broken their minds, spirits, and bodies. Sometimes it's been done in the name of science, and sometimes out of our own greed. We've destroyed their forests, devastated their habitats. There must be restitution for the crimes humans have committed against them. They are our closest relatives. I've come to know them, and to respect their intelligence and sensitivity. My parents, and SAC itself, made a fortune off their suffering. Now I, at least, am trying to balance the ledgers. Repay part of the debt I owe to them."

"How are you accomplishing that?" Valerie asked, looking up. His eyes had turned wistful, luminous.

"By giving them the tools they need to deal with the twenty-first century," Smyth-Archer replied. "The only way to do that is to make them our equals."

Equals? Valerie tensed, a hint of the implications dawning.

"Planet of the Apes?" Roberto asked.

"Oh, no, Mr. Naez. In that movie, they had been slaves. In the world I am building, they will be our equals."

"Jesus," Jim whispered. The glance he shot Valerie betrayed his dismay. He, too, understood the implications.

"Not Jesus," Smyth-Archer said evenly, missing the context, "but I hope they will remember me more like Moses."

Valerie observed his beatific smile. He meant it, every single word of it. Did the fool really think humanity was ready for a nonhuman partnership with apes? It was nuts.

They passed into the dressing room, stripped off the masks and gloves, and Smyth-Archer pulled off his cap and gown to free his graying shoulder-length blond hair. He wore a white button-down shirt, gray slacks, and brown oxfords. Jim grabbed his damp Rand hat from the counter where he'd left it. His face betrayed a tornado of emotions, but he was keeping his cool.

"You see," Smyth-Archer continued as they made their way

back through the maze of labs to the front of the building, "the plan was to attack the problem of ape augmentation from two directions. First, we needed the best and brightest of the augmented youngsters to be placed in homes such as yours, Dr. Dutton."

"That has been done before. Washo, Lucy, Viki, lots of chimps had been socialized through cross-fostering," Jim replied.

"Oh, yes," Smyth-Archer agreed. "They were placed in the families of psychologists, but when they outgrew the research design, they were cast off. In some cases those same animals ended up in cages, infected with HIV and hepatitis. The betrayal was morally reprehensible, but we've developed a society that believes in throwaway animals, be they dogs, cats, horses, or chimps. The research community was just as morally corrupt as anyone."

"Not all of us," Jim replied evenly. "Roger Fouts, Penny Patterson, and Sue Savage-Rumbaugh, among others, have practically gone begging in the streets to keep their apes."

"Yes, absolutely," Smyth-Archer agreed. "The trouble has always been that when the apes matured, they couldn't be let loose in our society without constant supervision. An ape doesn't have the same volume of frontal cortex. Their emotions overwhelm their good sense."

"I've got friends like that who are perfectly human," Roberto said from behind Valerie.

"Of course," Smyth-Archer agreed as they exited the security door and crossed the foyer. "But humans still have that extra gray matter that overrides the emotional drive of the paleocortex. My challenge was to provide the apes with the same advantages in emotional control, long-term planning, memory, and problem solving that humans have. Do that, and an ape is no longer threatening, or unpredictable. They cease being 'wild,' and can function within the parameters of human society."

Jim shook his head.

"Do you have a problem with that, Dr. Dutton?" Smyth-Archer asked.

"You put more faith in people than I do." Jim gave him a level stare. "I teach anthropology, Geoffrey. Over the last four million years the normal state was for several species of *Homo* to be alive at the same time. The last time we had two species of humans was during the Pleistocene, thirty thousand years ago. Moderns and Neandertals. From the data, it looks like the moderns wiped out the Neandertals, or at least outcompeted them for resources. We couldn't share the planet then, how do you expect us to do it now?"

"It's a problem, I know." Smyth-Archer sighed. "But, I mean, we *can* do it. Look here, at this project. These people, the Fang, used to hunt chimps for food. Now they work to protect them."

"That's here," Jim insisted stubbornly. "You're paying them to do that. Can you pay off the whole world?"

"It's a matter of education," Smyth-Archer insisted.

"I wish you were right, Geoffrey," Valerie said smoothly. "But it wasn't two weeks ago that I watched the excavation of a mass grave. Humans are still killing each other over religion, ethnicity, money, and any other thing they can think of, and you want them to reach out and embrace another species?"

Geoffrey turned his radiant gaze on Jim. "You did, Dr. Dutton. You embraced Umber. I hope that one day all of our chimps will be embraced, but that's for the future." He clasped his hands behind him as they walked out into the warm rain. "For me, all I need to do is level the playing field. This place, these apes, do that. I can die satisfied that I have done my share to give them a chance."

"A chance? What if they're hunted down as monsters?" Jim asked.

"I gave them what they need to compete, Dr. Dutton. Intelligence to match our own." He gave Jim a narrow-eyed look.

"I wonder, in a couple of years, how well do you think we'll do? One on one, I mean, with an adult Umber, or a Kivu? What if, Dr. Dutton, they turn out to be better adapted to technology than we are. After all, they have dexterous feet, that third hand we've always wished for. Ah, yes, I can see that you comprehend the implications."

Jim looked half stricken. In an agonizingly soft voice, he said, "Didn't it occur to you that having a human-sized brain may mean more than just greater intellectual ability? Think back to your basic primatology. Remember Passion and Pom, the two female chimpanzees at Gombe? They killed another female's infant. Bit it in the head and then ate it in front of the poor bereaved mother. That aggression is part of us as primates. Hardwired into our deep psyches. Chimp or human. Now, with bigger brains, you have given your subjects the capacity for more creative premeditated murder and genocide. In a couple of generations they can be slaughtering thousands in the name of God, or political ideology, or ethnic affiliation. Didn't SAC think this through before they decided to do it? If Kivu did kill someone, it's not his fault. It's *yours*."

Smyth-Archer gave him a sad look of incomprehension, and walked away.

Valerie trotted to keep up with Smyth-Archer's longer stride. "So, what *was* the original plan? The brightest apes go off to live with people like Jim. What about the ones here. What do you call them, feral apes?"

Smyth-Archer's eyes seemed to lose focus. "They serve a dual purpose. In the first place, they act as a control, giving us a comparative database to use against observations by people like Jane Goodall, Takayoshi Kano, and the Badrians. The results have been quite fascinating."

Jim spread his legs and took up a challenging stance before Smyth-Archer. "I don't think Vernon Shanks or Meggan O'Neil would agree."

"I *will* check into that, Dr. Dutton." Smyth-Archer led them over toward the dormitory building.

"My guess," Jim said ironically, "is that when you put human genes into a bonobo, you get human behavior."

Smyth-Archer stopped short, his hair sparkling with raindrops. "Yes, that would explain it, wouldn't it?"

"How can you take it so academically?" Valerie asked. "Your second in command is lying on a slab over in Compound A!"

Smyth-Archer resumed his walk toward the shelter of the dormitory. "Well, I don't . . . How did you say they were killed?"

"Machete." Valerie watched the man's face as she talked. His expression remained blank. "Shanks had the back of his neck chopped open. Then had his heart extracted. Meggan's whole head was lopped off. She was cut up into pieces and scattered around in the treetops."

They entered the lobby area of the dormitory, and Smyth-Archer sighed and shook his head. "I wonder where they learned that. We certainly haven't taught them any such behavior. We don't provide them with machetes. Rather, we encourage them to make their own tools. We wanted to see just how far they could take themselves here in this restricted environment."

"Did you know they had escaped Compound D?" Valerie asked. "They murdered Shanks and O'Neil in B. One of the researchers is missing from C."

"Oh, they can't," he insisted. "They can't get across the water."

"Apparently, Geoffrey," Jim said dryly, "there's a lot about your apes you don't know. For God sakes, you engineered the equivalent of human intelligence into an ape, and didn't expect him to figure out something as simple as a water barrier?"

Smyth-Archer paused, considering. "You make a very good point. We had thought to use electric fences in the beginning, but in this damp environment, and given the problems of generating that amperage reliably in this climate, we didn't think them feasible for the long term."

"So, tell me," Valerie asked, trying to remain nonconfrontational. "What do you call the blue-eyed guy with the propensity for things that are sharp?"

"Hmm? Oh, you must mean Sky Eyes. He's the leader of the Alpha Group. He's very bright, learned language extremely fast. There was a problem, though." A pained expression crossed his face. "We had placed him with a family in Denmark. Dickie told me there was an accident. Apparently one of the girls in the household fell down the stairs and broke her neck. I saw pictures of her. She was a pretty little blond child. The parents thought Sky Eyes was responsible. That was ridiculous, of course. Sky Eyes said he'd tried to save the girl. But we brought him here just to be safe, and thank heavens we did. He taught the other members of his band language, and tool use, and how to build things. Well, as I said, he's remarkably bright. The Alpha Group has been missing for a while, though. Something happened one night and they just vanished."

"I think what happened was poachers," Valerie said and followed Smyth-Archer into the cafeteria. The sound of pots clanging against silverware rang out. "From the stories told in Evinayong, your Sky Eyes killed two poachers that night to avenge two of your apes that the poachers killed."

"Retribution." Smyth-Archer led them to a long table with a gray Formica top and seated himself. He looked over to the kitchen staff standing behind the counter, more of the local Fang, and asked, "Tea all around, please."

"Retribution?" Jim repeated the word as if he'd never heard it before. "Dr. Smyth-Archer, do you realize what that means? You've got to stop this. All of it! At least four people are dead already, maybe more. When this comes out, no matter what your motives, the whole world is going to come down on top of you and your apes. And me and mine! Is that what you want?"

"Dr. Dutton, I don't think you understand what is at issue

here. We are talking about the survival of our biological cousins. But for an accident of evolution, we'd be them, or they would be us. Whatever separated us back in the dim past—"

"The Mitumba Mountains and the Great Rift Valley," Jim said tiredly.

"—the fact remains that history will judge us poorly if we commit genocide on our closest relatives. I'm willing to pay whatever price I must to save every last one of them."

"Including the murderers?"

Smyth-Archer gave Jim a sad smile. "Dr. Dutton, the latest census figures compiled by my people indicate that less than one hundred thousand chimpanzees exist on a continent that once supported over five million. Who are the real murderers here? With regard to bonobos, Dr. Kano estimated fifty thousand animals in the mid-seventies. Today, after the turn of the millennium and years of civil war, my best census figures suggest that there are less than ten thousand bonobos left in the wild. Within the next thirty years—in our lifetimes—they will be extinct. Since I cannot count on the milk of human kindness to save them, I must give them other skills."

Jim sat perfectly still, his flexed fingers perched on the Formica table. "You cannot know what you just said."

Smyth-Archer's lips curled into that beatific smile. He reached out across the table and grasped Jim's hands. "Dr. Dutton, I have changed the world. While others talked, and wrung their hands, I acted. Human beings are no longer alone on the top rung of the intelligence ladder. When you look into the blue eyes of one of my apes, you look into the eyes of an equal."

Valerie said gravely, "Doctor, on a planet that is fast running out of resources, how do you expect people to share those few that are left with apes, cousins or not?"

"You don't believe that they should have a chance?" Geoffrey asked, as if sensing her gravity for the first time.

"Sure they should," Valerie said, "but humanity isn't going

to give it to them. Smart or stupid, our species is the kind to exterminate on the spur of the moment and question the ethics of it years after the fact." She sighed. "God, we're a miserable bunch."

The sound of approaching feet could be heard in the lobby, then the door burst open. Shelly McDougal stormed in with four uniformed soldiers.

Valerie checked their polished Kalashnikovs. The soldiers had their hands on the pistol grips, thumbs on the fire-control levers. They were ready. Listlessly, Valerie said, "I think my point has just been made, Dr. Smyth-Archer."

Thirty-eight

"Hello, Shelly," Smyth-Archer greeted amiably, his curious gaze going to the soldiers. "Would you join us for tea? We were just talking about competitive intelligence, and I was just about to tell them about the next generation, and why they are going to be even—"

"I'm sorry, sir," she stated in her precise Scottish accent. "But these people have a plane waiting for them in Compound A."

"Oh, I don't think so," Valerie said confidently, rising to meet McDougal's hard eyes. "This is a meeting of two great scientific minds. It's too important to interrupt."

McDougal gave Valerie a thin smile. "I am sure Dr. Godmoore would disagree—the plane is waiting on *his* orders."

"Dickie?" Smyth-Archer asked. "Is he here?"

"No, sir, but he sent the plane specifically for these people. He is looking forward to seeing them in Sussex, soonest." McDougal lifted her chin. "That's why they have to leave now."

"Oh, yes." Smyth-Archer waved. "If Dickie wants them, we mustn't keep him waiting. He has something important to tell them, no doubt." He paused. "Oh, by the way, Shelly, Dr. Dutton tells me that Sky Eyes and the Alpha Group might be in

Compound B. You might look there. Girl is pregnant, you know. I'd really like to have her here for the birth."

McDougal narrowed an eye, jerking her head toward the door. "If you would, please, Dr. Dutton?"

Valerie could see Jim's anger in the stiff set of his shoulders. She gripped his arm, tightening her fingers, and said, "Come along, Dr. Dutton. Let's hear what Dickie has to say." When he got really angry, Jim's eyes always took on an unearthly blue glow. She gave him the same look in return, silently ordering him to back her up, and Jim read her expression perfectly. The muscles in his jaw bunched, but he relented.

"Yes. Of course," he said, voice clipped, and reached out for Smyth-Archer's hand. "Thank you for your time, Doctor."

Then Valerie took Smyth-Archer's hand. "It was wonderful to meet you, Doctor. I urge you to consider some of the problems we've discussed, especially the *human* aspect of the situation, and how to solve the backlash. That will be the challenge for the next generation of SAC apes."

"Yes, yes, I will consider the things you've said. All of them. I promise." Smyth-Archer stood, his eyes clear, apparently back in this world for the moment. "Dr. Dutton. Again, my thanks."

"Geoffrey, please," Jim said desperately, "don't let them take Umber away from me. It will break her heart."

"Of course we won't take Umber from you," Smyth-Archer said with a frown.

"Do I have your word on that, sir?"

"Why, yes, of course, we would never . . ."

McDougal hustled them from the room. Once the cafeteria doors had closed behind them, Valerie walked beside Shelly McDougal. "You've quite a place here. I'm Valerie Radin, Triple N—"

"I know who you are. And you've done quite enough already. I'm putting you on a plane. I understand that Sergeant

Bonoficio here has some questions for you in Malabo. After that, you're Dr. Godmoore's problem."

"Really? What if I refuse?"

As they stepped outside into the rain, McDougal said, "I wouldn't recommend that, Ms. Radin. I really would not. Sergeant, will you please relieve Mr. Naez of his camera?"

Roberto gripped his camera to his chest, shaking his head. "Sorry. This is Triple N property. It stays with me."

The sergeant stepped back, his right thumb clicking the fire-control lever down. The other soldiers followed suit, retreating to clear a line of fire.

"Roberto," Valerie said levelly as she read the sergeant's flat stare, "surrender the camera." Then, as Naez reluctantly did so, she turned to McDougal. "So, you're ready to kill us?"

McDougal's expression might have been carved in stone. "Accidents happen in the rain forest, Ms. Radin." She nodded at the sergeant. "No telling what native troops might do. They don't understand English very well."

"See to it that the camera, and the film in it, reach Compound A intact," said Valerie. "Because 'there's no telling' what reporters might do. Or, in this case, might already have done."

Valerie marched for the Kawasaki, her back muscles tense, waiting for the shot.

As Jim settled behind the steering wheel and turned the key, Valerie said, "It's not over yet. We still might end up floating in one of the canals before we get back to A."

Umber reaches for a branch as she climbs over a thick root. Her eyes are on the trail. She pulls herself up. The branch feels like rubber. Then it moves. Umber jerks back with a shriek and her wet feet fly out from under her. The huge snake curls down the trunk and into the shadowed roots. Its forked tongue darts in and out as it watches her through cold, alien eyes.

She cannot breathe.

The snake oozes through the roots, its sinuous length shining as the splotched sides become the shadows. Then the big triangular head lifts and the giant snake hisses.

In one panicked leap, Umber jets to her feet, screams, and runs.

After ten steps, she stops and looks back.

Brett needs her.

A whimper forms in her throat as she puts her left moccasin ahead of her right, then her right ahead of her left. Every root, branch, and vine watches her now, waiting to hiss and strike.

Umber holds the bow and machete over her right shoulder and bends to examine a place where the leaves have been kicked. On the side of a root, she sees a piece of red cloth. She reaches for it and sniffs it. Her heart pounds as she tucks it into the top of her moccasin. She sniffs again, flaring her nostrils at the breeze, trying to scent blood. But she smells none.

She hurries along the trail, casting terrified glances for snakes.

Brett's shirt on a root. A sock and a woman's panties at the waterfall.

Her lip pulls back from her teeth in a fear-smile. What will she do if she finds pieces of Brett?

An unfamiliar keening comes from her throat, driving her forward. Her fault. It will all be her fault. SAC made Brett and Jim come here because of her.

Umber's hair stands on end as she races up a steep hill on all fours and bursts out onto a road.

Tracks mark the mud. Ape feet, and Brett's running shoes.

Umber clutches her bow in her left hand and rushes down the road. Her pack, quiver, and machete bounce on her back.

Halfway down the slope, Umber sees where the apes pushed through the leaves into the forest.

Umber slips into the gloom and looks. Fear clutches at her throat as she sees the ape tracks. Umber follows, running headlong down the slick mountainside. When she bursts out onto the road, she sees the bridge rising.

Umber runs as she has never run before. Her lungs are heaving, her legs shaking, as she sprints onto the bridge approach.

Umber scrambles up the railing to the top span. There, on the opposite shore, three apes stand around Brett.

Umber throws her head back and screams.

The apes turn.

"Umber?" Brett cries, her voice breaking.

The apes hoot.

Umber rocks back and forth, panting, then points to Brett and signs, "Coming!"

"No, Umber!" Brett cries. "Run! Get back and tell Dad!"

The ape behind Brett slaps her hard, sending her staggering, and Umber squeals in terror, jerks her bow from her shoulder, and climbs hand over hand to the top of the bridge. Holding the bow on her shaking knees, she nocks an arrow and lets it fly.

The thin shaft arches through the rain and buries itself in the mud just to the right of the tallest ape. He jumps and peers down at the feathered shaft.

Hooting at the top of her lungs, Umber rushes toward the canal.

Brett screams, *"Umber, no!"*

With two soldiers in a Mule in front of them, and two other soldiers and McDougal in a Mule close behind them, Jim had no alternative but to obey McDougal's order to follow the lead vehicle. Rain poured from the gray sky as the Kawasaki bumped and growled down the forest road. Valerie, sitting in the passenger seat, and Roberto, in the rear, both seemed locked in thought.

"I don't get it," Jim said. "Why didn't you ask Smyth-Archer what he wanted done with us?"

"Because, Jim, he's a messiah leading a holy war, and McDougal is his general. Our lunatic Geoffrey isn't about to upset his sacred vision because some pilgrim begs him from bended knee. No, we'll fight this out with Mighty McDougal. Actually, we'll get further with her because, unlike her messiah, she probably possesses a modicum of common sense. I can use that."

They crossed the last bridge into Compound A. "The man is insane," Jim said.

"A raving idealist is more like it." Valerie shook her head. "Totally self-absorbed. No reality beyond his project."

"I'm starting to understand Richard Godmoore now," Valerie went on reluctantly. "It's darling little Geoffrey, the genius golden boy with his private African ape preserve and his PCR machines to make recombinant apes, who's making Godmoore so nervous. No wonder Godmoore's such a hard-ass. If this blows up, SAC sinks, and so does Dickie's ten percent of the stock."

"That must be worth, how much?" Roberto wondered. "Twenty or thirty million pounds? That's more than enough to make him snuff a couple of nosy journalists and a scientist."

"I'll keep that in mind." Valerie turned and gave him a worried look.

"They can't do that," Jim said. "At least I don't think so. People know we're here."

They drove past the gate in the chain-link fence and into Compound A with its now familiar main street. All three Mules parked in front of the dormitory.

Jim climbed out, followed by Valerie and Roberto. His heart

had begun to hammer, and the shakes lay buried just beneath his calm.

McDougal walked over to Jim's Mule and ordered, "Go and pack your things. I'll accompany you, just to make sure it's done correctly."

Valerie, Jim, and Roberto walked all the way to the door and had entered the lobby before Valerie said, "Dr. McDougal, have you ever heard of a digital satellite phone?"

McDougal seemed to miss a step. The nostrils of her thin nose flared. "A what?"

"It's actually rather old technology. I see that one of your soldiers is carrying Roberto's camera. Let's go up to my room. I'll show you one of the stories we uplinked out of here last night. My boss is sitting on it back in Washington. In the business, we call it insurance."

Shelly McDougal's jaw hardened. "It's not that I'm doubting you, but I don't trust you."

"Good," Valerie said smoothly. "You and I have finally reached an understanding."

McDougal hesitated, her cold blue gaze burning into Valerie's. Then she turned to the soldiers, took the camera, and said: "Wait outside. If I need you, I'll call."

When their suite door was closed behind them, Valerie pointed to the cases. "Roberto, show Dr. McDougal how the system works."

Roberto explained the satellite system to McDougal, then took the camera. Within seconds his capable fingers had fitted the right cable to the room television. Hitting a button, the screen came to life and began to replay Valerie's report from the night before.

Shelly McDougal's face blanched. Halfway through the report, she said, "That's enough! All right, Ms. Radin, what do you have to say?"

Valerie folded her arms over her white shirt. "Here's how it lays out: If anything happens to us, you're going to be at the center of a tornado. My boss is going to want to know why we disappeared in the middle of a very big story. So will every other news agency in the world. You've talked to Sussex? Then you know that umpteen reporters are camped at their gates. The world media is scrambling to make up lost ground. My guess is that as we speak news crews are in Libreville, Bata, and Douala trying to book bush taxis and figure out how to get here."

"They will be refused entry." But McDougal looked unsure. She smoothed her gray hair with an unsteady hand.

Valerie laughed. "I can't believe I'm hearing this! Come on, Doctor, you know better than that. Don't you? Shelly, *think!* You're an intelligent woman." Valerie raised a clenched fist. "This thing is coming apart around you. Do you want to go down as Richard Godmoore's private little SS martinet?"

McDougal met her icy glare for a long moment, then her shoulders slumped. "Then what do you suggest, Ms. Radin?"

"All right, cards on the table. Your Geoffrey is a delightfully charming, gracious, and naive Frankenstein, but he's still building monsters. If—"

"We don't think so."

"Well, I admit that I like Umber myself, but here's the way things sit. This story could go either way, Shelly. In Geoffrey's version, Umber sits side by side with CEOs at the Smyth-Archer board meeting. In another, pictures of mutilated human bodies lead the prime-time news. That's it. Science gone bad, or a grand new species. The jury's still out."

Jim waited, watching the muscles at the corner of McDougal's lips trembling.

"What are you proposing?" McDougal asked.

"I want to do an in-depth story on the whole thing." Valerie began pacing back and forth. "I want shots of the labs with the technicians describing the process by which the apes are augmented. I want the neonatal unit and nursery. I want shots of Compounds B and C, success stories of lab chimps reintroduced to the wild. Then I want Geoffrey, candid, with that messianic gleam in his eyes as he talks about the things humans have done to apes. I want—"

"Why?" McDougal demanded hotly. "So you can finish digging our grave? Not a bloody damned chance!"

Valerie walked up to McDougal and stared her right in the eyes. In that instant, Jim fell in love with her all over again. She looked like Joan of Arc about to call down the destructive power of God.

Valerie said, "I don't care about SAC, or you, or your stockholders. But I do care about the apes. That's the real story here. It's not what you've done, or why, but how it affects them. We have to discover why they're killing people."

"You can't prove an ape killed Vernon!" McDougal protested.

"Watch me." Valerie narrowed her eyes, pinning McDougal. "Sky Eyes didn't just start killing people one day because he thought it would be entertaining. He was pushed to it. I didn't want to tell Geoffrey this, but that female in the Alpha Group, Girl, she was the only pregnant one, correct?"

McDougal nodded.

"She's not going to be found, Doctor. A poacher named Ngasala killed her with a shotgun. He cut the fetus from her womb, hoping it was old enough to survive until he could get it to Evinayong to sell it. But just after he cut it from her belly, he was attacked and killed. Only one of the poachers escaped by blind luck. He fell into the canal. But humans, unlike apes, can swim."

"Blessed Lord." McDougal's voice had gone soft. "You can prove this?"

"We couldn't film him," Roberto said. "But it's here." He lifted a tape recorder from one of the cases. "It was dark, the man was drinking, but enough of the story seems to match."

"The blue-eyed ape," Valerie said, "that was the key, and then Geoffrey mentioning the pregnant female. Sky Eyes and his group were hunted. Two of his band—no, three, counting the infant—were killed. The same thing with Kivu. He, too, was protecting his own. There's my story, Doctor."

"How do I know I can trust you?"

"You *can't* trust me, Doctor." Valerie's expression grew predatory. "I'll go where the truth takes me. So you'd better damned well give it to me straight."

McDougal took a deep breath, anger simmering in her eyes. "I'll have to talk with Dr. Godmoore. In the meantime, you don't leave this building."

After McDougal stepped out, Jim placed his hands on her shoulders and looked into the eyes that had just burned right through McDougal. He said, "You were brilliant," and spontaneously kissed her.

Electric sensations coursed through him. He backed away, a little stunned, and looked at Valerie. Her lips had parted, her breathing gone shallow.

"Thanks," Valerie said as she ran her fingers through her hair.

Jim swallowed hard and awkwardly added, "I—I'd better go check on the kids."

"Yeah, okay. Say hi for me."

In the safety of the hallway, he stopped and took deep breaths. What a day, angry enough to kill one minute, scared shitless the next. He filled his lungs and held it. *For God's sake, take your time, Jim. You're headed for a mess if you don't.*

He turned the doorknob, opened his door, and strode in, calling, "Brett? Umber? I'm back."

He found nothing but unmade bedding in the girls' room. When he stepped into his, he saw the note.

Thirty-nine

Brett's heart thundered as she watched Umber wade into the canal. She shouted, "Umber, don't! You can't swim!"

Suddenly there was a hoot, and Umber jerked her head up to see Blue Eyes and his band stepping out of the trees, circling her.

"Oh, God, Umber, run! *Run!*" Brett screamed.

Umber's hair stood on end. She tried to back away, then seemed to change her mind. She bared her teeth and charged the approaching apes. For an instant, they were too surprised to do anything but shriek and throw things at her, then Blue Eyes let out a hoarse roar, and two of the males leaped on Umber and wrestled her to the ground. Blue Eyes walked to the lock box, inserted his stolen key, and lowered the bridge. They roughly dragged Umber across.

"God, no," Brett whispered.

As they neared Brett's position, she held out her hands, and Umber thrashed free from her captors' grip and ran into her arms.

"Oh, Umber," Brett said in a choking voice. "I wish—" and she doubled over, cowering beneath the pounding of the big male's fists; he knocked Brett to the ground. For a moment she couldn't breathe, then she gasped air into her lungs and coughed.

Umber shrieked and ran at the big male.

In response, he braced his feet and lifted his machete. It glinted in the dim daylight.

Umber stopped, one hand on her bow, the other on the machete that hung from the belt over her shoulder. She glanced between Brett and the belligerent ape.

Blue Eyes cautiously walked toward Umber. When he crossed some invisible line, Umber pulled her machete and bared her teeth. Propping the bow, she used her hand to say "Stop."

Blue Eyes obeyed, his own hand on his machete.

Umber signed: "Brett sister. You hurt her. Let her go."

Blue Eyes cocked his head. His chimp lips stuck out as he signed: "What mean . . ." and tried to form the sign for sister.

Umber signed: "Brett is my soul," and tapped her chest.

Blue Eyes mimicked the palm-out curl sign for soul and drew a question mark in the air.

Brett said, "What a bunch of morons." She walked forward and tapped Blue Eyes on the shoulder. When he looked at her, she pointed to Umber, then to herself, and signed: "We teach you new signs. If you don't hurt us." She paused, then asked, "Who you?"

He pointed to the sky, then to his eyes.

"Sky Eyes?" Brett said. "Well, that makes sense. What's the name of this jungle trash to my left?" She pointed to Nasty.

Sky Eyes made a throwing sign with his arm.

"Thrower?" Brett said, and the big male turned and gave her a suspicious look. Obviously he knew his spoken name. "Hi, Thrower, you're a piece of shit."

He cocked his head.

Sky Eyes pointed to Umber's bow, touched his fingers to his thumb, and tapped his chest.

Brett frowned. A shorthand version of "give"?

Umber started to offer it, and then seemed to reconsider. She signed: "I give. You give Brett."

Sky Eyes growled deep down in his throat and ferociously shook his head, signing, "No, no, no. Give bow. Now. Now."

Brett said, "I think we'd better, Umber. There's a lot more of them than us." Then, in pig Latin, she added, "Our-hay ime-tay ill-way ome-cay."

"Wheep," Umber said softly. She walked forward and handed the bow to Sky Eyes.

He took it, fingering it carefully. When he plucked the string and it thrummed, he almost dropped it.

Umber ran to Brett and wrapped her long arms around Brett's waist. She whimpered softly, and Brett could feel her warm breath on her bare stomach. "I'm all right, Umber," she said and gave Sky Eyes a cautious glance. Then she whispered, "Where are the arrows?"

Umber jerked her head back toward the other side of the bridge.

"Clever," Brett said. "He's got a bow, but no arrows."

Sky Eyes waved to the band and pushed through the screen of leaves into the forest. The female, the other male, and the other three apes ducked through behind him, grunting to one another.

Thrower flailed his arms at Brett, trying to get her to move. Over his shoulder, she saw Umber surreptitiously pull the arrow she'd shot earlier from the mud.

Brett distracted Thrower by sticking her tongue out at him, then she turned and headed for the opening.

"Oh, great," Brett moaned as she crawled through the leaves. "Another hill to climb."

Umber came through behind her, followed by Thrower. Umber rearranged the machete hanging over her back. She no longer had the arrow. So what had she done with it? They could have used that arrow.

From the corner of her mouth, Brett whispered, "Where's the arrow?"

Umber grinned, and her hands formed: "Trail sign."

But beneath her calm exterior, Brett could see fear in Umber's brown eyes.

At the knock, Jim opened the door to admit a stern-faced Shelly McDougal; behind her came a worried Bradley Cummings dressed in a water-sleek raincoat.

McDougal said, "The guards at the main gate passed two people at about nine this morning. Both were wearing yellow raincoats, like Bradley's, the sort they sell at the shop here. The guard thought they were staff attending to their duties."

Jim stood up, powered by fear. "Then they're somewhere on the road to Evinayong. Let's go." He marched for the door.

McDougal raised a hand. "Wait. Bradley Cummings just drove in from Compound B. He has something to tell you."

"Um, Dr. Dutton," Bradley said, "I don't know what it means, but . . ." Bradley lifted his hand, offering a purple backpack and a familiar quiver of arrows with it.

Jim took the quiver. His fingers caressed the arrows as if they were Umber's soft black hair. "These are Umber's. Where did you find them?"

"At the B bridge." Bradley's green eyes darted as he glanced at the people in the room. "I thought it was strange that some-one left their backpack hanging off the key control. The words 'Brett,' 'Umber,' 'Blue Eyes,' and 'that way' were scratched into the mud with one of the arrows pointing across the water gap."

Jim's blood raced. He grabbed Bradley by the sleeve and dragged him for the door. "I want to see this. Now!"

Valerie said, "Jim, if Sky Eyes has the girls, they're in real trouble."

McDougal's stony face looked even grimmer. "What do you need from me, Dr. Dutton?"

Jim fingered the backpack in his hand, thinking about the note, the things Brett had written there. "Just a Mule, Doctor. Sky Eyes will take them into the forest. All we can hope is that Brett and Umber can stay alive long enough for us to find them."

"What makes you think you can track anyone through the forest, Dr. Dutton?" McDougal gave him a cold look.

"I was an elk hunter long before I was an anthropologist, Doctor. If they're out there, I'll find them."

"Your guards are carrying Kalashnikovs." Valerie stepped forward. "We need one, with four full magazines."

McDougal said, "Ms. Radin, this is not a hunting compound. Those apes are worth millions."

Jim stepped forward, fists knotted at his sides. "At least four people have been killed by those apes. Now they have my daughter. *Give me a goddamned rifle!*"

McDougal considered for long seconds, then turned to Cummings. "Bradley, go find Sergeant Bonoficio. Have him hand over one of his rifles and four magazines. When you have it, bring it here." She paused. "And bring one of the FM communicators." She shot Jim a withering look. "I want regular reports, Dr. Dutton. When you locate Brett and Umber, call us. We'll send a team in to capture them."

"Deal," Jim said.

McDougal's brow lined. "I'll put security on the other water gaps. If this really is Sky Eyes and the Alpha Group, he's found a way to cross the canals. Dr. Shanks's key, no doubt."

Jim said nothing as McDougal and Bradley stepped out of the room. Then he murmured, "By God, these people are fools. They knew their augmented apes had learned to make tools, to construct huts, and it didn't occur to them that when those same apes saw the staff using keys to work the bridges, the apes would learn how to do the same?"

Valerie came forward and put a hand on his shoulder and squeezed gently. "I think we still have a lot of surprises ahead of us."

Jim opened Umber's pack, finding packets of food, candy bars, and little bottles of aspirin, antibiotics, and other medicines. "Looks like they packed for a long haul. In fact, if we're going into the bush, there's everything we need."

"Not quite." Valerie opened one of the aluminum cases and lifted out a large black cone on a handle. Jim watched as she slid the grip off the bottom of the cone. "Long-distance microphone. And, yes, it really works, in addition to camouflaging the pistol frame." Then she unscrewed a tube six inches in length from the tripod. When she lifted it, he could see rifling in the pistol barrel. Next she slid a pistol slide from the rails on a battery pack. From a can of what looked like spare parts, she took a recoil rod with a double-wound spring. He watched in amazement as she assembled a semiautomatic pistol from the parts.

"My God, Val," Jim said admiringly as she opened a film canister and removed two pressed-metal magazines.

She looked up at him. "Would you mind unscrewing the rubber feet on the bottoms of all the cases?"

It took effort, but the little rubber knob broke loose and he rapidly unscrewed it. There, tucked into the rubber, was the unmistakable base of a bullet with its lacquered primer. The Winchester headstamp read "45 AUTO."

She arched an eyebrow at his expression. "Jim, I go a lot of places where I can't rely on the charity of the locals." Valerie's four cases, at six rubber feet apiece, turned out twenty-four bullets. One by one, Valerie loaded them into the magazines.

He picked up the pistol. "What kind is it?"

"An HK Mark 23 . . . the pistol the special ops units use. The special ops guys didn't like the Beretta nine-millimeter. When people are shot with forty-fives they fall down and don't get up again."

"Where'd you learn all this?" Jim pointed to the cases.

Valerie shrugged into the straps for the shoulder holster. "I did a piece on SEAL Team Two a couple of years ago. I ended up in a relationship with one of the guys. It lasted about six months." She glanced down at the big pistol resting beside her left breast. "The thing was, I could talk to him. He understood."

"Understood what?"

"Horror, blood, death. That feeling you get when bullets whiz over your head. It's not something that most Americans can relate to."

"I suppose not." He indicated the pistol. "Aren't you afraid you'll get caught with that?"

"Not really, airport security people and customs officers are paid minimum wage. You're not exactly talking about a brain trust manning security checkpoints. Most of them are technological illiterates. They don't know a microphone handle from a polymer pistol frame. And journalists don't fit the profile for smugglers. Customs expects press equipment, and that's what they see."

"I thought media types were ninety-five percent antigun liberals."

She gave him a melancholy smile. "I've watched journalists die within five feet of me. My antigun liberal days vanished the first time someone shot at me with intent to kill. Most journalists believe press credentials will protect them. I don't, and I don't ask my people to."

Roberto knocked and stepped in at their call, an ugly-looking AK rifle slung from his shoulder. Rain had slicked his black hair down over his ears, and his mustache drooped. "I must have missed something really important. Doc McDougal had a soldier give me this out front. We going to war?" He unslung the rifle and a canvas pouch full of magazines. "Which government are we overthrowing this week, Fuerta?"

"Smyth-Archer Chemists, Taco." She took the AK, pressed the metal magazine release lever, and separated the curved clip from the rifle. With a thumb she pressed down on the staggered row of pointed bullets. "Spring's good. It'll feed." Then she slapped the clip back into the gun. "Pay attention, Jim. This fire-control lever on the right side of the receiver doubles as a dust cover and safety. Up is safe. The rifle won't discharge and you can't work the bolt. Push down once to the first click, it fires full auto. Push all the way down to the second click, and you shoot semiauto." As she spoke she demonstrated the way it clicked, then cycled the bolt. "You're loaded." Snapping the fire control up to safe, she handed it to Jim.

He took it, shouldered it, and sighted out the window at the forest.

"So, where we going?" Roberto asked. "How many battery packs do I need?"

"You're staying here, Taco." Valerie reached into one of the cases and handed him what looked like a cell phone. "You're our insurance. I don't trust our friend Dr. McDougal. I want you here, running the transmitter. I'll be filing periodic reports. If Jim and I don't get back, someone has to keep the story alive."

"Hey, Val, you need me out there." Roberto took the phone, nervously fiddling with it. "Who else can you count on?"

She slapped him on the shoulder. "I *am* counting on you. If anything happens, you need to finish this. Jim and I are leaving right now. Time is critical. You need to download everything on the camera to the sat net. I want Murray to have that material on file. And I think I can count on Jim."

"But I—"

She interrupted, "She's my daughter, Taco. I'm going after her."

A thin smile made his bandido mustache curl. "Yeah, Fuerta. She's a good kid. Go get her."

She hugged him. "Take care, Taco."

"*Y tu, tambien.*" Roberto turned to Jim and shook his hand. "Good luck."

"Thanks." Jim swung the pack over his shoulder, then slung the AK and the canvas magazine pouch.

The Mule was waiting, its canvas top soaked with rain. A small knot of people stood beside it, all looking uncomfortable.

Bradley Cummings met them halfway down the walk, handing them a radio. "I'll drive you to the spot where I found the backpack."

Jim climbed into the back as Valerie took the passenger seat. Marcus Yamasaki stepped out from the watchers and leaned in to say, "I'll be monitoring with Shelly. If you need me, Dr. Dutton, I'll be there, soonest."

"I hope we won't need you, Doctor."

Bradley started the Mule, turned a tight circle, and accelerated down the road. Jim looked back to see high rooster tails the chevroned tires threw from the red mud.

Blue Eyes? Did that mean Sky Eyes? The deep-seated worry he'd been holding at bay began to sink in.

"I should never have let her come," Jim said. "She blackmailed me. Blackmailed Smithwick. Told him she'd spill the whole story to you unless she could come. He promised me she'd be safe."

"Blackmail, huh?" Valerie considered. "Quite a kid."

They slowed at the switchbacks, and Bradley pointed. "I saw this earlier. Look there, you can see tracks. One person, running. The rain has ruined them, but when I came by you could still see the pattern. Small running shoes."

Jim leaned out of the side of the Mule, straining to catch a clear glimpse of Brett's prints. He saw nothing more than pockmarks as Bradley drove them down the long hill.

At the bridge, Bradley pulled to a stop and pointed to the

gray plastic key box. "That's where the backpack and quiver were hung. You can still see the writing in the mud."

Jim jumped out and crouched to look at the lettering, already fading under the pounding of the rain. "Umber did this."

"She writes?" Valerie asked, amazed.

"She hasn't penned *War and Peace* yet, but she's still young." He picked up Umber's directional arrow before Bradley used his key to lower the bridge into place. Jim ran ahead, his boots hollowly thumping the wood.

On the opposite side, he studied the mud, trying to read the tracks. A second arrow, carefully placed, pointed at the wall of leaves. The indistinct pattern of tracks led right to where the arrow pointed.

"Here," Jim called, waving the Kawasaki forward. "They entered the forest through that hole. From here on, we go on foot."

"Right," Valerie agreed, picking her pack up from the floor. Jim lifted Umber's purple pack out of the back and slung the rifle.

Bradley passed Jim a machete in its scabbard. "You'll need this. The vegetation can be like a prison. I'll call in what we found. Good luck."

"Thanks, Bradley." Then he looked at Valerie, read the concern in her eyes, and said, "Let's go."

As he ducked through the leaves and stems, his heart hammered at the back of his throat.

They waited a moment for their eyes to adjust and then Jim pointed. "There's our trail. Somebody, probably Umber, kept her wits about her."

Valerie glanced at her watch. "We'd better make time. It's almost five. We've only got another couple of hours of daylight."

Jim nodded. He unbuckled his belt and ran it through the loops in the machete scabbard, then rebuckled it.

"God help us if they've hurt those kids."

"No," Valerie said, patting her pistol. "God help them."

Forty

Richard Godmoore rubbed his tired eyes and exhaled. He leaned forward and propped his elbows on the big desk's rich-grained teak; his eyes focused vacantly on the expensive paneling. The office, once the center of his world, had changed. Where it had been the nerve center of his empire, it now confined, more of a prison. With each breaking news story, the walls seemed to close in, ever tighter, as if they would smother him.

The burgeoning Kivu problem was even now expanding out of proportion. The legal team he had sent to Texas was running into one roadblock after another. But, he had been informed that pending a preliminary hearing, Kivu would most likely be declared property. If so, a SAC team would be right there to euthanize him immediately. Then the corpse would be destroyed.

And if, by some means, this Harriman managed to have Kivu declared a person? Godmoore winced, fingered his chin, and used his keypad to pull up information. A list of names appeared. Well, Parnell might no longer be available, but there were other individuals, innovative men that could make Kivu's death appear natural. Surely then the courts would have no reason to deny SAC the body.

The corner of his lip twitched when he noticed the time. Reaching out, he manipulated the touch pad, calling up the day's financial stats. SAC had closed down two points on the FTSE. New York had just opened, and he was already down one and a half points in the first twenty minutes of trading. His wealth was vanishing before his eyes.

The chime sounded on his console. He wheeled around in his desk chair, tapping his touch pad as he opened the communications link. Shelly McDougal looked hardmouthed, brittle. Throttled anger brewed behind her blue eyes.

"Good evening, Shelly," Godmoore greeted. "I hope that just for once, there is some good news to report."

The muscles at the corners of her jaw tensed. Godmoore's heart dropped. "What's wrong now?"

"That Radin woman had a portable satellite link. She filmed the discovery of Shanks's and O'Neil's bodies. The compound, everything. By the time I got to her, she had already transmitted most of her film to Triple N. Beyond that, she knows about Compound D, had found her way to Geoffrey."

The cold fist of dread tightened in Godmoore's belly. "I want her stopped, Shelly. I don't care how, but you will take whatever means are—"

"No, Richard." The words, uttered so precisely, sent a shiver along his spine.

"No, Shelly? I would like to remind you that—"

"I am employed by Smyth-Archer Chemists, Dr. Godmoore. That doesn't mean that you own my soul. This is coming apart around us. My career is in jeopardy. I have dead people here. This project is under *my* administration. Since the proverbial cat is out of the bag, I am doing what I have to to save my skin, Doctor. As long as I am in charge here, I will manage damage control as I see fit."

"What does Radin want?" His throat felt as if it were swelling closed, choking off his air.

"The truth." Shelly cocked her head. "Maybe I can provide it in a way to spin it to our favor. But before I do, ask me what I want."

Instinctively, he stiffened. No one threatened Richard Godmoore and got away with it. "Very well, Shelly, what do you want?"

Shelly's lips pursed as she met his eyes. Her Scottish brogue emphasized her precise words. "You have a choice, Richard. Either I handle this my way, and salvage what I can, or my employment is terminated. Now, while I have the chance to escape this with as much of my reputation intact as I can. Rather than fall on my sword for Smyth-Archer Chemists, I will retreat while I can and take my chances on a lucrative book deal."

He saw no give behind her steely blue eyes. Instead, she bristled with all the thorny single-mindedness of her ancestry.

"Very well, Shelly. Do as you must." He swallowed hard. "Where is the woman now?"

"She and Dutton are out in the bush. It seems that the girl, Brett, and our ape, Umber, have run off."

"What?"

"You didn't give me the chance to make my full report. Ms. Radin is full of surprises, sir." Shelly leaned forward, monitoring his expression. "It turns out that Brettany Dutton is Ms. Radin's daughter."

"Daughter?" It took a moment for the implications to sink in. "Radin and Jim Dutton?"

"Apparently so." The quirk had returned to Shelly's thin lips. "It would seem, sir, that our own information was either lacking, or no one took the time to put all of the pieces together."

"So, Radin and Dutton are out in the jungle," Godmoore mused.

"Yes, and if Sky Eyes has taken the girl, Ms. Radin's daughter might be dead."

Brett's muscles had that loose feeling, and her coordination had begun to seep away. She stumbled through the prop roots, grabbing on to anything she could to stay on her feet. Her stomach growled continually. Her soaked shoes and socks had given her blisters. Numerous cuts and scrapes pained her. In all of her life, she'd never felt so miserable.

Umber reached out to catch Brett when she staggered.

"Tired," Brett muttered. "And hungry, and thirsty, and sore, and just generally pissed off." Then she added: "I want to go home."

"Wheep." Umber nodded.

"You know, I think even sauerkraut is starting to sound good."

Umber made a choking sound deep in her throat and signed, "Brett hates that."

"Not right now."

Thrower grunted at them in warning, and Brett climbed another of the endless ridges and scrambled over a log so rotten it felt like sponge. Brett looked back at Thrower, and he smacked her with the flat of his machete. "Ow!" she cried. "Why did you do that?"

Thrower gave her a blank stare.

Brett signed: "Where you taking us?"

Thrower frowned and signed: "Girl."

"Weird," Brett murmured, dragging her feet through the humus as they crossed the ridge top. "They keep talking about Girl. I wonder who she is?"

Thrower signed: "You bring Girl."

Brett looked at Umber, the feeling of desperation growing, and then she carefully formed the signs: "Bring Girl where?"

Thrower grunted, shrugged his black shoulders, and pointed to the sky.

"Am I dense? I don't get it," Brett whispered miserably. "Girl is in the sky?"

Umber held her hands so the others couldn't see and signed: "Think Girl dead."

"Yeah, right," Brett said. "How in hell do I manage this?"

Brett's eyes strayed to the machete that Sky Eyes clutched as he led his band farther into the twilight forest.

As the light failed, Jim reached into Umber's pack and pulled out the compact flashlight. He looked up at the ridge they climbed. The trail stood out as a darker streak in the gloom. Even so, the trailing had been easy. The moldy compost that made up the forest floor had been scuffed just enough by Brett and Umber, and in places where the trail crossed rocky outcrops, sticks had been cunningly rearranged by an artful hand to point the way.

Jim flicked on the beam, surprised at its brilliance. "So here's the question, Val. Umber's flashlight will probably take us another two hours up the trail. I—"

"I've got a small Maglite. Call it good for three hours."

"All right." He nodded. "That's five. Let's go." He took a deep breath and started up the slippery incline. "I don't think I've ever been so wet." As if to accent it, drops plummeted from the dark canopy overhead, splatting on his soaked felt hat.

"I've been this wet before. And a whole bunch hotter." Valerie rubbed her face as she climbed beside him. "How far do you think they are ahead of us?"

"I can't say." Jim blinked and gasped for breath as he struggled over a slippery root. He reached back and offered a hand to Valerie. "If they left by the main gate and ended up in Compound B, who knows? They were at the river crossing before

Bradley drove across it at about three. They could have as much as five, maybe six hours' head start."

"And we don't know how fast they're going." Valerie slipped, and Jim just managed to catch her before she tumbled back down the slope.

"Careful. The last thing we can afford is for one of us to get hurt."

"Got that right, Jimbo." She committed herself to the climb. She suddenly asked, "So, there's no woman in your life?"

"No!"

"Touchy, Jimbo. Did I strike a raw nerve?"

"Don't be ridiculous."

"Am I being ridiculous?"

"Yes."

"You never married? What's wrong with women?"

"Nothing. I just never found the right one, that's all. And given your record with men, I wouldn't be casting stones." Her face reflected palely in the flashlight's glow. "Let's see, a bad relationship with your station director, another one with a Navy SEAL, do I detect a pattern here?"

"Don't be a bastard, Jim."

"Is that defense I hear in your voice?"

"If you're going to be an asshole, I—"

"Me?"

He caught sight of another twisted stick on the ground and spotted a dragged toe mark. "Sorry, Val, neither one of us is what you'd call a model of success with the opposite sex."

Her voice was forgiving, and genuinely interested when she asked, "So, why didn't some woman marry you, Jim?"

His attention focused on the trail, on the place where a scuff mark led out onto a branch that spanned a leaf-choked gully. "I guess I never met your equal."

She was silent as they crawled out onto the branch. It creaked and swayed under their weight.

"Better pull out that Maglite of yours. I think this is a one-at-a-time crossing." Jim flashed the light out along the branch, seeing where it twined with another halfway across.

"Are you sure you don't want to go around?" Valerie asked nervously.

"Ask me that when we get to the other side. If we're there, I'll give you one answer. If one of us is lying down there in the bottom with a broken leg, I'll tell you something else."

He worked out along the branch, bracing himself on smaller offshoots. For an ape, this wouldn't have been much of a challenge. For a man in hiking boots carrying a flashlight, pack, and rifle, it proved a little more demanding. But he made it, stepping into the interlocking branch and shining his light upward to where the branches leafed out in a solid canopy.

Valerie came slowly, testing each step.

"Come on, Val. You can do it," Jim said as the branch swayed. She crossed the worst part and then made the transition to the second branch. Within moments she reached him and took his hand for balance.

"I felt my heart beat a little that time," she said, smiling at him.

"With good reason," he told her, and realized that he was holding her hand longer than he needed to—and that she didn't seem to mind.

Valerie shut her flashlight off. "Jim, what happens when we catch up with them? They'll see the flashlight beam coming from a long way off. When I interviewed Masala, he said that they killed his companions and almost got him by using the light against them."

Jim considered. "What time is it?"

"About eight."

"We'll travel for two more hours. Then we'll call it a night. At first light, we'll start off again."

At ten P.M. Jim located a hollow under a decomposing log. The space was scarcely drier than the surroundings, and just large enough for the two of them. He batted the cobwebs out of the way and huddled in under the protective overhang.

Valerie crawled in beside him, took out her handheld FM unit, and called to update Roberto. She then settled in, shifting to try to find a comfortable position. "God, I'm tired. My legs are going to kill me tomorrow."

"Mine, too."

He lifted his arm to put it around her, then thought better of it. His arm hovered uncertainly over her back.

Valerie smiled and snuggled against him, her head on his shoulder. "You know, Jim, I wish to hell we could start over again. Redo it all. Remember dancing out at Bruce's, that little bar in middle-of-nowhere Colorado?"

"Severance. The town was called Severance. They specialized in Rocky Mountain oysters."

"That was great training. After those plates of bull balls, I could eat anything. Even stringy camel meat in Australia."

They sat silently while the forest dripped around them.

"Earlier, you were right. About the men, I mean." She shook her head. "I'm tired of always being a nasty bitch. I'm tired of . . . of . . ."

"Hating yourself?" he asked gently.

Valerie drew up her knees and wrapped her arms around them, hugging them to her chest. "Yeah, I guess. No wonder Brett despises me."

"You should see your daughter's eyes light up when you come on TV. Neither one of us hates you."

She nodded, then laughed. "You're a saint, Dutton. A goddamned saint."

"Right," he said wearily. "With feet of clay."

Around them the jungle sounds seemed to intensify in the darkness.

Godmoore sipped a tonic water in an effort to still his dyspeptic stomach. On the monitors in his office, the security cameras showed the group of journalists camped at the plant entrance. Cold October rain slanted from the gray skies to shine on their umbrellas, camera vans, and raincoats.

Here, locked away in his plush office, Godmoore knew how the Nazis must have felt as the Russians closed in on Berlin. His idiot leader, Geoffrey Smyth-Archer, was in Africa, living in a fantasy future where apes and humans lived and worked side by side, unaware that the cold world was about to descend on him with all of its ugliness, bigotry, and hatred.

He glanced at the digital clock and winced as his stomach churned. Three phone calls from Dr. Johnson already. Godmoore had refused them, Kevin claiming he was in conference with a solicitor.

Is it time to run? He wheeled his chair back and opened the top drawer to his desk. Against his hot fingers, the little passbook felt remarkably cool. Bound in red leather, the cover had a small Swiss cross, and the bank name emblazoned in gold.

He tapped it absently on the polished wood of the desk. How much was enough? Surely the amount in that account would stand him in good stead for the rest of his life. He shot a scathing look at the computer monitor that tracked the FTSE. SAC was down another four points, and falling.

Still, it would stabilize, rise again once the news crews found another mass murder, war, or typhoon to exploit. If he could just make it past the next stockholders' meeting, he could divest and clear another thirty-seven million, even after the bath SAC was taking on the exchange. Thirty-seven million. The number stuck in his head. On top of the account, it would give him a total of . . .

The phone buzzed.

Godmoore glared at the golden handset, its polished wooden handle so beautifully deceptive. "Sir?" Kevin Clark's voice demanded urgently over the speakerphone.

Godmoore sighed and picked up the handset. "Yes, Kevin?"

"A reporter, sir. A—"

"I told you, I *will* not speak to any reporters. Do I need to make myself clear? What part of that don't you—"

"Sir!" Kevin's frantic voice interrupted. "He said if you don't speak to him, he's going to run the story anyway."

Godmoore tensed at the fracturing of Clark's voice; a tickle of fear slipped up his spine. "Very well, what story, Kevin?"

"It's crazy, sir. This reporter, Myles Edwards, he was out here that day with the Triple N crew. Well, sir, he claims he's been looking at some figures, specifically those for the IAR compound, sir. I don't know where he could have—"

"Yes, yes, go on!" Godmoore had stood, ice in his veins.

"Sir." Kevin swallowed hard. "Mr. Edwards claims that fifty million pounds can't be accounted for."

Dear God, they've found it. How could they . . . He closed his eyes. It didn't matter. Somehow, some way, they had.

"Sir?" Kevin's panicked voice intruded into Godmoore's private disaster.

"Yes, Kevin. Tell him . . . Tell him I'll meet him tomorrow at noon, in London. At . . . at my club. I'll talk to him then." And without waiting for confirmation, he hung up the phone. For what seemed an eternity, he could only stare and feel the hollow sense of terror welling inside him.

When he finally moved again, it was to pluck up the little red bankbook and slip it inside his pocket. Was his life, his freedom, worth the chance to nail down another thirty-seven million?

In a dry voice, he buzzed Kevin. "My car, please." His voice cracked. He tried to keep his legs from shaking as he walked hurriedly toward the door.

Brett jerked awake from the horrifying nightmare: Meggan's head lying beside Umber's, both bloody, covered with ants. Brett took a deep breath. She had a killing thirst and her stomach ached with hunger. The gray light of dawn streamed through the trees. The ground lay a good twenty feet below, but she rested on a bed of leaves in the hollow of Umber's arm, her head pillowed on Umber's soft black breast. Dew coated both of them, beading on Umber's hair and Brett's welted skin. Scratches and bites covered her face and arms. Bits of leaves, twigs, and pieces of bark matted her blond hair.

To Brett's left, Thrower lay in the nest he'd built in the Y of a branch the night before. She looked down at the rude cushion she and Umber had built, mimicking the wild apes in the hopes they'd look like they knew what they were doing. Her first real nest, made of branches and leaves. She'd seen similar ones on television. Her preference, however, ran to fireplaces, beds, and down comforters.

The sounds of the forest seeped into her. High above, brightly colored birds flew from branch to branch. A rope squirrel trilled, then a monkey screeched.

Brett's muscles felt like they'd been pulled through a sieve. Every square inch of her body ached. Today they would have to find food. She wished desperately that she and Umber had their packs with their medicines, food, and water bottles.

Umber let out a breath and blinked her eyes open. She yawned as she sat up. Umber signed, "Good morning."

Brett said, "I'm taking a 'wait and see' attitude about that."

Umber sighed and looked around. Thrower still slept, but

the other apes had gathered on the branches below them, grunting and chirping.

Umber looked down, and Brett leaned over, too.

Ten feet below, Sky Eyes squatted on a limb the width of Brett's shoulders, carefully picking through his hair. His machete rested across his lap. The female and another male sat on a branch below Sky Eyes, grooming each other and making soft "feel good" sounds. A huge snake stretched out on a branch in a tree thirty feet away. Its eyes glinted.

Umber started to climb down and Brett grabbed her shoulder. "Where are you going?"

Umber lifted her two index fingers to her lips and moved them to and from her mouth in opposite directions, then pointed at the sky, and at her eyes.

Brett said, "Talk to Sky Eyes! What on earth for?"

Umber patted Brett's hand and dropped to the branch just below, then climbed down to where Sky Eyes sat.

Brett got down on her stomach in their nest to watch.

Umber signed, "Why take Brett?"

Sky Eyes bowed his head, formed a fist with his right hand, touched the extended thumb of his fist to his temple, and drew the thumb down to his chin.

Umber tilted her head and signed: "For Girl," then drew a question mark in the air and pursed her lips. "Thought Girl was dead?"

Sky Eyes nodded and Brett thought he looked suddenly weary. His black shoulders slumped.

Umber scratched her neck and swung her legs over the tree limb. She signed: "Girl with God."

Sky Eyes shook his head. "What God?"

Umber pointed to her eye and then to her chest.

Sky Eyes peered at her intently.

Umber gestured at her heart, and the sky, and the rocks jutting up from the forest floor at the base of the tree. Then she made her eye-chest sign for God again, breathed in and out while she moved her hands in opposite directions in front of her chest, and formed the word for "world."

Brett's mouth fell open. She whispered, "God breathes the world? Damn, Umber, that's profound. I think."

Sky Eyes seemed mesmerized. He extended his hands in front of his chest and moved them back and forth, signing: "Wind?"

Umber nodded.

Sky Eyes mimicked Umber's eye-chest sign, turned his right palm down, his left up, and flipped them over.

Brett blinked and slid closer to the edge of the nest. Sky Eyes had just asked Umber if God was death. Considering Brett's present circumstances, that was a damned good question.

Umber tilted her head. She seemed to be thinking about that. She watched the birds flitting through the trees for a while. Finally, she nodded.

For a long time Sky Eyes seemed lost, his eyes focused across some terrible distance.

Umber plucked a bit of mud from the hair on his leg. Then her nimble fingers went after a twig, and before Brett knew it, Umber was busy grooming Frankenstein's child. She squished something between her fingernails, probably a louse, and Brett winced.

Sky Eyes looked at Umber, made the sign for "dream," then "Girl," pointed up at Brett, and added, "bring back."

Brett whispered, "Oh my God. He thinks I can bring Girl back from the dead? He saw it in a dream? Who's he fooling?"

Umber shook her head while she signed: "Can't. Dead forever."

Sky Eyes hunched and whimpered.

Brett saw Umber's eyes go tight, and watched as she stroked Sky Eyes's back. When Brett looked at him now, he seemed smaller, less threatening. In a shared understanding of grief, the six-million-year gap that lay between them had closed a little.

As mist curled through the morning-gray branches, Umber groomed Sky Eyes and made soft sounds.

Brett eased onto the branch and let herself down, placing each foot carefully. She clung to one of the vines and watched as Umber's hands flashed signs about souls, and God, and life and death.

"Great. I'm starving and Umber's into eschatology."

Brett had always liked the word. She had learned it from Mrs. Redderson in English class. At first hearing, she thought it sounded like something her father would disapprove of. She'd been a little miffed to find out it described abstract religious concerns about the end of time.

The young female chimp climbed up through the branches and approached Brett, her brown eyes wary.

"Hungry," Brett said, and made the sign.

The female nodded and scrambled up the tree with an agility that left Brett wondering. Having nothing better to do, Brett began the climb, levering herself up from branch to branch. Here and there, she had to rely on the ropy vines that wove around the trunk.

She found the female out on the end of a branch, plucking some sort of fruits. Brett glanced around. Up above, gray sky shone through the mottled tracery of leaves. It looked like rain again. Across from her streamers of mist clung to the treetops.

The little clusters of fruits lay just out of reach. Her stomach growled, and she swallowed against the angry knot in her belly. The female gestured for Brett to come, held on to one branch with her right hand, another with her left, and yet a third with her feet. In doing so, her weight was distributed evenly. Brett glanced down at her muddy running shoes. They weren't the thing for branches. Nevertheless, she inched out, mimicking the female's position, and reached a small cluster of the fruits by bending down an overhead branch. She pulled off a cluster of four, gripped the slender stem in her teeth, and inched back to the relative security of the thicker branches.

The fruits were curious, covered with a brittle skin. She nibbled at one, tasting bitterness, and then bit into the whole. Once past the skin, they tasted sweet, a little like plums. Brett ate as the other apes spread out in the tree below her. The best of the fruits, however, defied her, swaying just beyond her reach.

She clambered carefully back to the middle of the tree and searched around. There, perfect—a finger-thick vine with lots of curves. She used her pocketknife to cut the vine in two just beneath one of the curves and grinned. The section of vine reminded her of a shepherd's hook. Something to pull the fruits closer to her reach.

To free her hands for climbing, she slipped the hook down between her back and her bra and edged out onto the swaying branch. Using the hook, she neatly snagged the branch she wanted and pulled. In victory, she chuckled as she grabbed her bounty, a cluster of the brown-skinned fruits. The bitter stem grasped in her teeth, she retreated to a more solid purchase to eat.

Umber climbed toward Brett, her moccasins tied together and dangling around her neck, her machete over her left shoulder. Her yellow pants were smudged and her orange T-shirt was torn. She touched her fingers to her lips.

"Yeah, and it's not bad," Brett answered around a mouthful of the delicious fruits. "Here, try this." She tossed one to Umber.

Umber nibbled tentatively at first, then grinned, squatted on the branch beside Brett, and began to plunder Brett's treasure. In no time, the fruits were gone.

"This time, you climb out and snag some." Brett handed her the vine hook. "I almost fell and killed myself."

Umber took the vine hook and worked her way toward the end of a branch.

"Show-off!" Brett called, but grinned when Umber returned with another cluster of fruit. As Brett ate, she asked, "So, did you talk him out of killing us?"

Umber shrugged uncertainly and signed: "Sky Eyes crazy." Then she bit into a fruit.

"Oh, well, I feel better."

Umber finished her fruit, tossed the seed down, and watched it thunk the branches below. After wiping her hands, she casually pointed at Sky Eyes and signed: "May have to kill."

Brett's mouth gaped. "God, Umber! How can you say that? You've never killed anything. You even hate mousetraps!"

Umber waved a hand, her mouth working on another fruit.

Brett gnawed around her seed and threw it as far as she could. She listened but didn't hear it land. "I don't want to kill him," Brett said.

Umber tapped her machete where it hung over her shoulder, and one by one pointed at the big males.

Brett squinted at the female Umber had left out. "You know what Dad says, never underestimate a woman."

Umber's eyes narrowed at the female, then she said, "Wheep."

Brett picked up another fruit. She studied it thoughtfully. Little bugs crawled over it, and a worm wriggled from a hole, things that would have left her retching back in Fort Collins. Here in the forest, she picked them off and ate like it might be her last meal.

Of course, it might. And she'd need every last bit of strength today.

"Waaa-Waaa" came the rusty cry from Brett's right.

The female swung down, artfully dropping through the tree by allowing gravity to do the work. Her very weight bent one terminal branch to a lower one which she grabbed, and then it dropped her to the next. She stopped long enough as she passed Brett and Umber to point downward.

"I guess we're going," Brett said and stuffed her mouth with as many of the little fruits as she could.

Umber formed K letters with both hands and tapped them together twice, telling Brett to be careful, and pointed at Sky Eyes.

"Right," Brett muttered, grabbing on to a vine to lower herself.

Thick fog blew around the gnarled prop roots, warm and muggy as it rose toward the towering canopy. Water droplets pattered onto the leaf mat. In the trees, bush babies and black colobus monkeys shrilled at each other in accompaniment to a chorus of birdsong and the ratcheting whir of insects. Jim watched Valerie spooning out the contents of an MRE packet. According to the label the brown stuff was "beef stew."

"I'm preparing myself," she said woodenly. Her khaki shirt and pants had a thousand wrinkles, but her face shone in the morning gleam. She'd braided her blond hair. "You don't know it, but over the years I've kept track." She sucked the spoon clean and folded the wrapper over the plastic tray. "I made a habit of it. At least once a year, sometimes more if I was feeling rocky, I'd take time off, fly to Denver, and rent a car. I'd drive up, check into one of the motels, and follow you around Fort Collins for a day or two."

Jim heard the misery in her voice, either at the memory, or the admission. "You could have called. I would have made it easier."

She stuffed the empty MRE into her pack. "Hell, Jim, I didn't know that. I had convinced myself that you hated me. Jesus, I never even said good-bye when I walked out of that hospital. If you'd done that to me, I would have hated you for the rest of your life."

He smiled. "You gave me the greatest gift of my life, Val. How could I hate you? You had a right to see our daughter."

Her lips twitched, dimpling her smooth cheeks. "You amaze me. After everything I did to you, you'll still forgive."

"You carried her to term for me. Because I begged you to."

She smiled. "Yes, well, Jimbo, I never knew how it would haunt me for the rest of my life. The thing was, I didn't expect to be constantly drawn back, just to see how she was doing, to wonder who she was and what she was like. Damn it, I couldn't stay away. A break would come up and I'd catch a flight. Then I'd sneak around with my telephoto and take a picture of her." She rubbed her legs, making a face. "I suppose that's some sort of weird psychological disorder. If I believed in therapists for fucked-up old ladies, I'd have myself committed."

Jim stuffed his empty container into his pack and shouldered his rifle. "I think the only thing you need for therapy is to forgive yourself, Val. Actually, both of us could use a little of that. I've always blamed myself for the fact that you left."

She smiled, stood, and stretched like a tigress. He was acutely aware of her breasts, her slim waist. God, she was beautiful. Then she looked him squarely in the eyes. Hurt and confusion lay in those cerulean depths. He could read her longing, and bent down to kiss her gently. Her arms went around his waist. For a long moment, they stood there, locked together as the forest clamored around them.

Then he pushed away. What a fool. He loved her as passionately now as he had the first night they'd made love. In her parted lips and startled eyes, he could see her response. Her breasts were rising and falling as if she couldn't get enough air.

He smiled. "Come on. We've got tracking light."

As he bent over, he saw where a foot had slid through yesterday's mud. The track lay beneath a huge cluster of leaves, mostly protected. It looked like a shoe print. Fear twined through his guts. He felt as if his very life depended upon Brett and Umber being alive. If they weren't, no matter what the future held for him and Valerie, Jim's world would end.

Rain fell from a slate gray sky to batter the rusty tin roofs of Malabo. Rainwater sluiced from the corrugated metal and cascaded in streams to the packed earth below. Stippled pools reflected the dull light in overlapping rings.

Green fronds drooped on the lazy palms and shed the rain. The entire city with its shabby concrete and cracked pavement had taken on a lush sheen.

Don Amando stood at his high window, thumbs tucked into his belt, and watched as occasional people scuttled along the weed-infested walkways. A battered Citröen, faded blue mottled with blood-brown rust, splashed its way down the Avenida Tres de Augusto and made the left onto the Avenida de la Independencia. Beyond the green belt he could see Malabo harbor, the ferries lining the docks and one cargo ship snugged to the decrepit wharf at the "old port."

The chime from his computer system brought him around, one eyebrow lifting as he considered the blinking light. Leaning forward, he accessed the system to find himself facing Richard Godmoore.

"Good day, Dr. Godmoore. How can I help you?" Don Amando smiled, exposing his perfect white teeth.

Godmoore steepled his fingers and smiled. "Are you in contact with Sergeant Bonoficio? Do you have a way of communicating privately with him?"

"We do have military band radio," Don Amando said dryly, "even in benighted Equatorial Guinea."

"Yes, I'm sure you do." Godmoore missed the irony completely. "In the past, you have told me a great deal about your man, Bonoficio. I may have a little job for the sergeant. One particularly suited to his rather peculiar appetites." Godmoore took a moment, nerving himself. "Radin and her companions are currently in the forest, searching for a lost girl. I don't want any of them coming out, Don Amando." Godmoore managed to force a grin that resembled a rictus. "People disappear in the forest all the time, don't they?"

"For a price, Doctor, they can vanish in ways where no questions will ever be asked."

"My point exactly."

Brett looked at the waterfall that plummeted down over the black rocks into the green pool, and her stomach churned. Three days ago two people had been murdered here . . . but this was her first opportunity to drink, and she was suffering from the worst thirst she had ever known. On either side of her, the apes, including Umber, were sucking it up.

The rocks ate into her hands and knees as she knelt, touched her lips to the water, and drank. Once committed, she drank, and drank some more. God, it seemed she couldn't get enough. Finally, she rolled back and stared up at the misty veils streaming down from above. Right in front of her lay the place where her father had picked up the trail that had led to Shanks's mutilated body and the tree with Meggan's head in it.

Sky Eyes stood, his machete in hand, his hairy black body tensed as he watched the falling water. One of his black ears flicked, as if tormented by a fly. Something about his posture—not ape, not human, but piratical with his rusting machete in hand—triggered Brett's unease. All morning he had seemed un-usually preoccupied, his attention riveted on something inside that made him surly and uncommunicative—even when the fe-male, that Umber called "Sue," had approached to ask him a question. Once, Sky Eyes had even taken a swipe at Thrower with the machete. The hissing blade had come close enough to send the bigger ape shrieking in panic.

Umber shifted uneasily, rocking back and forth on her feet.

Brett whispered, "Do you feel it, too?"

Umber looked at Sky Eyes and signed, "Crazy."

"Yeah, well, right now I'm more worried about the water we just drank." She glanced at the glistening pool. "You think we'll get worms?"

Umber signed, "Hope we live long enough to see."

Brett laughed. "Yeah, I'm starting to think that just making it to see sunset would be way cool."

Sky Eyes turned his head from the heavens as the first drops of rain stippled the pool and burst in star shapes on the cob-bles beside Brett.

She looked down at her arms, at the crisscrossing scratches. She had torn her bra on a stick, and the thin fabric now hung in tatters, but modesty made her refuse to take it off, rag though it might be. Only one leg remained of her jeans.

Sky Eyes uttered a hoot-grunt, gestured for the others to stay, and waddled down the path where they'd dragged their last human victims.

Brett looked at Thrower, who squatted on a rounded rock, his machete in his hand. She signed: "Where go?"

"Gone to get . . ." he finished with a sign Brett didn't un-derstand.

That was a problem. They could communicate the basics, but Sky Eyes's band had signs for things that Brett and Umber didn't understand, just as they had signs for things beyond the apes' understanding.

As they waited, Sue picked shoots from the edge of the pond, stripping them open with her teeth and eating the pithy insides. Finally, she offered one to Umber, who took it, sniffed it, and tried to emulate Sue's ability to shred the tough stem.

"Here," Brett said, pulling out her pocketknife. She cut the stem in two, then split it lengthwise. Brett picked up the piece she'd split and looked at it. She bit into it experimentally and made a face. "That's strong stuff. It tastes like raw ginger."

Umber rocked back and forth, brandishing her machete, until it was apparent that the other two apes were purposely avoiding her gaze. Then she sat beside Brett and picked up a piece. She sniffed it, bit into it, and likewise made a face.

"Best eat it," Brett said unhappily. "It's better than that caterpillar Sue tried to make me eat earlier."

Umber signed, "Caterpillar good."

"You ate that? Yuck!" Brett bent down to drink more water and caught her reflection. She fingered the knot on the side of her head. "Gonna have a real nasty bruise there." Brett glanced back at the forest. "You know, these guys really play rough."

"Wheep."

They were still chewing the acrid ginger stems when Sky Eyes emerged through the gap in the leaves bearing two heavy packs, and Thrower appeared under a third.

Brett paled at the sight of the shotgun, while Umber cried out, jumped to her feet, and ran forward, signing, "Keyboard! Keyboard!" She stopped when Sky Eyes leveled his machete at her.

"Mine!" Umber signed. "My keyboard."

Sky Eyes dropped the packs, pulled the shotgun and keyboard out, and carefully placed them in the pack he'd stolen from Brett. Then he indicated the two packs on the ground and pointed to Brett and Umber. "Carry. We go."

Brett finished chewing the last of the crunchy pith out of the African ginger and sighed wearily. "He thinks we're mules."

Brett picked up one of the packs, judged that it weighed nearly twenty pounds, then lifted the other. It had to be thirty pounds. Brett started to shoulder the bigger pack, but Umber shot her a warning glance and took it from her.

Sky Eyes threw back his head and roared, "Waaa-Waaaa," then turned into the shadow of the trees.

Brett shrugged the lighter pack over her shoulders and took one last glance up at the cloudy sky. Warm rain fell steadily. Could her dad track in this? She had no idea.

Thrower waved an arm hostilely, and Brett followed Umber through the hole and into the hidden depths of the forest.

They climbed upward, toward the road, and Brett made sure she stepped on every dry patch of ground she could find, under deadfall and leaves and tangled vines, leaving clean imprints of her running shoes.

"Damn, I've come a long way in a short time." She shook her head, feeling the aches in her body. Had she ever really been young and naive?

At the pullout by the road she looked back down, wondering if anyone could find them, or if sometime soon Thrower would hit her with a machete instead of a fist.

Sky Eyes led them across the road and started across the flat-topped *meseta* toward the Compound B buildings.

Brett whispered to Umber, "If they go past Compound B, we can do a Roadrunner to their Wile E. Coyote. Ditch the packs and boogie."

Thrower gave Brett a suspicious look and brandished his machete.

Brett grinned at Thrower and said politely, "Have a nice day, microbrain."

Overhead, thunder rumbled, and the endless patter of water dripping from the leaves reestablished itself. Brett followed the apes across a deep ravine, climbing hand over hand up the roots and suckers. When she reached the other side, the cramps hit. Her belly tightened. She groaned, fighting the need to bend double, and took a deep breath of the humid air.

The next cramp was more demanding. She staggered to the side, her desperate fingers fumbling with her fly, and barely managed to drop her pants and rip her panties down before her bowels voided.

Her gut twisted and heaved again. Brett gasped and sat there, waiting. She wiped at a bit of rotten leaf clinging to her bare calf. When it wouldn't dislodge, she wiped again and realized in horror that it was something alive.

"Dear God!" Another convulsion knotted her intestines, and she reached down with shaking fingers. The leech was stuck firmly to her skin. She knew you couldn't just pull them off. She'd seen *The African Queen*. She reached into her pocket and extracted her pocketknife. With the blade, she shaved the leech off, watching in horror as the wound gushed blood.

When Sky Eyes grunted, she looked up in surprise to see a ring of apes, all watching her curiously, except for Umber, who knelt at her side with worry lining her brow.

"God! Go away!" Brett waved at them. "Jeez, disgusting! Go on! Leave me alone! Don't you people know anything about privacy?"

Sky Eyes's face looked genuinely bewildered.

Thrower bent down to examine Brett's nether regions, and she yelled, "Quit that!"

Umber lowered her pack, pulled her machete, and walked behind Brett. When she shrieked and bared her teeth at Thrower, he backed away, but grudgingly.

Umber lowered a hand so Brett could see and signed, "O-K?"

"Yeah." Brett swallowed hard. "Wow. It feels like my guts are tying themselves in knots."

Brett looked up to see Sky Eyes signing: "Come."

Brett watched Umber's hands sign: "Better come, Brett. I carry your pack."

Brett said, "Yeah, all right," and glanced around suddenly. "Oh, Jeez, who would have thought."

With her pocketknife she cut a strip off the bottom of her pants and used it to wipe. "At this rate, I'm going to run out of clothes before they can get around to killing me. I take back everything I said to McDougal about going naked in the forest."

Umber grunted, slipped her machete back into its scabbard, and shouldered both of their packs.

"You don't have to do that," Brett said, reaching out for one as Sky Eyes resumed the lead and Thrower shoved Brett forward.

She staggered, got her balance, and flipped him off as she stepped out after Umber. She didn't make more than fifteen paces before her bowels twisted again.

"Oh, God. Umber? I've got to stop." Brett looked back at Thrower and made the defecate sign.

He pulled his machete and gestured her forward, taking a couple of swipes at the air to make his point.

"I have to stop!" she said, but suddenly it was too late.

Thrower wheezed in laughter behind her.

Brett endured the indignity and shame. She had to keep up. If she couldn't, the machete-waving moron might really kill her.

All right, Brett, I guess this is where we see just how tough you really are.

Forty-one

After two hours of travel, Brett could feel the trembling being borne down around her bones. Worse, she no longer cared about the watery brown diarrhea that trickled down her legs and smelled so bad. The last time they'd stopped to drink, she'd seen her sweaty red face and the glazed shine in her blue eyes, one that looked crystalline and fevered.

Brett weaved on her feet, walking in a daze.

Sick, real sick.

Umber kept frowning at her, panting in worry. She signed: "O-K?"

Brett didn't have the strength to answer; she forced her feet onward, the movements mechanical. The other apes seemed oblivious. Sometimes they would pluck a treat, a fat grub, a succulent leaf, or a tender shoot, as they passed and pop it into their mouths. But they hardly spared a glance for the weaving and stumbling Brett.

Brett took a bad step, tripped and fell, and doggedly staggered to her feet again. Smelly and drawing flies, she gritted her teeth, willing herself to walk.

Umber turned, and Brett saw her glance at Thrower, who

now brought up the rear, periodically whacking roots and suckers with his machete.

Brett fell again. Thrower cocked his head and uttered a low, threatening hoot.

Brett dragged herself to her feet. Then, Sky Eyes led them up a steep trail. Brett had to crawl her way to the top, whimpering. At the crest, she stood, blinking, her body feeling rubbery and disjointed.

Umber must have known the very second when Brett's feet went out from under her. Brett sank soundlessly onto the rotten leaves. Umber was right there beside her, shrugging out of her packs and bending down with concern in her worried eyes.

"Umber," Brett moaned, choking on tears. "Umber, h-help me up?"

Thrower lifted his machete and took a step forward.

Umber signed, "Brett rest now."

Thrower made a deep-throated hoot-bark that brought the rest of the band back to gather around. Umber cautiously drew her machete as Sky Eyes approached, his bright blue eyes on Brett.

Umber formed the letter R with her fingers, then crossed her hands at the wrists over her chest, repeating, "Rest."

Sky Eyes's lips quivered as if in anger, and Brett said, "Umber, don't. Please, I . . ."

Sky Eyes signed, "She walk now."

Umber shook her head.

Sky Eyes pointed at Brett and signed: "Want me send you to God?" He swung his machete.

Umber signed: "Walk where?"

Sky Eyes looked down and Brett saw the fanatical glitter in his eyes. His hands made the words: "Girl's tree."

Umber shook her head, heaved a sigh, and picked up Brett.

"No, Umber," Brett slurred, unable to get her blurry eyes to focus. "You . . . you can't carry me."

Thrower signed: "Carry her in pieces," and stepped forward with his machete raised.

Umber's hair bristled as she slipped Brett off of her shoulder and waved her machete.

"No, Umber, no!" Brett tried to blink her vision clear.

This was a terrible place to fight them! Here on the ridge crest, they could surround Umber, and while she faced one, another could sneak in behind her.

Brett struggled to rise to her feet but collapsed on her side, sobbing, crying: "Umber, put down the machete! They'll kill you! Please, listen to—"

Thrower leaped for Umber, chopping sideways at her legs. Umber jumped out of the way, and as the momentum carried Thrower around, Umber screamed and ran at him, swinging the machete with all her strength. The blade struck his arm just above the right wrist.

Brett had expected the machete to stick in the bone, so when it cleaved neatly through, severing the hand, she could only stare in wide-eyed disbelief.

Thrower's hand and the machete both bounced off the thick leaf mat, and Thrower staggered backward and fell, his good hand clasping his wounded forearm above the stump. Blood shot out in spurts, and Thrower's chest heaved in short, panicked breaths.

The big ape's broad mouth worked as he backed away. Sue cried out and hurried over toward Thrower, but he shrieked and snapped at her with his teeth.

Sky Eyes dropped his pack with the keyboard and shotgun. Umber whirled around, breathing hard, her machete raised.

Desperation reflected from Sky Eyes's expression. The wrinkled black lips curled back to expose yellowed canines. His blue eyes had turned glassy as he advanced, back stiff.

Umber rocked from foot to foot, her machete ready. She removed one hand long enough to sign: "Stop!" then grabbed the hilt in both hands again.

Sky Eyes let out a long soft hoot, touched his eye, then his chest, and flipped his hands over.

Brett blinked, trying to clear her fever-bright eyes. The whole world had gone out of focus. "God is death?" she whispered. "What—"

Sky Eyes added: "Girl with God," and gestured to the big ape.

Big Guy bared his teeth, clearly uncertain about attacking Umber. Then he noticed that Sky Eyes had lifted his own machete, and a fear-grin split Big Guy's face.

Umber braced herself, one foot on either side of Brett's body.

Brett reached up and forced her swaying hand to grab on to Umber's hairy leg. "No, Umber, God, don't do this!"

Sky Eyes circled, and Umber looked over her shoulder at Big Guy. Brett saw Umber start to tremble, and used every last ounce of strength she had to roll to her hands and knees and reach for the closest rock.

Big Guy pant-hooted at the sight.

The fever, the weariness from walking and climbing and carrying packs, and the fear that charged her muscles all left Brett too weak to throw the rock, but she clutched it in her fist and managed to stumble to her feet. She drew a breath, ready . . .

"Stop!"

Sky Eyes froze, his machete over his head.

"Put it down!"

Brett glanced over her shoulder and cried, *"Dad! Oh, God, Dad!"* She tried to run to him, tripped and fell, and didn't have the strength to get up.

Her father approached the apes cautiously, a rifle in his hands. "Brett? Umber? Thank God you're alive."

"Wheep." Umber's voice broke in the pained utterance.

"Brett?" her father called.

"S-sick, Dad. I'm r-really sick."

"The killing is over," Jim called. "Sky Eyes? Do you understand? No more killing!"

Sky Eyes trembled, his leg muscles shaking, and he lowered his machete.

"All right, no one gets hurt. Sky Eyes, I won't hurt you. Understand? I'm a friend. A friend of Umber's. I'm here to help you if you'll let me."

Umber signed, "Truth."

But Sky Eyes didn't seem to see her gesture. His blue eyes had a haunted look. His lips moved as if talking to himself. The machete fell from his nerveless fingers and he backed away across the irregular ground.

Big Guy, too, threw down his machete and grabbed Sue, hugging her for reassurance.

Brett saw Umber look over at Thrower. He'd curled on his side, his arm still spurting blood.

As Jim stepped closer, Umber signed, "Help Thrower. Help Thrower, Jim."

"What about Brett? Is she injured?" Jim's expression looked hard, unforgiving.

"No, Dad, no, just . . . sick."

Umber looked around, made sure the threat was gone, then began to shake with relief. Again she signed: "Thrower. Help Thrower."

Jim glanced hesitantly at Brett, and then stepped over to Thrower. He set his rifle aside and bent down, muttering, "Jesus."

Brett watched as he whipped his belt off, looped it around the stump, and pulled it tight. The jets of blood slowed to a trickle. Thrower moaned. After jerking the knot tight, Jim fished a small radio from his pocket and raised it to his lips, saying, "Shelly, we've got them. We're just west of the waterfall. You can follow my—"

"Jim!" Valerie shouted. *"On your three!"*

Brett screamed as Sky Eyes stumbled forward, the old rusty shotgun in his hands. His eyes glittered oddly, and his lips were pulled back. He made the eye-chest sign again and mumbled something unintelligible as he lifted the shotgun and pointed it at Brett.

Jim screamed, "No!" and dove for his rifle.

Brett covered her head at the loud *crack!* like the snapping of a mighty timber and saw Umber fall to the ground.

Brett screamed, "Umber!"

Another *crack!* sundered the air, and she saw Sky Eyes's body jerk and totter. The shotgun slipped from his hands and he sank to the ground.

Brett turned when her mother stepped from behind a tree with a large black pistol in her hands. She walked forward carefully, the weapon still aimed at Sky Eyes.

Sky Eyes sat with one hand braced on the ground and the other hand stretched out to the clouds, signing: "Girl, Girl, Girl." A smile touched his pink lips as he turned to Umber. His hands said, "Girl with God. God death."

Then he sagged onto his side, and blood bubbled from his mouth. The frothy holes in his chest ceased their rasping, and the forest sounds, stilled at the shots, slowly grew in volume.

Umber stared at Sky Eyes's motionless right hand, formed into a fist with the extended thumb against his cheek in the sign for "Girl," then she hunched forward.

Brett said, "Umber? Are you shot?"

"Scared. Scared." Umber reached out for Brett and started rocking back and forth, whimpering.

Forty-two

Sergeant Bonoficio stepped aside as Melody Hinsinger led two of the captured renegade apes to a Kawasaki Mule fitted with two cages on the rear. She was saying to the apes, "This is just a short ride. I promise, you will both be all right. We need to check you, make sure you are well, and then you will be released."

Bonoficio controlled the urge to smirk at such nonsense. His clan had come from the eastern town of Mongomo, where his uncle and cousins still hunted the forest for apes. Didn't these white fools know they were food, not pets? The old stories told the way of it. Apes were made in the form they were because of the gods' anger.

Bonoficio lifted a finger and caught Nguema's attention. Then he ducked through the wall of leaves and into the perpetual gloom. His booted feet sank into the leaf mat, and old, familiar forest odors came to his nose. Perhaps it was in the blood, this love-hate for the forest. The roots of life lay here, for all things came from the forest. But so, too, did the hidden things, the dangerous spirits and miasmas of illness, evil, and death.

But this day, the death won't be mine. He glanced back to meet Nguema's gleam of anticipation. The private clutched the short entrenching tool as if it were a rifle. They had talked about the woman. About her golden hair, and how her breasts pressed against the fabric of her shirt, as though longing to be freed.

Bonoficio had tagged Nguema for this duty. He had worked with Nguema before. The man had special qualities. He acted according to orders, never boastful and without hesitation. He did what needed to be done without fuss or bother. A professional who guarded his silence.

The forest seemed to press down around Bonoficio as he stepped over the prop roots and followed the winding trail toward the sound of voices. Nguema's stealthy tread followed closely behind.

"Here, take my hand." That was the doctor, Yamasaki. "That's it. Easy there."

Bonoficio could see them now. The doctor was helping an ape to its feet. A white bandage swathed what looked like a stump. Another of the medical people steadied the ape as it was loaded onto a stretcher.

Just beyond them, another team had placed a half-naked blond girl onto a second stretcher. Bonoficio spotted his quarry as they leaned over the stretcher, talking gently to the girl.

The stretcher bearers passed him, answering his nod with one of their own. Bonoficio stared down at the wounded ape, marveling at the reflection of agony in its expression. The animal cradled the stump of its right arm, hairy black fingers caressing the white bandage.

The girl came next, borne by two young white men. In a passing glance Bonoficio read the fever in her glazed blue eyes. She looked up at him, seemed to see into his soul, and called out, "Dad?"

"Right behind you, angel," Dutton called. "I just need to get Umber."

Bonoficio reached out and snagged the last man. "Don't wait

for the rest of us. I will bring Dutton and the woman in my vehicle. I have to make a report of this."

The medical tech nodded and hurried on his way. Bonoficio unsnapped his holster, anticipation rising within. The man and woman were alone.

Raising a hand, Bonoficio motioned Nguema to one side. He stepped forward, saying, "Doctor, I am Sergeant Bonoficio."

They both turned, looking surprised, but not yet suspicious. Bonoficio again stepped forward, a disarming smile on his face. "I must make a report to my superiors. I hope you understand. I am sorry for having to do this now, but we have our rules."

"What report?" the Radin woman asked, the first glimmering of suspicion in her eyes.

"You have shot an animal," Bonoficio replied calmly, buying time. "This is considered as hunting in our country." He pointed to the pistol hanging by her breast. "That weapon, well, it must be explained to my superiors. Where did you get a pistol?"

"Jesus," Dutton muttered, "where's the NRA when you need them?"

Bonoficio smiled easily. "Please, these things are just a matter of formality. We know that you are with the project. I think the illegal pistol and the hunting permit can be taken care of. If there is only a little money, you know, for the paperwork."

The woman's suspicious expression dissolved to one of comprehension. "How much?"

"Oh, say, ten thousand *cefas*." Bonoficio shrugged. "I think all of these misunderstandings can be overlooked."

"Done," Radin told him.

Bonoficio extended his hand. "If you will surrender the pistol to me, well, there will be no more violations of our law to necessitate more . . . 'paperwork.' "

She hesitated, then reluctantly drew the big black pistol from its holster. "Sergeant, if someone were willing to pay for the additional paperwork, could they obtain a 'permit' to retain their pistol?"

Bonoficio vented a genuine laugh. "Perhaps another twenty thousand. But it will have to wait until the appropriate fines have been paid, yes?"

"I think I can arrange that," Radin said and reluctantly handed him the black pistol. As if in perfect timing, the distant muttering of a motor could be heard, and then began to fade.

"We'd better go," Dutton said. He had watched the preceding, a disgusted look on his bearded face. "I need to get—"

"Not so fast, please." Bonoficio handed the pistol over to Nguema and slipped his own worn Browning Hi Power out of its holster. "We are going back down the ridge." He indicated with a nod of his head. "Please, do not make this difficult. If you run, I will shoot you dead. The others are gone. They will not hear the shot."

"What is this all about?" Dutton stepped forward. As if on cue, Nguema slapped him on the shoulder with the flat of the entrenching tool. The blow knocked Dutton sideways, and Radin cried out, catching his arm.

"Get up," Bonoficio ordered. "Walk, now." He raised the Browning, staring at them over the front sight.

"Come on, Jim," Radin said, a hardness in her voice. She helped him to his feet. He winced as he massaged his shoulder. Then he started forward.

"I can make this worth your while," Radin said. "Come on, Sergeant. Think. If you kill us, the whole world is going to come down on you like a big brick. Done the other way, one hundred thousand *cefas* could find its way into your possession if you let us go." She surreptitiously thrust her hand into a hip pocket.

"Maybe you better take that hand out and walk nice-like."

"Look," Dutton said as he sidestepped down the steep slope. "It's me you want. Let Valerie go."

"No, man. It's both of you." Bonoficio lowered himself carefully down the slope. "This is good. This flat place here."

A tree had fallen in the past sometime, its trunk lying parallel to the slope, creating a pocket of mulch. Years of leaves had fallen and gave the ground a soft, yielding feel. Bonoficio pressed it with his boot and glanced at Nguema. "Like a mattress, eh?"

Nguema barely cracked a smile as he threw the entrenching tool at Dutton's feet and unslung his Kalashnikov. He swung the muzzle in Dutton's direction, saying, "Dig."

Dutton stared for a moment before understanding settled into his brain. He swallowed hard and whispered, "Sweet Jesus."

"*Two* hundred thousand *cefas*," Radin said, turning to face Bonoficio. A bitter desperation had settled behind her blue eyes, giving them a glassy look.

Bonoficio laughed from the belly. "Maybe you don't know, eh? We been paid a *lot* more than that for killing you."

"I might be able to cover three hundred thousand *cefas*," Radin said woodenly.

"Dig!" Nguema said, raising his rifle and centering it on Dutton's chest.

"Wait!" Radin lifted her hand. Sweat had begun to bead on her brow; the anxiety in her eyes had intensified. "Look, we're going to die, right? So tell me, who paid to have us killed? For God's sake, you can at least tell us that!"

"Sure, why not." Bonoficio used his pistol to gesture Dutton to dig.

Dutton shot a frightened glance at Radin, caught her slight nod, and picked up the entrenching tool, touching it like a live snake were writhing in his hands.

"You think maybe it was McDougal?" Bonoficio laughed. " 'Cept for her, you'd be dead the day we got you over at Compound D."

"Then it was Godmoore?" Radin asked. Her breath was coming in gasps now, pressing her breasts against the tight fabric of her shirt.

"Yeah, Godmoore. He tells Don Amando, Don Amando tells me." Bonoficio leveled the pistol on her face. "Take them off. The clothes."

"What?" Dutton cried, straightening from the shallow trench he'd scraped.

"Do it!" Bonoficio pivoted, pointing the Browning at Dutton. "Or I shoot him down low. Let him bleed out through the guts. You want it like that? Him screaming while we fuck you?"

"Valerie, no!" Dutton cried, his body trembling.

Bonoficio thumbed the hammer back, settling the sight blade on Dutton's fly. "I count to three. One, two . . ."

"All right!" Hands trembling, Radin reached up and began undoing the buttons on her shirt. "But you be merciful to him, you son of a bitch! Quick! Clean!"

Dutton shook his head, saying, "Valerie, don't do this."

Nguema chuckled and nodded. "One shot. But you be worth it, bitch."

Dutton had frozen, his lips parted. "No, Valerie."

"It's all right, Jim." Radin peeled her shirt off of her shoulders, revealing smooth white skin. Her fingers were fumbling with the belt when Dutton clenched the entrenching tool and stiffened, shoulders broad, his eyes fastened on the distance above. "Bonoficio, you are not going to rape her."

"Nguema, when I give the word, you may break one of his knees."

Dutton took a step forward, his eyes still lost in the high canopy, a look of desperation in those blue depths. Sweat was trickling down the side of his face to bead and glisten on his beard. Bonoficio had seen that look before. How often did they look up like that, as if for deliverance? When all hope had vanished, they insisted on believing salvation lay in the air, like a Catholic miracle.

"If you are going to shoot, you had better do it now!" Dutton said in a voice too loud. "Now!"

Radin gasped, eyes wide as she struggled for words. Nguema sighted on the man's chest . . .

The rifle's loud *crack* mixed with the pop of a bullet through skin, bone, and meat. The sudden jerk of Nguema's body, the flap of his uniform shirt as bits of red tissue were blown out of his belly, made Bonoficio flinch. A weird, high-pitched scream broke the air. Nothing torn from a human throat. Dutton was moving even as Nguema's body sagged, the knees buckling. The rifle fell from nerveless hands, and Bonoficio started to turn.

"Jim! Run!" Radin screamed and leaped for Bonoficio.

Bonoficio hesitated, then started to turn back, bringing the pistol to bear. The Browning's front sight settled between the brassiere's two white cups. He saw the blur of movement. Dutton! The entrenching tool caught him in the ribs, slashing through his shirt, spinning him just enough that his shot missed, the nine-millimeter slug ripping wood from the fallen tree trunk. Pain lanced his side as he caught his balance and pivoted. Bonoficio thrust the old blue Browning in his direction. Dutton looked into the pistol's bore in that instant of frozen realization that he was about to die.

Then the very sky crashed down upon Bonoficio. A flash of something black dropping from above. The impact drove him to the ground. He heard his pistol discharge. His face was driven hard into the rotten leaves, a ringing in his ears. He fought, twisted his head, and caught an image in the corner of his vision.

Black, hairy, two hands reached down for him, fastening on his head. He tried to scream, but his paralyzed lungs refused. The strong hands tightened their grip and twisted. The sensation of pain, of tearing ligaments, and then, he heard—*felt*—the bones in his neck pop. The roaring grew in his ears, and before the gray veil shaded his vision, a ludicrous image burned into his brain: It was an ape! An ape wearing brightly colored clothing!

Umber is rigid, every muscle tensed and thrumming, as if strung and plucked like her bowstring. The man's limp head is heavy in her hands, twisted three-fourths of the way around so that it looks over the left shoulder. She can feel the warmth of his skin, the moisture of his sweat.

Umber can't move. She cannot will her muscles to let loose of this hideous head. She cannot back away from this twitching husk of a body. Her fear-grin is a rictus; her heart hammers as if to burst her ribs. Despite the choked scream she utters with each panicked breath, her lungs are starved for air. Horror sends electric pulses through her contorted body.

Images flash through her mind: The two men with guns. Jim and Valerie being led away. Her timid pursuit as she followed behind them through the trees. The terrible understanding, and then her desperate race to retrieve the rifle—Jim's rifle. The one he leaned against the tree when she demanded that he take care of Thrower.

Was that me? The question hangs within her as she relives that moment when Jim looked up, met her eyes, and their souls touched. He had seen the rifle that she clutched, read her fear and indecision, as terrible as his own.

If you are going to shoot, you had better do it now! Now! His words echo in her memory. She had lifted the rifle, looked down those sights at the soldier's back. The shot had taken her by surprise, coming before she was ready. The awful *crack!* and the rifle jumping in her hands, like a thing alive. Instinctively, she'd dropped it, the way she would a writhing serpent.

Then she'd had no choice. The soldier with the pistol would kill them in the end. They had only Umber. So she had launched herself, falling like a wingless bird, and landed full on his back.

That moment would creep out of her dreams. In the deepest nightmare, she would remember the wide brown eyes staring sightlessly into the eternal distance of death.

"Umber?" Jim's voice comes from somewhere far away. "Umber? Are you all right?"

The panting, hot in her chest, is beyond her control. Her muscles are jerking now, making the soldier's head jiggle in her grasp. She is losing herself, bits of her are fading, falling away like leaves in the autumn.

Then the familiar hand touches her shoulder. The gentle voice says, "Umber, it's all right. You're okay. We're okay. You saved us, sweetheart. You can let go now."

The terror crashes. It is a windowpane, splintering into a thousand silvered shards. She blinks, swallows down her dry throat, and lets Jim's hands pull her away from the hideous body.

The mewing starts deep in her throat, and she looks up into Jim's tear-streaked face. She throws herself against him, clasping him to her in a crushing grip. Never wanting to let go. She feels Valerie, hears her sobbing with relief as she hugs them both. Together, they collapse.

Alive. All of them. Alive.

But the Eye Inside looks at her, and she can hear it asking: *What have you done? What have you become?*

Forty-three

Your daughter is sedated," Marcus explained as Jim bent over the hospital bed.

He reached out, placing the back of his hand on Brett's cheek, and winced at the heat he felt there. "Will she be all right?"

"I think she will. She's young and strong. It just might take a while." Marcus crossed his arms.

Jim grunted and glanced toward Valerie. She stood on the opposite side of the bed, her expression hollow. A dark smudge marred her cheek and bits of forest detritus had stuck in her uncombed hair. But then she looked pretty good for having just passed two days in the forest, having performed a rescue, and having so narrowly escaped rape and execution.

The mere thought of how close they had come, of the dark muzzle of Nguema's rifle, and the pistol pointed at Valerie as she unbuttoned her shirt, made him clench his fist to stop the sudden shudder.

"She needs rest," Marcus said in a mild voice. "So do you. Go back to your room. Take a shower and get a good night's sleep. I promise, if there's any change, I'll call you first thing."

Jim straightened and glanced at Umber, who gripped the

stainless steel railing on the bed, her eyes vacant as she watched Brett's deep breathing.

"Marcus," Jim's voice lowered. "I am assuming that you're your own man here." He met Yamasaki's mild brown eyes, saw the man recoil from the pent violence. "Godmoore just tried to have us killed. Valerie had a tape recorder in her pocket. I am assuming you didn't have any knowledge of that, and that my daughter will be perfectly safe. Am I understood?"

Yamasaki's eyes widened, then he unconsciously stepped back. "Godmoore tried . . ." He took a deep breath. "Look, I don't want to know, all right? I run the clinic. She'll be safe. I promise." Then he smiled wearily. "Go. You look like you need some rest. All three of you."

Jim nodded, his steely gaze unbending. He reached down, took Umber's hand, almost had to pry it off of the rail. "Come on. Let's go get cleaned up."

Outside the hospital room, Roberto slouched against the wall. He was fingering the old rusty shotgun, snapping the action open and closed.

At sight of it, Valerie stiffened and swallowed hard. Jim took her hand, tightening his grip on both her and Umber. "We're all right, girls. Just hold it together until we cross the street and make it up to the rooms, then we can collapse into jelly."

Umber's plaintive "wheep" didn't carry much conviction.

"Right, Jimbo," Valerie said, the tremors barely hidden.

"Close one, eh, Fuerta?" Roberto's eyes probed hers.

"Too damn close." Valerie bit her lip. "Taco. We've got to move. Tomorrow. Evinayong. We've got to show that shotgun to Masala. And then . . . we've . . . we've got to . . ."

Roberto raised a hand, shutting her off. "I'm on it, Val. It's covered. I want you here. God, look at you. You're about all in. You ain't gonna do me no good falling apart in the middle of an interview and cutting that damn poacher's throat for starting this whole mess, huh?" He lifted an eyebrow. "Trust me on this? Just for once?"

A thin smile crossed her lips. "You get the story, Beaner. Just make sure it has your byline when it runs."

Roberto winked, then glanced at Umber, the concern growing behind his soft brown eyes. "You head back to the barn. I'll bring dinner and then split. I gotta be in Evinayong by first light." He locked eyes with Jim and tilted his head toward Valerie, the message clear.

Jim nodded slightly and led the way out into the early-evening rain.

Valerie walked, eyes focused somewhere in the distance. She shivered again. "Being shot at in war, that's one thing. Walked off at gunpoint to your own execution . . . That look in Bonoficio's eyes . . . that's going to haunt my nightmares forever."

"Yeah," Jim said, glancing worriedly at Umber. She might have been a robot. The glassy horror reflected in her eyes scared him.

Valerie gave him a sidelong glance. "Back there. What was that look Roberto gave you?"

"A promise not to leave you alone tonight."

She frowned slightly, a bit of relief etched into her expression. Running fingers through her matted hair, she said, "Lord, yes, I don't want to be alone. Let me get some clean clothes. Take a shower."

The climb up the stairs, the walk down the hall, it all might have been a dream. Jim closed the door behind him and Umber and turned on the lights.

Umber stopped short when he released her hand. She stood motionless, eyes fixed on eternity. Then he lifted her up on the bed beside him. For a long moment, he stared into her miserable eyes.

"Want to talk about it?"

She fidgeted, started to form signs, then shook her head, dropping back into that wounded place deep inside.

"We have to talk about it, sweetheart." Jim took her hand and kissed it. "I'm so sorry these things had to happen to you. My dear, sweet Umber. Never a single violent or hateful thought in that pretty head, and then all of this."

She withdrew her hand and signed: "Heart sick. I feel dirty. Inside, dirty. Why did this happen to me? What did I do wrong?"

"Nothing, Umber. You didn't do anything wrong." He scratched a bug bite and said, "Umber, sometimes you have to take a life to live. Today, you saved your sister's life. Then you saved ours. You kept the people you love alive."

Her soft brown eyes pleaded with his, her hands moving haltingly as she formed the signs for, "Why? the eye inside asks. Umber cannot answer."

He placed his hand in hers. "Feel, Umber. Put your finger right here on my wrist. That's my pulse. My heart beating, sending blood through my wrist. Look into my eyes. See me here, looking back?"

"Wheep."

"That's what you did today. I am alive, here, holding you. Your sister is over in the hospital. She's breathing, healing. Tomorrow, when she smiles at you, she will do so because you kept her alive. And Valerie is in the next room. But for you, she would be cold and dead now, buried out in the forest under the leaves. She'd have dirt in her eyes and insects crawling into the bullet hole in her head."

Umber hugged herself for a moment before her sad eyes met his and she signed, "Umber wants to go home now."

Jim patted her arm. "Valerie has enough information that we can bury SAC if they don't let us go."

"Will bad memories go away?" She looked up at him hopefully.

"No. That's just part of life. You'll have to live with them from here on out. Just like the rest of us do."

"Long time sad."

He ruffled her hair. "Well, next time you're feeling sad, remember, you're our hero, Umber."

She shook her head. "Umber doesn't feel like a hero."

Jim smiled sadly. "Real ones never do."

Valerie was leaned back in the chair in Jim's room, her feet spread, head back. Her nerves had finally loosened enough that the trembling had passed. Nevertheless, she wasn't about to let her big HK pistol out of sight for a while. The events of the afternoon kept replaying in her mind.

Damn it, bitch, that was one close call. She'd been able to smell the grave this time, and its memory was going to send shivers down her soul for a while.

She looked up when Jim stepped out of the shower. He savaged his head with the towel, a vain attempt to dry his hair and beard. He had donned a clean shirt and shorts, but his feet were bare.

"How's Umber?" She studied him through lowered lids.

He indicated the other room. "After her shower, she folded. I put her to bed. Damn it, Valerie, what's this going to do to her?" He wadded the towel, as if unsure what to do with it. "Hell, what's it going to do to all of us?" After a pause, he added, "God, I've never been so scared in all my life. The thought just kept rolling through my mind that this couldn't be happening."

"It almost did." She tried to smile. And failed. "Not quite like the movies, is it?"

"That man, Nguema . . . he was going to kill me with no

more emotional involvement than disposing of an empty beer can."

"I wouldn't have made it but for you striking with that shovel." She worked her hands into fists, fidgeting again. Powered by nervous energy she stood and walked over to sit beside him on the bed.

"Out in the forest . . . you said . . ." She frowned, running her fingers down the back of his hand. "Jim, I'm so sorry I hurt you." A pause. "You know, we came awfully close to being real dead out there. If it weren't for Umber, you and I . . . My God, there are times when the simple act of breathing can be its own fulfillment."

"I will never take life for granted again." He tightened his grip on her, pulling her close. "We were lucky today. Damned lucky."

Impulsively, she let her lips touch his, remembering how he had held her out in the black forest night. For the moment, her soul seemed to float, to drift in an airy lightness.

"Val, are you sure?"

"Let's just savor the moment. It's a gift, Jim. Were it not for Umber, we'd be dead." She slipped an arm around his neck, feeling the rush of her blood, the warming in her loins.

"Amen."

She kissed him harder and tensed, a tingle running through her body. One by one, the buttons on his shirt came undone and she ran her hand over his chest, twining it in the thick hair. She let her tongue glide down the side of his neck. That, she remembered, always drove him wild.

His hand slid under her shirt, across her stomach, and under the elastic of her bra. In all the years of frantic male groping, she had forgotten that a man could touch her with such tenderness.

She sighed as he slipped her shirt over her shoulders and freed her breasts. As in a slow dance, they undressed each other.

He eased her onto the mattress, covering her with his warm body. The sensation of his skin against hers was like salve on a raw wound. He took her in his arms, conforming to her, and a honeyed warmth was kindled at the base of her spine. It spread through her like a golden dawn. She wrapped her arms around his back and pulled him tightly against her, holding him. When she finally guided him into her, the joining was as fulfilling as it had been that night by the campfire alongside a high mountain lake.

Valerie stepped through the doorway into the quiet hospital room.

Brett sat propped on pillows watching a silent rebroadcast of the latest Triple N report on the SAC preserve. On the screen, Valerie sat on a log, her microphone in hand, while Jim Dutton translated the story Big Guy and Sue narrated with their hands.

That had been the important story, the interview with the killer apes. The reason they'd gone over the edge all tied back to a poacher named Ngasala who had killed Sky Eyes's beloved Girl and his unborn child. The solid bit of evidence: Masala's story on tape and the shotgun with Ngasala's name hand-carved into the stock.

The scene changed to a cutout of the shotgun—the one Sky Eyes had clutched in his hands when Valerie shot him dead. She stopped cold, her heart skipping as she watched the last of the interview. Roberto had shot the segment yesterday in Evinayong. Masala, looking into the camera with half-dead eyes, identified the shotgun and asked to have it now that Ngasala was dead.

Valerie whispered, "I didn't know it was unloaded. How could I have known?"

Brett glanced at her. "What if he'd had a shell in it, Mom? He could have blown Umber and me away."

"I know, Brett, but I don't have to feel good about it." The scene on the television changed to show a harried Richard God-moore as he tried to avoid the cameras by draping a jacket over his head. She smiled grimly. "Ah, the power of the media. I had my tape recorder in my pocket. That son of a bitch Bonoficio . . . I recorded him saying that Godmoore ordered our murder. That hit the airwaves yesterday. Somehow I imagine life is going to be a little difficult for the good doctor."

"What an asshole."

"I'm supposed to tell you to watch your language." Valerie stepped up to the bedside and looked down. "How are you feeling?"

"The doctor says I'll be out of here in another couple of days." She made a face. "So, I've got malaria. In spite of SAC's hot new vaccine. That's bad enough. But what's worse, Marcus says I've got worms. He cut tumba fly larvae out of my back where my bra got wet. And I've got amebic dysentery. And it caused an infection, you know"—she rolled her eyes—"down there. But the doctor says the fever's under control."

"You're in fine company. I've had all of those things. Well, maybe not the tumba larvae, but I'm young yet. And to make up for it I've had some other things you haven't."

Brett smiled at that.

Valerie asked, "Have you seen Umber?"

"Yeah. She's gone down the hall to reassure Thrower. He's pretty scared. Not only did he lose his hand, but he's certain that because he helped Sky Eyes cut people up, someone's going to kill him. Umber has been explaining things to him. She's been real weird. All adult like."

Valerie nodded. "I've been checking on you, too. The first two days, your dad and I were here every chance we had. You were awfully sick, raving and fevered. And we were pretty busy."

"You had things to do." She pointed at the TV. "What's going to happen to them?"

"The apes?" Valerie shrugged and reached down, resting her hand on the bed railing. "We'll see. That's for the future, Brett. For now, let's just look for the truth, determine who the victims were, and let the facts speak for themselves. If the story is presented fairly, people usually make the right choices." She gave her daughter a crooked smile. "But a little journalistic slant might not be a bad thing."

To her surprise, Brett reached out and grasped her hand. "I'm real proud of you, Mom."

Valerie's throat constricted. She swallowed and smiled. "I'm proud of you, too, Brett. Umber, Thrower, and Sue said you showed a lot of guts."

"I couldn't even stand up," Brett said. "Umber had to protect me. If it hadn't been for Umber, they would have killed me."

"If it hadn't been for Umber." Valerie shook her head. "That might just end up as my epitaph. And as to you, no wonder you couldn't stand up. You had a temperature of one hundred and five, Brett." Valerie shrugged. "The miracle is that you kept your wits and marked a trail."

Brett's grip tightened on Valerie's hand. "Dad says you made the difference. That he'd never have made it in time without you. That you were pretty scared, too."

"I was terrified. I was afraid I'd mess this up, too. That I'd just found you, only to lose you again."

Brett released Valerie's hand and lowered her eyes, peering at the white sheet that covered her. "Mom? Taco said to ask you sometime about the picture. The one in your purse." She looked up, straight into Valerie's eyes. "So, I'm asking."

Valerie smiled, but it must have looked very much like a chimp's fear-grin. She pulled her purse around, fished the laminated photo from her wallet, and handed it over. "I took it just before I flew off to Colombia to do that mass murder story."

"So that's how you knew I went to Blevins Junior High School." Brett fingered the plastic, a faraway look in her eyes. "You really did care, didn't you?"

Valerie's eyes blurred. She nodded. "I cared a great deal, Brett."

"Why didn't you ever call?"

Valerie lifted a shoulder. "Because I'm a coward. Thirteen years ago, when you were born, I made a mistake. The worst one of my entire life. I've been trying to pay for it for years. I was afraid. If I'd called and you said you hated me, dear God, Brett, what would I have done?"

That old familiar sense of desperation stung her chest. Valerie sniffed, hoping she could keep the emotion from over-running her defenses. "Hell, I didn't even know if your father had told you I was your mother. If I only saw you from a distance, I could keep the illusion that you didn't hate me." She dared to look into Brett's blue eyes, and added, "You must think I'm a pretty miserable excuse for a mother."

"I might—"

"Well, I'd be the first to agree with you. I know I—"

"But then I might not." Brett smiled at her. "Though, I don't know, if you'd showed up I might have tortured you a little. You know, just to make sure you didn't take me for granted. But I always hoped you'd come."

Of all the reactions, Valerie hated tears the most. She had always thought women who cried were beneath loathing. The warm rush from her eyes, the hard ache under her tongue, caught her by surprise.

Brett handed her a facial tissue to sop up the excess and to blow her nose when it was over.

"Well, Brett," she said, "look what you've done to me now."

"Awesome. I love power." Brett grinned in satisfaction. "Uh, maybe you could make a basketball game sometime?"

"And maybe you could come and see Washington with me? I know the hot spots. The Old Ebbit Grill, the roof of the Washington Hotel, the best of the museums. I could probably get us an exclusive tour of the White House." She paused. "Brett, I can't make up for past mistakes. But I'd like to get to know you."

"Yeah, Mom . . . Neat ring to it, don't you think?" She yawned.

"Maybe you'd better sleep now." Valerie clutched her hand again, then stepped back. "I'll see you in the morning."

Brett smiled. "Good night, Mom."

Valerie stepped out into the hallway. For a long moment, she leaned against the wall, trying to collect herself.

At the sound of feet, she saw Jim round the corner, his old battered hat in hand. He wore a clean blue shirt and dark blue jeans. He said, "How is she?"

"Just drifting off to sleep."

He stopped in front of Valerie, surveyed her face, and said, "What happened? You're a real mess."

"I've never known a man who had such a smooth way with words. You really know how to buck a girl up, don't you?"

"What did she do, stick the stiletto in and twist it around a little just to hear how loudly you could scream?" He started past her. "That's our dear little Brett, Torquemada's younger blond sister. I'd better—"

She caught his arm, pulling him around. "No, Jim. She was really super. Not only did she forgive me, I actually think she understood. She's a bright, intelligent young lady."

He absently curled the hat brim in his hands. "She must want something from you."

Valerie laughed and punched him in the ribs. "Come on. Walk me home."

"I'll just take a minute."

Jim walked in and Valerie saw him bend over the bed and kiss Brett on the forehead. They murmured to each other, and then he kissed her again and eased back to the door. He whispered, "I couldn't leave without a good night kiss."

Valerie took his arm. They walked out past the nurse, down the main hall, and into the warm night. A light rain was falling. Jim put his hat on.

"Damn, Jimbo, we did all right. Brett and Umber are safe. We're still alive. The apes had a chance to tell their side, the story's knocking the ratings dead, and CNN still hasn't come busting the doors down to hog the story. Not bad for you and me."

"I guess we make a pretty good team." He lifted his handsome face to the warm rain. In the glare of the compound lights, she admired the line of his bearded jaw, the perfect profile of his straight nose. A softness entered his eyes. Even after all these years, that vulnerable look still melted her heart.

Arm in arm, they walked to the dormitory doorway and climbed the stairs. At her door, she said, "Come in for a minute? Roberto won't be back from Evinayong until tomorrow, if he's lucky."

He hesitated, and Valerie reached out and took his hand. "Come on. I've got a bottle I keep handy for celebrations. I think this one's been stretched over four continents already."

She found the Camus XO cognac and held it up to the light. At least three-fourths full. "Come to think about it, this is almost a year old." She poured two glasses and settled on the couch beside him. "Isn't that a pisser. There are maybe two drinks gone in a year. We certainly didn't toast in Colombia. Nor in Azerbaijan. Nor in Korea. Whoops, that's five continents." She shook her head. "God, I'm tired of seeing people dying, dead, or in misery."

"You know, we're only getting started with this," he told her solemnly. "I talked to Shelly today. Kivu's being charged with murder. I have to be there . . . testify on his behalf."

"I can't think of a more qualified witness," she murmured.

"We'll need someone from the press on our side. Got any ideas who that might be?"

"It would have to be someone with experience. And, please, God, no dead bodies." She paused and smiled crookedly. "You know, if Kivu is acquitted, it will change the world. The fact that he's being granted a trial smacks of *human* rights."

"Well," he said, lifting his glass. "Here's to a better world."

"A better world." Valerie clinked his glass and sipped the smooth cognac. "You're starting to sound like darling Geoffrey. And when you think about it, this whole thing went sour because of people: Ngasala poaching, Godmoore in search of power and profits, your Mr. Morrison, or Parnell, needing to compensate for his own inadequacies by debasing another human being. What kind of creatures are we?"

"I said a better world, not a perfect one. We all make mistakes."

"Yeah, I know." Her brow furrowed. "I wish to hell I'd known that shotgun was empty, Jim." She shook her head, that sick feeling tormenting her again. "What was Sky Eyes saying? Those signs he was making as he died?"

Jim frowned down at his cognac. "He was talking to Girl. I think he could see her there at the end." He swirled the cognac and watched the amber liquid wash the sides of the glass. "He saw her killed, saw their baby cut from her womb. Sue said that Sky Eyes sat by Girl's dead body for days without food and water. He loved her, Val. So much of this happened because Sky Eyes loved."

She frowned down at her drink. "I'm not saying that anything might come of it, and it could be a can of worms for the both of us, but I keep thinking about the other night when we made love. In fact, I can't stop thinking about it." She glanced at him uncertainly. "Maybe later, when Umber is finally asleep . . ."

He reached over and kissed her.

Epilogue

Umber held Brett's hand and watched the workmen load the last of their luggage into the Gulfstream jet. The big white plane was different from the one that had brought them here. This one had been sent by Triple N, and it had more windows.

The smell of jet fuel mixed with the odors of the forest; the clank of metal on concrete couldn't compete with the forest's song. The warm muggy air lay close around her, almost suffocating.

"So, like, the sooner we're out of this burg the better," Brett muttered out of the side of her mouth.

Umber looked over at Jim and Valerie where they talked to Shelly McDougal. She pulled Brett over a step or two so she could hear.

"I'll not tell you that Godmoore's finished," she stated in her Scottish brogue. "There's to be a fair fight at the next board meeting. Godmoore and Geoffrey Smyth-Archer go back a long way. Godmoore always took care of Geoffrey. But I understand that Dr. Johnson and some of the other stockholders are rallying." Her face grew even more pinched. "And your reporters have discovered a problem with the books. About fifty million pounds can't be accounted for. There are rumors of some hidden Swiss account, and no one has heard from Godmoore in the last twenty-four hours. He seems to have missed an appointment with a Mr. Edwards. One of your reporters, I believe. It should be an interesting next couple of days."

"What about you?" Valerie asked. "How will the corporate shake-up affect you?"

McDougal's cold blue eyes remained expressionless. "Last thing they want is to dismiss me. I might go shopping for a publisher down in London. Given what I know, I could make a very nice book deal."

"Always on top? Shelly, you'd have made a great archaeologist."

"No need to be insulting, Dr. Dutton." McDougal stiffened. "I do what I must." She stared down her nose at him. "But then, I've discovered, so do you."

Jim said, "Yes, I do, so let's make sure that Umber's involvement in the affair remains between the three of us."

"Agreed, Dr. Dutton." She offered her hand and Jim shook it.

"Dr. McDougal." Valerie offered her hand.

Shelly returned the grip. "You've done all right for us, Ms. Radin. I still don't trust you, but I'm glad it worked out."

"Wish us luck in Texas," Valerie replied. "We're not out of the woods yet."

At that moment, a rattly old jeep careened around the edge of the hangar. The exhausted brakes screeched, and mud-spattered men stepped out. One carried a camera, losing no time in taking a panning shot.

From the steps rolled up beside the Gulfstream, Roberto called, "Hey, that's CNN! 'Bout time they got here."

"Damnation!" McDougal muttered. "Journalists!" To Umber it sounded like a curse word.

Jim motioned, and Umber led the way up the stairway and into the aircraft. This Gulfstream had more seats in it than the last one. The fold-down beds were missing in the back.

Umber climbed into one across from Brett and watched Jim and Valerie settle into the seats behind the bulkhead. She noticed that they were holding hands, talking in hushed voices.

"Quite the thing, huh?" Brett asked, indicating her parents.

"What you think?" Umber asked.

"I don't know." Brett shrugged. "It's kind of weird to think about my mom and dad being lovers."

"Oh, I don't know." Roberto leaned forward, his chin on the seat back behind Brett's head. "She might be ready for a real man. Your dad, he's a cool guy." He made a tsk-tsk sound. "But he's gonna have his work cut out for him to get her to settle down."

"Naw," Brett replied knowingly. "Dad wouldn't try to turn her into a housewife. He's smarter than that."

Umber watched the co-pilot step through the cabin door and listened as he talked about seat belts and safety features of the Gulfstream. He kept staring at Umber, as if having trouble believing what he was seeing. She nodded at the appropriate moments, amused that his expression grew even more stricken.

After he had gone forward and closed the door to the cockpit, the engines began to whine. Umber tensed, her fingers digging into the armrests.

Pressing her face to the window, she watched as the jet turned and rolled onto the runway. It stopped, the whine growing louder.

There, just beyond the gleaming white wingtip, lay the wall of leaves. A bird flitted through it, fluttering into the dense cover.

Umber could see beyond, into the shadowed depths. She could smell the leaves, the mold and moisture. She could sense the rhythm of the place, the sap in the lianas, the chatter of the rope squirrels, the squeals of the monkeys, the musical birdsong. There, among the roots, the big snakes passed on shining scales.

The jet whine rose to a fevered pitch and the plane rolled ahead, gaining speed. Umber watched the forest slide past, moving ever faster. The rumbling and shaking ended as the aircraft lifted and they cleared the trees.

Africa.

Sky Eyes was back there. His soul locked with Girl's wherever God had allowed them to go. Meggan O'Neil's sightless eyes stared across the tops of the forest giants, her soul caring for the apes. Vernon Shanks's ghost walked the project, searching, no doubt, for the shades of Ngasala and Ntogo.

And where are you, Umber? Here, on this airplane, or back there? How much of yourself did you lose to Africa?

She raised her hands, flexing the long black fingers. Did Thrower's severed right hand have a soul? Did it search among the trunks of the mighty trees, seeking the arm that had extended it? Did the two dead soldiers, their bodies rotting in the hollow of a fallen tree, search in vain for their killer?

She put a hand to her aching chest, the gesture in recognition of the eye inside, with its endless questions.

Acknowledgments

This novel could not have been written without the work of people like Sue Savage-Rumbaugh, Franz De Waal, Takayoshi Kano, Alison and Noel Badrian, Roger and Debbi Fouts, Jane Goodall, and others. Without their commitment and hard work, bonobos and chimpanzees would remain unknown to the world—and even closer to the perilous edge of extinction than they are today.

We wish to acknowledge Pat Rochefort of McCord Zenith Travel in New York for providing information on flight schedules and the minutiae of traveling to Equatorial Guinea. Pat has coordinated our professional travel for years, and her help in making this a better book is appreciated.

Our agent, Matt Bialer, believed in the book from the beginning. Our editor, Betsy Mitchell, devoted a great deal of thought, time, and effort to this project. She and Frances Jalet-Miller did some of the finest line editing we've had the pleasure to know. We would like to recognize and acknowledge the hard work and commitment of Mark Lee (for taking us to the zoo), Jennifer Royce, Cassandra Leoncini, Lynn Sutherland, and the rest of the field force. They are the unsung heroes of the business.

The Thermopolis Holiday Inn graciously maintained a private stock of Guinness and Red Hook ale for those late-afternoon skull sessions when we needed to brainstorm plot and character or argue about the inclusion of scientific data. Thanks, guys.